Flesh

Flesh

by
Hollis Seamon

*For Nina —
With all best
wishes —
Hollis Seamon
September 2005*

MEMENTO MORI MYSTERIES
New York

Memento Mori Mysteries
Published by
Avocet Press Inc
19 Paul Court, Pearl River, NY 10965
http://www.avocetpress.com
mysteries@avocetpress.com

AVOCET PRESS

This novel is a work of fiction and each character in it is fictional. No reference
to any living person is intended or should be inferred.

Library of Congress Cataloging-in-Publication Data
Seamon, Hollis.
Flesh : a Suzanne LaFleshe mystery.— 1st ed.
p. cm.
ISBN 0-9725078-3-3
1. Women graduate students—Fiction. 2. Poets—Crimes against—
Fiction. 3. Overweight women—Fiction. 4. Albany (N.Y.)—Fiction. 5.
Windigos—Fiction. 6. Witches—Fiction. I. Title.
PS3569.E1755F58 2004
813'.6—dc22
2004007273

Cover: Photograph by Caitlin Brennan-Cant ©2005

This novel is dedicated to my mother, who passed on to me her love of good mysteries and great desserts.

Priscilla Elmer Rowan
1915-2001

It has occurred to me that I am rather strong on Voyages and Cannibalism and might do an interesting little paper....

Charles Dickens, Letter to W. H. Willis, Editor of *Household Words*

...what a feast run amok the whole earth was, only how could you tell the eater from the eats?

Jaimy Gordon, *Bogeywoman*

Part I: *Wind*

...the Wendigo is a cannibal...a giant spirit creature with a heart and sometimes an entire body of ice...it can travel as fast as the wind.

Margaret Atwood, "Cannibal Lecture"

1

Suzanne Brown (aka Suzanne LaFleshe, sexiest fat woman in New York State and true connoisseur of everything corporeal) put her hands over her weary eyes and rubbed. Palms against eyelids, she gathered what psychic strength she could muster. She took her hands away and opened her eyes. They verified her first impression. The office she'd just inherited was indeed a pigsty. Under the glare of the fluorescent ceiling light, it revealed itself: curly-edged papers piled in monstrous heaps; styrofoam coffee cups six weeks old and growing molds of many colors; a dead Christmas cactus, spreadeagled across the top of a rusty file cabinet; four petrified bagels; two gray metal desks; one rolling chair. One bare window, black with night sky, reflecting her own face, the fierce winter wind hissing around its frame. One computer, vintage.

Okay, then. She'd come alone, late on the last evening before the so-called spring semester began, Sunday, January 19, 2003. She'd come to see for herself what she had gotten herself into. Well, okay. Now she knew. She could handle it. She'd ignore the mess—she'd only look at the computer, for the moment. She wedged her butt into the too-small seat of the rolling chair. (She'd have to see to that, wouldn't she? They'd have to supply larger furnishings, to accommodate her. She'd insist on it.) She pushed the computer's on button and waited, a long time, for it to boot up. But it did, at last, adding its whine to the noise of the wind. Well, then. The first task, she'd been told, of the new editor of the departmental literary magazine was to decide on the name of this august publication. A name suited to its brand new slant: a journal dedicated to fiction, poetry, photography, art, literary theory, cultural theory, film theory, and whatever else they could find, all on the theme of fat. Fat bodies. Fat female bodies, mostly. Fat as a feminist issue. Fat as fun. Fat as cultural monster. Fat as oppression. Fat as oppressing. Fat as oppressor. Fat as …. Well, she hoped, anyway, fat as sexy, fat as sensuality run amok, fat as excess, fat as carnival. Fat as fleshy flashy fun.

Because that's why she'd taken this job—one of her missions in life was to convince people that fat *was* beautiful. And that's why she'd gotten the job, most likely. Because she was Suzanne LaFleshe, in the flesh, after all. Who better to serve as editor of this particular publication than some who was, well, large? A deluxe-sized woman: six feet, two-and-a-half inches tall. Big breasts, big butt. Lots of heft. Lots of healthy, happy flesh. Fat, some might say, fat—and proud of it.

And, of course, she'd also taken the job because she was a poverty-stricken graduate student who needed the stipend and tuition remission the job provided. Because even fat women—especially fat women—need to eat, after all.

She leaned over and reached into the wire basket that was full of scraps of paper, a post-it note stuck on top, proclaiming: Potential Names!! Do Not Throw Away!! There had been a suggestion box outside the office door, all through December, with a note taped next to the slot: Name the Fat Magazine. Good God. People must have actually put suggestions in there—there were a zillion little bits of paper. She began to spread the papers out next to the keyboard. She'd just make a neat typed list, to start. Tomorrow, she'd decide.

Most of the suggestions, it turned out, were too obscene or offensive or just plain nasty to even type. Those, she stuffed into the most disgusting of the coffee cups. Out of the others, she created her list of the thirteen top contenders, neatly alphabetical: Big is Beautiful, Bulky Babes, Consuming Desire, Fat Attitude, Fat Chick, FFB (Fat is Fucking Beautiful), Fleshpots, Largesse, Plenitude, Pulchritude, Trip to Bountiful, Your Mama, Zaftig!.

Suzanne leaned back in the rickety little chair and realized that she was smiling. The names were cheering her up. Everything, maybe, possibly, could be turning out all right. The magazine would flourish, she'd finish her doctoral dissertation in her own lifetime, she'd get a real job. Maybe. She pried her ass from the chair, stood up and went to the window. She leaned her forehead against the icy glass and cupped her hands around her eyes, looking out over the frozen concrete campus. From here on the 3rd floor of Humanities, the white stone below glowed like the mountains of the moon. The wind tunneled into every crack, howling through archways, skidding bits of snow and paper down the endless corridors of modern architecture that made up the State University of New York at Albany uptown campus—a campus that was all angle, alley, and swoop. She sighed. No trees, no red brick, no ivy, no traditional quad. No softness, no charm. The queen of flesh was imprisoned in an ivory tower of pure cold stone.

She turned back to the desk and shut off the computer. In the sudden absence of electronic sound, the wind seemed to scream even louder, first in one sharp burst, then a long descending wail. At the end of its riff, there was a slight, thick thud—a dull sound, as if a rock had rolled into an empty well and finally struck bottom, somewhere in the depths of the earth.

Wind with weight. Weird. Very weird. The shudder that shimmied down her back made Suzanne realize how silly it was to have come to work in the middle of the night, in the middle of the winter, alone. She dreaded her walk to the bus stop, alone. But there was no help for it—none of her fellow grad students was back yet, and certainly none of the professors. Not one of her lovers, from either group. Well, okay then. She threw her bright red scarf around her head and drew her purple coat around her shoulders. She headed for the long stairway—she'd be okay. She knew that. She'd just have to run for it, that's all.

2

Sam Tindell was leaning against the railing that guarded the deep well at the center of the building. The glass windows of the inner circle of faculty offices overlooked this well. With no outer view, the professors in these offices got natural light only from here, this space lit from above, during the day, by skylights. At night, it was lit only spottily by moonlight and flickering fluorescent bulbs. The glass windows of the empty offices were full of shifty reflections. What they mirrored, one minute, was Sam, looking down, a forbidden cigarette in his hand. What they reflected, the next minute, was just blurry, shadowy motion. A sudden swing. An arc of legs. A body suspended, then a body in flight.

What the walls echoed was the scream and then the small, dull thud.

A body in motion gains momentum as it falls. That's called gravity.

A body, when it meets solid stone after a swift, spiraling flight, four storeys down, shatters rather spectacularly. That's called death.

Blood, bone, hair, skin, viscera, muscle, tendon, heart—all blend, all coalesce into something that no longer has discrete parts. What's left then, is something you could just call "flesh." If it needed a name.

3

Suzanne, as always at 6:30 a.m., was in what she called her "crucified on a cross of dog" position—a canine yanking on each arm, heading in opposite directions, leashes taut, noses deep in the leavings of even earlier doggy walkers. Suzanne's armpits hurt, as muscle and tendon strained under the pressure. "Come on, Pear," she said, tugging at the right-hand leash. The heavy head of her elderly quasi-labrador retriever came up and he waved his thick tail, but he didn't budge from the fascinating damp spot on the tree trunk before him. "Come *on.*" She leaned her weight against the leash and towed Pear from his spot, gradually. On her left hand, Apple was bouncing and quivering, making constant vertical leaps that rattled the leash and jarred the shoulders. The little beast couldn't help it, Suzanne knew—it's what Jack Russell terrorists do. But it was still irritating, this early in the morning, to have such energy vibrating your wrist. And it was cold. Face-freezing, bone-aching cold. Clear dawn sky, promising bright sun, but treacherously cold. Icy sidewalks, unshoveled for weeks. Snowbanks gray with dirt, lining the walks.

"Come *on,*" she yelled. "I'm dying out here and I have work to do." She pulled both dogs in a line toward home, moving steadily but surely, like a tug with two barges in its wake. Her moon boots—fifteen years out of fashion, she knew, but reliable on ice and easy to put on when she was half asleep—pounded at last up her driveway and around the back of her house. Well, not her house, as in actual ownership—just her half of the duplex. A very old, very shabby duplex, the crummiest house on this upscale street of tastefully restored Victorians. And the only reason she even could afford to rent half of this house was because Molly, her landlady for the past two years, was over ninety and needed company more than she needed money. Or so she said. Suzanne suspected that Molly needed both, but company was the most, really, a poor graduate student like herself could offer.

Inside the back mudroom, she dried eight dog feet and wiped down two dog bellies. She slipped off her boots, climbed the two steps to the kitchen and went into its warmth with gratitude. The kitchen was cavernous and spectacularly unmodernized, its stove pre-World War II, its wooden floor pre-World War I. But it was blessedly warm, graced by three radiators—and Molly was generous with heat. The dogs galloped to the door of the pantry and sat down, staring at Suzanne. Obediently, she went into the pantry, found the box of dog biscuits and tossed one into each waiting mouth. Pear swallowed his whole, then walked with stiff dignity to his foam arthritic-dog bed, wedged up against the iron radiator. Apple danced off with her biscuit in her mouth, then bounced into the wicker rocking chair, circling and circling until the cushions settled into the perfect nest. She munched up her biscuit, then tucked her head under the stump of her tail. Both dogs heaved huge sighs, closed their eyes and went back to sleep, their day essentially over.

Suzanne leaned her backside against a radiator and poured herself a cup of coffee—the Mr. Coffee was the newest thing in the kitchen, her one indulgence in consumerism. A necessity, really. She added a nice big dollop of heavy cream and tipped a healthy swig of maple syrup into the steaming mug before carrying it upstairs to the little back bedroom she called her study.

There, on the screen of the laptop she'd sold her grandmother's complete 16-setting Royal Doulton china to buy, was the first paragraph of Chapter Two of her dissertation. It glowed at her, mocking. Like a skull on a shelf, she thought. That's what, she'd read somewhere, Alice Walker called an unfinished novel—a skull grinning down at you from a shelf, never letting you rest. Screaming its hideous little reminder into the air: You haven't done enough! You're nowhere near done! She scolded herself, just as she'd said to the dogs: Come *on*, come *on*. She sighed, adjusted the pillows on the little wooden chair in front of the computer and sat down, sipping the comforting, sweet coffee. She leaned forward and read what she'd typed so far: According to Raymond Hilliard, "They argue that in actual cannibal cultures in particular, the ritual killing and eating of victims is the paradigmatic gesture underlying all major forms of social action, just as it is in Clarissa, where the main action itself is the killing of a female scapegoat by unanimous 'blame,' by collective oral aggression represented as a displaced mode of cannibalism. They see ritual cannibalism as mediating between psyche and society in cultures marked, like Clarissa, by a preoccupation with such oral issues as nursing and weaning and by the all-embracing influence of the preoedipal mother imago" (1084). She took a bite of the jelly doughnut she'd left next to the computer, for just this sort of moment—in order to think at her best, Suzanne needed to chew. She closed her eyes and let her tongue do its work. Perfect: the powdery outside, the crisp dough surrounding the tart raspberry jam. That first bite through all three layers. Heaven.

She reached into the pile of Xeroxes in the drawer of the desk. Oral aggression, oral aggression: she'd seen something else on that recently, in some one of the nine thousand articles and book chapters she'd copied, right? Shit, where? Ah, yes—here, here: "...even the most apparently benign acts of eating involve aggression, even cannibalism." That one was from a book called *From Communion to Cannibalism* and in the margin someone—herself, in some midnight fugue state of research-induced exhaustion?—had scribbled, See Freud on the "oral or cannibalistic stage of development." Oh, God, now she'd have to re-read Freud. But which fucking Freud? She'd forgotten to write it down and now she hadn't a clue what she'd been thinking. The curse of working in your sleep. She picked up a pen and added another scribble— Totem and Taboo? Check.

She sat back, looking at the bit of empty, limp, sugary doughnut shell in her hand, sucked dry of its jelly. She tried to see it as her victim, as an object of displaced anger, as the flesh of a defeated enemy, drained of its strength, its spirit now melding with her own. Or as her mother's breast, and herself as an aggressive little pre-Oedipal infant, sucking it dry and demanding more, more, more. Bullshit, she thought—a doughnut is flour and water and sugar and shortening and…well, okay, yeast. Yeast was sort of a living thing—but hardly sentient and nothing she felt particularly aggressive toward. She folded the doughnut shell into a neat packet and put it in her mouth. She chewed, thinking. Then she scrolled backward through her document, all the way to the top, the title page.

She did this every time she got discouraged, every time she was certain she would never finish the damn thing, never earn her doctorate, never ever ever ever be done. This self-doubt happened about every three or four hours when her mind bit down on the recurring, angst-ridden thought: You're thirty-eight years old and you'll be working on this thing until you die. Your tombstone will read:

Suzanne Brown
[aka Suzanne LaFleshe]
November 15, 1964- ????

All But Dissertation.

Once again, she read the title page, the one she'd typed exactly as the university manual told her, the one that gave her the only hope she could muster:

CRUSOE'S CHILDREN:
EMBODYING CANNIBAL AND CARNIVAL
IN FOUR TWENTIETH CENTURY NOVELS

By
Suzanne Brown

A Dissertation
Submitted to the State University of New York at Albany
in Partial Fulfillment of
the Requirements for the Degree of
Doctor of Philosophy

Department of English
May 2003

She stared at the final line—the date. She'd already changed it three times: from December 2001 to May 2002 to December 2002. And now May 2003, completion projected again into the future. That ever-deferred date was the record of her procrastination. Her failure to get a grip. The skull on the shelf, grinning its toothy mockery.

She sighed, clicked the mouse to close the file and then to shut down the computer. When the machine, courteous as always, inquired if she was *sure* she wanted to shut down, she took it as a reprimand from the gods. But she clicked "Yes" and closed the top of the computer with a sense of relief. And she really wasn't goofing off—she had a meeting at 8 o'clock with Rachel Ellis, her dissertation director, who was also the faculty advisor of Whatever-It-Would-Be-Called Fat Journal. She had yet to meet her assistant editor, a brand-new, shiny graduate student, one who wasn't already beaten down and broken. Only a new grad student and a totally gung-ho advisor would have set up a meeting at 8 o'clock on a Monday morning, a time when most English departments are quiet as graves. But these two had, so she needed to get dressed and go. It really wasn't goofing off. Or avoidance or denial or passive aggression or any of those things.

Really, it wasn't. Fuck Freud. She carried her cold coffee into her bedroom and lifted the cat off the long wool skirt she'd chosen to wear on this, her first official day on the job. "Thanks, Plum," she said, "for warming up the outfit." The cat glared at her as she brushed

brilliant orange cat hairs off the dark green wool, then burrowed under Suzanne's quilt, becoming a quiet round lump in the covers.
Suzanne sighed again. Her animals were warm and happy; she had to
go out and face the cold. "Fine," she said, aiming her voice toward
the lump in the bed. "Someone has to be the kibble-winner in this
house, right? And that seems to be me."

After the brutal air she'd breathed on the way from the university bus
stop to Humanities, air so cold it made her teeth and sinuses ache, the
stuffy heat of the building felt like the tropics. Suzanne unwrapped
the red scarf from her face, fluffed up her hair, and headed for the
stairs. Her one bit of exercise—besides vigorous sex, whenever she
could get it, which was gratifyingly often—was taking stairs instead
of elevators. If truth be told, though, this wasn't for health reasons.
She liked stairs; her long legs took stairs two at a time, easily. And
Suzanne was scared of elevators, as she was of any space that seemed
too small to hold her safely. Anyway, here in Humanities, the elevators were very, very small. And very slow and jerky. Terrifying.
    As she was turning into the doorway for the stairs, however, she
saw a cluster of people down the hall, gathered into a little circle, just
where the skylight from four floors up poured its sunshine into the
center of the building. She stopped to stare. It was way too early for
students to be in the building, surely. And one of the backs bent into
the circle was wearing the blue uniform of a security guard, always a
worrisome note. And surely, someone in the group was crying—or
retching. Now that she stopped to really listen, there was definitely
some sort of gasping, choking noise going on. She let the heavy steel
door close behind her as she walked down the hall.
    The security man turned at the sound of her high heeled boots
clicking on the stone floor and he held up a hand, palm out, to stop
her from coming any closer. But the minute he'd turned, opening a
gap in the little circle, she'd seen what was on the floor and she'd gone
down on her knees, hard, skidding. She felt the crack of her kneecaps

against the cold floor, but the sharp pain seemed to come from a great distance. All she could really see, really feel, was the body in front of her.

The blood and pulp had dried into a deep brown, crusted puddle. There was no face. But the clothes, the khaki pants and black sweater, were familiar. And so were the tan work boots, bent at odd angles. Everything twisted, everything smashed. But the hand, flung out to the right of the pile of clothing and flesh, was intact. Bent backwards, wrist broken where he must have tried to stop the hideous fall, but still recognizable. From her knees, Suzanne knew exactly whose hand that was—knew it in her bones. She closed her eyes and saw that hand as she had seen it last, cupped under her breast, holding fast. She opened her eyes, reached out one finger, and touched the blue wrist with its crisp curling blond hairs. "Sam?" she said. "No. Sam. No."

A hand grabbed her, pulling her back. "Don't touch anything, m'am. University police are on the way. Do you know this man?" The security man kept his hand, warm and heavy, on her shoulder.

She sat back, rocking on her wobbly heels. She tilted her head back and looked up. Four floors up, the skylight was brilliant with light, clear dazzling blue. She stared, up and up. She remembered, suddenly, last night's wind. Wind with weight. Wind that screamed. Wind with an awful thud at its end. Oh God, oh God, oh God. It came to her with absolute clarity. This was her fault. If she'd left her office three minutes sooner, he wouldn't have done it. He'd have seen her or heard her on the stairs. And he wouldn't have done it, because he never, ever would have wanted her to see him like this. Oh God. She grabbed the security man's arm and hoisted herself to her feet, her legs trembling. She took one last look at the body on the stone. "Yes," she said. "I do. He was my...friend. He was a grad student here, last year." She looked into the guard's face, then around at the two other faces. One, she knew—Rachel Ellis, standing with a hand over her mouth, the fingers making white marks in her cheeks.

"Rachel," she said. "You know him. It's Sam Tindell. You remember, he finished last May." She wanted to cry—at least someone could put PhD after Sam's name, on his tombstone. God, what a waste. What a sad, pathetic waste.

Rachel shook her head and whispered through her fingers. "Jesus. It is. I didn't recognize…." Her voice trailed away, then strengthened, as if she'd suddenly thought of something practical she could do. "Someone will have to call his wife."

Suzanne looked down at her boots.

The security guard took hold of her elbow. "You okay, m'am?"

She nodded.

"You know this man's wife?"

She shook her head. "Not really. Just her name. Her name is Diana." She thought of how sadly Sam had said that beautiful name: Diana. How, just after Thanksgiving, in her bed, Plum tucked behind his knees, purring, Sam had leaned into Suzanne's neck and said, "If only Diana were my friend. If only I could talk to her, you know? But she's not. She's my wife, but I think she doesn't even like me, most of the time. So I guess you're my only friend, Suzanne. The only true friend I've got."

Rachel stepped out of the circle. "If he finished his degree just last year, their phone number will still be in my files, in my office. I'll go get it for you." She walked away, briskly.

The other woman, a skinny, freckled woman whose face was so pale and sweaty that it was obvious who had been retching, moved closer to Suzanne. She held out a bony hand, offering a formal handshake. "Hi," she said. "I'm Ronelle Graham, your assistant editor." She smiled, showing a mouthful of crooked yellow teeth. "Hell of a way to start the semester, ain't it?"

4

"You better sit," Ronelle said. "You look pretty pukey."

Suzanne nodded, then lowered herself into the rolling chair in her office. Her knees throbbed; she guessed that they were turning many shades of blue. She smoothed her skirt over her thighs, pleating the dark green wool in her fingers. It was one of her favorite skirts—a great find, $2.75 at the Goodwill store on Fuller Avenue, a bonafide Ann Taylor skirt, made of fine, soft wool. She always liked to think about the original owners of her clothes—the tall, large, rich women who bought beautiful things like this, then discarded them when they were hardly even worn. Her fingers gripped the fabric and she held the bottom of the skirt up to the light. "Is there blood on the hem?" she asked. "Do you see any blood here?"

Ronelle crouched down and put her nose almost on the fabric. She scrutinized it, carefully, then looked up at Suzanne. "Nope," she said. "Not a drop of gore. You're good to go, girl. Lucky the stuff on the floor was mostly dry."

Suzanne stared down. This woman didn't look more than fifteen—she was thin as a thread, with dark hair twisted into fuzzy dreadlocks. Her eyes were the palest blue Suzanne had ever seen and her freckles the darkest brown. *Her* face looked like it had been splashed with blood, now that she thought of it—darkly spattered. And she was smiling, looking perfectly happy, even though she'd been barfing in the hall ten minutes before. Unbelievably odd. But, of course, Ronelle hadn't known Sam—that mess in the hall was just a mess, to her. Not a man. Not a friend—a lovely, funny, sexy friend. Suzanne nodded. "Yeah, lucky."

Ronelle stood up and put her hands on her hips, looking around the office. "Well, this is some piece of crap office, isn't it? Jeez." She began to gather up the coffee cups, holding them in her arms, looking for a waste basket. When she spotted it, jammed under the window, she dropped the cups in. She brushed her hands off and turned back to Suzanne. "Look," she said, "I'm not a total ass. I know you must feel awful about that guy. I just don't know what to say, okay? I mean, what the fuck is there to say?" She tilted her head. "You know? I've had a couple of friends off themselves and there just isn't a thing to say about it, after. I mean, people want to go, they go. The rest of us just don't know shit about it—what was in their heads. Their hearts. And we can't know, ever, so there isn't a thing to be said. You know?" She rocked on her heels, her bunches of hair bouncing, her hands jiggling in the air.

God, Suzanne thought, I've got a Jack Russell terrier for an assistant editor. But the girl was right. She couldn't think of a thing to say, not really. "I know."

"Right." Ronelle slid her butt onto the desk top and swung her legs. She was wearing only thin black leggings and her ankles were bare above her heavy black boots.

Suzanne put a finger on one ankle—it was icy. "How come you aren't wearing socks?" she said.

Ronelle drew up a leg and looked at her foot as if she'd forgotten it existed. "I'm not?" She shook her head. "Must not have been any around. I couldn't see much this morning in my apartment, in the dark." She smiled. "It's a basement flat, on Dove Street, downtown. It was really dark."

"Why?"

"Ni Mo didn't come yet. No power." She shrugged. "And, you're not my mother, you know. I think we ought to establish that, real quick. Okay?"

Suzanne looked at the square, spotty face and the clear eyes. This kid would be fine, she realized. She was going to be just fine. "Sorry," she said. "It's just that I'm nearly double your age and twice your size, so I might forget and go all motherly on you once in awhile. Just smack me if I do." She held out her hand. "I didn't introduce myself, did I? I'm Suzanne Brown." She waited a beat, like she always did, then added, "Also known as Suzanne LaFleshe, Queen of the Fat Women. That's how I got this job."

Ronelle looked blank for a minute, then she giggled. "Cool," she said.

When Rachel joined them, she set the rules for the morning meeting. They would not discuss the mess in the hall. It was being taken care of and nothing they could say would help. They would not engage in gossip or worry or elegy or grief. There would be time for those later. This morning, they would work. Work worked, at distracting people from tragedy. Work, in fact, for Rachel was the only thing that really mattered. She'd gotten her doctorate at twenty-eight, written three books of feminist criticism by thirty-four, received tenure at thirty-five, become department chair at thirty-eight and Suzanne's dissertation director the same year. Now she was forty, with short silvery-blond hair, spiked into points around her head, and a boxy, compact body. She had one of the best brains Suzanne had ever come across and she never wasted a minute, ever, that Suzanne had ever seen.

So, they were working. Ronelle was on her hands and knees on the floor of the office, sorting manuscripts into piles according to genre: fiction, essay, poetry, literary criticism, film criticism, other. Last September, in a fit of enthusiasm about the new slant of the literary magazine, Rachel had issued calls for manuscripts in all sorts of places: Call for submission: Literary journal focused on the positive aspects of fat is looking for thoughtful, insightful, theoretically-informed creative and critical works. Cutting edge stuff only. No misogyny, no violence, no self-help, no whining, no porn (unless it's very well written and turns us on). NO DIETS!! Deadline: October 15, 2002. And, God, they'd come in: great heaps of manila envelopes. And

then, on October 14, the graduate student hired to be the editor had
flaked out, dropped out of the program and gone to Guam. Then
there had been only one poor student aide, a freshman, whose main
job was to collect the mail and put it somewhere. Which she had—
the floor. In November, Rachel and her committee had offered
Suzanne the Managing Editor position for the spring semester: tuition remission and a cash stipend in exchange for bringing the magazine to life. Just simple editorial work, part time. Nothing to interfere
with the completion of her dissertation and certainly better than teaching a section of freshman composition, which is what all the other
graduate assistants were doomed to do and which Suzanne had done
for years, with only moderate success. And, Rachel had promised, an
Assistant Editor.

So now the Assistant Editor was scrabbling on the office floor,
Suzanne was trying to locate the computer disks with the addresses
and names of all the people who'd submitted something, and Rachel
was washing the desk top and file cabinet with Lysol that she'd gotten
from the custodian's closet. They kept the door closed, so they couldn't
hear the noises from three floors down, the heavy footsteps of the
police or the squeaking wheels of the covered stretcher being rolled
away.

When the disk was located and its files printed out, when the piles
of manuscripts were neat and all surfaces shiny and mold-free, they
looked at the potential names for the journal. Rachel liked *Zaftig!*
best.

Ronelle frowned. "I don't even know what that means," she said.
She was perched on the windowsill, looking down at the white campus. Classes started tomorrow and students were coming back. But it
was too cold for them to gather on the concrete walkways. Most likely,
they were scurrying through the underground corridors, like mice in a
basement.

Rachel was sitting on the floor, her back against the file cabinet.
She put on what Suzanne called her in-class lecture voice and said,
"It's a Yiddish term. A lovely term. It means—well, like all Yiddish,

it's difficult to translate, exactly. It means big, buxom, beautiful. Like that."

"Oh, okay." Ronelle nodded. "Sorry, I should know that—but there ain't much Yiddish where I come from. And, anyway, I like *Fat Attitude*. But, hey, how about this?" She jumped from the sill and grabbed a piece of paper. "Look! How about we spell it like this?" She took a pen and wrote, in big block letters: *Phat Attitude*. She grinned, bouncing on her heels, waving the paper. When she saw the confusion on both faces, she shook her head. "It's a pun. Get it? Like, phat, you know? It means, sort of like, cool. Great." She made a face. "Groovy."

Suzanne laughed. "Oh, I see. That's pretty good."

Rachel nodded, thinking. "Not bad. What's your choice, Suzanne?"

She looked at the list and, suddenly, she heard Sam's voice, as it had been in her ear, two months back, before the Christmas break had separated them. The last time she'd seen him, she realized, alive: "Suzanne," he'd said, sipping sweet red wine and plunging a fork into the chocolate mousse cake she'd baked, "what I like best about you is your generosity, your warmth…your, I don't know." Suddenly, he'd grinned, pointing his fork across the table. "Yes, I do. It's your largesse. That's what I like best."

She bent over, looking for the little scrap of paper where she'd found that word. He must have submitted it. That must have been Sam's suggestion, dropped into the box. "Where are the scraps?" she said. "The little scraps with the names?" She felt her face flush. "I need the scraps. I think one was Sam's."

Rachel stood up and put her hand on Suzanne's shoulder. "I threw them away," she said. "They're gone. We have the list. I didn't think we needed the papers. And you can't know if any was Sam's—they were all anonymous, right?"

Suzanne let her fingers go limp on the desk. "Yes. It's just that— well, I know it was Sam's. I just know. I wanted to have the paper, to hold it, keep it, you know?"

Rachel's fingers tightened. "It's gone, Suzanne. But what was the name? We'll use it, if you want."

"Largesse," Suzanne whispered. "It means generosity."

Ronelle sighed. "That's pretty boring. I still think that phat...."

Suzanne stood up, towering over Ronelle and Rachel, pulling her-self up to her full height. Six feet two inches, plus. She only remem-bered when she needed to, that she was taller than almost all women, and most men, and that she could use her size. "Largesse," she said. "I'm the Managing Editor. The name of this magazine is *Largesse*."

After Rachel had gone back to her own office, Suzanne asked Ronelle, "So where are you from?"

Ronelle looked up from the stack of manuscripts she was shoving into her bookbag, to read at home, she said, if she ever got her lights turned on. She'd volunteered to slog through the literary criticism submissions, getting the worst over with. "What?"

"Where there's no Yiddish? Like you said." Suzanne leaned back in the rolling chair, rubbing her knees. Her eyes ached; she wanted a chance to cry, but she wouldn't, not while anyone else was around.

"Oh, that." Ronelle zipped the bag and slung one strap over her shoulder. The bag looked like it weighed more than she did. "You won't have heard of it. Livingston, New York." She put her hand on the doorknob, then turned back. "My dad worked on dairy farms, his whole life. Not his own farms. Other people's. We always lived— well, my folks still do—in trailers next to barnyards. Knee deep in cow shit. I grew up chewing on silage for a snack. It's kind of sweet, you know—they mix it with molasses sometimes, to get the cows to eat it." She smiled, a crooked little grin. "I'm as white trash as the great Northeast allows."

There was a tap on the door and Ronelle jumped, then swung it open. On the other side was a tall, white-haired man. Handsome, Suzanne noted automatically. Younger than the white hair would have you think. Good face, strong bones. He nodded briefly at Ronelle, then stared at Suzanne. "Ms. Brown? I'm Charles Clark, head of

University Police." he said. "I'd like to ask you a few questions."

Ronelle scurried out under the man's raised arm. "See you, Suzanne," she said, and fled.

Suzanne stood up. She was exactly Charles Clark's height. "Come in," she said.

When he'd settled himself on the window sill, she sat back down. He didn't look like a cop, exactly, except maybe for the steady watchfulness in his eyes. He was dressed in ordinary clothes—a tweed wool jacket, khaki pants. He sat quietly, just looking at her, and she thought she'd better think of something to say. "I read somewhere that you guys carry guns now. Is that true?"

Mr. Clark smiled. "Since four, five years ago, yes we do. We're empowered with all the rights of regular police officers these days. Think about it, Ms. Brown—I'm in charge of the safety of a small city here. Nearly 20,000 people are on this campus every day and night during the academic year. Most of them between the ages of 17 and 22. Often stoned. Very often drunk. Sometimes crazy and sometimes armed. Wouldn't you want a gun?" He took a notebook out of his pocket.

Suzanne thought about it, just as he'd asked. She remembered the kid who'd held a whole class hostage, a couple of years ago, and the other kid, the one he'd shot in the groin, the kid the newspapers called a hero. She thought of all the dried blood in the hallway, three floors down, Sam's blood. "No," she said. "I don't think I would."

He laughed. "Well, that's real nice—a true pacifist. But I do want a gun and the law says I get to have one. And I just need to ask you a couple of things about the death of Sam Tindell. All right?"

"All right." She leaned back in her chair, running her hands through her hair. She'd had it cut short over the break and wasn't used to the way it felt, wrapping like little springs around her fingers. She dropped her hands to her lap and folded them tightly together.

"We've spoken to his wife," Mr. Clark said, easily, as if it was no big deal. "And she suggested that we speak to you—she seemed to think that you and Mr. Tindell had a kind of close relationship."

"Dr. Tindell," Suzanne said. "He'd earned his degree. He was entitled to be called Dr. Tindell."

"Okey doke." He made a note in the pad he was holding. "So did you and Dr. Tindell have a close relationship, like his wife said?" He held his pencil loosely in his fingers, the eraser beating a little tune on his thigh.

Suzanne sighed and closed her eyes. "Okay. I slept with Sam a couple of times. I've never met his wife. I had no idea…." She paused, her throat tight. "I didn't know she knew that Sam and I were friends." She opened her eyes and looked directly at Mr. Clark. "I'm sorry if that's made this any worse for her. I really really am."

Mr. Clark made a little check mark in his notebook and then flipped back a page, reading from earlier notes. "She just said you and her husband were friends, Ms. Brown. Classmates. That's all she said. She said you read his poetry for him and gave him your reactions. Suggestions. She said she couldn't do that, that she's just an accountant. A numbers person, not a word person. She said she paid the bills and he wrote poetry. That right?"

"I don't know. I don't know what arrangement they had. But it's not fair, the way that sounds. Sam worked hard—he taught four courses as an adjunct, at four different colleges, driving all over the whole capital district. For slave wages. And, yes, he wrote poetry. Lovely poetry." Her eyes started to fill and she shook her head, hard, to clear her vision.

"Uh huh. Well, do you know of any reason why Mr.—Dr. Tindell would want to kill himself? Was he depressed? Worried?"

Suzanne stood up. She'd meant to do it with grace, growing tall before him, but it took a minute to wrench her butt out of the chair and when she stood the pain in her knees made them buckle, ruining the whole effect. She forced her legs straight. "He couldn't find a full-time job. He sent out 300 applications in November and didn't get one interview at MLA—not one. He was sad about that. And his poems were always being rejected, all the time. He sent them to about a zillion places and every damn one sent them back. He was sad about that." She stood in the center of her newly neat office and remembered Sam, showing her the pile of rejection slips, all colors: blue, ivory, lavender, pink, green, yellow. He'd said he liked the yellow ones best. Yellow, he'd said, was the color of the jaundiced eye, the color of bile, the color of cowardice. He'd said it was perfect, to convey rejection. She nodded. "So, yes, he was often sad. But not suicidal." She felt that she was swaying and she tried to steady herself, find her balance. "Oh God, I'd have known that, wouldn't I? I'd have seen that?"

Mr. Clark stood up and put a hand on her shoulder. "Not necessarily. Believe me, I know. In this job, you learn. Some sorority girl chucks herself out a window and none of her sisters knew a thing was wrong. Some poor dumb jock takes five hundred Advil and none of his teammates knew a thing was wrong. Some brilliant physics student gets an A- on an exam, instead of his usual A+, and he slits his wrists. No one knew. Parents sit sobbing in my office—they didn't know anything was wrong." Mr. Clark's voice was soft. "It's not your fault, Ms. Brown. It's never really anyone's fault."

She tried to smile, welcoming the steady weight of his hand on her flesh. She was starting to tremble. "But I think I heard him fall." She was whispering, her head turned, her lips almost brushing his fingers. "Last night—I thought it was the wind. But there was this screaming sound, a wail." Her throat closed and she couldn't speak.

Mr. Clark's hand tightened and he said. "Sit down, Ms. Brown, and tell me about last night."

At home, Suzanne mixed the ingredients for rice pudding and put the pan in the oven, before she walked the dogs. That way, it would be warm and comforting when she came back. Nothing, nothing was more sustaining than her grandmother's recipe for rice pudding. She let herself picture only that, as the dogs pulled her through the icy streets, already dark at 4:30 p.m., and she limped behind them. Only that, food and warmth and sweetness.

When she'd cleaned the dogs' feet and washed her hands, she noticed the plant on her kitchen table—a graceful bit of green in a mossy clay pot. There was a piece of paper under the pot. Suzanne pulled it out and read the note: *Rue. It protects against bad spells. Which, by the way, someone is sending your way, dear girl. Very bad spells! (Who is your enemy?) Rub rue over your skin, drop some leaves in your bath.* She shook her head. Molly's writing—still strong and spiky, prickly all over with jabs and swoops of the pen. Just like Molly. She ran a finger along one branch of the rue plant and its lacey leaves. Then she turned to stir the rice pudding in the oven, thinking: Who is my enemy?

Because she believed Molly. She had learned to over the past two years she'd shared Molly's house, since Molly was always right, about everything. Well, almost everything. Molly was certainly odd. She claimed, in fact, to be a witch, the oldest practicing witch in Albany, she said. As evidence of her prowess, she always pointed to her spine, still straight as a wand at ninety-four, because she knew the herbs to counter weakening of the bones and she'd been eating egg shells and white clay since she was a girl. Yes, she was blind in one eye, but she had the hearing of an eagle. Molly herself said that she was failing, that time was devouring her powers—as it should, she always added, as it should—but her coven still gathered at the house every once in a while and she was still its leader. She still walked Munchie, the little white poodle she called her familiar, three times a day, without fail. Suzanne didn't know if she believed in the craft Molly said she practiced. She couldn't quite get herself to believe that Molly was a witch, with any kind of special powers. But, still, she believed in Molly's wisdom, her humor. Her strength.

So she kept the rue in the center of the table as she mixed a custard sauce for the pudding—butter, sugar, egg yolks, rum and vanilla—and she looked at the plant as she ate, spoon after spoon of warm, plump grains of rice, softened and flavored by the sauce. She rolled each grain on her tongue. The she closed her eyes, picturing Sam Tindell, alive and laughing, as she spooned and swallowed, spooned and swallowed. When she opened her eyes, the pan of pudding was almost gone and she'd almost erased from her mind the terrible picture of Sam's pathetic hand on the cold stone floor of Humanities. She stood up and noticed Plum, lying on the radiator, and Apple and Pear at her feet. Six animal eyes, canny and alert, focused on her face. She bent over and spooned the last bits of the pudding onto the plates that were lined up on the floor in the corner of the kitchen, next to the sink, cracked china plates, each one bearing a picture of the appropriate fruit, gifts from Molly. She put a dab of sauce on each plate and waved her hand toward them. "Treats," she said. Apple raced to her plate and Plum leapt from the radiator to hers. But Pear—solid, worried, sensitive Pear—leaned his heavy head against her leg, butting her thigh. She took one of his silky black ears in her palm and rubbed. "I'm okay, Pear," she said. "Really. It's all right. You can eat." The dog's tail raised in an arc and he walked to his dish, nosing Plum away just in time.

Suzanne was in the tub, soaking in hot water scented by bits of lavender, white sage and rosemary, dried and saved from Molly's garden, with bits of fresh rue floating on the surface, when she heard steps climbing her stairs. She sat up in the water, her heart pounding: Who is your enemy? But then she remembered Pear and relaxed. He would not let a stranger into the house. And she hadn't heard any frenzied barking from Apple. So it had to be one of the people the dogs considered to be part of their pack. She made an educated guess and called out, "In the tub, Morris." She hadn't seen him in some time, but still, the dogs remembered. She thought about covering herself with the washcloth, then realized how ludicrously inadequate that little square of fabric would be. And Morris had seen her naked before, anyway. "Come in," she said.

The door of the bathroom swung open a crack and a voice floated to her through the steam. "It smells a bit like you're making a stew in there, love. Has all that work on cannibalism crazed you at last?" Morris stuck his head around the door. "Oh, how lovely you look. If you are stewing, may I please have a bite?"

Suzanne laughed. "Of course. Come on in."

Morris walked into the bathroom, wearing an overcoat and woolen hat pulled over his ears. He had to bend his head to get in the door— Morris was six and half feet tall, even with his perpetual stoop and rounded shoulders. His body, Suzanne always thought, must have been cloned from the scarecrow from the Wizard of Oz. But his brain—ah, his brain was a wonder. He was fifty-three years old, had once been a poet of some fame—a Yale Younger Poet, in his youth, now a professor at the university. Her one-time lover and her buddy, the first person to befriend her when she'd come to the university two years ago.

Suzanne's eyes filled with tears at the sight of the three red roses he held in his mittened hand. "Oh Morris, roses," she said. "In the middle of winter."

He looked down at the flowers, as if surprised to find them there. "Oh, yes. The miracle of florists." He sat down on the toilet and pulled off his mittens. He touched Suzanne's cheek with one cold finger. "I heard, love. About your friend Sam. I thought that you might—well, need the company of roses this evening, you know?"

He lifted the roses to his face and inhaled. Two dog snouts appeared in the doorway, sniffing loudly. Suzanne gestured toward the door. "Close that, okay? It's letting all the warmth out—and letting beasts in."

Morris sent one long leg across the bathroom, pushing the door shut with the toe of a huge rubber boot. "Get, beasties," he said. He pulled his hat from his head and slid his arms out of the old coat, letting it slide to the floor. He turned back to Suzanne, his eyes traveling over her body. "God, you are a glory. Look at how those gorgeous breasts float. My God. Aphrodite rising from the waves." He slid from his perch on the toilet, kneeling next to the deep Victorian tub. He began to pluck petals from a rose, dropping them one by one into the tub. The heat of the water released their scent and brought June into the January night. Petals swam across the water and adhered to

Suzanne's skin. Morris rolled up the sleeves of his sweater and put his hands to work, denuding each rose, sending more and more petals into the bath, until Suzanne's whole body was covered with spots like wet red velvet—her arms, her belly, her breasts and thighs. Then he sat back, smiling. "There. Now you look like a different painting. Ophelia, but better. Not mad. Far sexier."

She smiled, looking down at her petal-bedecked skin. "Thank you, Morris," she said. "I needed some cheering up."

He nodded. "Yes, I thought you might." He leaned back, dabbling a hand in the water. "I could, you know, do much more, my dear. To make you feel better." He tipped his head, his eyes asking a question.

She felt his hand brush her hip. She closed her eyes. Why not? Why the hell not? "Yes," she whispered. "You could." She heard the little hiss of his intake of breath, the surprise and joy in it.

Then he rose up on his knees, bending his long spine over the tub. He lowered his head and kissed the petals that lay on her skin, one by one, until his mouth was under water and Suzanne's hips were rising to meet his lips. She slipped her shoulders down into the water, as he raised her hips with his strong, long hands and bent above her. She let the water fill her ears and mouth and eyes, as his tongue slid into her body and drowned her.

In her bed, Suzanne sat up and toweled his hair dry, rubbing his head hard. He'd already done her hair and it swarmed in damp curls around her head. Her bare shoulders were covered by the handknit afghan her grandmother had made her, years and years ago. He rested his forehead against her belly and his mouth tickled as he spoke. "I cannot imagine it. I simply cannot imagine anyone casting himself over that railing and into the air." He pushed his face deeper into the softness of her flesh. "I am not a coward, Suzanne. I know that. But I cannot imagine making that fall, watching that stone floor fly up to meet me." He rolled over, suddenly, and sat up. "And who would choose to die in the fucking Humanities building? I mean, really."

Suzanne dropped the towel on the floor and slid down under the covers, curling on her side and resting her head on her hand. "I know. Really—and this was Sam. Sam, who hated to make a scene. To have anyone even notice him. That's what I can't figure—I mean, even if Sam decided life was just too terrible to bear and it was time to check out, I can't imagine him making such a——well, you know."

Morris nodded. "Such a splash."

Suzanne flinched.

"Oh, God. Bad choice of words. Will I never learn to control my tongue?" Morris ran a hand over Suzanne's shoulder.

She shrugged. "Well, yes—terrible word choice. And you happen to control your tongue very nicely and you know it. But it's true— you know what Sam did when he was teaching? He always knocked on the door before he went in. I mean it, he used to stand out in the hall and knock on the door of his own classroom before he'd enter." She started to laugh, remembering. She sat up, still laughing. "He said he didn't want to startle anyone by going in unannounced. I mean, my God. He didn't want to embarrass some kid who was sound asleep or someone who was bitching about a grade or something. So he knocked!"

Morris smiled. "Did he really? Well, that's how I'll choose to remember him, then. A polite, hesitant young man, standing in the hallway, knocking on his own door. Thank you, love, for giving me that image." He stretched his arms over his head. "Well, I'd better make my way into the cold, cold night. You need your sleep." He pushed to the edge of the bed and bent for his socks. "Tomorrow begins the next great adventure in state-sponsored education."

Suzanne curled back into the covers. She thought how much she'd have liked Morris to stay, to sleep curled around her, his stalky body a wall against loneliness and nightmare. But she knew that he wouldn't want to stay, that Morris lived alone, wrote alone, slept alone, dreamed alone. That was a given, a fact. She'd never been to his house, never intruded into his private space. And that was fine, usually. Their relationship had always been casual, intermittent, easy. And usually

Suzanne, too, preferred her own space and her own pillow and her own dreams. But, tonight, the wind rattling the thin panes of glass was cold and it howled like a banshee. Who is your enemy?

She would have liked his company. But she wouldn't ask. She drew the comforter to her chin. "Let the dogs out for a minute, okay? And, Morris, lock the door when you go." She closed her eyes, but felt him still breathing in the room.

"You never lock your doors. You always say that Pear is security enough."

She squeezed her eyes even more tightly closed. "Just lock them, okay?" She listened to his steps moving down the stairs and hoped that she would fall asleep quickly and that the night would pass without dreams.

Sometime in the night, the phone rang. Suzanne's hand shot out to pick it up and her sleep-numbed tongue said, "Yes?"

A thin, high voice on the other end sighed across the wires. "It's your fault, you fat bitch. He did it because of you."

Then the voice was gone.

Suzanne sat up, the blood in her veins turned to ice, crystalline, slow-moving. She stared at the phone, and gently replaced the receiver. She pulled the covers to her chin and sat very still, listening to the wind slicing through the trees.

5

Suzanne woke to the white glare of snowlight at her window. In the early morning hours, when she must have finally slept, the wind had died, the sky had clouded over and soft, heavy flakes had begun to fall. She shook her head, ruffling her hair around her skull. She looked at the quiet, innocent phone. That voice, that incredible accusation—a dream? It might have been a dream. It could have been. Really—it must have been.

She stood up and looked out onto the back yard. Molly's herbs and shrubs and trees were curtained with three inches of fresh white, all pure and veiled, like virgin brides. All converted to magical, gentle shapes, as if even the possibility of evil had gone out of the world. That voice must have been a dream. And she would shake it off, forget about it. Let the new day begin. The snow really was lovely. But she still sighed, thinking about walking the dogs over sidewalks where the treachery of ice was now hidden beneath the beauty of fresh snow. Plain old walking on her bedroom floor was bad enough. Her knees were stiff—not terribly sore, just a spectrum of colors and aches.

Then she sniffed the air—coffee. Someone had already made the coffee. She opened her bedroom door. Pear was not in his usual guardian spot just outside her door. Apple was not bouncing up and down the stairs. Her animals had abandoned her and they did that for only one person. She bent over the railing and called down: "Molly?"

"Are you up, then, you lazy slug? Come down. We've made you breakfast, Plum and me."

Wrapped in a bathrobe, Plum curling around her feet, Suzanne sat at her kitchen table and stared at the plate Molly had set in front of her. You had to be suspicious of Molly's food. It always tasted wonderful, but it was often also dotted with odd green flecks and unidentifiable bits. But this looked all right—and, really, what could anyone do to a pair of soft-boiled eggs? And they were lovely, each set on its slice of hot buttered toast. Toast cut into perfect crust-free rounds, so that the eggs looked up at their eater like a pair of startled eyes. Suzanne cut a bite and slipped it into her mouth—and it was perfect. Warm, salty egg, dusted with pepper. Buttery, crunchy toast. Very crunchy toast. She chewed for a long minute and then asked, "Molly? What kind of bread did you use?"

Molly smiled at her across the table and her blind eye winked. Her white hair stood up in a crown of spikes and she was wrapped in layers of sweaters—at least three that Suzanne could distinguish, all the same sort of purply-brown. "Multigrain. Homemade," she said. She sipped from her cup of coffee.

Suzanne took another bite and chewed it for a long while. "Uh huh. And what else? Besides all those healthy grains, I mean."

Molly looked out the window. "Multigrain with a bit of bone meal mixed in."

Suzanne put down her fork and also looked at the window. The dogs were romping in the snowy back yard. Well, Apple and Munchie, Molly's tiny white poodle, were romping. Pear was ignoring the others, walking about with great care, trying to lift each paw above the snow as he went. A shawl of new snow was piling up on his broad back. "Whose bones, Molly?" she asked.

"Oh, no one you know. Just bone meal. Like you give to tulips, when you plant them. You can buy it anywhere. And it's full of calcium, minerals. It's good for you." Molly stood up. She leaned her hands on the table and bent over, staring hard at Suzanne's face. "And it would be even better, you know, if they really were the ground-up bones of your enemy. So you'd absorb your enemy's strength. And cunning. Shoot. You write about cannibals and you don't know that?"

Suzanne looked into Molly's eyes. The right was just a cloudy ball, covered with thick gray cataract. But the left was as clear and blue as yesterday's sky. And dancing with light. "I do so know—fee fi fo fum and all that. But, who is this enemy I'm supposed to devour?"

Molly shrugged and straightened up. "I don't know. But I heard her voice in the wind, last night."

Suzanne felt a chill in her own bones. "Her? Is it a woman?"

"Ha. Isn't it usually a woman, who hates another woman that bad?"

She smiled, her teeth perfectly straight and white. At ninety-four, Molly had no fillings. No missing molars, no gold crowns—she'd probably been snacking on bones her whole life. Probably had bone meal in her baby bottles. "But I couldn't tell, not really. Man. Woman. Ghost. They all sound alike, in the wind." She shrugged again. "You just take care. I don't want to lose my tenant." Molly turned and walked into the pantry. "And I walked those pesty dogs hours ago, so you don't have to take your aching knees around the block."

Suzanne shook her head. "How did you know my knees hurt, Mol?"

The door that separated her pantry from Molly's swung open with its usual groan. It wasn't easy to see, that door—it was just a panel next to the shelves in the back, but it connected the two halves of the old house. Molly's voice came from the other side, just before the door swung shut behind her. "Because you're gimping around like a downed cow, that's how. Elementary, my dear Watson—don't need witchcraft to see that. But you take care today. It's easier to fall when you're already hurt." The door closed with a little click as the latch fell into place on Molly's side.

She heard Molly's sharp whistle from her own kitchen door and knew that Munchie was being summoned inside. Suzanne thought about what Molly had said—how being hurt made you even more vulnerable, as if misfortune was some kind of magnetic field, pulling in more of the same. That seemed true, actually, when she thought about it. It was the old rule of bad luck coming in threes; it was the whole "never-rains-but-it-pours" thing. Okay, but was that true of Sam—that he was already hurt? That he'd chosen that horrible fall because he'd already been so very badly hurt, somehow? But how? And how could she not have known? No matter what Mr. Clark had said, she should have known. She'd taken Sam into her body. He'd moved inside her flesh. She'd come around him, for God's sake, saying his name. Sam. Of course she should have known.

She stood up, scraping the rest of the egg on toast onto the three plates on the floor. She went to the back door and called the dogs. Apple charged inside and slid directly to the egg, toenails screeching on the floor. Pear stood perfectly still while she brushed the fresh snow from his back. She could see individual snowflakes, intact and delicate, resting lightly on his black fur. She picked one up on a fingertip, trying to see its facets, its intricate crystalline structure, but the instant it touched her skin, it was gone.

Upstairs, in her study, the messy heap of pages that was her dissertation stared at her from her desk—its little bony eye-sockets mocking. She put her hands on her hips and stared back. She really wasn't in the mood. But she opened the file with the first page and she added a new line. Then she pondered the words on the screen—this line wasn't authorized by the university and it didn't follow the prescribed format, but fuck it. The new words, in the very center of the page, might change everything. Maybe, with this line, Sam's ghost would rest and the dream-phone would never, ever ring in the night again. And maybe, with this line, she'd have the motivation to get the damn dissertation finished. It was a simple line, but maybe it would change everything. Right under "Doctor of Philosophy," she'd added:

Dedicated to the Memory of Sam Tindell, PhD

Then she sighed, started a new file, and began typing:
Chapter Three: The Carnival of Flesh in John Dollar.

But an hour later, she only had half a page of typing and three of hand-scribbled notes, all saying "Look up…" with lists and lists of things she needed to know before she could go any farther. Every fact she uncovered needed checking for accuracy. Every analysis she proposed needed checking, to see if someone else had already done it, already stolen her scholarly thunder. It wasn't even one step forward, two back—this whole process was one step forward, ninety-two steps around in circles, forty-three steps back. It was unbearable. She closed the file, shut down the computer and slammed down the lid of the laptop. It was just too horrible to face, alone. She'd go to the library, where at least she had the company of real scholars—successful scholars, who presumably had survived their dissertations and then had actually gone on to write other books. She loved the thought of all those books. She loved libraries, all that knowledge, stored so neatly. Categorized and laid out in perfect order. That's what she needed—a sense that there was some discernible order in the universe. And she needed to create some order, in her own life, as well. That was obvious—but where, how? She thought of Robinson Crusoe. (She was never supposed to stop thinking about fucking Crusoe, was she? Her topic, her kind, the lynchpin of all her research. She'd had Crusoe on the brain for years and years—a curse, droning in her intellectual ear like an eternal gnat.) Crusoe, for most of the book, alone. Castaway. Survivor extraordinaire. Crusoe, the king of order, the guy who'd created a universe on his island, all alone. Food, shelter, clothing, an umbrella—order created one tiny piece at a time. Crusoe, the great list-maker, enumerator supreme. Crusoe knew that to make a world, you just had to start with one little bit, control that one thing and then move on to the next. Well, she was in control of one thing—her new job. So, first, she'd stop by her office and make a sign for the door. EDITORIAL OFFICE: *Largesse*. Then, she promised herself, she'd spend the rest of the day in the library, a dedicated scholar, hard at work.

Cheered by the prospect of all this self-descipline and productivity, she went downstairs to pack a lunch.

Ronelle had gotten to the office first. When Suzanne went to put her key in the office door, it swung open. Ronelle was sitting at the computer, her skinny legs wrapped around the rolling chair like tendrils. She was wearing the same black leggings and black sweater and black boots—still sockless—that she'd been wearing the day before. She pushed the chair back from the desk, rolling backwards. She looked, Suzanne thought, like a giant black spider who'd fallen into a baby carriage.

"Hey," Ronelle said. She began to untangle her legs from the chair. "Hope you don't mind. I like to work in the mornings." She stood up and stretched, rubbing her eyes. "Old farm girl habits, you know? Up with the chickens." She smiled.

Suzanne plopped her bags onto the floor. "No, it's fine. How did you get in, though?"

"Oh, the door was open. Was it supposed to be locked?"

"Yes. It was. I'm pretty sure I locked it after that Clark guy left." Suzanne leaned over and jiggled the doorknob. It wobbled. "Maybe it just doesn't work. I'll get security to look at it."

Ronelle was shuffling some papers on the desk. "I'll get a key, right? I mean, I'd like to have a key, boss, if that's okay with you. And this was on the floor this morning, like it had been slipped under the door, you know?" She held out an envelope, addressed in ink. "Another submission, I guess."

Suzanne took the envelope. It was light—not a full manuscript, then. The handwritten address read "To the Editor: Fat Magazine." She laughed. "I guess. I knew we needed a sign on the door with the real name. They can't just keep saying 'Fat Magazine.' This envelope is pretty skimpy—probably a poetry submission from someone just back for the semester. I'll put it with the pile of poetry I'll be reading."

"Okay. The poetry's there—in that blue folder." Ronelle pointed. "I put everything in different colored folders, so it'd be easy, you know, to tell what's what. Pink for critical articles, blue for poetry, red for non-fiction, green for fiction. And yellow for 'whatever.' You know, all that cross-genre, experimental crap—poems inside essays, stories written in rhyming couplets." She made a face. "That kind of shit."

Ronelle's pointing finger wasn't exactly clean, Suzanne noticed. There were grimy lines around the knuckle and the bitten nail. In fact, now that she was standing inside this hot little office, Suzanne noticed a smell, as well. Not terrible, but vaguely unwashed. A kind of stale smell that drifted up when Ronelle moved around, lifting from her clothes. Wonderful, she thought. Just great—an office mate who doesn't bathe. But then she looked at the neat, color-coded folders—Ronelle might not be scrupulous about hygiene, but the girl understood order. "I take it you don't like avant-garde stuff?" she said.

"Is that what you call it—avant-garde? I just can't swallow it." She made a gagging noise in her throat. "You know, I just don't *get* it." She dropped back into the chair. "And then I feel stupid and I hate that."

Suzanne tucked the envelope into the blue folder and nodded. "Well, no one likes to feel stupid. But some of the weirder stuff is good. It just takes some effort. We won't reject anything without really trying to understand what it's doing, okay? That's our editorial policy—give everything a fair chance."

The chair rolled, as Ronelle began to walk her feet around the floor, moving in a little crablike wobble around the office. "Sure. But, remember, I'm just a lowly master's student. Just a few years away from the barnyard. So I may not get avant-garde, okay?"

"Ronelle, you'll be fine." Suzanne leaned her butt against the desk. They certainly needed a second chair. She grabbed a piece of paper and started a list: TO DO: 1. Get lock checked. 2. Request chair. 3. Make sign for door.

Ronelle's chair scooted over and she read the list. "Request chair?" She put her head back and hooted. "Request? Do you know how long that will take? Can you just imagine how far down on whatever list the university keeps of furniture needs we'd be? Come on. We're in the column marked 'Never.' The 'Fat Chance' category. At the end of the 'Don't Hold Your Breath' page in the 'When Pigs Fly' file. Jeez." She stood up suddenly and the chair rolled backwards and cracked into the wall. "You want a chair? I'll be right back." She slipped out the door.

Suzanne had barely had time to slide the blue folder into her back-pack when the door flew back open and Ronelle staggered in, push-ing an armchair in front of her. A very big armchair, new and cushy and upholstered in heavy teal brocade. She manuvered it into the corner of the office, facing the window. Then she turned to face Suzanne, grinning. She waved an arm. "Madame Editor, your read-ing chair," she said.

The chair looked perfect in the corner. It gave a bit of comfort to the office. But Suzanne made herself frown at Ronelle. "That's from the faculty lounge down the hall. And it's one of the new ones—they just put those in there last week, Ronelle. You can't just take one."

Ronelle sat down, wriggling her skinny butt into the cushions. "Why not? There are about thirty damn chairs in there. No one will miss one. Besides, do the taxpayers of New York state really want over-paid, underworked faculty to have cushy chairs more than they want underpaid, overworked editors to have chairs? I don't think so."

"It's brand new. And everyone will recognize it. They'll know we stole it."

Ronelle's eyes narrowed. "Come sit in this chair, Suzanne." She jumped up and brushed a hand over the seat. "Just put your ass right here and tell me if this chair wasn't made for you. I mean custom-designed to LaFleshe specs. I mean it. Plunk your butt down, boss."

Suzanne sighed, then lowered herself into the chair. It was per-fect. It was over-sized and fit around her like a lover's arms. She put her head back and noticed how she could see out the window, could look out into the swirl of falling snow. Noticed how nicely the light from the window fell into her lap, where she could sit with her manu-scripts and a cup of tea. How she could put her feet up on the window ledge and sink back into the chair. Perfect. She stood up. "No. It's too recognizable. Everyone knows they just put these into the lounge."

"Uh huh." Ronelle reached over and took a fat black marker from the desk. With one quick stroke, she drew a wide streak down one arm of the chair.

Suzanne stared.

Ronelle nodded, looking happy and satisfied. "Gosh. I didn't notice before but this particular chair must have gotten damaged when they moved it up here. What a shame. Damaged during the move, over the break, when none of the faculty were here. Donated to us by the embarrassed guys in Facilities, who fucked it up. Otherwise, a loss—a waste of taxpayers' money. Lucky we were here to take off their hands, huh?"

Suzanne looked at Ronelle. Her spotted face was glowing, her pale eyes lit with laughter. God—her assistant editor was a thief. A natural-born thief and liar.

Ronelle squinted into Suzanne's shocked eyes and nodded. "Yep," she said. "The girl doesn't fall far from the trailer." She snapped the cap back on the marker. "So, want to look at the manuscripts I read last night?"

Suzanne sighed and sat back down in the chair. She leaned her elbow over the ugly black mark on its arm so she couldn't see it. "You read some of the literary criticism manuscripts already?"

Ronelle laughed. "Not some—all. Hey, boss, I'm quick. You'll find out—I got lots of talents."

The knock on the door interrupted the argument Suzanne and Ronelle were having over whether an article on the British mystery *The Sculptress* could be considered appropriate for *Largesse*. Ronelle, wrapped around the rolling chair, was saying, no, no it certainly could not, because the fat woman in that book was hideous, had probably slaughtered her whole family and then cut them into pieces with a great big knife, sliding all over the kitchen floor in their blood. Not exactly fat-friendly, she maintained.

Suzanne, comfortably ensconced in the armchair, was trying, patiently at first, then with some yelling, to explain that the article was saying exactly that—that the Sculptress character's disgusting fatness was emblematic of how the world views fat women, to the extreme. That the author of the book was deliberately tapping into that cultural iconography. That the character was the perfect embodiment of how horrifying most people find fat. Fat equals evil. Ergo, the fat woman becomes the perfect murder suspect. That the article itself wasn't anti-fat; that it was, instead, performing a valuable service in showing anti-fat sentiments at work. That it was nicely written, assumed some knowledge of feminist cultural critique, used solid theory. And so on.

Ronelle was shaking her head. "Theory, shit. Listen to the first paragraph of the book." She held up a copy of *The Sculptress*. "I just got this from the library and I read it. Now, listen."

"Wait." Suzanne pointed at the book. "You got the book? You read the article, when, last night? And you already got the book? This morning? And you read it, already?"

"No—I got it last night. I read the article, went to the library, got the book, read it. Re-read the article. Now listen."

Suzanne put a hand to her head. "No, wait. You took the bus home, then took the bus back up here, went to the library, got the book, and took a bus back home to Dove? And now you're back here? Good lord. When did you sleep, Ronelle?"

"I don't need much sleep. Now shut up and listen." Ronelle held the book almost to her nose and started to read: "*It was impossible to see her approach without a shudder of distaste. She was a grotesque parody of a woman, so fat that her feet and hands and head protruded absurdly from the huge slab of her body like tiny disproportionate afterthoughts. Dirty blonde hair clung damp and thin to her scalp, black patches of sweat spread beneath her armpits. Clearly, walking was painful. She shuffled forward on the insides of her feet, legs forced apart by the thrust of one gigantic thigh against another, balance precari-*

ous. And with every movement, however small, the fabric of her dress strained ominously as the weight of her flesh shifted. She had, it seemed, no redeeming features. Even her eyes, a deep blue, were all but lost in the ugly folds of pitted white lard." She slammed the book closed and said, "See? It's cruel. It's horrible."

Suzanne had to catch her breath. She felt tears rising to her eyes. "Yes, it is. That's why it's so good. That's what the article says." She lifted the manuscript from her lap and found the passage she wanted. "Now you listen: *The extremity of the imagery here is simply taking our culture's hatred of fat women to its logical end. Anyone who looks like this—this horrific, this gigantic, this powerful—must be evil. So evil that she kills and dismembers her own mother and sister. In the kitchen. With a butcher knife. As if she were preparing the ultimate meal. This kind of body, our culture screams, is the embodiment of not only gluttony, but also of overweening lust, anger, and murderous envy. The body of the Sculptress, it seems, hosts a veritable catalog of the seven deadly sins.* See?"

Ronelle shook her head. "I *get* it. I guess I just don't want that description in our magazine, okay? I don't want anyone to have to read that. I mean, think about it—all the fat women who will pick up this magazine, feeling like they're safe, like they won't be insulted here, and then they have to read that? It's a cruel trick to play on them, don't you think?"

Suzanne leaned back in her chair. "Come on. Toughen up, kiddo. Ain't a fat girl out there who hasn't heard much worse than that. If you'd ever been fat, you'd have heard worse. From first grade on, you've had heard worse, every day on the school bus."

The book crashed onto the floor, where Ronelle flung it. "How do you know I didn't? I mean, listen…."

Just then, the knock sounded on the door, and the voice. "Ms. Brown? Charles Clark, from University Police—can I come in? I'd like to speak to you."

Suzanne jumped guiltily out of the purloined chair. "Oh, shit," she whispered. "We can't let him come in here." Then she raised her voice. "One second, Mr. Clark. I was just leaving for the library. I'll walk with you." She grabbed her bookbag, lunch and coat and glared at Ronelle. She opened the office door just enough to slide out, then slammed it quickly behind her.

Out on the campus, snow was piling up. Even under the concrete roof covering the inner campus, snow had blown onto the walks and was over an inch deep. When Mr. Clark stepped out the door of Humanities in front of her, Suzanne stared at the boot print he left in the doorway. She remembered, suddenly, how Crusoe's whole orderly little self-made universe had come crashing down, the day he saw the cannibal's footprint on the beach.

6

Suzanne put her foot into Clark's footprint, exactly. Her boots, good leather, fleece-lined, with high heels, $6.95 at Salvation Army, were almost as big as Clark's. It made her feel better, for a minute, to see her own print obscure his. But only for a minute. Clark was striding through the snow so quickly that she had to rush to keep up and her boots didn't have much traction. She could feel their leather soles sliding on the slick concrete and she remembered Molly's warning. *It's easy to fall down when you're already hurt.* She slowed her pace, thinking how undignified a very tall, fat woman falling on her ass in the snow would look.

Mr. Clark turned his head around and then stopped walking. "Huh," he said, his words blowing out on puffs of white breath. "I've never understood why women cripple themselves that way." He backed up and took Suzanne's arm. "You're obviously a smart gal, Ms. Brown. But you're wearing stupid shoes."

She snatched her arm back. "They're boots. They're warm." She tried to step more briskly, ignoring the pain in her knees and the unsteadiness of the footing. "They're fine."

He grunted and walked beside her. "Do you know how many young women we pick up at the bottom of staircases, because of stupid shoes? Flimsy little things with no backs—what do they call them— slides? Things with heels six inches high, wobbly as all hell? Every Saturday night, I swear to you, there's a whole slew of broken femurs, sprained ankles, cracked elbows, not to mention hurt pride and bruised fannies. All because of dumb shoes."

Suzanne kept pace with him. "Of course. It's all the shoes' fault. The monster amounts of alcohol those young women have consumed isn't a factor."

He laughed. "Sure it is—being drunk gives them an excuse for wearing such silly shoes." They'd reached one of the four corners of the inner campus, facing the empty pool with its frozen fountain. Here, snow swirled, propelled by the winds that always funneled along all the walkways, converging here in the center and twisting into mini-whirlwinds. Mr. Clark spread his arms in two directions. "The library? Or would you prefer we talk in the coffee shop? There won't be too many people there yet."

"The library. That's where I'm heading anyway." Suzanne turned to her left. Besides, she thought, the library was where she felt safe. She wasn't sure why she needed that assurance—surely she wasn't in any trouble with University Police, with their guns and their full powers under the law of New York State. She wasn't a factor in Sam's death, in any way. But as the snow hit her face, she remembered the voice on her phone in the night and she shivered.

They settled into one of the study carrels on the top floor. The new library provided comfy seating for groups in some of these. Group projects, collaborative research—Suzanne could never get used to the concept. In her world, scholars worked alone, swimming through the pages of the work of others who'd gone before them, of course, but never, thank God, having to meet those others in person. She believed in solitary scholarship, old-fashioned, time-consuming, but somehow also soul-satisfying. She'd never made her own students work in small groups, even though it was the pedagogical fad of the moment and saved the teacher from always having to teach, because she herself had so hated it when she'd had to rely on her own classmates to get anything done. Once a loner, always a loner, she thought. But she sank with relief into the warm soft chair of a group carrel.

She slid her bags to the floor and shrugged off her coat.

Mr. Clark left his jacket on, but sat down across from her and crossed his long legs. His feet, she noticed, were encased in solid L.L. Bean boots, which dripped water onto the new carpeting. He reached into the pocket of his jacket and pulled out a folded sheet of paper. He held it out to her. "We found this in Dr. Tindell's pocket. Look familiar?"

Suzanne looked at the paper. It was white, shiny. There was no blood. "That was in his pocket? When he fell?" Her stomach felt tight, her throat tighter.

"Not this exact page, Ms. Brown. This is a Xerox copy, of course. The actual paper is being looked at in the State Police lab."

"Looked at?"

"Examined for fibers and so on. Standard, in cases of sudden death—just routine." He moved the page toward her. "Would you just take a look please?"

She took the paper and unfolded it. It was a poem.

Shooting the Moon
   To the one on the ledge
        [one on the edge]
   The crowd howls:

> **JUMP!**
> GO FOR IT!
> DO IT!
> JUMP!

And a voice mounts above the others:

> **SHOOT FOR THE MOON!**

The one on the
    (l)edge looks up, hears music: fly me to the moon
                                     moon river
                                     moon dancer
                                     moonlight sonata
                                     claire de lune

    and laughter: straight to the moon, Alice, straight to the
moon

    advice: quit mooning around for something you'll never

                    ever

                    get

    warning: Don't look down!! You moonstruck, moonshine,
moonie-tune.

    Lunacy, lunacy, lunacy, lunacy, lunacy, luna….

And over you go.

(You go. Over
and over and over,
again.)

                    31 December 2002

She closed her eyes. She didn't realize that she was rocking back
and forth on her chair until she felt Mr. Clark's hand on her shoulder,
stopping her.

"Ms. Brown?" he said.

She opened her eyes and looked into his. They were dark and clear, sympathetic. Then she looked back at the paper in her lap. "It's one of Sam's poems," she said. "It looks like it's from the poem cycle he started last summer. Like this is the last one in the cycle. The final piece." She remembered the title of the whole cycle: *Moon Dancer: An Elegy*. She looked down at this one—New Year's Eve, that auspicious date. On New Year's Eve, as the world celebrated with champagne and funny hats, Sam was writing about a man on a ledge. Oh God. He really had been hurt, hadn't he? And then, a few weeks later, he'd fallen. Molly was right, of course. He'd been desperately hurt and she hadn't done a damn thing to help him. She remembered when he'd shown her the others from the cycle and she'd read them and made little wording suggestions. That's all she'd done for him—fixed some fucking words in poems full of pain. Oh, yes—and she'd made love to him. As if that were enough. As if pleasures of the flesh really could heal a shattered heart.

She looked at Mr. Clark. His eyes seemed kind, but he was clearly waiting for more information. What more was there to say, really? She'd utterly failed her friend. Utterly.

He took his hand from her shoulder and dropped it gently on her knee. She winced, but then welcomed the pain. "Do you think he meant this a kind of suicide note, Ms. Brown? That he was carrying it with him for that purpose?"

She shook her head. "I don't know. I don't know. Honestly, I have no idea. It's just one of his poems. He had hundreds."

He nodded. "Okay, but is this one different, somehow? Specifically? Different from the others in this cycle he wrote?"

"I don't know. It seems to fit." She tried to push the lump of sorrow from her throat, but it was lodged there and she had to whisper around it. "I remember the whole cycle. It's wonderful—full of hope and terrible sadness, combined. Most of the poems are addressed to the same person. Someone he just calls 'you.' The moon is his metaphor for the person the poems are written to."

"Uh huh." He took the paper from her hand and refolded it. "And who's this 'you'? I mean, did he write these poems to any particular person, Ms. Brown?" He stood up, slipping the paper back into his jacket pocket.

She stood up, too, trying to attain his height, look him in the eye. "I'm not sure. He never really said." She pushed her hair off her face. "Look. I treated them like *poems,* Mr. Clark. Not like diary entries. I read them for their aesthetic value, not as some kind of clues to Sam's life. That's what I'm trained to do—read literature as literature, not autobiography." She felt her hands trembling and she shoved them into her pockets.

"Uh huh—so this is just some literary artifact, right? Not a cry from the heart of a desperate man? Is that what you're saying?"

She stared at him. His dark eyes were impossible to read. Was he making fun of her? Was he blaming her? She stood up as straight as she could. "Yes. That's what I'm saying, Mr. Clark."

He leaned toward her, just slightly. "Okay then." He opened the door of the carrel, then turned back. "They weren't written to you, then, were they? You're not 'you,' are you, Ms. Brown? I mean, you were his lover, so I just wondered."

She felt herself shrink. She shook her head. "No. They were not written to me, I'm certain of that. He let me read them because they *weren't* for me. Do you understand that?"

He smiled. "I think so. But it's too bad. You deserve a poem cycle, Ms. Brown. You really do."

The door closed softly behind him and Suzanne's knees collapsed. She found herself sitting back in the soft chair. She put her head in her hands. She knew perfectly well who Sam's poems were for. Why hadn't she just said it? Was it some sort of stupid pride? Silly vanity, like her high-heeled boots? Was there some particular humiliation in admitting it aloud? Actually saying that a man whom she, Suzanne LaFleshe, had been fucking—frequently, lustily, happily—was all the while writing poetry to the woman he loved? Was it particularly awful to have to say that Sam's poems—all of Sam's poems—were for his wife? For beautiful, beautiful Diana? For cool, flawless Diana? For Diana, young, lithe, slim? Diana, huntress, virgin, goddess of the moon. For Diana.

Part II: *The Creature has No Name*

The word for the creature is not a proper name, for the creature
has no name. No one may know it and live to tell about it, so the
Windigo must remain nameless.

John Robert Colombo, *Windigo*

7

Diana rested in her bathtub. There were little swirls of pink in the water and bits of floating clots—nothing to worry about, she was sure. The people at the clinic had been very kind. She smiled, soaping her flat belly with tenderness. They'd given her some kind of pills to take for the cramping and the pills made her ever so slightly woozy. Not enough to be alarming—not so much that she feared sliding down in the tub and drowning, her face white and wrinkled under the warm water. Couldn't have another sudden death in the family, could they? She giggled. The effects of the pills really were quite pleasant.

She raised the washcloth to her breasts and soaped even more gently. Her breasts were still a bit tender, but the doctor at the clinic had told her that the soreness would subside quickly. Now that the pregnancy was terminated, the doctor had explained, her breasts would return to their normal state.

She had nodded. And would they shrink back to their normal size, she'd asked? She'd like that. She hated the swollen, blue-veined things they'd become. She'd like to have her own breasts back—small, neat breasts. Could she, she'd asked, almost flirtatiously, could she count on having her very own breasts back? She'd cupped them in her hands, as she spoke, smiling at the gray-haired doctor and lifting her breasts for him to see.

He'd backed away and nodded. Then, he'd asked her to slide her hips down the table and to put her feet in the stirrups.

And that's what she'd looked at, the whole time—her own bare feet in the silver stirrups. Dancer's feet, misshapen but very strong. She'd wriggled her toes, whenever there were sharp jabs or pulling aches from her belly. She'd flexed her calf muscles, using the discipline of her dancing days to get through the procedure without a sound.

She raised one leg and rested the foot on the edge of the tub. The leg was still strong, with muscle like taut rope. She hadn't had much time to practice, since she'd been married. She'd been tied to a desk in an office, tied to her columns of numbers. It had been no easy life, supporting a poet. But now she was free, wasn't she? Her womb empty, her body her own.

She leaned forward and rubbed the washcloth along her thigh. And she hadn't lost that much. She'd get it back—the hardness, the absolute tone, the marble quality of a dancer's leg. She smiled. Soon, she'd have legs like stone. Legs like stone, to match her heart, which had iced over long ago. She giggled, resting her head on the porcelain tub.

8

There was snow on her shoulders and a chill deep in her bones by the time Suzanne got back to the Humanities building after her trek from the library, this time solo, only her own footprints marking the snow. The blast of heat that came with the opening of the heavy glass door into the building was welcome, but one glance down the corridor to the place beneath the skylight where Sam had died froze her flesh more than the snow ever could. There, in a little cluster of hunched backs, was a group of students, weeping. They carried bunches of those horrible plastic-wrapped bouquets of super-market flowers—scentless carnations, pale chrysanthemums, limp daisies—that had become the standard popular memorials for the fallen. Was there anything more pathetic? Sam would be hooting from heaven, if that's where he'd gone. Sam, whose own little backyard garden, he'd told her, was full of big, bright flowers: iris, hollyhock, sunflowers, all flung along the chain link fence behind his apartment, hiding its ugliness. She'd never seen his garden, of course, since they'd never gone to Sam's house. Of course. Never gone into Diana's territory. Still, in August, in September, in October, even, Sam had come to her house bearing big messy bunches of flowers, still warm from the heat of the sun. Real flowers, smelling of earth and water. Essence of summer. Like the taste of his sun-warmed skin.

Suzanne stamped snow from her boots, hard. The slap of her heels on the stone floor echoed, a sound so loud it startled her—and the kids. They dropped their plastic bundles and turned to stare.

One of the girls, a chubby, pale-faced kid who'd been in one of Suzanne's classes two years ago, called out a snuffly greeting: "Oh, Ms. Brown. Isn't it awful? We just heard. Isn't it horrible?" The girl came down the corridor, her shoulders bowed, her eyes red. She wasn't even wearing a coat, just some kind of sleeveless shirt that exposed her goose-pimpled arms.

Suzanne could not, for the life of her, remember this girl's name. She was just one of the many round-faced girls who had floated through her composition classes. She nodded, stamping her boots one more time. "Yes," she said. "It's very sad."

The girl was joined by a male friend, as the other students drifted away down the hallway. This one, Suzanne knew—he had a name not to be forgotten. Ajax Swenson. A poet, self-declared. Sam had talked about Ajax with a kind of horrified humor, this mega-weird kid in his poetry workshop. The kind of kid, Sam said, who reads at all the open mics in town, who never leaves home without his yellow pad, who drinks coffee and scribbles about the cream swirling on its dark surface like a nebula in space, who eats a bagel and scribbles about its perfect circular force, who takes a shit and scribbles about—well, you get it, Sam had said, laughing. The kid who emails his teachers daily with new drafts of awful poems and quotes from Rilke. The kid whose eyes water and whose sinuses are always stopped up. The kid with rashes on his hands and zits on his face. The kid who worships his poetry teacher and hates his classmates, afraid all the time that one of them—maybe that pretty blond in the corner? maybe that earnest returning adult student? maybe that attitude-filled black guy?—will show him up, prove that he isn't the most talented kid in the room. The kid who follows you to your office and stands in the doorway, talking talking talking, until you say, as kindly as you can, "Well, it's been nice talking to you, Ajax," and you actually close the door in his intense face. The kid who is still there when you open your office door again, sitting on the floor in the corridor scribbling on his pad, and who walks with you to the bus stop and who sits with you on the bus and whom you can only escape by leaping off the bus at your

stop. And then, all the way home, you worry that now he knows—
approximately—where you live. And you imagine him, Sam had said,
loitering under the lamp-post outside your apartment, writing writing
writing through the night, so that in the morning he can greet you
with a new sonnet cycle—forty-eight poems, every damn one rhymed
abab, cdcd, efg, efg—before you've even had your first cup of coffee.
The kid who loves you to death. The kid who has to get an A on
every paper, every time, or he'll die. The kid, Sam had said, voted
least likely to live until his 21st birthday, because his teachers will gang
up and kill him, each striking one blow, *Murder on the Orient Express*
style.

Ajax sighed, shaking his head. His long greasy hair fell onto his
shoulders. "Hello, Professor Brown," he said. "What a terrible tragedy."

Suzanne started for the stairs, moving fast. "Yes," she said over
her shoulder.

She almost ran up the first flight, but Ajax and the anonymous girl
were right beside her. She took the next flights two at time, but the
kids kept pace.

By the time she reached her office, she was winded and Ajax was
wheezing like an ancient radiator. Clearly, his asthma/allergies/mi-
graine/chronic fatigue syndrome had kicked in. Still, he had enough
wind to catch hold of her office door and stand there. His heavy
wool coat reached to his ankles and his face was slick with sweat. The
girl kept two steps to his rear, hugging her bare arms.

Suzanne sank into her editor's chair and tried to smile at him. "Is
there something I can do for you, Ajax?"

He nodded, trying to catch his breath. "I think—you know." His
eyes filled with tears and his voice failed. He tried again. "I want to
know if we can dedicate this whole issue of this literary journal." He
paused to wave his hand toward the office. "To the memory of Sam.
Like, you know, everyone writes a tribute, all his students."

"But, Ajax, it's a fat magazine." Suzanne tried not to giggle. "I
mean, it's got a theme."

The boy's face was starting to get very red. "Fat? What?"

The girl stepped forward and pulled on his coat. "Yeah, didn't you hear? It's like a journal about how mean people are to fat girls. It's…." Her own round face lit up. "It's like all about—well, all about, like fat." She smiled into the doorway. "But, you know, Dr. Tindell once told me he liked women to have flesh, you know? So maybe it would be okay?"

Suzanne leaned forward. "He told you that? That he liked women to have flesh?"

"Oh, yeah. I wrote a poem—like a sestina, you know, the kind with all those lines?—and it had a kind of chubby girl in it and she wants to get liposuction and Dr. Tindell said in class that he liked women with flesh and all and that 'liposuction' was a kind of hard word to use seven times in a poem because it's kind of, like, limited." She nodded. "And that…."

Ajax grabbed the girl's arm. "Bullshit. He just said—in class, in workshop—that characters in poems should have bodies, not just heads. He said that characters—not *real* women but *characters*—needed to be flesh and blood. You didn't get that? You thought he was talking about real people?" His fingers were tight on the girl's arm, making deep indentations in her skin.

The girl's face turned pink. "Well, I just implied, you know and…."

"INFERRED! It's not 'implied,' it's 'inferred,' you jerk." Ajax was shaking the girl's arm. He started shouting into her face. "You need to get words *right*, Jennifer,"

Suzanne stood up. "Listen, you guys," she said softly. "Everyone's upset, okay? But there's no need to yell. And this magazine is not the appropriate venue for a tribute to Dr. Tindell. But perhaps, Ajax, the student affairs office would give you some funds to create a little chapbook of poems in his memory. Maybe you could be the editor?"

The boy's sweaty face turned to her and he dropped the girl's arm. He shook his head, nodding. His pale eyes lit up. "You think so? I mean, I could pick the pieces? And reject some?"

"I guess so. You'd make editorial decisions, I imagine. Sure you would."

Ajax squared his shoulders and cleared his throat. "Come on, Jennifer," he said. "Let's go to student affairs."

Suzanne watched them walk down the corridor. Ajax was already scribbling on his yellow pad and Jennifer was sucking on a strand of her wet hair. In her arm, there were four moons, little red crescents where Ajax's fingernails had dug in. That kid was more than weird; he was nuts. She shook her head. The world was full of poets. And Jennifers. Hundreds and hundreds of Jennifers, always.

It was, she decided, time to go home.

9

Diana stood in the back of the chapel, thanking the guests who'd attended her husband's very simple memorial service. She was wearing a slim black dress, with black tights and ballet flats. She knew that she looked lovely—sad and young and bereft. She'd brushed her hair until it fell like a silvery sheet down her back and she'd worn no makeup. Pallor, she'd thought, becomes a youthful widow.

She'd been shaking hands and accepting kisses on her cheek for a very long time now and she was weary. She still had some cramping in her uterus and biting twinges of hunger from her belly. But she kept her spine straight and her shoulders back. Whenever she felt faint, she flexed her thigh muscles, as she'd been taught. Those muscles were enormously strong and they sent blood pumping back to her head. She did not smile; she kept her expression somber and grave. Yes, grave.

She was surprised at how many people had actually come, on such a cold Wednesday morning in January. And on such short notice, too. She'd made the arrangements quickly, efficiently. No sense in waiting, even though the police wouldn't release Sam's body for cremation. The body wasn't important, anyway. And neither she nor Sam had any family to speak of, so there were no relatives to worry about. And, apparently, the ever-efficient University gossip system had been enough to notify anyone else who'd known Sam that the service was today. Indeed, the little chapel she'd chosen for the ceremony was nowhere big enough and people had had to stand at the back and around the sides. Who'd have thought so many people cared about Sam? There were streams of students, badly dressed, and of faculty, almost as badly dressed, dowdy frumpy women and paunchy middle-aged men. It was all she could do not to wipe their handshakes from her skin, they were so utterly unattractive. Then there were dozens and dozens of people she could not identify—probably Sam's classmates or maybe even his students. They murmured their sympathy and one or two expressed their appreciation for the poem she'd recited at the service. She nodded, pleased. Yes, that had been a good choice—no God, no eternal rest, no platitudes to send Sam off. Just his own words. And it had certainly gotten to the one person she wanted to feel it—the red-haired slut, LaFleshe. It certainly had.

Diana had stood in the front of the chapel, her head bowed. Then she had lifted her head and swept the audience with her eyes. Mostly, there was no one there she cared about. Just a sea of boring, winter-pale faces. But, there, standing in back, as if she'd come in late, was the Slut. Well, of course, she was late, she was a disorganized, sloppy, undisciplined person, after all. The Slut was clearly visible. She was not wearing black. Or navy blue or gray or brown or any other sub-dued funereal shade. Oh no—that kind of woman always needs to call attention to herself, doesn't she? So the Slut was wearing some kind of brilliant amber dress—silk, it looked like from here—all shim-mering over her breasts. The dress caught the light from the stained glass window and held it. The Slut's short red hair curled out around her head in another flash of light. Her face was a round white globe beneath her hair. She was staring attentively at Diana.

Fine. Perfect. Diana knew that she had her audience and she drew her spine up into perfect alignment as she spoke. "Thank you all for coming. I will recite one of my husband Sam's poems, in his honor." She raised her head and began:

To the Old Goddess Artemis, Alive Again at Beowulf's Funeral

As though all this noise
might wake her into being,
again, the moon ducks

behind the clouds
of mist-spitting smoke
that rise from the pyre.

You, moon, who only reflect
Sun's light. You, who
only mirror, distort.

You, whose skin is dark and pitted
and dry. You, Artemis, who leap
upon the throat of the rabbit

and sip his blood like
nectar from the vine and marrow
from the bone.

Artful, artificial, many-arrowed Artemis—you
are not all. The smoke lifts, the
fire burns, the heart blisters and flames.

But above the pyre, farther
deeper, milky-way starshine flows.
There is something higher than the moon.

In story, in song, in
the breasts of men and monsters alike,
the Hero can not die. Flesh becomes light,

and light seeks light. Swallow the smoke,
Artemis. It is all
you're due.

When it was over, she had glanced at her audience. They were very still. Some had tears on their faces. Some just looked baffled. She looked to the back of the room. The Slut had covered her face with a handkerchief and her shoulders were shaking. The flashy silk dress trembled over her chest. Diana shuddered. Flesh, quivering. It was disgusting. She spoke out into the chapel: "As you heard, Sam believed in the next life and that it would be better. Let us take comfort from his faith. Thank you." Then she had stepped down.

Now, she was waiting for the Slut to come through this endless line and shake her hand. The line was thinning, but she still didn't come. The nice man from the University Police came and shook her hand. Some awful student with pimples and greasy hair—he'd stood and talked to her for a full five minutes, yammering on about lost genius, until the next person in line shoved him along. Well, perhaps the Slut hadn't the courage to face the wife of the man—one of the men, only one of them—she had seduced. Perhaps not. Diana felt a deep spasm in her guts, pulling her down. She was afraid that her spine would begin to sway and she pulled the bones up, aligning them one on top of the other, creating a straight column of vertebrae.

When the line of people was at last over, Diana drew her coat over her shoulders and stepped outside. The sky was dark with clouds, although no snow had fallen for two days. The ground was covered, but the walk in front of the chapel had been cleared. Diana walked to the limousine the funeral people had waiting for her. There would be no morbid graveyard ceremony. Later, Sam's body would be cremated, privately. Clean and simple. No fuss. No bother.

As the car slid quietly from its place by the curb, Diana saw her, the Slut, standing on the corner with two other women. Diana leaned forward, staring. One of the women was thin as a twig, homely, her hair an utter rat's nest. She had her hands on her hips and she was talking to the Slut, a mile a minute. The Slut was just shaking her head, looking down into the filthy snow piles at her feet. As the quiet black car passed, Diana could see that her fat face was whiter than the snow, but her eyes were stained with red, swollen almost shut. They looked bruised, as if she'd been beaten. Perfect.

It was the third woman that Diana saw last, as the car turned the corner. And it was that one who sent her belly into another spasm of cramping. An old, old woman with one dead eye. But she kept her live eye sharply focused on Diana's face. Even through the tinted glass, Diana felt the intensity of that eye and she shrank back against the plush seat.

She put her right hand over her face, as if she were weeping, and let the left drop to her belly. The cramps would pass. And so would the faintness, in a minute or two. Perhaps she should have eaten breakfast. Her stomach was growling, and she could feel its acidity, burning itself. She could have eaten a half of bagel, on this of all days. But no. She smiled. Better to stick to the regimen, to exercise perfect self-control. She was paring herself down to bare muscle and bone. Hunger was her friend.

10

"That is *not* what that poem meant," Suzanne was saying. She was stamping her feet in the snow. Like a kid having a tantrum, she knew it. But also like someone just trying to keep the blood flowing to her frozen toes. God, why hadn't she worn boots? Because she didn't have any that went with her good silk dress, that's why. Stupid, stupid vanity again. But this dress had been Sam's favorite, that's why she wore it. She stamped harder, remembering Sam's head resting against the amber silk, his blond hair curled against it. Like an angel. She shook her head. "He didn't believe in some perfect afterlife. That wasn't it at all. He was just saying something about art, how it preserves the best, the true heroes. That some people are bold sources of light, not just mirrors. Did you hear the last lines? Did you?" She glared into Ronelle's face.

Ronelle's lips were blue with cold. She was wearing only a thin jacket over her inevitable black leggings. "I heard them. I just think that maybe you could take those last lines as meaning…."

Molly sighed. A huge, juicy sigh. "You girls going to stand here all day in this cold and argue fine points of literary criticism?" she asked. She put a hand on Suzanne's arm. "I'm too old for that shit. Either take me home or take me out to lunch, girls." She shook Suzanne's arm. "That little wife was enough to freeze the balls off any man. No wonder he came to you, my dear. Bedding that one must have been like sleeping with a stone. Or a coyote. That poor man."

Suzanne looked down into Molly's shining eye. "But she's so beautiful. Do you think she's cold? Why?"

Molly leaned forward, staring down the street. "Ha. Cold ain't a big enough word for what she is. No name, really, for what she is. At least not one you'd want to say aloud. Where's the bus got to?" She closed her eyes and said, loudly, "Bus, bus, bus, get your ass to us." She opened her eyes and added, "I've met some like her in my days. That little wife is someone you don't want to hate you. But I'm afraid she does. Oh, yes, she does."

The number 30 bus appeared suddenly in a steaming cloud of exhaust and stopped directly in front of them. Suzanne took Molly's arm and helped her up the high step. Behind her, Ronelle whispered. "How'd she do that? Did she conjure the bus, or what?"

Molly stopped on the steps and turned back toward Ronelle, craning her head around Suzanne. "*She*, little miss smarty-pants, can do all sorts of things. And, *she* hears very well, so you shouldn't go talking about her behind her back." Molly dropped her coins in the box, nodded to the driver and walked to a seat.

Ronelle whispered in Suzanne's ear. "Jeez. She really is a witch, isn't she?"

Suzanne laughed. "So she says. But she also knows the bus schedule like some people know the Bible. She's lived in this city her whole life and never driven a car." She let her coins drop into the box. "But she likes to put on a show. I think that's like 90% of witchcraft, anyway—it's performance art." She glanced back at Ronelle, who was scrabbling in her pocket for change and coming up with paper clips and candy wrappers. "Never mind, I got it." She pulled out four more quarters. "It was nice of you to come along, to a service for a guy you never even met."

Ronelle shrugged. "All in a day's work, boss."

The Corner Café was warm and fragrant with coffee and homemade bread. Molly settled into her seat with a happy sigh. The owner, a tiny woman with a perpetually hoarse voice, poured Molly's coffee before the others were even seated. Molly smiled at her and handed her a tiny packet. "Here you go, sweetheart," she said. The woman dropped the packet into the pocket of her apron and walked to another table.

Ronelle sat down across from Molly. "Do you sell drugs?" she whispered.

Molly leaned forward. "I don't *sell* anything. Those are a gift— some lozenges for that poor girl's throat."

"Oh. What's in them?"

"Nosy, aren't you?" Molly sat back in her seat. "Let's see—cherry bark, feverfew, honey, orange juice, bits of this and that."

Suzanne sat down, fitting herself into the small chair carefully. She and Molly came here often. The food was good and the prices unbelievably cheap. Well, when she came with Molly, they were cheap. Otherwise, they were not. She knew that Molly had some kind of scam going here, but what the hell. Good food is good food and her stipend didn't allow her to eat out much. Whatever Molly's charm was, she'd take it. She grinned at Ronelle. "It's the bits of this and that that make Molly's medicine so interesting."

Molly nodded. "That's true—the special ingredients make all the difference."

"So what's so special in those lozenges?" Ronelle nodded toward the woman, who was slipping one into her mouth.

"You are really one nosy girl. Well, that's not necessarily a bad quality in a young person. That's how you learn." Molly whispered across the table. "I add some things to take the swelling out of her throat and give her back her voice. Simple things—a bit of cannabis, bit of good whiskey. And a good shot of opiates."

"Opiates!" Ronelle's voice went up an octave.

"Molly grows a lot of, well, interesting plants, right in our back yard." Suzanne winked at Ronelle.

"God. Can I have some of those lozenges?" Ronelle's eyebrows shot up hopefully.

Molly's face grew solemn, the deep lines around her mouth etched tight. She put a hand on Ronelle's arm, holding it down on the table.

"Listen to me, nosy girl. I don't play, okay? I make serious medicines for serious people. That woman there—take a good look at her. See the circles around her eyes? All blue and sunk? See the way her face sort of folds in, so you can see the shape of the bones underneath? See the yellow in her skin? The little bit of hair on her head? The way pain pulls one corner of her mouth down, like she's always biting on her cheek to keep from crying? She's got throat cancer. The doctors did what they could, with their knives and their radiation and their poison chemicals. And it won't be enough." Her hand tightened like a claw on Ronelle's arm. "Don't play with what you don't understand."

Suzanne watched Ronelle's face grow pale, so that the dark freckles seemed to float above the skin. She spoke loudly, to break Molly's spell. "Okay, ladies, what'll we have? The omelets here are wonderful, Ronelle."

Then she watched as Ronelle ate hers so quickly that she was finished when Molly had just barely begun, swiping the melted butter from her plate with the crusts of her toast. She just smiled when Ronelle tipped the container of jelly packets into her pocket—just a petty bit of thievery, after all. And she smiled again as the cashier waved them through, presenting them with a bill for all of five dollars.

On the sidewalk out front, Ronelle turned right. "Thanks," she said. "For the lunch. I'll walk home from here."

"Long cold walk to Dove Street," Suzanne said. "Why don't you take the bus? The number ten runs up and down Western every twenty minutes. See? I've learned a lot from Molly."

Ronelle shook her head. "I like to walk. Clears the brain."

"Okay then. See you tomorrow. Thanks for coming today. I appreciate your support."

Ronelle nodded, then walked away, fast, her bare ankles blue in the winter afternoon sunshine.

Molly took Suzanne's arm as they walked the two blocks home. "That girl didn't have bus fare, you know. And she's hungry. More than just a little. That girl can't afford food."

Suzanne looked back but Ronelle was gone. "Really? She's that bad off? I mean, we're all poor, all the grad students. But I didn't think anyone was actually starving."

Molly shrugged, pulling Suzanne along. "You got to learn to notice more, my girl. Pay attention to the signs. Pay attention to the smells people give off. It's obvious. That child is cold and she's hungry and she doesn't sleep in a bed. Her teeth are rotting away in her jaw and she needs a hot bath. You got to learn to notice the things around you. I won't always be around to point things out, you know. Now, come on, get a move on. Dogs' bladders are only so big and we've been gone all day. I can almost see Munchie piddling on my clean floor now."

Tucking her arm into Molly's, Suzanne looked at her feet, in their thin shoes, moving down the sidewalk. "I didn't notice what was wrong with Sam, did I? Even when he tried to tell me?"

Molly tucked her head into her collar. "Damn wind's coming back up. No you didn't. You didn't see enough, that's for sure, didn't pay enough attention. What did he tell you?"

Suzanne tried to remember some of Sam's exact words. "He said he couldn't talk to Diana. That, at first, when he'd first met her, he thought her silence was wonderful—a sign of her inner serenity."

"Ha! If that woman has inner serenity, I'm a Lutheran." Molly's head dipped farther. "That woman's full of something but it sure ain't serenity."

"Wait—I remember what he said." Suzanne could see Sam's face. He'd been stirring the pan of turkey gravy on her stove, while she chopped the giblets to drop into it. He'd been looking at the pan, his shoulders sort of drooping. "He said, 'You know what it's like? It's like keeping a wolf as a pet. You try, but you just can't communicate with the wolf. It's not like a dog. It's not domesticated. It's just too far away from you. It's just too alien, too wild. And you never know, ever, when it's going to lick your hand and when it's going to tear your arm off.'" Suzanne stopped walking. "Oh, God, Molly. He said that and I was just so pleased to have his company for Thanksgiving dinner that

I didn't really listen, did I? I was so happy, cooking the turkey and baking the pies and thinking about how he could even stay overnight, because Diana was away, that I didn't really think about how lonely he was, living with someone he couldn't talk to. A wolf! God, what a jerk."

"Keep moving. That dog's ready to burst, I can feel it." Molly tugged Suzanne's arm again. "You're right. You didn't listen very well, did you?"

Suzanne felt the tears start down her face, freezing into little tracks of ice. "If I had, Molly, would Sam still be alive?"

"I don't know. I can't judge that. And neither can you. A man living with a wolf is always in danger, isn't he?"

11

There were two possibilities for the evening: work on the dissertation (aka the skull on the shelf) or read the blue folder of poetry submissions for *Largesse*. Hardly a tough choice. Suzanne told herself that she'd had a hard day and deserved a relatively peaceful evening. There should be some kind of rule, anyway. If you had to go to a funeral in the morning, you did not have to work on your dissertation in the evening. Only fair. Not really procrastination or denial, just common sense. And besides, she would be doing her job, fulfilling her editorial duty. Keeping up with her staff. Hell, Ronelle had probably read all the essay submissions, checked three or four books out of the library, read those as well and was now typing up neat notes on all of the above. Suzanne carried her cup of hot chocolate to the wicker chair in the warmest corner of the kitchen. Apple was curled on the cushions, a perfect doughnut of white with black specks, nose hidden under butt. "Sorry, small dog," Suzanne said. "Out." She pointed to the floor. Apple raised her head and gave a soft growl. "Okay, that's it. Out, you ungrateful little wretch." She grabbed the chair and tipped it, sending Apple tumbling to the floor. The dog stood up and shook, looking wounded, her ears flat against her head, her pop-eyes rolling. Suzanne settled into the chair, the blue folder on her lap. She'd changed into an ancient sweatsuit earlier, returning the amber silk to its plastic bag, sighing. When would she ever want to wear it again? She had also changed her wet shoes and was now wearing old moccasins with a pair of thick wool hiking socks she'd discovered in her laundry basket a while back—not hers. Left by one of her visitors, she'd guessed. Or by some benefactor at the laundramat on the corner. No matter— they were warm and thick and cushy. She was comfortable, she was in her own kitchen, she was safe.

Apple sighed, a long dramatic indication of resignation, and curled up on Suzanne's feet, adding another layer of warmth. Suzanne smiled. "See? I am the Alpha Female of this pack and you are a mere drone, despite your terrier delusions of grandeur. But if I had any other chairs, pup, I would sit in one of them and give you this one. You know that." She thought about her empty living room—a gracious Victorian parlor, with shining hardwood floors, a high ceiling, oak moldings. She called it the "ballroom," as if she kept it empty on purpose, just in case some evening a chamber orchestra showed up and began to play a waltz. Just in case women in long gowns and men in tuxedoes came over, expecting to dance. *Yeah, right,* she could imagine Ronelle saying, *when little pink piggies fly.* Or, maybe she could just have Ronelle "find" her some furniture. That was an idea. She opened the folder and pulled out a piece of paper, sighing as dramatically as the dog. "Someday," she said. "Someday, Apple, there will be chairs enough for all." But then she remembered that Ronelle was cold and hungry and bedless, at least according to Molly, and she stopped feeling so sorry for herself.

And the poem in her hand made her laugh, then cry—happy little sniffles of appreciation. It was that good. Praise be to the goddesses of flesh, *Largesse* was going to get some good stuff and it was going to be a fine, fine publication. She sipped her chocolate, real old-fashioned cocoa, rich with cream, and re-read the poem. She turned the page over and read the hand-scribbled note on the back: *Hope it's okay that this poem is about a guy, by a guy. Fat men get a bad rap, too, you know.* The signature and campus address were of no one she knew. But she read the poem again and thought she'd like to know the guy who wrote it. "Hey dogs," she said. She nudged Apple with a toe. Pear lifted his head from his foam bed and cocked his ears, obediently. "Listen up." She cleared her throat and began to read aloud:

THE ALOE SYMPHONY

I have big dreams, even for a 300 pound man.
I grow Acapulco Gold in my closet and flip
through Orvis catalogs, thinking about fried
brown trout. I once rescued a dog runover
by the milktruck. I called him Guernsey
and he's alive to this day.

My wife left me 4, maybe 5 years ago.
The night she walked out I began to compose
a symphony dedicated to my aloe plants.
She took our daughter Ruth with her.
I used to call her "Babe" and told her she'd hit
about a million homeruns. Though war appalls me
I'm an avid supporter of women's lib, kettle drums and State's Rights,
and every year I read Homer's *Iliad* cover to cover.

Long time ago I owned a '48 International.
I rolled that truck into a pond when I didn't quite make
the curve around Kerley's Corners. I still think
about my '48 International, when I take Guernsey for long
walks past the pond. Maybe one day I'll throw a line
in and pluck a few bass up off those sunken running boards.

I have a girlfriend named Linda. She's got a good
job with the telephone company. We met when I spent
all my money on a new Casio recorder and she was forced to turn
off my service. She drops by the trailer, we drink virgin
pina coladas, play chinese checkers. I don't mind
the company but I wonder sometimes if
Linda knows the real me.

When I finish my symphony, I'm gonna save
up my disability checks and have that '48 International
dredged from the pond at Kerley's Corners. Then I'll drive
North and find Ruthie, who's somewhere in Vermont.
I'll lean on a chainlink fence, smoke Acapulco Gold
and watch my daughter hit one homerun after another
into that thin, green mountain twilight.
I have big dreams, and Guernsey does too,
though he mostly keeps them to himself.
Being runover can sometimes do that to a dog.

Suzanne let the silence linger after the word "dog." She almost expected applause. She looked at her own canids—Pear was still politely pretending to pay attention, his head tilted to one side. But his eyes kept drifting shut and the minute her voice stopped his head clunked back onto his bed and he resumed snoring. Apple had removed herself from Suzanne's moccasins and was licking her own feet. "Well, I like it a lot," Suzanne said. "And I'm the editor. So there." She penciled a big "YES" on the top of the poem and put it back in the folder. There—one acceptance letter to be written already. This job might actually turn out to be fun.

She pulled out the next thing her hand found—the slim envelope that had been slipped under the office door the other morning. She lifted the flap and pulled out the single sheet of paper. It only took a minute to read it. In big block letters, written in black marker, it read:

QUESTION: HOW DO YOU FUCK A FAT GIRL?
ANSWER: ROLL HER IN FLOUR AND AIM FOR THE WET SPOT.

Below that, in green marker, was another line:
See? A man will fuck anything. Even you.
She set the paper down, her hands shaking. There was no signa-

ture, of course. People who write things like this never sign them. Oh, yeah, she'd met these people before; she was the fat girl that served as their target. Oh, yeah. These kinds of people put shit like this on bathroom walls or else they shouted it behind your back, after you've walked away. She knew that. And she'd been taught to ignore it. It wasn't personal. It wasn't Suzanne Brown that they hated. It was flesh itself that they hated. And feared. Even though it was what their very own bodies were made of. It was their very own selves, somehow, that they hated. Their very own bodies that terrified them. They were sick, they deserved pity. That's what she'd been taught and she'd tried, really tried, to learn to pity rather than to hate and fear.

She turned the paper over. Blank. She turned it back, read it again. She remembered the lessons of her life as a fat baby, fat child, fat teenager, fat young woman, fat mature woman. She remembered her grandmother, herself a very tall, very large woman, stroking her hair, her cheeks, and saying, "Oh, sweetheart, it's just some ignorant, evil-hearted people, that's all. Just nasty, stupid people. Ignore them and they'll leave you alone." And then her grandmother would fix them both a snack, to cheer them up—something warm and sweet and full of comfort. For her teenage years, Suzanne remembered, it was biscuits. Hot buttermilk biscuits, yellow butter soaking into their creamy insides, homemade strawberry preserve topping the butter. She closed her eyes. She could still taste those biscuits. The first bite through the brown crust, salty and sharp, into the hot, soft innards, sweet and fruity. She opened her eyes and looked at the joke on the page. She supposed that's what someone thought it was, after all, a joke. She thought, suddenly, about her dissertation. All those strange conjunctions between food and flesh. Flesh as food. Hell, that's what Crusoe's faithful cannibal companion, good old Friday, might think, right? It was just a recipe, after all: Take one fat girl, naked, and roll her in flour. Heat the oil in the pot. Toss her in. (Ignore the screams; she'll shut up soon enough.) What have you got? The perfect fuck and the perfect meal, all rolled up in one.

She crumbled the paper in her fist and threw it on the floor. She stood up. Just a joke. "I know, Gran," she whispered, "it's just a stupid ignorant joke." But her legs were trembling and her grandmother had been dead for ten years. There was no one here to listen or to comfort her. So, okay, she had a choice. She could go to the pantry, pull out the flour and make biscuits, then slather them with jam and eat them all. Or she could go out and find someone to stroke her cheek and her hair. She stood up. Hell, the silk dress was right upstairs in the closet. The bars that ringed the campus were open and would be full of newly returned students and faculty. An easy choice: stay home and wallow or go out and party. Before she'd even walked across the kitchen, Apple was back in the chair, curling up with a happy sigh.

Or, she thought, she could avoid relying on the luck of the draw and call someone to meet her. She had some choices there, too. She wasn't exactly without resources. Yes, Sam was gone. But she'd never been able to call Sam anyway, for fear that Diana would answer the phone. When she and Sam met, it always had to seem like an accident, a chance encounter in Washington Park, an afternoon in the library, a stolen sunny morning when they'd both just happened to take a walk around the campus pond, where there were quiet woods and deep, soft grass. In the afternoons, Sam always went home, to fix supper for his working wife, to be there when she came in. At night, Sam slept beside his beautiful Diana. She shook herself. What difference did it make now, where Sam had slept? Sam slept somewhere out there in the cosmos, now. Sam was gone.

She took a deep breath. Okay. There was still Morris, wasn't there? Morris still existed in the here and now, didn't he? And when she'd needed comfort, he had come to her, and provided it. She slipped the silk dress over her shoulders and shimmied it down over her body. She loved the way it slipped over her bra and skimmed her hips; she loved the sensation of silk on silk. She picked up the phone and dialed Morris's number. His phone didn't even ring before the message machine kicked in. She knew what that meant. Morris was in his hunker-down, do-not-disturb mode. She listened to his new message:

I'm working. Do not leave your name and number. Do not tell me the time you called. I will not get back to you. Leave me alone.

She sighed and hung up. Really, he meant it; she knew that. When Morris was working—and that meant writing, not grading papers or doing any other academic chore—he would not return calls. So, okay, she'd just go out, shoot a few games of pool and take her chances. And, she'd wear high-heeled shoes with her silk dress. Take that, Mr. Charles Clark—vanity over common sense, with no apologies. She hummed to herself as she outlined her eyes in blue and fluffed her hair into a halo of soft waves. She looked into the mirror before she threw on a coat: Okay. She was tall; she was large. She was, as her grandmother always said, a deluxe-sized woman. Or, as Arethra had sung, a natural woman. So be it.

And anyway, she'd never had trouble getting someone to share her bed. Never. Not since the day she'd made a startling discovery. A simple, huge discovery, like gravity or how to split an atom. A simple law of physics, of physicality: Men love flesh. Men have always loved flesh, lots of it. They love to rest on it, roll in it, bury their sorrows— and their dicks—deep inside it. They love to taste it, lick it, burrow into its rich deep clefts. They get hard five times a night, just looking at it. This was the great secret that all the slick magazines and all the gyms and all the spas and the whole fucking fashion industry con- spired to hide, to keep from girls and women of all ages. It was the biggest secret of contemporary culture and it was so simple. They may not take them home to meet Mama, but, still, men love fleshy women. She shook her head. Too much sometimes. Way too much. Love them damn near to death.

Still, she was all right. She was, after all, Suzanne LaFleshe. When- ever she wanted to be. And, tonight, she did. Because, when you are Suzanne LaFleshe, you know another secret. You know that it is not only men who love your flesh; you know that it is your own flesh you most love when making love. When your flesh moves, wave after wave, around you. And you—the you who lives inside this flesh, feeling, feeling it all—you are like the core, the tight core at the center of a storm of sex. The man, he provides the hard axis on which you turn. The man, if he's good—and most men are, really—then he joins you, somehow, on the inside of the whirlwind. Together, you set the flesh in motion, with your primitive bumps and grinds and shivering sliding thrusts and pulls, but once begun, the flesh moves you. From your thighs to your breasts, the waves heave and peak, heave and peak. The man is lost; you are lost. He comes once; you lose count.

Really, it is so simple, the knowledge of LaFleshe: pound for pound, your flesh multiplies your orgasms. And that's that.

She made a concession to the cold and to her high-heeled feet and called a cab, instead of waiting for the bus. So when she got to the campus hangout called Down the Road, she stepped in dry and warm, full of confidence. She slung her coat on a hook and walked to the bar. It was packed, steamy with bodies. She had to tap shoulders and say "Excuse me" all the way across the room. And all the way across, people turned to look at her. In her heels, she was a good six inches taller than most of the men in the room and nearly a foot taller than most of the women. Often, when some guy turned to let her go by, he found himself face-to-bosom, his mouth nearly crushed against one of her silken breasts. She always smiled down at the guy's startled face and moved on, brushing herself gently against him. By the time she'd reached the bar, there was a trail of interested eyes behind her. And, of course, a trail of snotty remarks, too, mostly made by skinny women. She could shrug those off, once she'd had a vodka tonic or two. She could even feel sorry for those women, the poor hungry little things, believing the great big lie, constantly dieting, starving all the curve out of their hips, suffering for flat bellies and hard abs and solid gluts. When, all the time, their boyfriends were starving, too, hungry for real thighs and bellies, longing for the soft welcome of real breasts. Suzanne heard a voice at her elbow.

"Hey, Suzanne. Glad you're still around."

She turned and looked down. It was Leon, one of the shortest, smartest grad students in the English program, another perpetual ABD, struggling to finish his dissertation. His, she recalled, was on something even more horrible than her own—something on 17th and 18th century American sermons and captivity narratives. Endless tracts written by white God-fearing Christians who had been carried off by the people they called heathens, held as slaves in the wilderness by those they considered painted savages. Tortured, and all the while hollering out praises to their merciful God. Horrible, horrible stuff, as she recalled. But Leon was always cheerful and now he was grinning up at her like she was the angel of mercy herself. "You look great, girl. Like you're ready to celebrate," he said. "Did you finally finish that little paper you've been writing for two years? You all done with cannibals?"

She sighed deeply, knowing that Leon would be happy to watch her breasts heave, just above his head. "When little pink piggies fly. In my dreams. You?"

He shrugged. "I think I'm going backwards, you know? I deleted ninety pages over the break, typed twenty new ones. My committee hated the new stuff, said I should put the old stuff back in—the same old stuff they'd told me to ditch in the first place, naturally. But I'd really and truly deleted it, so it's gone. Poof. Into the ether." He sipped from his beer. "Well, as Edward Taylor liked to say 'Praise be to an afflicting God.'"

She laughed. "Yeah, well, what did he know from dissertation committees?"

Leon put his hand on the small of her back. "Want to sit down? I can find us a booth in the back, I bet."

"No, thanks. I want to play some pool. I'm afraid I lost my touch, over break. Gotta get the ole body English back."

"Sure, like you'd ever lose that." As they began the long trek toward the back room where the pool tables were, Leon said. "Guess what? I think I grew over break. No kidding. I stood against the marks on the kitchen wall and I swear I was one and three-quarters of an inch taller than I was in November. Pretty soon I'll be a full-sized guy and you'll be sorry you never agreed to sleep with me. Women will be crawling all over me and it'll be too late."

She laughed again, putting an arm over his shoulder. He'd been telling her for two years that he was growing, that she'd be sorry she'd scorned his manly charms. She always laughed. They both knew that it wasn't his height that had kept her from taking Leon to bed; it was his wife. They both knew that she'd made a rule about that, years and years ago—no married men. It was just not necessary to screw around with married men. There were plenty of single, or more often these days, divorced, men to pick from, around any university. Some widowers, even, so grateful for a happy fuck that they just broke your heart. But no married men. Except for Sam. The one exception to her lifelong rule—Sam, so beautiful and so sad that he'd broken *her* heart. Sam, who looked to *her* like an angel, all gold and shiny and tarnished around the edges, his natural light dimmed by some kind of indefinable sorrow. No one knew that she and Sam were lovers, though. Everyone knew that they were friends, that she read his poetry, that they shared lunches and coffee breaks, but no one really knew anything about them. Morris—always observant, always poking around for characters and plots for his long poems, his epics—had guessed but she'd never confirmed it. She'd kept their secret; at least she'd thought she had. But she'd never really thought about Diana, that Diana might have known, all along. Even here in the overheated bar, Suzanne shivered. God, she had never meant for Sam's wife to know.

She stopped in mid-crowd and leaned down to Leon's ear. "Did you hear about Sam Tindell?"

He tightened his arm on her waist. "Yeah. Just this afternoon. I didn't get back in time for the service. I'm really sorry. Sam was a sweet guy."

She held fast against the bulwark of bodies pressing against her. "Yeah," she said. "He was."

Leon took her hand and moved forward. He yelled up into her ear. "Not that I'm surprised, you know. I always thought that someone like Sam, so intense, you know, might do something like that. I always had a feeling he was really really fragile, you know? That any little thing would send him off."

She let herself be towed behind him. "You did? You thought Sam was fragile? Like so fragile that he might be suicidal? That he might actually want to die?"

In one of those odd hushes that sometimes fall into noisy rooms, her voice bounced above the crowd, and hovered there. There was a long echo, before the bar noise flowed back in, covering up all but the last of those words: "Die?"

Suzanne listened to the word lift into the air and then get washed away. She stumbled into the pool room and immediately sent Leon back into the fray for another drink—she wanted, suddenly, lots and lots of drinks.

She felt better once she had a cue in her hands. It was a skill she'd learned in junior high, something she could always do at parties, when no adolescent boy would be seen dancing with her, no matter how much he wanted to get his hands on her swelling tits. She was good at it and it showed her off to her best advantage, she knew that. She balanced on her high heels and bent over the table, showing lots of pale cleavage above her amber silk. She swayed her hips and rested the cue between her breasts between shots. Always, always, she had men watching. They admired her skill with the stick; they clearly wanted her hands on their own sticks; they clearly wanted to rest theirs against her chest, too. It was so simple that it was almost laughable. She'd had enough vodka to play it all up, too, letting the silk dress hike up her thighs and cling to the damp, perfumed spot between her breasts. She wasn't sure, any more, that she really wanted to take one of these men home, but she was willing to let them look. Leon had given up, gone home to his wife, and she didn't really need anyone else around. She was feeling confident enough to be okay on her own, after all. Maybe she just wanted them to look at her like that, to see the appreciation in five or six sets of eyes. To see the hope that a sexy full-fleshed woman created in the whole male gender. So she just bent and shot, bent and shot, her face flushed with warmth.

When she'd finished her game, she stepped back, leaning against the wall. She saw that Morris had come in and was watching her from across the room. She waved and he came across, weaving a little. She watched him carefully. Morris tended to drink too much, especially when he was writing. When he was into a new project, he would work like a demon all day and then start drinking. And then he'd keep drinking. He got his best ideas when he drank, he always said. Slightly wild, offbeat ideas that he could use the next day, in a new stanza, a whole new spate of elegant couplets. That was one of Morris's great gifts as a poet, actually, his ability to put dark, disturbing content into lovely, scintillating verse. She admired him for it. But she'd seen him turn mean, too, when he was drinking, and she'd learned to avoid him during those bouts. She'd seen him be caustic, cutting with his words. He'd once made some little undergraduate student cry, one of those worshipful workshop girls who followed him around from bar to bar. Suzanne had seen that poor child run off, snot and tears running down her perfect little face, and so she was wary. But Morris was her friend, too. And she remembered his mouth on her skin, sipping rose petals. He stopped beside her and kissed her cheek, leaning hard against her side.

"Wonderful show, my dear," he said softly.

She felt his breath misting her cheek and drew back. He was definitely over-the-top drunk. "Hey, Morris," she said.

He pressed against her. "Hey yourself, sweet lady. I was hoping to find you here."

She moved away, putting her cue in front of her chest. Morris's breath was sticky with bourbon and his eyes were bloodshot. "Sorry. I'm about to take off, Morris," she said. "Lots of work to get done tomorrow. As always, I've got a date with Crusoe."

His eyes snapped and he backed up. "Fine." He took a sip from his glass and leaned on the wall beside her. "Perhaps before you go, you'd like to hear about my new poem? Just a quick synopsis?"

She laughed, ready to forgive him for drinking too much. Who didn't have their weaknesses? Jelly doughnuts? Bourbon? "Sure."

"Okay. Let's see if any of this sounds familiar, shall we? It's about a beautiful, talented man. A young man, full of promise as a poet." He sipped again. "Not a washed-up middle-aged poet, mind you. A young one. No aching prostate, no droopy prick for him. No, no, he is at his peak. Peak prick." He closed his eyes and bent his head toward Suzanne's ear. "So this young, beautiful, well-hung poet, he finds a beautiful, tall, full-breasted woman and he fucks her blue, whenever he gets the chance. You'd never guess that this polite young man, a man so diffident he knocks on the door of his own classroom, would be so bold in bed. But he is. He just turns his lover inside out, he's so good at it. She can't stop coming, around his oh-so-sturdy young prick. In fact, she's so taken with this young, poetic stud that she stops wanting to see her other lovers. She just drops them flat. But she and this poet-fellow, why they suck and fuck like bloody mad. And that's just the first section—lots of sex to get my reader hooked."

He drank, coughed, then continued. "But now we've got to have a real conflict, right? People don't read for sex alone. No, we need Trouble, capital T, to keep our audience entranced. So let's pretend that our hero finds that he's having so much fun fucking this great broad that he just can't write his sad, sensitive little poems anymore. And then the little wifey at home—the one who pays his bills, by the way, the one who supports him so he can play around and get his fucking useless PhD and fuck his lovely, lovely lover—well, that little woman gets just a tad pissed at this beautiful young poet and she says she's going to toss his handsome ass into the hard, cold world where he will have to earn his own damn living. So, there he is, poor sap. He can fuck like a bunny, but he can't write and he doesn't have a job and he hasn't any marketable skills, not a one. And so he's kind of disgusted by what he's done to get his wife all upset and he blames the lovely lovely lover for the whole mess—because, of course, he's never blamed himself for anything, not this handsome lad, oh my no—and so, one dark and stormy night, he does the most dramatic, most poetic thing of all. He throws himself over a railing. And he lands, splat, right where his lovely lovely lover will have to find him. And that's only part two. How do you like it so far?"

Suzanne felt her heart thudding against the fine silk of her dress. There was sweat sliding down her ribs and she thought about the stains it would leave on the fabric, white, salty, indelible stains. "You wouldn't," she whispered. "You would not exploit Sam's death like that, just for some lousy poem."

Morris stood up suddenly, splashing bourbon onto her dress. "Oh, yes, my dear. I would indeed. I'm getting old, Suzanne. I am not, surprise surprise, a hot commodity in the publishing world. Yes, indeed, I would sell my mother into white slavery for just, as you so kindly put it, one more lousy poem." He shook his head. "But, perhaps you're right. Perhaps the dramatic suicide is just a bit of a cliché? And, would my hero have the guts—the basic balls—to take that plunge? No. You're right. He can't have done it—it must have been someone else. Someone who hated his handsome guts. Someone with the balls to give him one good shove. The little wifey perhaps? Or—here's a thought—the scorned lovely lover herself? Is that better, my dear?"

She turned to face him. His eyes were staring into hers and suddenly he didn't seem so very drunk after all. Suddenly, he seemed like a cop, interrogating a suspect. She felt dizzy. "God. Do you have a heart, Morris? Do you have a human heart under there?" She poked the cue into his chest, hard.

He put a hand on her shoulder. "You have to ask? Don't you know, Suzanne? Jesus, don't you realize?" His eyes lost their focus and went all swimmy with tears.

Her blood was pounding in her ears. She could breathe, but just barely. She tried to swat his hand away but his long thin fingers were very strong.

Another man's hand fell onto her shoulder, and for one horrible moment she thought that she was being accosted by not one drunk, but two. But then she heard Charles Clark's voice. "Is there something I can do for you here, Ms. Brown?"

Morris's hand slid down her arm, caressing and soft. It lingered on her wrist, then dropped. "Oh, I'm sure you can, Officer. I'm sure there's something you can do for Ms. Brown, a fine young man like yourself." His voice was soft and hoarse and when Suzanne looked into his face, she saw that the tears had actually spilled down his cheeks.

In the University Police car, Suzanne began to shake. "I thought Morris was just a friend, really," she said. "God. I'm not much of a judge of character, am I? Molly's right."

"Oh, come on. The guy was drunk. Don't judge him by whatever he said to you tonight."

She looked over at his face. It was a good face, lined, but much younger than the white hair would make it seem. "Did you hear what he said?"

He laughed. "Nope. I just didn't like the way he was putting his hands on you, that's all. But, really, I see more drunks in a week than you do in a lifetime. You can't worry about what they say. He won't remember a word of it in the morning."

She shook her head. "I hope not." She sighed. "So, what were you doing Down the Road, anyway, Mr. Clark? I don't think I've ever seen you there before."

"No? Funny, I've seen you there. You do tend to turn a few heads, Ms. Brown. Tonight, though, I was drinking a beer. Just drinking a beer." Charles took a hand off the wheel and laid it on her knee, gently. "Even a cop gets to have a night off now and again, right?" His hand was warm and suddenly she couldn't think of anything to say.

He cupped his fingers over her knee and they drove silence until they'd pulled up to her house. "So you really do live with old Molly Highsmith?" he said.

Suzanne turned in her seat. "You know Molly?"

He nodded. "Sure I do. All my life. And I took a class with her once, years and years ago."

"A class? My God, I didn't know she taught. What kind of class?"

"Not a whole class—just one session. On natural poisons. She told us how to recognize someone who'd been done in by the ordinary stuff that grows in little old ladies' gardens. Very informative." He leaned over and unsnapped Suzanne's seat belt, his arm heavy against her left breast. "You okay, now, Ms. Brown? Want me to walk in with you?"

His voice was neutral, quiet. He might have just been checking to see if she would be all right alone. Or, he might have been inviting himself in for the night. She'd like that, she realized. But if he wasn't, she'd look like a fool. She looked at his face again. An honest, tired face. Not someone playing games.

She lifted her hand and set it against his cheek. "Are you married, Mr. Clark?" she asked. "Tell the truth, please."

He turned his face just slightly, so that his lips moved against her palm. "No, I am not married, Ms. Brown." He raised his left hand and waved it slightly in the air. "If you look real close, you'll see a slight indentation on the ring finger. It's been empty for about three years now but that damn skin just won't fill in. Go on, look."

She had to lean across him to take his hand and she stayed there, letting the weight of her breasts rest on his chest. She lifted his left hand close to her face and looked at the empty ring finger. "Divorced?" she said.

He nodded. "Yep. Want a copy of the legal papers? I carry them in my wallet, everywhere I go. Right next to the condoms."

She smiled. "I believe you, Mr. Clark." She lifted his hand to her lips and ran her tongue around the tiny smooth groove on his finger. "Feels legit to me," she said. "Come on in."

12

They hadn't been asleep long when the phone rang. Suzanne had just drifted off, savoring the beat of Charles's steady breathing beside her. Each small eddy of breath ruffled her hair and the weight of his arm across her hip anchored her perfectly. But she came out of this bliss with a heart-pounding start when the phone screamed into life beside her. She sat up, staring at the lit numbers of her alarm clock. It was 2:15. Charles was already sitting up. "You got a machine? Or you going to answer that?" His voice sounded perfectly alert.

She swung her feet to the cold floor, pulled the comforter over her bare breasts and reached for the phone. "Yes?"

"I am so very sorry, love. I am sitting here in abject remorse, with a cup of instant coffee and a piece of humble pie. And I wondered if you might, by any chance, welcome the company of a sorry, sorry man." Morris's voice was loud enough to bounce beyond the phone, into the room.

Charles groaned and lay back down.

Morris went on. "Are you there, Suzanne? Or do I, god forbid, have the wrong number? Am I speaking to some poor sleepy soul who doesn't know me from Adam? Did my poor, shaking, utterly remorseful fingers push the wrong little buttons? Answer me, love."

Charles ran a finger down Suzanne's spine. "Go on. Answer the asshole, Ms. Brown. Or, if you prefer, I will," he said. "In fact, I'd love to. Give me that phone." He made a grabbing motion.

Suzanne shook her head and spoke clearly into the phone. "Mor-

ris, go to sleep, okay? I'll talk to you later." She set the receiver down
and turned back toward Charles. She let the comforter drop and leaned
over him. She smiled. "Just what I've always wanted—a man who
carries a gun, in my bed, keeping watch, scaring off the drunk and
disorderly."

He reached up, taking a breast in each hand. He pulled her down,
burying his face between the swells of her flesh. Voice muffled, husky,
he said. "God. Just what I've always wanted, Ms. Brown. This is a
place a man could die, happy."

The second time the phone rang, just about twenty minutes later,
Charles said, "Shit. This jerk is really getting on my nerves now. Let
me get it." He stood up, his erect penis bobbing in the air. Suzanne
reached out to touch him, but he turned his back and grabbed the
phone. "Listen, asshole," he said. "Ms. Brown is busy, okay?"

Suzanne could hear the voice on the phone—the sound of it came
shrilling over the wires: "She's a fat slut. Slut. Slut . Murdering, filthy
slut."

By three a.m., they were sitting at the kitchen table, drinking hot coffee. Suzanne had almost stopped crying. She knew her face looked all
blubbery and ugly. Nothing, she thought, nothing looks worse than a
fat woman crying. But she hadn't been able to stop. When that voice
had come into her bedroom, all sibilant and full of fury, she'd just
started to bawl, curling into her pillows like a two-year-old. Charles
had stared at the phone and then said, calmly, "Who is this, please?"

But the line was dead. So he'd hung up, tried a quick *69, but
nothing happened. He'd run his hands through his hair, then turned
back to Suzanne. He'd put a hand on her shoulder, but his voice wasn't
sympathetic or even friendly—it was official, cool, just like he was
interviewing her for a case. "Get these calls often, Ms. Brown? Someone mad at you or something?"

She took a sip of coffee and pulled her bathrobe tighter around her shoulders. She patted Pear's head. When Pear had seen her come into the kitchen, crying, he'd risen from his bed and put his head against her thigh. No matter where she went, moving from the coffee maker to the fridge to the pantry, he kept pace, his head pressing her leg. Now that she was seated, he stood beside her chair, head heavy on her lap, eyes closed. "It's okay, sweetie," she whispered into his soft black fur. "I'm okay." Sure, as okay as someone who'd been accused of murder twice in one night could be. Murder. The thought brought back the chill of that terrible wind in her office, that screaming wind. She'd thought Sam's suicide was unbearable—but murder? Someone killed Sam? She wiped a hand over her eyes.

Charles sipped his coffee. He'd gotten completely dressed, as if he was now back on duty. His hair was neatly combed and he looked every inch a cop. Except that he was holding a quivering Jack Russell terrier on his lap, scratching behind her ears. "Why didn't you tell me you were getting threatening messages?" he said.

Suzanne ran her hands over her face and through her hair. "I'm not. I just got one other call and I thought it was a dream or something, it was so quick and weird." She wanted something to eat, but she was embarrassed to admit it, to let Charles think that she was dependent on food for comfort. She lifted one of Pear's ears and held it in her hand. "I didn't think anything of it."

"Right." He leaned over the table. "Don't kid a kidder, Ms. Brown. No one hears a voice like that in the middle of the night and doesn't think a thing of it. Christ, that voice was enough the peel the hair off your head. Wendigo voice." He lifted Apple in two hands. "You know, this dog is built just like a rump roast. Put her on a spit and you'd have a meal."

Suzanne stared at him. "What?"

He laughed. "Sorry. I'm hungry, that's all. Got anything to eat?" He pushed Apple off his lap and brushed little white hairs from his pants. "Go along to bed, you little pork roast, you."

"Eat?" Suzanne stood up, gently shoving Pear away from her thigh. "I can probably find something." She opened the fridge and brought out half of a key lime pie. She cut two pieces and set one before him.

He looked up. "Is this homemade? Did you make this?" He put a fork into the perfect meringue, touching one of the little brown swirls she'd created. He took a bite and closed his eyes. "My God. I've died and gone to heaven, haven't I?"

She smiled, dipping into her own piece. She wouldn't tell him that not only had she made the pie, she'd made two—one for herself and one for Molly. And she wouldn't tell him that she'd eaten half of this one all by herself, for breakfast, before going to Sam's funeral, for strength. She just said, "I like to bake. My grandmother raised me and she was the best baker I've ever known. I learned a lot from her."

He finished the pie in three more bites and sat back with a sigh. "You're not telling me what I need to know. You're plying me with pie and not mentioning who you think this might be who's bothering you."

Who is your enemy? She shrugged. "I really don't know who it is. Molly says I have an enemy, but even she doesn't know who it is, for sure." She licked the last sticky bit of meringue from her fork, letting the sugar and egg white soothe her.

"Uh huh. Ms. Highsmith said that? Interesting. When was the first call?"

She looked into his eyes. They were fine eyes, dark brown, with soft black lashes. His cheekbones were high, showing clearly under his skin. His nose was big, hooked and slightly bent to the left. She noticed, for the first time, really, under the fluorescent kitchen light, how dark his skin was, what a sharp contrast to the thatch of white hair, how tawny and smooth. She reached a finger out and touched his cheek. "Are you Native American?" she asked.

He took her hand in his, wrapping it in his big, warm palm. "Yeah, I'm an Indian. Partly. On my mother's side. My grandmother was full-blood. When was the first call, Ms. Brown?"

She sighed. "The night after Sam died. I thought it was part of a nightmare. Really."

He nodded. "No one else here with you that night, Ms. Brown?

Anyone else hear that call?"

She remembered Morris and how she'd lifted her hips to meet his mouth. How even in her sorrow for Sam, she'd welcomed Morris into her body. How easily he'd made her come, in the bath and in her bed. And how, in the bar, he'd pushed himself against her, like he'd had the right. She felt a flash of pain behind her eyes—maybe the voice in the night wasn't so far wrong, calling her a slut. A filthy slut, taking them all in, wanting them all. Greedy for food, greedy for men, sucking them up without a thought to the consequences—Sam, Morris, and now Charles. Right now, right this minute, her cunt was still swollen from Charles's thrusts. And if he wanted to do it again, right this minute, she'd be ready. She was always ready, always easy. Always, always hungry. So, maybe that voice was right—maybe she was just a slut, pure and natural. "No," she said. "There was no one here that night."

He squeezed her hand. "Okay. But maybe you ought to get caller ID, you know? And an unlisted number." He stood up, stretching his arms above his head. "Well, no sense trying to sleep anymore tonight. Might as well go back to work, see what's up at the university." He dropped a kiss on her hair. "You going to be all right, Ms. Brown?"

She stood up, facing him, trying to smile. "I'll be fine. For an accused murderer, fine." She waited for Charles to say something, something about how no one could possibly suspect her of killing Sam. No one sane. It was just so ridiculous. But he didn't. He just looked steadily into her eyes and the silence grew long. "Don't worry, really. I'm fine," she said. "Hell, I've got Pear to watch over me."

Charles looked at the big dog sitting at Suzanne's feet, upright but asleep. "Right. And how old you say that dog is?"

She reached out, laying a hand on Pear's head. "Not so old."

"Uh huh. Well, I'm off. Where'd you put my coat?"

Suzanne shrugged. "I think we dropped our coats on the living room floor."

He laughed. "You're right. Kind of in a hurry to get our clothes off, weren't we?"

They walked together to the living room. Plum, happy that everyone was up in the night, was playing with a ball of paper. Her orange
fur was fluffed into a halo of night-time energy, full of static and
fuzz. She pounced on the paper, then batted it with a paw. It shot
across the empty floor and hit Charles's foot. Suzanne bent, quickly,
and snatched it up. "Sorry," she said. "These animals. It's a zoo."

Charles slipped his arms into his coat, then turned to her, lifting
her face with both hands. "Thank you, Ms. Brown," he said, "for a
swell evening. You unplug your phone, get back into bed and pull the
covers up nice and tight, okay? Get some sleep." He kissed her cheek.

Icy air streamed over her bare ankles as he opened the door. She
locked it behind him. Then she stood in her empty living room and
opened the paper in her hand, smoothing it out in her hands. She
couldn't have borne to have him see it. She just couldn't have stood to
stand there and watch him read: Question: How do you fuck a fat
girl? She began tearing and she didn't stop until the paper was nothing
but a heap of smudgy, tiny scraps. Then she went upstairs and flushed
it down the toilet. Plum watched it go, tail twitching.

Sleep wasn't possible. The air in her bedroom swarmed with hissing
voices and she spent the rest of the night curled up, listening to them.
What had he called the voice? A wendigo? That was a new one on her.
She'd have said it was the voice of a banshee, her Irish grandmother's
favorite terror. She'd have to look up the wendigo thing—one more
bit of research. When the first light of the winter day appeared, she
heaved a sigh and got up. She made a pledge: she'd get to the office
super early, take care of few things there, then go to the library and do
the research she'd planned to do three days ago. Then she'd come
home and tackle the dissertation. She'd have a well-organized, productive day. She'd eat nothing but salads. She'd be disciplined, calm, in
control of all her desires. She really would. The first university bus ran
at 6:53 a.m., in optimistic hope of early-bird scholars. It usually ran
empty, but today, she'd be on it.

It had been awful, waiting for that bus in the icy dawn, freezing. She'd worn the heavy wool socks and her moon boots, just to show that she wasn't so vain, so silly about her footwear as some people seemed to think. So her feet had been warm, even while the rest of her shivered in the wind. But it was even more terrible, coming into Humanities and hearing the heavy door slam behind her in the empty building. She looked down the long hallway to the spot where Sam had died, as if she would find his spirit there, bits of white mist rising to the sky-light, four floors above, just now glowing with the silvery light of morning. But there was no mist—just something lying on the floor where his broken body had been. She walked very slowly, very steadily to the spot, determined not to be spooked. When she got close, she could see what it was—just another of those awful bunches of flow-ers rolled in a cellophane wrapper. She bent down and touched one of the blossoms, a cold, pale, winter carnation, pink. She crouched down and lifted the flowers—what an awful little bouquet. Insipid, waxy flowers, fresh from the Mobil station. No fragrance, no vitality, barely any color. Two white mums, three pink carnations and a bit of stiff baby's breath. One leathery piece of fern. The saddest thing she'd ever seen. Still, someone was remembering. Someone had tried. She laid the bouquet back on the floor, stood up and headed for the stairs, her boots pounding.

When the office door swung open, the smell hit her. A combina-tion of unwashed skin and Ramen noodles, thick in the overheated air. She stood in the doorway, staring. Ronelle was curled in the tur-quoise chair, sound asleep. Her thin jacket was slung over her shoul-ders and her bare feet hung over the edge, ankles rimmed in grime. On the radiator was an empty carton of noodles, unwashed, and a styrofoam cup that smelled of sour milk. On the floor were a pair of black leggings, a black shirt and black boots. There were also stacks of books and manuscripts. And a toothbrush on the windowsill. Hang-ing over the arm of the desk lamp, a little black bra and panties. Suzanne walked into the office and closed the door behind her. In the printer was a paper with the heading:

ENG 564—Response paper #1: Country of the Pointed Firs. There was a paragraph or two below that, then in capital letters: THIS IS ALL BULLSHIT!!! Then nothing. Obviously, Ronelle had tired of doing her homework for one of the three graduate classes she was taking.

Even more obviously, Ronelle was living in the office. Suzanne sat down in the rolling chair and put her head into her hands. It was really too much. She didn't need this much to deal with, did she? She stamped her moon boots on the floor and the chair rolled backwards, crashing into the desk.

Ronelle leapt up. She was naked, holding a penknife in her hand. Her eyes were wide. When she saw Suzanne, she sat back down. She folded her legs, yoga style, and slipped the knife between the bottom cushion and the arm of the chair. She shoved her arms into her jacket and crossed them over her chest, pulling the jacket close. "Hi, boss," she said.

Suzanne closed her eyes and leaned her head back. She wanted to erase the sight of Ronelle's body from her vision, but she couldn't. The girl was a twig, thin and brittle. Her belly was concave, dipping between sharp hipbones. Her breasts were just two loose sacks with brown nipples. Her armpits and legs were thick with hair. Her chest and shoulders were sprinkled with the same dark splotches as her face. "Why didn't you tell me, Ronelle?" she said. She opened her eyes and looked into the girl's pale eyes. "Why did you lie about having an apartment down on Dove?"

Ronelle put one hand to her mouth, biting at a nail. "Sure. You'd have been real pleased to know that your assistant editor was a home-less piece of shit, right?" She sat up and pointed at Suzanne. "What's your stipend for this job?"

"A pittance. Six thousand a semester. Why?"

"Yeah, well. Mine is half a pittance—three thousand. And I haven't gotten one fucking cent yet. Want to try to rent an apartment on promises? Want to stand there and offer some landlord spit?" She gestured around the office. "This is better than giving daily blow jobs to some sixty-year-old landlord so he'll let you stay in his little roach-closet, right? Listen, I told you—the girl doesn't fall far from the trailer. What the hell else was I supposed to do?" She stood up and bent to gather her belongings from the floor. "Don't worry, I'll split. I'll find some other hole. I'm good at this survival shit—I've done it before. Dog eat dog; survival of the fittest; the sneakiest, slickest gene-pool wins. And my DNA is slick as hell. I'll find something."

Suzanne looked at the girl's skinny bare thighs and sighed. "No you won't. This is okay—until you get your stipend, that is." She stood up and put a hand on Ronelle's shoulder. She could feel every bone, sharp against her palm. "But, listen, there's a women's locker room you can use free with your student I.D. And, girl, it has showers. Hot running water. Probably some soap lying around, too. Maybe even shampoo."

Ronelle blushed, blood rushing up her face, pink behind the freckles. "Yeah? I never thought of that. You mean, I can just go in there, any time, flash my ID and they won't throw my ass out? I was afraid, you know, if anyone found out I was living here, they'd toss me."

"Well, maybe. But they don't have to find out, do they? Get your butt dressed and we'll find you some breakfast. *Largesse* cannot have such a skinny assistant editor. Ruins our image, totally."

13

Suzanne tucked into her scrambled eggs. Ronelle was already on her second stack of pancakes, her third order of sausage. They didn't speak for quite some time, just chewed and swallowed, chewed and swallowed. The coffee shop was all but empty. Just a few dedicated students getting their first coffees of the day, sleepy-eyed and silent. When her egg was gone, Suzanne sat back and watched Ronelle eat. There was something comforting about it, like a mother must feel, seeing her child well-fed. Maybe. Suzanne had never been a mother and had never really known her own. Still, it seemed oddly familiar, the satisfaction of watching the thin, hungry girl filling herself up.

Ronelle set down her fork at last. She swept one finger over her plate and raised it to her lips, licking at the maple syrup. Then she sat back, smiling. "Thanks, boss," she said.

"No problem. Breakfasts are cheap."

"Yeah, well. Still. I owe you one." Ronelle began swiveling in her chair, looking around. "Not many kids about. Where are all the thousands that go to this school, anyway?"

Suzanne laughed. "Ronelle, it's 7:30 in the morning. Students don't get up for another four hours. Jeez, where did you go to college, that you think people appear before noon?"

"Me? First two years, Columbia Greene Community College. Lots of nursing students and criminal justice types who worked nights and took their classes during the day. They were up early—or never went to bed. Then, for the last two years, College of Saint Rose. Nuns get up early, too. Okay, not many of the kids did. But the old nuns, the ones who'd been teaching there for forty years, hell, they were up and eating at sunrise. Probably had already said their prayers, too. Gone to Mass. All that." Ronelle twirled a piece of her hair in her fingers, dragging it in front of her nose and sniffing. "Think I can go to the locker room now? I stink."

Suzanne leaned forward. "You don't stink. Well, a little. And that's mostly your clothes. You need some extra stuff, so you can wash those."

"Yeah, well. I had plenty, but then someone stole my bag, on the bus I took from home last week, coming up here. I mean, I had a lot; even in my family, you get some new clothes for Christmas. I had sweaters, jeans, all sorts of shit. I put my bag under my seat. But I fell asleep and it was gone. Had my cash in there too—not a lot, but some." She stood up. "So, can I take a shower now?"

Suzanne looked at her watch. "Not yet. I'm sure they don't open the athletic building until eight. Sit down. Tell me about your undergrad studies." Even to herself, Suzanne felt stuffy, all motherly and middle-aged. What was wrong with her? She pointed to Ronelle's chair. "Sit your butt down. I'll get you some more coffee."

Ronelle slumped back into her chair. "No thanks. I'm all buzzed already. So, you want to trade life stories? Okey-dokey. Mine is short. Trailer in the barnyard, I already told you about. Dad, his name is Ron. Get it? Ron, Ronelle? The other two girls in the family are Ronette and Ronita. No shit." Ronelle grinned at Suzanne and shook her head. "Dad likes to declare his paternity, big time. We're El and Et and Nita, around the house, to save on confusion. Anyway, Ron has only two teeth that meet in his whole mouth, just enough to hang a cigarette from. He milks cows, twice a day every day. Ma breeds like a prize heifer, so the trailer gets pretty packed. Nine kids at Christmas, one due any day. But this one, this Ron-girl, who happens to be the oldest, gets to be high school valedictorian, much to the utter amazement of everyone involved—I mean, Ron can't even read, although Ma is big on Harlequin romances. Anyhoo, Ronelle gets a scholarship to Amherst but has no real money, to even buy books or live on campus. Besides, she's scared of all the snotty Little Ivy League types. So, off to community college for this kid. Liberal arts major—started with computer science but got bored. 4.0 average. Scholarship to Saint Rose, where they love to take in the poor and disadvantaged. It's part of their mission, I swear. They even bought my books. Lots of books. English major— I couldn't believe they'd let me read books for credit. 4.0 average. Accepted into SUNYA grad program in English, with a grad assistantship, as you know. No tuition, little bitsy stipend. I always worked two or three jobs, before, but this gig is supposed to be a serious full-time thing, as you also know. I'm not supposed to work anywhere else. I signed a paper that said so. Thus, the office as crash pad. End of story." Ronelle sat up, tapping Suzanne's wrist. "Your turn."

Suzanne laughed. "Mine might take a little longer. I'm a lot older."

"Yeah, well, you only got until eight. I really do stink."

"Okay. Let's see. My parents died when I was three, both of them, on March 17th, 1968, so my grandparents raised me. My grandfather was a…."

"Wait a minute! Whoa. You can't just say that kind of thing and not fill in." Ronelle was glaring over the tabletop. "What do you mean, they died? And on the same day, yet?"

Suzanne dipped her finger into some spilled sugar and raised it to her lips. "It's simple—Saint Patrick's Day in Boston. They were walking home from work—they both taught at BU—at four o'clock in the afternoon and a very drunk fake Irishman, so full of green beer he couldn't see the hand in front of his face, ran them down on Commonwealth Avenue. By the time the first cop arrived, they were lying together on the sidewalk, still holding hands, I'm told, dead. The drunk was standing there puking up his corned beef and cabbage."

"Jesus, Suzanne. That sucks, big time."

"Oh, it doesn't matter. I don't even remember them, except for little snatches. But I'm not even sure those are real memories. They might be things my grandmother told me. Anyway, my grandparents came down from Maine and took me back with them. My grandfather had a little printing shop in the back of their house. He always had ink on his hands. He never said much. He used to let me sit in the shop and watch him work. I loved the smell. And seeing the words appear on the pages, like magic." She smiled, feeling it again, for a minute, the old man with the black hands, lifting her up to see a freshly inked page. She shook her head. "Sorry, this is getting long. Anyway, my grandmother ruled in the house and the garden. She was the queen of food, growing everything, canning, freezing, baking. I had a wonderful childhood, Ronelle. Those old people loved me like mad. It was perfect. Really." She thought about that, for a minute. She wasn't saying it just so Ronelle wouldn't feel sorry for her, poor little orphan. It was true—she had been a well-loved, cherished child. A great gift.

She went on. "But I was not valedictorian of my class. I did okay, though, and I went to Bates College and then I went to New York, thinking my English degree would get me a job—ha! And then I moved upstate and did get one, finally, writing copy for a small town PR firm. Mostly secretarial, really. A little writing, a lot of word-processing. Pretty boring. And, so, finally, I got up my nerve and decided to get my doctorate, so that I could be a genuine college professor, like Mom and Dad. The rest, my dear, is history. I'm thirty-eight, I'm here, I'm perpetually poor, I haven't finished my fucking dissertation and probably never will. Et cetera. Ad nauseum. Yadda, yadda, yadda. Blah, blah, blah."

"Yeah. I hear you. But what about, you know? Like life? Marriage? Kids?"

Suzanne leaned back, squinting into Ronelle's face. "You didn't tell any of that, did you? Why should I? I thought this was all just sort of a professional resume, with some basic ancestry thrown in. Curriculum vitae and all that."

"Curriculum what? Spell that."

Suzanne did. "Life, it means. Just life. Your CV is the curriculum of your life, just the highlights, the parts you want people to know."

"Cool—I'll look it up later. But, I just want to hear, you know, some of the real stuff. Like how did you live, in New York, when you couldn't find a job?"

"Oh, that. Okay. Well, I did find a job—oldest job in the world, being somebody's wife. I was an artist's model. And then I married the guy, the artist." She felt her throat growing tight, just saying it: the artist. Scrambled egg rose in her throat, choking, like a reminder of that whole time, the paintings, the endless endless paintings. Sitting, naked, for hours and hours, chilled and stiff, while he painted and painted and painted. In between the sessions, the food. The endless endless food that he cooked for her, then watched her eat, his eyes following every morsel down her throat. The husband obsessed with her flesh, with making it grow, with adding rolls and rolls of it, to be painted, to be worshiped. To be fucked. To be owned. She swallowed a sip of tea, forcing the memories down.

Ronelle's eyebrows shot up. "You were a model? Like, nude and shit?"

Suzanne rolled her eyes. "Yes. Nude. And shit. At first, for draw-ing classes at NYU. My therapist—yes, I had a therapist in the 80's, who didn't?—told me that it would help me with my body image if I did that. I was big. I mean, really big, much bigger than now, if you can believe that. Anyway, I did it, the modeling thing. And it did help." She laughed, trying to keep it light. "I sat there and all these intent art students stared at me and they loved my rolls, absolutely adored my flesh. It gave them a chance to practice their shading techniques, get some major proportions going. After class, I used to walk around and look at my naked self, drawn from every possible angle. Every bulge lovingly traced in charcoal, every bit of fatness carefully sketched in ink. It was great. The other model was an opera singer—her drama coach had told her the same thing, to model and learn to appreciate her own body. "Great sopranos are not fat, my child,' her coach told her, 'great sopranos are *zaftig.*' "

Ronelle nodded. "Yeah. I looked it up in a Yiddish dictionary. Great word."

"To wrap this saga up: one of the art professors liked me. A lot. He painted me, over and over and over. Then he married me, carried me off to his country hideaway in Woodstock, damn near locked me in his studio, kept me barefoot and naked, painting and screwing, screwing and painting. And eating, always always eating." She swallowed, hard. "I got bored, eventually, and escaped to Kinderhook, New York, where I got the PR gig and lived in a nice little cottage, all by myself, with just my good dog Pear, who was a tiny black bit of fluff when I got him. And lots of men, as visitors only. I like my privacy. The artist remarried, another one of his students, another *zaftig* girl, this one thirty years his junior, had a nice chubby baby, I hear. I lost some weight, not all, but a lot of it. I got back to being myself, that's all. Then I moved to Albany and once again, here I am." She let her breath out. Told like this, it was just a story. A funny, odd kind of story. Not the nightmare it had been. Maybe she should tell it more often. Maybe it would lose its power to haunt her dreams.

"What happened to the paintings? I mean, are you on any famous walls or anything?"

Suzanne stood up. " As in 'That's my last Duchess, painted on the wall'? Yeah, I am, actually. I'm in the houses of rich people in New York City, rich people in Woodstock, a gallery at Bard College, some other places I don't even know about." She lifted her tray. "If you ever run into one of those paintings, maybe you'll recognize it. Won't be difficult—the paintings all have the same name, only with different numbers."

Ronelle picked up her tray, pocketing the extra packages of syrup. "No kidding. What's the name?"

"The name I picked, for a kind of joke, but he took seriously. The paintings are all called Suzanne LaFleshe. Suzanne LaFleshe 58. Suzanne LaFleshe 97. Suzanne LaFleshe 154. And so on."

"Wow. Cool."

Suzanne sighed, burying the vision of those paintings far, far back in her brain. "Yeah, way cool. Come on, kiddo. Bath time."

The time in the library was productive, in a perverse kind of way. Productive as in producing more work. Suzanne found three more books she had to read before typing another paragraph of her dissertation and one book on Native American legends, where she found the word "wendigo" in the index. She might as well know, she figured, what she was dealing with. The first thing she found out was that the whole concept of a wendigo was so common and stories about it so plentiful, and spread among so many tribes, that the word itself had, good grief, thirty-five variant spellings. By the time she'd copied them all into her notebook, her eyes and ears were ringing: *weedigo, weeghtako, weeghteko, weendago, weendegoag, weendigo, weetego, wee tee go, weetigo, wehndigo, wehtigo, wendago, wendigo, wenigo, wentiko, wetigo, whit te co, whittico, wiendigo, wihtigo, wiitiko, windago, windagoe, windagoo, windego, wi'ndigo, windikouk, wintego, wi'ntsigo, wintsigo, wi'tigo, witigo, witiko, wittako, wittikka.* And there were many other cannibals in the Native stories, too, in all sort of forms. She leaned over the *Dictionary of Native American Mythology.* Here was a doozy: *Stikini: "Man-Owls." People who transform into horned owls…and keep themselves alive by stealing and eating the hearts of humans. Stikini use their powers to put people into a deep sleep, then pull the victims' hearts out through their mouths.* Wasn't that a nice little bedtime story to tell the kiddies? It was all, really, just too much. Dizzy, she packed up and went home.

When she opened her door, both dogs cowered and crawled on their bellies toward her. She dropped her heavy book bag. "Oh no," she said. "What did you do?" It didn't take long to find the problem—a neat round puddle of urine next to the kitchen door. When she noticed Suzanne looking at it, Apple fell dramatically to the floor and rolled onto her back, exposing her bare pink belly. Her "Go ahead, kill me, I'm a bad dog and I deserve it" routine. Pear slunk to his bed. *He* had not peed in the house; *he* would never pee in the house; *he* would let his bladder rupture before he would defile the sacred den. But he always felt that he was implicated in Apple's crimes by dint of species alone. Pear had been born feeling guilty; from puppyhood, he'd borne the burden of original doggy sin.

Nothing made Suzanne sadder than seeing Pear feeling bad for something he didn't do. She swatted Apple once, just to get the requisite punishment over with, and sent both dogs out into the yard. She grabbed a handful of paper towels and dropped them into the puddle, cursing. Usually, when she was gone most of the day, Molly saw to the dogs. She knew that Apple couldn't wait. Where the hell was she? Suddenly, her annoyance turned to fear. Oh, God, maybe Molly had fallen. The woman was ninety-four, after all. Maybe she was lying over there, right now, in pain, hip shattered. Or worse. Stroke, heart attack, ruptured aneurysm. Suzanne left the soggy towels on the floor and ran to the little door in the pantry. She squeezed through, calling. "Molly? Are you okay?"

Munchie greeted her, tail down, fluffy ears drooping. She saw, immediately, that he'd peed, too, on Molly's always spotless kitchen floor. Her heart beat harder. "Molly?" She ran into the living room, so different from her own, so stuffed with furniture and knickknacks that there wasn't an empty surface. She skidded to a stop. Molly was sitting upright in her favorite rocking chair, her lap covered in a black mohair afghan. Her head was tipped to one side and her mouth was open. She was very still. Suzanne's heart pounded into her throat. She forced herself to walk the rest of the way across the room. She crouched in front of the chair and stared at Molly. The old woman's chest was moving, gently and regularly. Her skin was pink. Suzanne put out a trembling hand and laid it on Molly's hand. It was warm. She felt relief flood her chest and she sat down on the floor, hard.

Molly's eyes shot open. She sat up. "What the hell?" She stared at Suzanne. "What's the matter? Are you hurt? Did you fall? Why are you on my floor?"

Suzanne started to laugh, a hysterical little giggle. "Oh Molly. You're alive."

Molly kicked the afghan away from her feet. "Shouldn't I be?"

Wiping tears from her face, Suzanne slid forward on the floor, and put her head in Molly's lap. "Oh, yes, you should be. You have to be. I need you." Molly's wool pants smelled like dried sage and lavender.

Molly's hand fell onto Suzanne's hair. Her fingers lifted each little wave and gently scratched the scalp beneath. "Yes, you do, my friend." She sighed. "I had such dreams, Suzanne. Such dreams. I knew I should wake up, that the dogs needed to go out. But I could not break out of the dreams." Suddenly, her fingers lifted into the air and she stood up, tipping Suzanne's head out of her lap. "Oh, crap, the dogs. Munchie, if you messed my kitchen, you're a dead man."

Suzanne laughed, put both palms on the floor and pushed herself up. "It's all right. Munchie was a perfect gentleman. Stay there, I'll make you some tea." She trotted back to Molly's kitchen, scooped Munchie from his hiding place under the table and tossed him out the back door. She grabbed a rag from the closet—Molly did not use paper towels, or anything else paper, if she could help it—and mopped up the puddle. Then she tossed the rag into the garbage, destroying the evidence. She set the old iron kettle on Molly's stove and reached into the pantry for one of the many tiny jars that lined the bottom shelf, baby food jars filled with unidentifiable dried leaves and twigs and who knows what. "What kind?" she yelled. "Eye of newt or toe of frog?"

Molly appeared in the kitchen doorway. "Don't be a wise-ass," she said. "Mint will do. The one with the little bits of orange rind in it. Little flecks of raspberry." She pointed. "The one in the strained prunes jar."

"Of course. How could I miss it?" Suzanne grabbed the jar, opened it and sniffed. "Whew," she said. "Strong. What else is in here?"

"None of your beeswax. Just brew it."

As she rinsed the teapot and spooned in the leaves, Suzanne looked at Molly. She was rubbing her head with both hands, holding her temples. "You okay, really? You don't usually sleep during the day. You always say that only dotty old women take naps." Molly's eyes were ringed with black, she noticed. The blind eye seemed to move restlessly, as if it were searching for something in the air of the room, something that couldn't be seen by normal eyes. Her fear came back: Molly, who made fun of old women, was the oldest woman she knew.

Molly was ancient. Despite all appearances, despite her craftiness and wisdom and hard-earned powers, Molly was human. Ergo, mortal.

The kettle hissed and Suzanne lifted it from the flame. "Really, Miss Molly, are you all right?" She poured the boiling water over the leaves and an odd metallic smell rose from the teapot. Yes, there was mint and orange and maybe raspberry in there, but there was definitely something else too—something bitter, with a sharp edge that made her eyes water. Little white flecks floated to the top of the water, then dissolved.

Molly leaned back in her chair. "I'm weakening, my girl. There are holes spreading in my muscles. In my guts. I can feel them. But I ain't dead yet. Put some honey in that."

"Holes? What kind of holes?" Suzanne poured the tea into Molly's favorite mug, a silly kid's Hallowe'en mug, bright orange, with a picture of a witch flying across the moon. She stirred in a heaping spoonful of the honey Molly kept on the stove, dark honey, a rich russet color. She knew from experience how strong and sweet that honey was.

Molly sipped the brew, steaming hot as it was. She wrapped her hands around the mug. "Good. Oh, that's good. You have some, Suzanne." She took a great swallow and sat up straighter. "That warms the bones."

Suzanne poured half a cup for herself and then added two spoons of honey to mask the taste. She sat down opposite Molly. "Come on," she said, sipping carefully and wrinkling her nose at the smell. "What's wrong with you?"

"Oh it's not just me." Molly smiled, her strong white teeth gleaming. "It's the world, the way it's always been. I don't know why I thought I'd be able to slip out without a struggle, here at the end." She looked into her mug, swirling the foggy tea in circles. "It's just old-fashioned evil, my dear. It's here, as it always has been, always will be. It's just that, since your friend Sam died, it's gotten just a bit too pushy for my liking. There's something rotten in the state of Albany. The air stinks of it. Can't you tell? Go outside in the back yard and take some long deep breaths. There's a stink in that cold air—some nasty winter spirit farting into the sky. Gets into the head, into the dreams, that stink." She looked up, her good eye bright. "And, Suzanne? Keep your doors locked at night. Don't let that tall scarecrow man just walk in when-ever he wants. Don't let anyone just walk in. Except me, for course. Oh, shit." She put her mug down. "I didn't do your dogs either, did I? Did that stupid little Apple let her water down in the house? That bitch hasn't an ounce of self-control."

"Yes, she did. Pear damn near died of shame." Suzanne stood up. "And now they're all freezing their doggy butts off out there, as pun-ishment." She poured the dregs of her tea into Molly's sink. "Why shouldn't I let Morris in unannounced, Mol?"

Molly shook her head. "Oh, not him in particular—anyone, I said. I don't know. I'm just worried, that's all. Just lock the damn doors, okay? And, like that nice Indian policeman said, get caller ID. Better than expecting me to keep track of voices in the wind. Verizon is better equipped."

Suzanne stared. "How did you know about Charles?"

"Ha! I hear, girl. You're not always so quiet in that bedroom, you know. Or in your kitchen. Sometimes, nosy old neighbor ladies leave the pantry door open, to entertain themselves in the long nights. And, besides, I knew little Charlie Clark's grandmother, years ago. She was not a fool, let me tell you. That woman knew her stuff. A good sen-sible woman. Oh, that reminds me." Molly stood up and pointed to a cardboard box in the corner. "I made up a box of things for your skinny little friend, that Ronelle girl. Will you take it to her?"

"Oh, God. Poor Ronelle. She's living in the office—did you know that? She has nowhere else to go." Suzanne looked into the box. It was lined with cans of food: pineapple chunks, tuna, green beans, apple sauce, vienna sausage. Packages of hot chocolate mix, little boxes of raisins. A six-pack of miniature puddings. A box of Kleenex. A box of Tampax. Two pairs of heavy tights, black and purple. Mittens, blue. "Good grief, Mol. How did you think of all this stuff?"

Molly's good eye glared. "What? Do you think I'm some silly old witch who believes people live on herbs and spells? Get off it. That girl needs ordinary, everyday things. Maybe you could add a few your-self. Now go on, get out of here. You're going to have dog-popsicles if you don't let those poor beasts in from the cold. They've suffered for their sins long enough."

In her own kitchen, Suzanne looked at the clock. It was 5:30. She knew that Ronelle had class at six. She started adding items to Molly's care package, choosing carefully. What would she want, if she was living in an office? Easy, quick, comforting stuff.

She began packing items into the carton. Fig Newtons. Three bags of goldfish crackers: pizza, parmesan, and cheddar. One slim tube of Pringles. Cheerios. Zwieback toasts. A jar of cherry jam. Peanut but-ter. Slim Jims. A can of macadamia nuts. A jar of Cheez Whiz.

When she was done in the kitchen, she continued her gatherings in the bathroom. Shampoo. Panty liners. Toothpaste. Dental floss. Vaseline. Lip gloss. Three bars of Caress soap. A cherry red wash-cloth and matching towel. Six condoms, assorted colors. Then she went to her bedroom. Most of her clothes, of course, were far too big for Ronelle. She stood looking at the closet. But so what? Some things are meant to be big. She folded two heavy sweaters around two pairs of socks. She added two flannel shirts. Two pairs of lacey panties, hardly worn. No one likes second-hand underwear, but in desperate straits, a girl could make do. Then she added a wooly bathrobe. Ear-muffs. The long chenille scarf Morris had given her a year ago Christ-mas, a gorgeous vibrant blue with gold streaks like shooting stars—so beautiful she hadn't even worn it, saving it for something really spe-cial. She ran her fingers along its nap, ruffling it, then smoothing it back down. Maybe, she thought, generosity would win her points, somehow, with the fates. Maybe charity would count against whatever evil Molly smelled in the winter air. She rolled the scarf into a tight little cylinder and shoved it into the sleeve of the bathrobe. Then she packed all the things into the box and taped the top shut.

Everyone on the evening bus stared at her as she wrestled the obviously heavy box into an empty seat and then stood next to it. She didn't think it was fair to take up two seats on the crowded bus, so she swayed in the aisle all the way to the university. Then she hauled the box across campus and into Humanities. It was way too heavy to carry up the stairs and so she had no choice. She had to take the elevator to the third floor, no matter how much she loathed the thing. She got in, punched 3 and sweated as the tiny gray box lifted her into the air. It was slow and quivery, the worst elevator in New York State, she'd swear. She closed her eyes and fought panic, all the way. When the elevator finally reached the third floor and shuddered to a stop with three tinny dings of its bell, she leapt out, reaching back in for the box. Hoisting it once again, she fled down the hall.

The office was empty. It only took a few minutes to transfer all the things from the box to the drawers of the desk nearest the window. She could tell which drawer Ronelle had already adopted, by the strange assortment of items stashed in the very back, including a toothbrush and the stolen packages of jelly and syrup. Suzanne arranged her items neatly by category—food in the top drawer, sundries in the second, clothing in the bottom. She stood up, with a flush of satisfaction. There, she thought, there you go, Ronelle. It was almost like watching the girl eat, the warmth of this feeling. Feeding, clothing. Providing. It was weird, how much she liked this sort of thing—how natural it felt. Good grief, she thought, what next? Will I want to tuck her in, read her a bedtime story?

She grabbed the empty box and started down the hall toward the stairs. The faculty offices were all empty. People either taught at this time or were home having supper, like normal human beings. Suzanne stopped for a minute and listened. There was no wind this evening. The building was very still. She heard a funny whir, though, and turned. The elevator was still on this floor, its doors half open, vibrating, stuck. She walked over and looked in. It was empty—just stuck. Stupid thing. She reached out and joggled one of the doors. It wouldn't budge and the whirring noise got louder. It really was a piece of shit. She dropped the box in the hall and stepped gingerly inside the elevator. She held the doors open and pushed 1, then jumped out as the doors suddenly came unstuck and slammed together. She watched the little lights above the elevator doors. It didn't go to 1. It went up. To 4. She heard the four little dings and doors slide open, then nothing. She waited but it didn't come back down. She waited some more. Then, feeling like an icy hand was on her shoulder, steering her, she walked to the open well of the building, leaned over the railing and looked up. She could see nothing above but the closed glass doors of the faculty offices that surrounded the well and the black skylight above them. She leaned just a bit farther, feeling the pull of gravity, the frailty of the railing against her thighs.

Maybe, she thought, it was just an accident. Maybe Sam was just looking up at the stars, just like this, and he leaned too far. That was like Sam—to want to see the stars from inside a building, to want to see more than humanly possible. And to lean too far, too dangerously over the abyss. Sam was always tottering above some kind of abyss, wasn't he? She was only now realizing that—how unstable, slippery, Sam's existence had been. A bit of one of his poems came into her head, in his voice, as clear as if he were whispering in her ear, a poem he'd called "Rumination on Resuscitation": *"I lean against the walls of your ribs/I blow hot breath into the ice of your smile/Every day, I try to make you melt/And, every day, I freeze."*

She stared up, into the dark square of sky in the center of the ceiling, and then at the four office doors. "Sam?" she whispered. But, of course, Sam was not here. And why, she wondered, would he have been here that night? Sam had graduated, his program was complete. He had no reason to come back here, to see any of these faculty, any more. He'd escaped. No one wanted to come back, once their dreadful dissertations were done. Who would? Who would Sam want to see, late on an icy January night? Sam hated cold; he wouldn't go out unless it was important, unless he'd had something he wanted to do. She let her eyes circle the offices above, trying remember whose offices were up there. Well, everyone on the writing program faculty, of course. So writing students hung around up there too. And then there were some classicists she didn't know. And a few literature folks who didn't fit down here, like Dr. Elmer Redding, the early American specialist who was Leon's dissertation director. Some others, too—a whole floor of offices, just like this one, only higher up. She pulled back, dizzy, her hands slick on the metal railing. She looked up once more and then down. The stone floor of the first floor was clean, shiny, empty—no flowers now. Just a cool square of white, far below. If you stared at it long enough, that square of white stone, it seemed like it was rising up to meet you. Or that you were going down, to meet it. As if, one way or another, the meeting of flesh and stone was inevitable, already on the books, unavoidable. Accident, suicide, murder? In any case, death.

Very carefully, one step at a time, she backed away, then turned and headed for the stairs. As the stairwell door shut behind her, she heard the whine of the elevator, finally coming down.

Part III: *Cannibalism in Winter*

…Darwin was influenced by his exposure to the Tierra del Fuegians, a people who practiced cannibalism in winter rather than eat their dogs.

Nigel Rigby, *"Sober Cannibals and Drunken Christians"*

14

Diana laid out her supper: four Ritz crackers, one slice of American cheese. One can of Diet Coke. She was sweaty and warm, from her workout at the *barre* she'd erected in the bedroom. She wiped her hand across her forehead. She cut the cheese into four perfect squares and put one square on a cracker. She frowned. It didn't fit, quite. Its little pointy edges draped over the cracker, folding down onto the plate. She should have gotten square crackers. She stood up, swallowing the spit that had risen in her mouth at the smell of the cheese. She went to the blackboard hanging on her wall and wrote, in white chalk: *Buy Saltines.*

Then she sat back down. She raised her knife and trimmed the messy edges away from the cheese and set them on the edge of the plate. She looked at the newly rounded piece of cheese. It was fine, really. It would do. Slowly, with great care, she took a tiny bite out of the cracker. It hit her mouth with the force of a blow—the first food she'd allowed herself all day. The salt swelled on her tongue. She closed her eyes. She would not chew. She would just let the salt and the sharp flakiness of the cracker melt. She would take her time. She felt the saliva flow into her mouth, as if it would drown her. But she wouldn't swallow yet. She waited until the cheese was liquid, until the food was a pulsing mass, pushing against the back of her tongue. Then, finally, she opened her throat and let it in, shivering with pleasure.

Four times, she trimmed the cheese. Four times, she let the crackers melt on her tongue, controlling her urge to swallow until the very last minute, teasing herself, tempting herself. Daring herself to be so greedy, so hungry that she lost control. But she knew she wouldn't. She knew just how far she could go, just how much the pressure in her mouth had to build before she would open herself up, suck it down, the muscles of her throat vibrating like strings.

And she wasn't stupid, either. She knew that it was masturbation—Sam had screamed that at her, one night: "You don't eat food, Diana. You make love to it. You're not dieting, you're fucking." But Sam was wrong, too, as he so often was. It wasn't fucking, her affair with salt and crumbs and creamy cheese. It was much, much better. Because she was in control, right up until that last second, when she allowed herself to let go.

When the four crackers were gone, Diana stood up and briskly brushed her hands on her leotard. She tilted the plate into the garbage can, pushing the little scraps of cheese away with the knife. No matter how her stomach pleaded, she would not eat them. She wouldn't give them the satisfaction. They hadn't fit on the crackers and that was their own fault.

She went upstairs to run her bath. She bathed three, sometimes four times a day, after every exercise session. Sam had said, once, when they'd first met, that she was the cleanest, the sweetest-smelling human being on earth. She frowned, letting the steamy water run across her hand. Sometimes, she'd thought that Sam understood her, appreciated her. But he hadn't, obviously. Because he'd gone and put his prick inside that woman who was not clean—who had no control. Greedy, gluttonous, dirty woman.

Diana lowered herself into the bath. It was so hot that it hurt, especially hurt the newly shaved lips of her private parts. But that was fine—the hot water was cleansing. She looked down at her body, pleased. There wasn't a hair on it. She could see the thin crack between her legs. Keep an eye on it, so to speak, in case it ever acted up again, as it had once or twice in the past, making its own silly demands. She lay back, spreading the washcloth over her chest and closing her eyes. The mouth, the stomach—they were bad enough, always demanding, always crying out, always wanting more, more, more. She certainly didn't need to take any shit from her tulip, did she?

She sighed. Sam had been wrong about that, too. He nearly cried the first time she'd shaved herself and shown him the way it should look, told him the name her mother had taught her, to avoid all the bad words: such a pretty little pink tulip, her mother had said, that's what you've got. She had even posed for him, leaning back on the bed and holding herself open, all clean and shining, a gift. But Sam had gotten terribly upset, saying she looked like a child and he wasn't turned on by children. Saying it was unnatural, sad. He'd gotten angry and left their bedroom, left the house, leaving her there with her own hands against her own flesh, forcing her to touch the soft, damp, shining places all by herself, tears streaming down her cheeks.

It made her angry just remembering that day, the way he'd left her there, naked and alone. But she'd gotten over it. She'd decided that it was just fine. If he liked hairy, dirty women, she was better off without him, wasn't she? But, still, someone should suffer, for all the times he'd left her all alone. And someone would. Someone surely had to pay for the horror she'd suffered, when on one of those nights, a horrible cold, windy night, she'd run the test and found out that he'd planted a seed in her belly. Around her diaphragm, around the sticky, sloppy jelly she had to coat it with whenever she let him into her body—around all of that, all of that armor, all of that protection, his sperm had swum. Even though she rarely had periods, it had found an egg, somewhere. Up and up, taking root inside her. A parasite. A worm, deep inside her. He'd done it deliberately, to torture her, she knew that. He'd refused to wear a condom, saying that surely her precautions were enough—he'd been cruel, pushing his naked flesh into hers. She had closed her eyes and prayed. She'd smelled the Slut on his skin, though, and known that prayers wouldn't help.

And she'd thought she would die a few weeks later, that night when she sat alone in the bathroom, looking at the little strip she'd had to hold under her stream of urine. She really thought that she would die, mortally sickened by the thought of it all: fat belly and milky breasts, some squalling pink brat fastening itself onto her flesh and sucking her dry. She'd sat there on the edge of the bathtub, staring at the paper strip, thinking that she would die and knowing that Sam was with that woman, at that very moment. Sam, no better than a squalling brat himself, attaching his mouth to the Slut's tit and sucking for all he was worth. She'd really thought she would die, that night. But she hadn't, had she? No, Sam was the one who had died. She'd gone on, calmly, quietly. She'd gotten rid of the worm, and she had not died then either. Sam was the one who died. And it was his own fault.

Diana turned on her side in the tub, curling up. She put her right index finger in her mouth, sucking gently.

15

...Star's mother began to feel, in the agony of starvation, a yearning for human meat. This meant she was turning into a windigo, a kind of cannibal giant, which terrorized the Messessagey winter camps. Star's mother told Star what she feared and asked him to kill her, which is their custom. But Star refused. One day he came home and found his mother skinning the corpse of one of her own daughters. This time he clubbed her to death and built a pyre for her body, which is the only way to kill a windigo, whose heart is made of ice. Good God. Suzanne closed the book she'd brought home from the library, a novel called *The Life and Times of Captain N* by Douglas Glover.

It was incredible. Cannibalism everywhere she looked. Everywhere, people sinking their teeth into their enemies, their friends, and worst of all, their families. Suzanne sat propped up in bed, next to stacks of books on Native legends. She had thought that this would be light reading, a vacation from her dissertation—that skull still gaping on the shelf—but no. It was all tied in. This kind of unrelenting coincidence was spooky and annoying, almost silly. Surely there was some realm of her life that was *not* about flesh-eaters. She rubbed Plum's purring belly and put a caramel into her mouth. She loved the burst of burnt sugar across her tongue, the slow melt of the toffee. She picked another book from the pile, at random. She started reading again, making little stars in pencil in the margin. What the hell—it would become another source for the damn dissertation, showing her eclectic research skills, her grasp of the whole interrelated matrix of cultural, aesthetic, economic, and literary ramifications of eating your friends and relations. Rachel and the rest of the committee would love it. She popped another caramel and read. According to Morton I. Teicher, in a paper called *"Windigo Psychosis Among Algonkian-Speaking Indians,"* "The outstanding symptom of the aberration known as windigo psychosis is the intense, compulsive desire to eat human flesh. In many instances, this desire is satisfied through actual cannibal acts, usually directed against members of the individual's immediate family....The individual who becomes a windigo is usually convinced that he has been possessed by the spirit of the windigo monster."

Suzanne closed her eyes and put her head back on her pillows. Well, jeepers. Who knew? She thought about that. Jeffrey Dahmer, apparently. Thomas Harris, who wrote about Hannibal-the-Cannibal Lector, books too terrifying for her to read, even though they were related to her research. Apparently he knew. Hell, Crusoe knew, even though he didn't call it a psychosis. He, as always, called a spade a spade, a cannibal a cannibal. She slid down under the covers, Plum burrowing in beside her. What had Crusoe said, exactly? She knew the damn book almost by heart. Something about Friday's having a "hankering Stomach after some of the Flesh." Friday, Crusoe sadly admitted, even after his conversion to Christianity, was "still a Cannibal in his Nature." Well of course he was. People didn't change their spots any more than leopards did. She turned on her stomach, searching for Charles' scent in the pillow. He hadn't called her and that was a breach of the rules of sexual etiquette, as she understood them. The guy was supposed to call you, the next day, just to let you know that he hadn't been so drunk or indiscriminately horny that he'd forgotten your name. Suzanne sighed. She knew that Charles knew her name, although he hadn't yet progressed beyond "Ms. Brown," despite their enthusiastic evening. And perhaps he, like Morris, harbored some suspicions that she was a murderer, that she had pushed Sam over that railing. God, Sam. Beautiful, beautiful Sam. No one could want to hurt Sam.

She rolled back over, staring up at the ceiling, tired. She was afraid to fall into dreams, though, with all these cannibals prancing through her head. Friday, still following his Nature; those horrid little girls in *John Dollar*, watching their fathers devoured and then snacking on some thigh meat themselves. Wendigos, howling through the winter nights, preying on their kin. No wonder Molly had strange dreams. No wonder at all. What was a wonder was that anyone ever slept at all, in this world. That anyone ever felt safe enough to close their eyes.

Early the next morning, Suzanne woke with a start. She had slept, obviously, soundly and well. No one had called her, nothing had coming screaming into her dreams. Instead, she had happy, warm dreams, dreams where she was in her grandmother's lap, her toes in the sand of the beach in Maine, comfy and safe. She sat up. There was a steady dripping outside her window—she got up and looked out. The icicles that had been hanging there for a week were melting. That meant that overnight, some warm air had appeared, from somewhere. The vaunted January thaw. She stretched. It never was much of a thaw, in Albany, but any trickle of warmth was welcome. She pushed her arms into the sleeves of her baggy dog-walking sweater and went downstairs.

She stuck her head through the pantry door and whispered. "Munch? You want to walk with us? Hey, Munchie?"

"Just come in," Molly said.

Surprised, Suzanne slid through the door, leash dangling in her hand. "I thought I'd save you a walk, Mol. I didn't know you'd be up. You're not usually a morning person, exactly." She saw that Molly was fully dressed, fiddling with some leaves on her table. She looked utterly weary, her shoulders drooping. Munchie was sitting at her feet, head low, tail barely wagging, fur flat. "Hey, you guys okay?"

Molly nodded. "We're fine. Yes, take the Munchkin with you. I'll take a break from dog duties this morning. Go, sweet spirit," she said, pointing at the little white dog. "Get your ass out of here."

Munchie rushed for Suzanne, growling happily at the leash. Behind her, Apple made steady vertical leaps, yapping madly. As soon as Munchie was in range, Apple started jumping on his back, snapping at his furry neck, making him roll over and acknowledge her superior pack status. Back in Suzanne's kitchen, even Pear started to bark.

"What a bloody racket. Get them out of here, Suzanne," Molly said. "Really, I'm not in the mood."

When Suzanne got to the office, Ronelle was freshly showered. Her hair was still a mass of lumpy dreadlocks, but they were clean dreadlocks, fluffy and fragrant. She was wearing the purple tights Molly had supplied, with one of Suzanne's sweaters as a dress. It came to her knees and was neatly belted with a black leather Harley Davidson belt, with an eagle wing buckle. Suzanne whistled. "Wow. You go, girl! You look great."

Ronelle blushed, smoothing the sweater down her thighs. "You like?" She put her hands on her hips. "Listen, I'm going to pay you back, Suzanne, the minute our stipends come through. I'm not taking charity, you know."

Suzanne shrugged. "I haven't the faintest idea what you're talking about, Ronelle. Not a clue." She pointed to the belt. "That's nice. Where did you get that?"

"See? You immediately recognize the one thing you *didn't* supply. It was a test, this belt, and you failed." Ronelle grinned, sticking her thumbs in the belt and standing like an old-fashioned movie cowboy. She pointed her index fingers like six-shooters at Suzanne's chest. "Bang, bang. Gotcha."

"Okay. Molly and I played Santa. But it was fun—no need for paybacks." She sat down in the big chair. "But, really, I haven't seen the belt before. Where did it come from?"

Ronelle looked at the floor. "Okay, okay. From the locker room. It was just lying there, on one of the benches. Next to someone's clothes. By the jeans. Well, in the belt loops of the jeans, really." She lifted her eyes, defiant. "The guys' locker room, right next to the girls'. I don't steal from women; it's against my principles."

Suzanne looked out the window, trying not to laugh. There was water streaming down the window, ice melting off the roof. Warmth. "Uh huh. What were you doing in the guys' locker room, anyway?"

"Looking for a belt, what do you think? Come on, boss, get with it. I couldn't wear this sweater without a belt, could I? It would have looked like a tent. No offense."

Suzanne swung back and looked at the outfit again—her favorite soft angora sweater, a turtleneck, dark blue with thin purple stripes. Perfect with the tights. "No, you're right. It's perfect. You deserve the belt, just for putting it all together so well. In fact, I think I'll call *Vogue* to come over for a photo shoot. They'll want you for the Campus Fashion section. You've got a flair, El."

Ronelle smiled, then slipped into the rolling chair. "Yep, they teach us *haute couture* on the farm. Okay, so listen to this great article I found. Man, it's wonderful—and it's by a woman who taught me at Saint Rose. No shit, I know this woman. Listen."

She scrabbled around in the pile of papers on the desk and lifted one out. "It's called 'The "Deluxe-Sized" Woman: Atwood's *Lady Oracle,* Grenville's *Lilian's Story* and the Postcolonial Experience,' by April Selley. Isn't that cool? Deluxe-sized?"

Suzanne nodded. "Yeah, cool. It's from some ad or something."

"Like Queen-Sized pantyhose?" Ronelle giggled. "Chubby chick tights?"

"Yes. Bras for the full-figured woman. Jane Russell."

"Who?"

"Never mind. So what does the article say about these deluxe models? I never read the Grenville book."

Ronelle settled back in her chair. "I got it out of the library. Grenville's Australian. They don't mind fat so much in Australia, apparently. Anyway, listen: it starts like this. *Why are there so few positive representations of large women in American literature—and, indeed, in American culture as a whole?* Then, a little later, Selley says *...white American writers, both male and female, are operating within a cultural imperialism, traceable back to Victorian England, which declares that fat—at least for women— is evil.*" Ronelle looked up. "She even gets into films—remember that huge, horrible mother in *What's Eating Gilbert Grape?*"

Suzanne sighed. She could see what was coming—cannibalism, metaphoric or otherwise. The gods just would not let her forget the skull on the shelf at home. "No. I don't see films much."

"Jeez. Why not? They're pretty cheap. If you go the Norma Jean on Madison, with a student ID, really cheap."

"I don't go to films because I'm always afraid that the seats will be too small for me, okay? I just can't get over feeling that way. American culture does not allow for voluptuous hips and long legs. I mean, really. I've had people give me glares you wouldn't believe, when I tried to squeeze past them to find a seat." She watched Ronelle's face, to see if she got it. Admiring the complex issues of fatness on the page is one thing; understanding the discomforts and problems of fatness in person—in the flesh—is a whole nother ballgame.

Ronelle nodded, chewing the end of one of a dreadlock. "I never thought of that. I bet I do it too. Glare, I mean. But not just at fat people—anyone who comes down my aisle. I hate it when anyone sits next to me at a movie. I hate having strangers that close, you know. And I always think I'll catch something."

Suzanne stared. "Catch something? That's pretty weird. Like what?"

"I don't know—nothing specific. I can't explain it. Like, I just feel viruses crawling around. Especially in winter, you know, when the theater's all hot and everyone is coughing and shit." She shrugged. "I have a thing about viruses. I was real careful, all through high school, not to get sick."

"Any particular reason?

"Jesus, it's obvious, isn't it? If I got sick, I had to stay home. And home had a zillion little brats in it. Home had my mom, puking with the next little brat, milk running down her chest from the current one. Home had me and Et and Nita and the smallest kid sharing one bedroom. Come on—think about it. Home smelled like manure. Hell, why do you think I was valedictorian? From never wanting to go home, that's why. From living every day in school and every night in the library until it closed. Weekends, too."

Suzanne tried to picture it and couldn't. She had had her own room in the little salt box house high on its Maine hill, scoured clean by sea winds. She had had her grandparents all to herself. Maybe, she thought, there were worse things than growing up as a fat orphan. She looked at Ronelle's pale, spotted face. "I see. So, what *was* eating Gilbert Grape, according to Dr. Selley?"

Ronelle laughed. "What do think? Listen, there's a 500-pound mother in the film and Selley says that, '...the title hints darkly of some primal monster, a "what," that "eats," or destroys everything in sight, including her own children. It is fitting that only the death of the mother and the burning down of the family's house in *What's Eating Gilbert Grape?* finally free the Grape children for an undisclosed future.'"

Suzanne stood up, putting her hand against the window glass. It was cold, but not bone-chilling. "Mrs. Grape sounds like a wendigo," she said, hoping her voice sounded light.

"What?"

"Nothing. Just another cannibal. Something I'm reading about for my dissertation. And, speaking of which, I'd better get to the library." She turned and reached for her backpack. "You can compose two letters, okay? One a form rejection thing—you know 'The editors of *Largesse* thank you for your submission but regret that, blah blah.' We'll put those on yellow paper. And then, more fun, an acceptance one. We have to get final approval from Rachel on stuff we want to take, but at least we can have the letters ready. Oh, that reminds me. Look at this poem, okay? I really like it." She rummaged in her pack, found the blue folder and pulled out the copy of "The Aloe Symphony." She handed it to Ronelle. "Let's start an Accepted file, okay? Some new color, your choice. You're the color maven."

Ronelle looked at the poem. "But it's about a guy. A fat *guy*."

Suzanne slipped her arms into her coat. "So what? Read what it says on the back. Fat guys have problems, too."

"But I thought—I don't know, I just thought we were doing women."

"We are, mostly. But I like that poem, Ronelle. Read it. It's a hoot."

Ronelle shrugged. "Yas'm, boss lady." Suddenly, she smacked her forehead with her palm. "Jeez, in all the excitement about new clothes and lit crit, I forgot. I checked your departmental mail slot and found this. I mean, there was a whole lot of junk mail in there, notices and shit and I threw those out. But this looks real." She held out an envelope.

Suzanne looked at it. She'd forgotten that she even had a departmental mail slot, but as editor, of course she did. And someone, apparently, had remembered that. She took the envelope from Ronelle's outstretched hand. God—not another anonymous piece of filth. It had her name written in green ink on the front and suddenly that writing became very familiar—it was Sam's. She felt her knees weaken and she sat down, hard, in her chair. She swallowed. "It's from Sam," she whispered.

Ronelle's eyes grew huge. "The dead guy? Oh, shit." She began to bounce. "Open it. Open it."

Suzanne's shaky finger slid under the flap and the envelope broke open. Inside was a sheet of paper with typing on it—and Sam's signature at the bottom, in bright green ink. Her eyes blurred.

"Read it, read it."

"I can't," Suzanne said. "Here, you read it." She handed the paper to Ronelle, who snatched it up like it was edible.

"Okay," Ronelle said. "First, there's a date: it says January 3, 2003. Suzanne nodded, numb. "Okay. Then what?"

Ronelle cleared her throat. "It goes, 'Hey, Suzy-Q.'" She turned to stare at Suzanne. "Jesus. Suzy-fucking-Q?"

"Never mind. Really, never mind. Just read the damn thing." Suzanne folded her shaking hands in her lap. "Straight through, no comments."

"Okay. Ahem. 'Taking off for break tomorrow—going to D's old place in Vermont. But got news, great news, to tell you. Hint: it involves a whole new life.' Then there's three exclamation points. Then, 'Not certain-sure yet, but I will be by the time we're back in Albania.'

Albania, like in Europe?" Ronelle's head tilted with the question.

"No, no. That's just what he calls Albany. Just read, Ronelle."

"Oh, cute. Okay, after Albania it says: 'So, see you on or around the 19th, K? Full moon, Suz, full moon rising.' Then, just 'Luv' with a 'u.'" Ronelle made a face. "Why do people do that, use a 'u'? Who do they think they are, John Lennon? Anyway, then the signature. That's it." She laid the paper in Suzanne's lap.

Suzanne's heart was pounding her chest. And her face felt scorched. "Maybe—maybe he didn't kill himself," she whispered. "See?" She poked her finger into the date on the top of the page. "He wrote this *after* that shooting the moon poem and he was making a date to see me after break." She stood up, shaking the letter near Ronelle's face. "And he had good news to tell me. He did not kill himself."

Ronelle nodded. "I don't know what poem you're talking about here. But, still, I'd say that this thing doesn't sound exactly suicidal, boss. So, does that make it better? Do you feel less, like, responsible? And this thing about 'new life.' I mean, does this mean his wife was pregnant? Is that what he doesn't know yet, for sure, do you think?"

Suzanne shrugged. "Maybe. He wanted kids. He always said he wanted kids. But Diana didn't. Really did not, no way, he said. So I don't know. Or, it could mean he got a poem accepted. He was always waiting for that to happen, the day, he used to say, he could start calling himself a real poet. That would be a whole new life for Sam, too. Or, wait, maybe a job offer. Maybe he'd finally gotten an inter-view, even."

"Well, yeah. Lotsa maybes there. But, let's just say, for the sake of argument, that it's pregnancy, okay? His wife is preggers. Jeez. A guy happy about knocking up his wife doesn't off himself, for sure. Does he?"

It hit Suzanne like a slap in the face then, the obvious: No, a man happy to have a pregnant wife—he does not kill himself. Or a man happy to have a poem accepted—he does not kill himself, either. Or a man with a job offer. A man happy about anything big enough to be called "a whole new life"—he does not kill himself. And that means that someone else did.

"Man." Ronelle was tossing her hair. "You got to show this letter to that cop, then. They've got to rethink this whole thing. Right?"

Suzanne's head was aching. "I guess so. Yes."

"Yeah. But hey—you know who I'd suspect, if I was that cop? I'd suspect *you*, boss!" Ronelle giggled. "I mean, just think. Here you're in love with this guy—look, don't bother to deny it, I can tell you were—and he comes in all happy, all buzzed to tell you his *wife is pregnant*." Ronelle tapped Suzanne's arm with each word, then repeated them "*Wife is pregnant*. So, of course, you just freak out and you shove him, in a fit of fury." She was grinning, poking Suzanne's arm. "Hey, isn't that a riot? They'll think it was *you!*" She danced backwards, laughing.

"Oh yeah. A riot." Suzanne's voice was hoarse. She crumbled Sam's note into a tiny ball and shoved it in her pocket.

Ronelle looked at her face. "Come on, boss. Lighten up. I was just kidding. Really, it was, like, a joke. Really."

Suzanne fled the office. Just outside the door, she slammed into Ajax Swenson. The boy grabbed her arm. His eyes were furious, his cheeks bright red. "Listen," he said, before Suzanne had a chance to draw breath. He leaned into her face, spitting his words. "I just got my grades from last semester. There's a mistake. There's a huge fucking error here and I want to know how to fix it." He shook a crumbled pink grade sheet in her face. "Somebody's got to fix this shit."

She shook her head. "I have no idea what you're talking about, Ajax. And I'm on my way to the library. I have work to do."

The kid was trembling. "No. Look. Right here." He shook the grade sheet again. "English 312—Poetry Writing. Instructor—Dr. Tindell. Look. It says A-." He spoke very loudly, spitting each word. "A. Fucking. Minus."

Suzanne nodded. "Yes. I see that. So, what's the problem?"

The boy's eyes closed into slits. "Minus. Minus. Minus. Look. I was the best poet in the class. I mean, the best. This fucking minus is a piece of crap. How do I get it changed? Sam made a mistake, that's all. It's a clear error. You have to get this fixed."

Behind Ajax, Jennifer appeared. Her face was all crumpled, like she'd been crying, but she reached out and touched Ajax's back. "Relax, okay?" she said. "It's not her fault."

Ajax dropped Suzanne's arm and swung around to face Jennifer. "Look, you stupid cunt, somebody's got to take care of this," he said. "The registrar just told me that no one can change a grade except the instructor who gave it. Get it? So I said to her, 'But, listen, lady, this fucking instructor is *dead,* man.' And she's all like, well, yes, that is a problem and I'm like, so *fix it*, bitch. And she fucking calls security." Suddenly, the boy's shoulders dropped. "I mean, I just want justice, that's all. There's no way I got a minus from Sam. No way." He sounded like he was going to cry. Jennifer put her arms around him and patted his back, making little soothing sounds.

Suzanne took the moment to squeeze past the students. She made it to the top of the stairway before Jennifer reached her, calling out, "Oh, please wait, Ms. Brown."

Suzanne stopped and let the girl catch her breath. "I've got work to do, Jennifer," she said, as quietly as she could. "What is it?"

"Oh, it's Ajax. I just wanted to apologize for him. He's so bummed and he's really acting crazy and all. I just wanted to tell you that he'll be okay, though. He'll calm down." She leaned closely to Suzanne, whispering in her ear. "I mean, he *knew* he might not get an A. He told me, at the end of last term, that he'd gotten like a B on his final portfolio. I mean he went nuts—totally bonkers for about a week. But then he said he'd talk to Sam about it and then, after break, he told me that he did, that he met with Sam and that Sam said it was all a big mistake and he'd still get an A for the course. You know? So Ajax was fine about it and all. But then he got his grades and he just freaked again, you know? Like Dr. Tindell must have forgotten to fix his grade and now he's dead and all. Isn't that just like so fucked-up?"

Suzanne shook her head. "Yes," she said. "That is just so fucked-up." And she ran down the staircase, two steps at a time.

Outside, the campus was dripping. From every concrete arch, every concrete corner, every concrete roof and window ledge, water ran. Suzanne, standing in the walkway between Humanities and the library, raised her head and sniffed. The air was damp. Just enough warmth to bring the smallest hint that spring was possible—not that it was imminent or even nearby, but possible. She could, at least, believe that in some future time, the gray campus would be abloom with greenery. The azaleas bunched at the campus's east end would crown themselves with purple and ivy would burst from the square stone beds.

And Sam would never see it. Never start the new life he'd wished for. And right around then, she thought suddenly, in the midst of all that bloom and blossom, her dissertation was supposed to be finished. As in done. Complete. All done. Her head dropped and she plodded forward. All around her, students were laughing and shouting to their friends. They were up early, snorting the damp air. Some, she noticed as she rounded the corner, were lying on their backs on the concrete steps of the empty fountain, in shorts and sunglasses, as if it were already May and they could catch a tan. The watery, thin sunshine trickled down onto their bare legs and traced the edges of their skin with light. Youth. Foolish, lovely youth. Not one of them had a skull on the shelf or sorrow as heavy as lead as their shoulders. Not a one.

She settled into one of the old-fashioned, single-occupancy carrels in the basement of the library. On even the brightest of days, these were dank and dreary, with only little square windows at head level, but they were private and quiet, too, with doors that closed. So at least she was alone and she could put her head into her hands and think. What did all of this mean? Sam's letter. Sam's news of a new life. She leaned forward and thought. He might have gotten news of some poetry acceptance. Or maybe a job? Maybe that was it, a job. Not that Diana was pregnant. No matter what Ronelle thought, that wouldn't be it. Sam always said he hardly ever had sex with Diana.

He'd told her this horrible story about once finding his wife with her crotch shaved, looking like an eight-year-old and how sad he'd felt, looking at her tiny smooth body. How troubled he'd been. How worried about her whole state of mind. So surely not pregnancy then. But, what? And who? That was the terrible thing: who? She took Sam's note from her pocket, smoothed it out and read it again. But she couldn't really see the words because her eyes kept tearing up. She could only see that green-ink signature.

She sat up. She would not think about this now. She couldn't. She had work to do. She really did. She carefully smoothed the little note. She sat straighter and reached for the stack of new books she'd ordered through interlibrary loan: literary cannibals abounding. She put Sam's note between pages 604 and 605 of the bottommost book— there, when she got to that page, then she'd think about it. There. Out of sight, out of mind. There.

She sighed and pushed her hair out of her face. Cannibals were proliferating, that's what it was. Since she'd begun her dissertation two years ago, they'd bred like bunnies. Every time she thought she'd covered the territory, there was another cannibal's footprint in the sand, another trail to follow, littered with bones and scraps of flesh. Always, she had another book to order. To read. To take notes on. To swallow. To digest. And finally, to enter into her bibliography file, which now took up an entire disk of its own.

Still—she did love the smell of a fresh book and often she was the first reader of one of these new tomes. She cracked the spine of the heavy book on the top of the pile and buried her nose in its pages. Ink. Good clean new ink. Her grandfather's scent. She took out her notebook and a pen and settled in to read *The True Story of the Novel.* An hour later, she was puzzling at Margaret Doody's odd prose and copying passages into her notebook: *Cannibalism in the Novel is treated as a social concern, rather than as the absolute sign of the monstrous. If every-thing is hungry, it's no wonder this mistake is sometimes made, that the pit people fall into forever is the esophagus of somebody else"* (425).

She sat back. Everything *is* hungry. Indeed. She remembered that she'd packed herself a nice lunch—a comforting lunch. She put down her pen and reached into her backpack. Of course, eating in the library was forbidden, but what the hell. She was alone in her little carrel with its closed door. She opened the tupperware container of key lime pie she'd brought, and dipped her fork inside. But before the sweet smooth tartness met her tongue, there was a knock on the window. She dropped the fork, spattering lime and meringue on her skirt. She stood up, wiping the mist from the window. Outside, Charles Clark was squatting in the slushy snow, grinning in at her like a madman.

16

Outside, Suzanne stood in the slush and looked at Charles's face. He was smiling. "How did you know where I was?" she asked.

He put a hand on her shoulder. "Detective work, Ms. Brown. It's what I do, remember?"

She nodded. "But…."

"But what? Have you ever thought about the physics of light and shadow, Ms. Brown? Now, I'm not talking metaphor here, mind you—good and evil and all that stuff. I'm talking about the way you can see into library carrel windows, basement level, from the outside." He took her arm. "Walk with me? It's too nice to stand still."

She fell into step behind him. She'd left her backpack and books in the library and felt lighter, without them. "So, you could see me working? But how did you know where to look?"

He laughed. "Didn't. I was just walking by the library, minding my business. But," he added, quickly, "thinking about you, of course. After last night and all."

"Of course."

"Yes, really. Anyway, I was thinking about you, kind of reliving the, um, highlights and all, and then I looked down and there you were. Odd. Behind a pile of gray slush, the light in the carrel was shining—the only one in the whole basement. So I looked in and there you were—hair glowing in the light. You were smiling and writing, all at once. Looking happy. Looking pretty." He leaned toward her, putting his weight against her hip, for a minute. "Hell, if I was a

137

university publicity guy, I'd get a photo of that. Stick it on all the brochures—label it 'Happy Student at Work in the Library.' Perfect."

"They never put thirty-eight-year-old ABD's in the brochures. And they never use fat women, ever," she said. Then she felt bitchy, for laying that on him. She didn't know why she'd said it. It just popped out of her mouth, sounding defensive and snotty. She tried to cover up. "Besides, they'd say 'Our new, high-tech, state-of-the-art, three-million volume library' or something like that."

He stopped walking. "Yeah, they would. You're right—they'd leave you off and put that shit on. Damn fools." He kicked some wet snow off the sidewalk. "Listen. I need to talk to you, officially. I'd like you to come to my office, all right? I have something there I want you to see."

Something rose into Suzanne's throat—officially, he wanted to talk? She stopped, too, noticing how the slush was soaking into her boots, leaving white salt stains on the leather. Officially? Now, of course, was the time to bring up Sam's note, to tell him that Sam had been happy, looking forward to his new life. But she remembered Ronelle's gleeful little dance: *I'd think you did it, boss.* And, behind that, Molly's blind eye blinked: *Who is your enemy?* And, really, she still wasn't sure about that, not at all. "Sure," she said. "I'd love to see your office."

He ran a finger down her cheek. "Uh huh. It's a high-tech, state-of-the-art law enforcement kind of place, I swear. Come on."

The University Police building was new, located on the far southeastern corner of the campus, on what Suzanne always thought of as the wild side of the university—the woodsy, grassy corner behind the athletic fields, where the campus pond shimmered in summer, reeds and grasses blowing gently in the wind. She'd read that it was a prime spot for bird watching, that pond, especially in the spring and fall, a kind of oasis in the concrete and asphalt now covering what used to be the Albany Pine Bush. A tiny remnant of the natural world where migrating birds rested, surrounded by dorms, strip malls, motels, and college bars.

Now, of course, the pond was frozen. The reeds were thin brown stalks, whispering and rustling in the damp air. Suzanne could just see it through the trees, a slick white surface behind the building, as Charles held the door open for her. She stepped inside. This wasn't wild in the same sense as the pond—but it was wild in its own way. Students in various states of misery were sitting on benches in the lobby—some obviously drunk, some bruised, some staring into space. Guys mostly sat alone, legs flung out in front of them, glaring. Girls sat in pairs, leaning into one another, whispering. Charles walked down the hall quickly, then turned into a private office space. He nodded to a secretary in the outer office, then opened the door into what was apparently his own inner sanctum. The office was bare and clean, all the surfaces shiny. The windowsill was covered with leggy, overgrown geraniums, with a few bright red flowers and a lot of pale, dry leaves. There was a photograph on one of the file cabinets.

Suzanne picked it up. It wasn't a good photo—the faces in it were out of focus and off-center. But they were grinning. A tall white-haired woman was holding the hand of a skinny dark-haired boy. They looked like they were standing on some kind of dock, water shimmering behind them. The woman was barefoot, wearing a summer dress, flowered cotton, it looked like. She held a bowl in the crook of one arm, full of some kind of beans. The boy was waving a hand, creating a blur of motion at the edge of the picture. She turned and held the photograph out to Charles. "You and your grandmother?"

He nodded. "Now who's the detective, Ms. Brown?"

"Lucky guess. I loved my grandmother, too. And Molly mentioned yours." She put the photograph back and turned to the chair facing his desk. She sat down, shrugging out of her coat. She tucked her wet boots under the chair and folded her hands on her lap. "What do you want to show me, Charles?" she said.

He sat down in his desk chair and opened the top drawer. He took out a sheet of paper, encased in a transparent plastic cover. He slid it halfway across the desk, but kept one hand on top, covering the surface.

Suzanne noticed how big his hand was, how long the fingers. She felt, for a moment, the way his fingers had cupped her whole skull, cradling it, pulling her head down to his lips. "What's this," she said, "a mash note?"

He shook his head. "Hardly. It was in my mail this morning—campus mail. I'm sorry you have to see this, Suzanne. Really, I am."

She noted the use of her first name, and smiled. "Come on. I'm tough. What is it?"

He lifted his hand from the paper and pushed across the desk, turning it so it was facing her.

She leaned over. At first, it didn't make any sense, then the wiggly black lines coalesced into a figure. Roughly drawn, crude, but effective: it was a very fat woman, rolls and rolls of flesh hanging from her body. At her breast, she held a very small man. His mouth and hands were clinging to her nipple, his tiny, erect penis was bobbing in the air. The woman was lying on her back, her legs spread. In between her thighs was a gaping vagina, lined with sharpened teeth. Just visible, being drawn into the vagina, was a pair of legs, flailing. Bile filled her throat.

"Turn it over," Charles said, quietly.

She did. On the back was black printing, big block letters: FAT FILTHY CUNTS KILL. ASK LaFLESHE.

She sat on the stone bench at the side of the pond. She was done throwing up—she'd finished that in the woods—but she was still shaking and wiping sweat from her forehead. Her skirt was soaking wet from kneeling in the slush; it was heavy and cold against her legs, but she was still sweating. She kept her face in her hands. She felt Charles sit down next to her and put a hand on her wet thigh. She started to shiver.

"I'm sorry," he said. "I should have warned you."

She spoke into her palms. "You wanted to see how I'd react, didn't you? You can't help being a fucking cop. You wanted to look for signs of guilt."

He took his hand away and leaned back on the bench. "What do you think I think you have to be guilty about, Suzanne?"

She lifted her head. "Oh, come on. Killing Sam. With my cunt, apparently." She leaned back, closing her eyes.

"It didn't say anything about Sam."

She nodded, eyes closed. "No. But I can't think of anyone else who's dead. Can you? I mean, anyone else that I've been fucking recently who's dead. Let's be fair. I don't generally kill them. Lucky for you."

He reached over and tapped her head. "Come on, Suzanne. Stop. And think. It's just a vile little picture with a vile little note. Obviously from some vile little person who has a bone to pick with you. That's all it is."

Her eyes flew open and she found he was leaning over her, looking into her face. "Bone to pick? Bone? Jesus, Charles. It seems like a bit more than that." She watched his face, his dark, quiet eyes watching her back. *Who's your enemy?* She sat up, turning away from his eyes.

The pond stretched in front of her, white and bare. The ground at her feet was softening, turning muddy, but the ice in the pond was undisturbed. It would take a lot more than one day of warmth to ruffle its cold heart. Just looking at it sent a chill circling down her spine. She looked into the bare trees beyond the pond, branches lifting into the sky. The sky was clouding over, losing its earlier washed-out blue. Oddly, for January, it looked like the sky was full of rain. She sighed. "I would never have hurt Sam. Never. I liked him immensely," she said. "I didn't love him, exactly, but I liked him. I liked him in class, I liked him in the coffee shop, I liked him in my kitchen, I liked him in my bed. He was a very beautiful young man. I know you only saw him when he was all smashed to hell. But, alive, he was beautiful. And sad. Troubled. Worried. Kind of tormented. You know, a poet." She turned back and caught Charles's face, for just a second, twisted into a kind of wince, hurt.

"Uh huh. I got it: a beautiful, young poet. Someone you enjoyed in bed. I got it." He stood up, stamping his boots in the muddied snow. "You know anyone who might have wanted this great guy dead, Ms. Brown?"

She stared up at him. This was the right time to tell him about the note Sam had left for her, his happy note, all chirpy about a new life. But she couldn't. She turned her face away. "Sam fell, Charles. Maybe on purpose. Maybe not. Right? That's what happened. There was no one else there. No one else involved." She stood up. "Right?"

He looked away, across the pond. He shrugged. "Most likely. We don't have a shred of evidence that says otherwise. Not a thread, not a fiber, not a footprint. Nothing that didn't belong to your friend Dr. Tindell. Or any of the five hundred faculty, students, and staff that run around that building all day long. Hardly a clean scene. And we've got that poem, that to the cop mind spells out 'Suicide' loud and clear. Disturbed poet flings himself over railing—end of case. And that's really what I think did happen. Usually, in this business, the obvious is the truth. But, still, when you get a nasty little message like this one, you wonder. Somebody with that kind of mind, walking around campus, maybe connected to the dead guy somehow, well, that's interesting, don't you think?"

She had almost stopped shivering, but now her skin glazed with sweat and she began to shake again. She stood up, turned away from the pond and started walking, stamping back toward the path that ringed the water, circling through the woods. "I've got work to do," she said. "I'm going back to the library."

He caught up with her, took her arm. "You're wet and cold. I'll drive you back," he said. "Come on."

She shook her arm away from his grasp. She looked into his face and said, "How did you know who 'LaFleshe' was, Charles? How did you know that I was the fat, filthy cunt? How did you decide it was me?"

His eyes were dark and clear but he blushed, a dusty red appearing on his cheeks. "I didn't. I just wanted your opinion, that's all. Come on, Suzanne, just listen."

She was walking away, fast. "Bullshit," she said, over her shoulder. "Bull. Shit, Mr. Detective."

"Come on." He caught up to her again, grabbed her shoulder. "Listen, Suzanne." He shook his head. "Okay. I did know. I saw a painting once—Bard College."

She felt like she would throw up, all over again. She kept swallowing hard.

Charles was talking fast, kind of patting her shoulder the whole time. "I was down at Bard for a campus cop meeting. And I got bored and went over to their gallery, just nosing around, you know. And I saw this painting—well, it's hard to miss. Canvas was about 8 foot long. And, it had this woman on it—this, well, big, big woman and...."

"I know," she said. "Don't say anything. I know."

"No." His voice was very low. "No you don't. I looked at that painting—Suzanne LaFleshe 883—for about an hour. I fell in love, Suzanne. I swear to God. Not with her body. I mean, that was just gorgeous, like a river of flesh, glowing. But kind of weird, over the top, all color and contour. No, I fell in love with her face. It was so sad. So beautiful and sad and, I don't know, trapped. I didn't know it was you until the other day, in the library, when you talked about Dr. Tindell. I watched your face and it was the same one. Sad, trapped. Beautiful." He cleared his throat. "Listen. I was already crazy about you before I ever met you. That's why I went home with you last night. I shouldn't have—I mean, I don't get involved with university women, ever. Ever. But, Suzanne, listen. I was already in love with your face."

For a minute, she could almost believe him. But then she saw the black lines of the scrawled drawing. She saw that version of herself— fat, filthy cunt—and she knew he'd seen it, too. Shame and horror filled her chest. She shook off his heavy hand. "Bull shit," she said. "Bull Shit."

It was a long walk back to the main campus and by the time she got there, a strange winter rain was falling. The sky was a heavy leaden gray, the day much darker. There were no students lying bare-legged around the fountain now. She splashed her way to the library for her things.

She left wet footprints on the marble floors and all the way down the steps to the basement. She opened the door to the carrel and stepped inside, slamming the door behind her. She piled the books into her backpack. She was shaky with cold and, she realized, hunger. It was mid-afternoon and her stomach was completely empty. She picked up the tupperware container and the fork. She sat down at the desk and began shoving forkfuls of pie into her mouth. As the last bite dissolved on her tongue, as she sat here, alone, she remembered. She recalled. She regressed. She was, again and forever, the woman in the paintings.

The meringue stuck to her lips, sickening. She opened her backpack and reached inside, down into its deepest bottom. There, her fingers found the folder that she always carried with her. It was her reminder, her conscience. It was her story, far more honest than the gentle version she'd told Ronelle. This version was just for herself. Memento mori. Cautionary tale. Red flag.

She looked at the cover of the folder where she'd written, nearly ten years ago, the title of the little tale she'd composed, her perpetual warning tale:

The Strange Sad History of Suzanne LaFleshe
By
Herself,
For Herself.

She licked the sugar from her lips and started to read.

Dear Suzanne Brown,
Once upon a time, you were an orphan. But your grandmother loved

Hollis Seamon 145

you. And the way you knew that she loved you, without a doubt, every day, was that she fed you. Not just the foods every kid needs to grow up big and strong, but extraordinary foods—desserts fit for a queen. Your grandmother should have run a bakery. She should have fed whole villages, whole cities with her breads and pies and cakes and cookies. Her puddings and baked custards. But by the time you were an orphan and lived in your grandparents' house on the top of a windy hill in Maine, she only had you and Gramp to feed. Gramp ate vegetables and meat and fish and bread, but he didn't much care for sweets. He'd take a tiny portion of whatever dessert Gramma had created each day and he'd declare it wonderful but he'd never ask for seconds or raid the pantry in the night. He left all the rest for you. Yes, you. Sweets were the only thing that you could get down your sad, scared throat, at first. When you couldn't even swallow a spoonful of homemade chicken broth, you could eat half a blueberry pie. A la mode. Gramma was in mourning for her daughter and in fear for you. She needed to feed you; you needed to eat. She baked; you sat in her sunny kitchen, humming to yourself, one of your mother's old scarves wrapped around your shoulders, and you breathed in the smells of cinnamon and yeast, nutmeg and flour. You were comforted and your heart healed.

Here is one, just one, of your Gramma's recipes—just so you'll never forget.

Gramma's Icebox Cake

Day One—Sponge Cake
Beat 6 egg yolks with 1 C. of verifine sugar
Add 2 tsp. Vanilla and ½ C. cold water—beat until lemon-colored
Add 1 ½ C. self-rising cake flour

Beat 6 egg whites until very stiff, adding ¼ C. verifine sugar

Fold white and yolk mixtures together
Bake in ungreased tube pan—1 hour @ 325 degrees
Turn pan upside down and cool cake thoroughly before removing.
Wrap and keep overnight.

Day Two—Chocolate Custard

Mix 1 ½ C. soft butter, 1 ½ C. confectioner's sugar and 2 tsp.
vanilla. Put aside.

In double boiler, mix 4 sq. unsweetened chocolate, ¼ C. water, ¾
C. sugar. Cook until chocolate is melted. Then add 6 beaten egg
yolks and cook until thick. Add 6 beaten egg whites (stiff) and
cook 1 minute.
Mix together butter mixture and chocolate mixture until well
blended.

Line tube pan with waxed paper. Slice sponge cake into 7 or 8 very
thin layers. (It doesn't matter if it breaks.) Starting from top of
cake, take one slice and put into pan. Cover with chocolate mixture. Continue until all mixture is used up and one slice of cake is
left for the top. Poke through all layers with skewer or long fork.
Cover and refrigerate overnight.

Day Three—Voila!

Take cake out of pan and cover with whipped cream. (1 pint whip-
ping cream, whipped stiff with 4 T. of sugar and 2 tsp. vanilla.)
Enjoy!!

So, there you are. One cake, one dozen eggs—typical and utterly de-
licious. Gramma grew old, baking and gardening and loving. You grew
fat, eating and reading and loving. By the time you left for college, you
were the girl with the pretty face, the gorgeous red hair—and the

body that was big, but not grotesque. And you were funny and smart and everyone liked you. Your ankles stayed slim and you wore jangly anklets and flowing Indian print dresses. You kept your feet bare. You never lacked for dates. Well, no, let's be honest. You never lacked for sex. In all kinds of places—dorm rooms with ties hung from the door knobs, cars in college parking lots, motel rooms in cheap downtown dives, Maine pine woods, Maine seashore—in all those places, boys loved your flesh. Some professors, too. Lonely, middle-aged grateful men, those professors, men who loved your body and liked your brain, too. And you liked yourself, as well. So it all worked out.

But, of course, you graduated and things changed. Big changes, terrible changes. Gramp died first and then Gramma followed, not long behind. You couldn't bear to live in their house. You sold it, for what little it brought, and you paid off your student loans and you banked the rest and headed for New York. Where you were alone. You began to bake your own desserts, for comfort and for love.

Let's skip ahead, shall we? None of that is the real story, is it? That is just what we're writing to avoid the real story. Which starts here: you posed, you modeled, and the art instructor at NYU fell in love with you. You were utterly flattered and head-over-heels. His name was Allen Gaynor—yes, the one we've all heard of, the one whose work hangs in galleries and maybe even, by now, a museum or two—and he loved you so much that he wouldn't let you model anymore. He loved you so much that he couldn't bear anyone else looking at you. He loved you so much that he took you to his tiny country cottage in the mountains near Woodstock and he got a job teaching painting at Bard College and he kept you fed and warm and nearly always naked.

You remember, Suzanne, don't you? You haven't forgotten. You can recall exact scenes, specific nights, certain mornings. (And if you ever do manage to forget, the paintings are available, aren't they? Aren't they just?)

You can't afford not to remember, so here's just one scene for you to look at. Keep your eyes wide open, Suzanne. Don't turn away. It's necessary:

There you are, on the red velvet couch. He likes to pose you on red, saying it tints your flesh with its warmth. You've gotten huge, Suzanne. You aren't just the big, easy girl you were in college. No. You are enormous, with breasts that spill to the sides like great billows of white cloud. Your legs are pillars. Your belly is a field of flesh, rolling like hills, shimmering in the bright light he's got shining on you. He likes to use old-fashioned movie lights, hot and terribly bright. He says they make you glisten (you know it's sweat; you feel it gathering in all the folds, spilling down the gullies of your body). He says he wants to see every crevice, every ridge and curve and valley and summit of your flesh. He wants every iota lit up like the fourth of July sky.

You must stay absolutely still. When you close your eyes, you can see the brightness of the lights on your eyelids, where the colors slide constantly across your vision: orange and red, the occasional arc of bright green. When you try to turn your head away from the glare, he speaks softly. "No, no, my love. Look at me. I want to see your eyes. Look, love."

When you open your eyes, he is close. He is naked, too, because that is how he needs to be, to capture the sensuality of the scene, he says. He is naked and pale, his legs dusted with dark hairs, his beard curling from his cheeks just as his pubic hair curls from his crotch. His penis is erect, dark with blood. He is always erect when he paints you. He says it can't be helped, that he is wild with desire for your flesh. And it makes him paint quickly, with fast sure strokes, so that he can—soon, very soon—push himself into you. He will keep the bright lights blazing in your eyes; he will splay you on the couch, pushing inside with his mouth, his paint-stained fingers, his prick. He will make you come, not once but over and over, until it hurts and you are choking in the paint-filled air and you are crying and asking him to stop. But he will not stop. He loves you too much to ever stop.

Afterwards, he takes you to the kitchen and watches you eat. If you say you are full, he chides. He wheedles. He whines. Eventually, when you've been married three years and you are so big you no longer leave the house at all, when you haven't a friend or job or anything, anything outside this house, outside this studio, he doesn't even bother to chide and cajole. Then, he just takes handfuls of food and he pushes it into your mouth. It all tastes like paint and it makes you choke. Afterwards, he holds you in his arms and tells you how much he loves you.

Sometimes now, in the studio, on the red couch or the dark blue rug or even the icy, cement-gray floor, he orders you to hold yourself open, so that he can paint you from the inside out. Then, almost gasping with desire, panting with the pain of his own excitement, he paints brilliant tunnels of pink, caves of damp pink inside mountains of flesh; these paintings, he calls "abstract." When he is done fucking you, on the cold hard floor, your back and buttocks bruised with the combination of his weight and your own, he whispers assurances. He claims that no one who sees these paintings will know that this is your cunt, your own, open, vulnerable, terrified cunt. He says no one else will even know what they are, these strange paintings—to the average eye, they are just design, color, form. He carries these paintings off, so you never have to look at them, but one day you see the catalog of one of his shows and there it is: a swirling, glistening, perfectly recognizable vagina, fringed with red hair. And the name of the painting is Suzanne LaFleshe 623.

And then you know you have to leave. You know that his love is a devouring, deforming thing—that your flesh feeds something terrible inside him. That you have lost control of your body and your life and you have to get the hell out.

This is the hardest part to tell and so it will be short, although in life, it was long. You had to make very careful, very secret plans. You had to save money, slowly, secretly piling the dollar bills in the box at the bottom of your closet. You had—at last, at last—to walk down that snowy, ice-bound hill one morning in January, when he was teaching. You could barely breathe, out there in that terrible air, the icy wind tearing the breath from your throat. You could barely walk, thighs rubbing against one another like intertwined trunks of trees. You could barely bear your own weight. At the bottom of the hill, a taxi waited and when he saw you, puffing and sliding down the walkway, the driver stared. And stared. And finally said, "Jeez, lady. I don't think the suspension of this old cab can take that much weight."

And you said, "Please. You have to help me. Please."

And he shrugged and said, "Well, hell. Okay. I'll try."

The rest—the hiding; the lawyers; the tear-filled, begging phone calls; the claims that you'd ruined his career; the promises to reform; the declarations of undying love; the fury; the whole rest of it—it's too sordid to recall.

The thing is, Suzanne, you got out. You did. You got away. You got thinner—back to your true self—your deluxe, not degraded, self. You got better. You learned what love is not. What is not love, but cannibalism. You learned that cannibal love devours what it desires. You learned. You healed. You got over it.

Just don't forget it. Ever.

> With all my love,
> Suzanne LaFleshe

Suzanne closed the folder and wiped the tears from her cheeks. She flipped open her notebook to the page where she'd jotted two quotes a while back, ones she might never use in her dissertation but would keep in her head: "*Cannibalism resembles exotic and taboo sex.*" Caleb Crain, "Lovers of Human Flesh." And "*...of all the teeming perils of the night and the forest, ghosts, hobgoblins, ogres that grill babies up on gridirons, witches that fatten their captives in cages for cannibal tables, the wolf is the worst, for he cannot listen to reason.*" Angela Carter, "The Company of Wolves."

She remembered what it was like to cohabit with a wolf and would not do it again. She dumped the remnants of her pie into one of the library wastebaskets, on her way out.

17

In just the time that she'd been inside the library, winter had returned.
Typical upstate New York weather—never held steady for more than
an hour. She carried her backpack against her chest like a shield as she
slid along the walkway outside the library. The rain was still falling,
even harder now, but the temperature was dropping and the wind was
picking up. The water beneath her feet had already begun to freeze,
becoming slick and treacherous. She decided that she just couldn't
face the walk to the bus stop in this, so she headed back to Humanities, to wait it out. Her heart was still beating hard from the resurrection of terrible memories and the invasion of new fears; she needed
to sit down in her editor's chair and have a cup of tea. She needed to
steady herself.

She walked very slowly and carefully, feeling her feet slip with every other step. All around her, students were laughing, sliding and
falling with the ease of children. Faculty were walking like cripples,
stiff and terrified. She shook her head. How time does make cowards
of us all, she thought, and tried to walk faster. She was still a student,
after all. But she was afraid to lift her feet up and only accomplished a
kind of brisk shuffle, an accelerated Uncle Waldo walk. An *older* student, no matter how she tried to mimic youth.

A tall kid with brilliant blue hair slid up behind her, his bare bony
arms held out like wings. "Just relax, man," he said, smiling. He had
three silver rings in his lower lip. "If you relax, you won't fall." He
spun in a circle, flapping his arms, skin bumpy with cold and festive

with tattoos. "And even if you do fall, you won't get hurt, if you're having fun." He sailed on by her, a gawky heron, grinning. "It's all a matter of mind over matter, you know?"

She nodded grimly, tightening her grip on her backpack. "It's just that I've got a whole lot more matter to mind," she muttered, admiring his style, his goofy confidence. Mental heaviness slowed her steps and dragged on her heart.

Her legs were still stiff and shaky when she opened the door to the *Largesse* office. It was empty and warm. It smelled better now. She sighed with relief and dropped her backpack on her desk. There was an envelope on the desk, propped up. It had "Suzanne" typed on the front. Her heart started pounding again. God, was it never going to end? She shook her coat from her shoulders and tore the envelope open, already angry at whoever was doing this, leaving disgusting little messages everywhere, dogging her footsteps, tormenting her. She pulled the paper out of the envelope and flipped it open. "Dissertation committee meeting: tomorrow at 10:30. Remember? My office." It was signed, "Rachel."

She sat down hard in the rolling chair, catching her breath. It wasn't her tormentor. She put the note down. Well, okay. It was a different sort of torment. At least that was something. She dragged her calendar out of her backpack and checked the date. Yes, she had written it down, sometime last semester, and since then, apparently, she had chosen to forget all about it. A meeting with her dissertation committee, tomorrow, January 22, at 10:30 a.m. Only Rachel would schedule a meeting on a Saturday, but there it was: tomorrow. In big letters, she'd even written, BRING NEW CHAPTERS!! Written in a moment of optimism, sure she'd have new chapters to bring. She couldn't even remember that little gleam of hope, anymore. She let the calendar slide to the desktop and lowered her head to rest on top of it.

The smell of peanut butter woke her. She sat up with a start, neck stiff. The window was already dark and the wind was howling outside it. Ronelle was standing at the window, looking out. She was holding a packet of peanut butter/cheese crackers in her hand.

Suzanne pushed her chair back and stood up. "God, I can't believe I fell asleep. I've got dogs to walk. I've got to get home." She shook her head, trying to clear muzzy afternoon sleepiness from her brain.

Ronelle turned around, chewing. She swallowed, then said. "I don't think so, boss."

"What do you mean? What are you talking about?" She reached out a hand. "Can I have a cracker?"

"Yep." Ronelle held the packet open. "But you can't go home. Look."

Suzanne took a cracker and bit into it, savoring its salt. "What the hell are you talking about?" She moved over to the window and looked down. She couldn't see a thing. It was nearly dark outside and the window was completely coated with ice, wavery and thick, like the kind of glass they use in shower stalls. She tapped on the glass with a fingernail. "What's going on?"

Ronelle shrugged. "A huge ice storm. They say the temperature dropped, like, forty degrees, in the lower atmosphere, within two hours. But the temperature in the upper atmosphere stayed high. Thus, freezing rain. Falls liquid, hits the ground and turns solid, instantly." She grinned. "See what you can learn on the weather sites? Anyway, the university buses stopped running about an hour ago."

"Shit. Why didn't you tell me? How do you know, anyway?" She turned to Ronelle, who was slipping the last cracker from its wrapper. "Give me that—I'm starving."

"Oh, and I'm not?" Ronelle looked at Suzanne's face. "Jeez, you look worse than me. Here." She handed her the cracker. "They sent out a message on campus email, about the buses. Look." She slipped into the rolling chair and brought up something on the computer screen.

Suzanne stood behind her, baffled. "We get campus email?"

Ronelle laughed, tipping herself back in the chair. "You are not exactly a techno-genius, are you, boss? Of course we do. We're on the network, just like every other office on campus. Lookie here. Our address is FATMAG@MAIL.SUNYA.EDU, by the way. Cute, huh?"

"Adorable." Suzanne was staring at the screen. *As of 4 p.m., University bus service has been suspended. As of 4:40 p.m., Capital District Transportation Authority bus service has also been suspended. A travelers' advisory has been issued and the New York State Police are asking that only emergency vehicles use the roadways. Evening classes will be held as usual.* "That's crazy," she said. "I mean, that they didn't cancel classes. How can you not go out on the roads and still get to class?"

Ronelle shrugged. "They only cancel classes if there's a state of emergency, I hear. Like, declared by the governor or something. This is just an itty bitty travelers' advisory. I think they figure that everyone lives on campus, anyway. In dorms or, like, me, illegal office-dwellers." She grinned. "And, I guess, like you, for tonight anyway. Looks like we're roomies, boss. Want to sleep in the rolling or the stationary chair? Lucky you brought all that food over, right?"

After Ronelle had left for her 5:30 class, Suzanne sank into the editor's chair and held her head in her hands. She couldn't work on her dissertation, because it was all at home, residing on disks and her laptop. She couldn't have a hot supper because she wasn't willing to walk across campus on sheer ice. She was worried about Pear and Apple and Plum. And Molly and Munchie, too. She'd called, as soon as she realized that she really couldn't get home. Molly hadn't answered until the twelfth ring and then she'd sounded confused, sleepy. Finally, Suzanne had gotten Molly to understand that she was stuck in her office and wouldn't be coming home, that the dogs had to be fed and let out and Molly was not, repeat NOT, to try to walk them—just to send them out back. Did she understand? DO NOT walk outside.

"Yes, yes. I get it. I'm old, not retarded, Suzanne. I am capable of handling three miserable mutts and a little lousy ice," Molly had said, just before she slammed the phone down.

Three minutes later the phone rang. It was Molly. "Pear refuses to step outside," she said. "He is large and stubborn and he simply will not go. I'm just letting you know. If he pees or shits in my house, I will hold you responsible."

Suzanne tried not to laugh. "He won't. He'll rupture something before he makes a mess. He's old enough to make up his own mind, Mol. He hates slipping on ice—I think it embarrasses him."

Molly snorted. "Me, too. It's really embarrassing to have a broken hip. Anyway, Apple and Munch went out, slid around like that stupid deer in *Bambi* and did their business on the slide. It was pretty entertaining, by the way, watching those two trying to shit with all four feet flying out from under them. Now that the show's over, we're all going to settle in for a sleepover at my place."

"You saw *Bambi?*" She just couldn't picture Molly sitting through that film, with all its Disney cuteness.

There was a sigh. "Yes. And I cried when his mom got shot, like a normal human being. Wailed through the mother elephant's song in *Dumbo*, too. Witches have their sentimental sides, just like anyone else." Then a snort. "Of course, we don't let it stop there. Take *Bambi*—if I'd been in that forest, I would have put such a curse on those hunters that they'd all have shot each other right square in the middle of their stupid orange jackets. Anyway, I'm going to make these dogs a nice warm supper, full of bone-meal and whatever else I can find. You just rest easy."

"Thanks, Molly. And listen—don't let anyone in, okay? If Pear barks, don't go to the door."

There was a moment of quiet on the line, then Molly said, "You got dogs in that office with you, Suzanne?"

She looked at the phone. Molly was really getting odd. "No, of course not."

"Ha. So who shouldn't open any doors tonight, huh? Me or you?"

"Oh. I get it. I won't let any strangers in, either. Ronelle and I will have our own little pajama party."

Molly grunted. "I'd think you'd rather roll around in your pj's with that handsome Charles Clark."

Suzanne tapped a finger on the phone. "I don't think I'll be seeing Charles Clark for a while."

"You're a fool if you don't, girl. That man comes from good stock. I'm just saying." Then she'd hung up, without a word of farewell.

Suzanne rifled Ronelle's food drawer and settled down with some Zwieback and Cheez Whiz, alternating with Zwieback with cherry jam. She'd found some tea bags in the faculty lounge and heated water in the official faculty tea pot, figuring, hell, it was an emergency. Even a lowly grad student couldn't be denied hot water, on this kind of night. It wasn't a bad supper. Then she opened her book bag and dug out the pile of books she'd gotten in the library. Okay, so she wouldn't be able to wow her committee with new chapters but at least she could impress them with her new research. If she sat up most of the night, reading and taking notes, she'd sound pretty good, anyway. The building was lively with stranded people—faculty who'd emerged from their 4 p.m. classes to find themselves having to to decide whether to drive home on sheer ice or stay the night in their offices and choosing the latter; graduate students in the same boat, except for not even having private offices; undergraduate students pouring in for their evening classes, loud and excited by the storm. It was festive. Suzanne had already been stopped in the hallway and invited to an impromptu slumber party by Leon, who seemed utterly delighted that he had a legitimate reason not to go home and who was inviting all the grad students to the office he shared with three other teaching assistants. "Come on, Suzanne," he'd said. "I'm growing as we speak." But she'd declined. She needed to read and she wasn't really in the mood for a party, she'd said. He'd tilted his head back and looked up at her. "Still feeling bad about Sam? Okay, so I'll comfort. All night—back rub, foot massage, sympathetic nods, sensitive listening, constant little bursts of amazing empathy and compassion, all that new-age guy stuff, I swear. I won't even try to cop a feel while I'm loosening your tense back muscles with my incredibly agile fingers. Come on—we've got all sorts of illegal substances and pilfered foodstuffs in there. It'll be fun. Like being fifteen again." But she'd shaken her head—no, she was much too old to be fifteen again. She'd said she'd tell Ronelle, though. It was a good way for Ronelle to meet her fellow grad students at their worst.

She'd shut the office door, to close out the sounds of hilarity and to munch her Zwieback in peace. She settled in with her books and notebook.

But it was hard to concentrate. Maybe it was that she knew that there was a party—or many parties—going on all over the building, without her. Or maybe it was the niggling memory of the last time she'd sat here in the dark, listening to the winter wind scream. Not listening hard enough, though, to hear the human cry beneath it. She sighed, leaning back in her chair and lifting her feet to the windowsill. She'd set her soaked boots on the radiator to dry and borrowed back the pair of warm socks she'd brought for Ronelle. The pen she was supposed to be using to take incisive, brilliant, perceptive notes began to slide over the notebook idly, making little swirls and squiggles that all managed to shape themselves into the letter S. Hardly needed Freud to figure that one out, did you? She capped her pen and sank farther into the chair, resting her head on its cushions. Hell, this was the day to dredge up all the old memories, right? Okay, so maybe it would be better to think about Sam, consciously, using her analytic powers, rather than trying to push him aside. That was taking up too much psychic energy, she decided, all that denial. Because really, Sam was always there, anyway, even if he was staying just out of her range of vision, like a speck on the eyeball. He was always standing there, hands in pockets, leaning against a wall, waiting for her to pay attention. There was always a little half-smile on his face, a kind of teasing grin: *Oh, come on, Suzy Q, look at me. Remember. You know you want to, Suzy Q.*

Her eyes washed with tears. No one, no one else, her whole life, had dared to call her Suzy Q. Even when she was a little girl—well,

never really little, always tall, always large—people seemed to understand that she just wouldn't be nicknamed. That Suzanne was not a
candidate for the cute, diminutive, "y" ending. That she remained
"Suzanne." But Sam, the first day he kissed her, the day they'd first
made love, called her Suzy Q. Sang it, actually, to the tune of Buddy
Holly's "Peggy Sue." Oh, Suzy Q-uh uh uh uh oo ooo. She folded her
hands on her lap, and smiled, with tears trailing down her cheeks.
Okay then, she'd let herself remember: Last summer, July, hotter than
blazes. She hadn't seen Sam much since May, since he'd finished his
dissertation and held a party for himself, Down the Road. At the party,
she hadn't talked to him, really, just handed him her gift—one of the
black velvet tams with the gold braid that you could wear with your
graduation robe, when you'd achieved, as they said, "doctordom."
Sam was going to the commencement ceremony, he'd said, and so
she'd sprung for the soft tam, one he could keep forever, to replace
the silly rented mortarboard. She'd even embroidered his initials inside, very inexpertly, formed with big loopy stitches in gold lame thread:
ST, PhD. Sam, already wobbly from many toasts to his future, had
loved it. He'd read the embroidery, grinning. "Hey, look," he said,
tilting the cap in the dim bar lights. "Look, if you look at it just right,
it says 'STUD.' See?" He held the tam up for Suzanne to see.

She'd smiled, saying, "Well, of course. That's the subtext, anyway,
Dr. Tindell. Your perspicacious literary eye picked up on it instantly."

Sam shook his head. "Nah. You just guessed my true attribute,
Suzanne, you foxy thing." He laughed and stuck the tam on his head,
crooked, throwing his arm around Diana, who stood at his side. Diana
had not smiled.

Suzanne shifted in her chair, trying to picture Diana as she'd been
that night, the night of Sam's big celebration. Diana had spoken very
little to anyone, just stood by Sam's side, glimmering with elegance in
the otherwise dowdy, messy bar crowd of students and faculty. She'd
been wearing some sort of silvery dress, Suzanne recalled, and her
hair was a sleek shine of white-blond down her back. Trying to capture even one clear image of Diana, Suzanne realized, was extraordi-

narily difficult. It was as if she wasn't made of flesh and blood but light. A kind of cool silvery light that shifted when you tried to capture it. She'd stood so close to Sam that she was a kind of shadow, but reversed, like on a photographic negative—a shadow made of light. One moment came back: Sam, getting very drunk on the vodka tonics everyone kept buying for him, holding a glass of the clear liquid in one hand and dropping the other on Diana's shoulder. A shoulder so thin, Suzanne remembered, that it looked as if Sam's heavy hand would break the skin, as if the sharp bones underneath the pale flesh would pop through, piercing Sam's palm. Diana had turned her head, for a moment, toward Sam's hand, and looked at it as if it belonged to a stranger. No, worse—as if it were some kind of attack, that hot, sweaty hand on her cool skin. She'd bared her teeth. Exactly, Suzanne had thought, as if she were ready to defend herself from Sam's hand with her sharp fangs. Or, as if the hand were food, the food her starved, bony body so clearly craved, and she was ready to devour it.

Oh, jeez. She really had been reading too much cannibal stuff. Suzanne shook herself and sat up in the chair, opening her eyes. There, reflected in the ice-covered window, was her own face. She looked at it, carefully, distorted as it was by the wavy silver surface. Her face was okay, really. Her eyes were big, deep blue. Her hair curled around her head, still mostly red, although shot through with a few white strands. In the glass, she looked pretty, in a thirty-something kind of way. She thought about Diana. If Diana was Sam's moon, she was just a thin crescent, barely there. It was Suzanne who looked like the moon at its full, at least in this glass. She shrugged. Yeah, well, it was Diana he loved, wasn't it? He'd never, ever said anything else. Every poem he wrote was for Diana, about Diana. Even when every line screamed his frustration, his pain at not being able to understand her, impress her, make her happy—well, they were, still, all for Diana.

But it was for *her*, Suzanne LaFleshe, that he sang "Suzy Q." She stared at her wavery reflection until it became Sam's face, lowered above her own, that steamy July afternoon when they'd gone to Washington Park in the heart of Albany. The temperature was in the nineties and the air as heavy as wet wool. Thunderclouds were piling up in the western sky, dark. But the sun was still beating down and they sought shade. They'd gotten together, supposedly, to look at some of Sam's new poems. He'd called, early in the morning, saying he just couldn't keep working all alone, that he needed her eyes to look at his stuff, to keep him on track. So they'd met at the park and settled under one of the huge trees in the quiet end west of the lake, far away from the playground and the romping canines in the dog meadows. She'd lain back on the grass. Okay, she'd known perfectly well she was being seductive. Something in Sam's voice on the phone and in his greeting of her that afternoon—the long, close hug, his hands moving on her back, his lips in her hair—had told her that it was time to give it a shot, to see how he'd respond. So, yes, she had been perfectly well aware that her thin white cotton shirt, damp with sweat, was clinging to her breasts and that the warm pink circles of her nipples were clearly visible. Of course she'd known that her skirt, also thin cotton, swirling with gypsy colors, was clinging to her thighs. Her legs, below it, were bare and she'd slipped her feet out of her sandals. Sam was wearing what he always wore, hot weather or cold: black jeans, white shirt, work boots. She'd laughed at him, that hot hot day, asking why he always wore those heavy boots. What was he hiding, anyway? Did he have webbed toes, like a merman? Cloven hooves, like the devil, like Arnold Friend in the Joyce Carol Oates story? Come on, why didn't he wear sandals, Tivas, like everyone else?

He'd sat down beside her, his eyes moving over her chest and then, slowly, he'd begun to untie his left boot. Then his right. He talked while he unlaced each boot. "Arnold Friend didn't have hooves. He was just short. He stuffed his boots with old socks or something, like girls used to stuff their bras, to be bigger. Okay, I'll show you my amazing secret foot thing." Then he slid off his white socks and wiggled his toes in the grass. "See?" he said.

She rolled on her side, looking at his pale ankles, lightly covered with curling blond hair. They were both misshapen somehow, swollen. She reached out and placed a hand on his right ankle, circling it gently with her palm and fingers. Under the skin, she could feel all sorts of lumps. "What happened to you, Sam?" she whispered.

He leaned back against the tree, his eyes on her hand. "God, your hand is cool. It feels great."

She let her fingers massage his ankle, very gently. "Does it hurt?"

"They both kind of ache, all the time. My punishment. Constant reminder of being such a jerk. Oh, man, keep doing that, okay? That's wonderful—it's been so long, since anyone touched me like that."

Suzanne sat up, moving until she could reach both his feet. She nestled between his legs, a hand on each ankle. He let his legs fall open, then put his hands on her shoulders, pulling her up toward him. She curled there, her head on his thigh, rubbing his ankles with her hands. Her heart was pounding; she'd never touched Sam like this before. They'd held hands, touched each other lightly on the back, brushed cheeks in greeting. But not this. Not this. She let her hands move in caressing circles, all around his feet, up his calves. "Reminder of what, Sam?" She heard her own voice, low and full of desire. He shifted slightly and pulled her up farther, until her head was against his ribs and her breasts lying heavy across his lap. She had to let go of his feet, and let her hands fall into the grass on either side of him. She could feel his erection under her breasts.

He lowered his head until his mouth rested in her hair. "Okay, Suzy Q, I guess I can tell you. I broke both ankles and most of the bones in my feet, when I was just a kid, seventeen. I wear boots all the time now, for support." His hips were beginning to move under her, rising and falling against her weight.

Suzanne reached one hand up to his chest. She found a button on his shirt and opened it, sliding her palm onto his hot skin. Under her hand, she could feel his heartbeat, strong, pounding. She rubbed the palm lightly over the damp hair on his chest and belly. "How? How did you break them?"

"I jumped off a bridge. I was trying to kill myself."

She sat up, lifting her face until she could see his eyes. They were green, clear in the hot air. There was a thin layer of moisture coating his forehead and his beard curled in perfect circles. A Greek statue, she thought. With broken feet. Feet of clay. She kept her hand on his chest, looking at him. "My God. Why?"

He smiled, cupping her face in one hand. "Oh, because I was an asshole, an insufferably intellectual teenager and no one understood me, of course. Because my parents were boring and cruel and my girlfriend broke up with me to date a jock and because I was reading all sorts of German romanticism. Honest to God, *The Sorrows of Young Werther*, I swear. And I was doing a whole lot of drugs and listening to Pink Floyd and Leonard Cohen. I mean, really. Who wouldn't want to die?"

"But you didn't, thank God."

"Shit, no. I floated. I mean, what a bummer, right? Here I'd made the grand gesture. I really did it—jumped off the fucking bridge and hit the water like a brick and went under and all. But, hey, I just popped to the surface like a cork. Just could not sink, ironically enough. So I floated there for awhile, looking up at the stars, and then I gave up on death and swam to shore and crawled out of the river. Only then, when I tried to walk home, did I realize that I had done myself some damage. Couldn't stand up, so I crawled over to the highway and was rescued by two guys driving a Pepsi truck. Romanticism ain't ever looked the same since." He brushed her damp hair from her temple. "So, am I a jerk or what? Want to disavow your friendship? Get up and go home?" His arms tightened around her. "Decide, okay? Because I really need to know. Are you going away, Suzanne?"

She ran her hand over his ribs and shook her head. "Nope. You were a jerk, but that's just because you were reading the wrong writers. If you'd been reading Virginia Woolf, you'd have known to put stones in your pockets before you jumped." She'd tried to make her voice light, but it cracked a little, torn between compassion and pure lust. She knew enough to want to laugh at herself, knew that she was tempted not only by Sam's physical beauty but by the irresistable urge to comfort, to heal his flesh, his spirit. A suicidal poet, after all—who could resist? A suicidal poet whose penis was rock hard against her

breasts, pushing up against the zipper of his jeans, calling for libera-
tion.

She let her hand move to his crotch.

He put his head back against the tree trunk, his throat working. He
closed his eyes. Then he'd smiled, and started to hum: *Suzanne takes
you down, to her house by the river.*

They'd taken the next bus back to her house, that hot July afternoon, and they'd been on her bed, naked and happy and covered with
sweat, by the time the first thunderstorm broke. While lightning danced
all around and split the sky, Sam had knelt naked on her bed, playing
air guitar and singing "Suzy Q." Who, who could resist?

She shook her head and Sam's image disappeared from the glass. She
stood up. Why hadn't she told Charles that Sam had attempted suicide once before? Why hadn't she really even let herself remember
that he'd told her that, until now? She leaned on the desk. Because
that made it worse, somehow. That she *had* known, all along, how
desperate he could be, how wildly sad Sam could get. But she also
knew that Sam didn't always tell the truth. Of course he didn't. He
was a storyteller; ergo, he exaggerated. And, anyway, she knew now
that Sam hadn't killed himself, hadn't grown up to learn that stone
was more effective than water for shattering flesh. He hadn't. He'd
been happy, excited. It was someone else who wanted Sam dead. Someone else was the enemy.

She slammed her fist on the desk and all her books jumped. Her
throat hurt and her eyes were swollen from crying. See? See why you
don't let yourself remember? It hurts. It stinks. And you have work to
do. Her mind roared at her and so she said it aloud: "Do your *work*,
Suzanne. It's really all you've got." With great care and determination,
she sat down, picked up a book, her notebook, and her pen.

She didn't let herself look up from the pages until her eyesight
began to blur. She rubbed her eyes. The print was fading, or something. She could hardly see it. She stood up. The computer screen,

that Ronelle had left on in case any more messages came, was doing something odd—sort of flickering and then swelling in a kind of nauseating pattern. She looked out the window. The rain, now that she stopped to listen, had stopped. Thick ice still obscured the window, but, through it, there was a bluish glow. She was staring out, wondering if the world was coming to some sort of unpredicted sudden end and feeling bad that she hadn't really said goodbye to Pear, when the phone rang. She picked it up, afraid. Afraid that the wailing wendigo voice had found her, even here.

But it was Charles's voice, sounding rough, rushed. "Listen, Suzanne," he said. "I've only got a minute. The campus is a madhouse, all these people trapped here, the god damn ice. But I want you to listen, okay?"

She nodded, then realized she'd have to actually speak. "Yes."

"I know you hate me right now, for being a cop and all. So I might just as well tell you one other rotten thing. You listening?"

Another rotten thing? How bad could this day possibly get? "Yes," she said.

"Okay. This girl—woman—came to see me. Before I got that drawing, even. Said that—well, she said that she'd been having an affair with Dr. Sam Tindell and that she thought that maybe he killed himself because—well, she wasn't too clear on that. Anyway, she seemed to think that he was just so crazed with love that he'd do something like this. Like kill himself for love."

Suzanne put a hand over her eyes. "She was lying," she said. "Or she's just nuts. Lots of girls think their professors are in love with them. It happens all the time, especially in writing classes. You tell them that they wrote a good poem and they think you want to marry them. Sam used to laugh about that."

Charles's voice got rougher. "Yeah, I bet he did. Except she has a pile of poems, Suzanne. Addressed to her. And, you know, to the untutored cop's eye, they look a lot like your friend Dr. Tindell's work. And they're signed, well, initialed. By one S.T." He sighed. "Listen. I'm sorry. I know this stinks. But I think your friend Sam got around more than you realized. I'd like you to look at these poems, see if you think they're his. Will you do that?"

Suzanne felt sour Zweiback in her throat. "What does she look like, this girl?"

"Who cares, Suzanne? I just need you to verify... ."

"I want to know what she looks like."

"Fine." Charles coughed. "She's all of twenty years old. Belongs to Sigma Phi, the sorority. Doesn't seem to have one solid brain cell in her whole head. And she's small, blond, skinny as stick. Satisfied?"

The picture floated from the phone to Suzanne's eyes: Small, blond, skinny as a stick. Like Diana, Sam's beloved Diana. "What's her name?" she asked.

"I'm not at liberty to say. In the poems, he calls her 'Stella.'"

Suddenly, Suzanne started to laugh. "Stella? Fucking Stella? Does he call himself Astrophil?"

"What?" The sound of pages being flipped filled the gap in his words. "He doesn't call himself anything. He just writes that she shines like the stars. Blah. Blah. Listen, I got to go. Will you look at these poems for me, tomorrow?"

"No." Suzanne swallowed hard, forcing down the hysteria and the Zweiback. "No, I will not. Let his fucking wife read them. She should recognize his style." She slammed down the phone at the exact same moment that Ronelle came crashing through the office door.

Ronelle slid into the seat in front of the computer, pushed all the "shut down" keys, then unplugged the machine from the wall outlet. The screen went black and the annoying wailing noise that had been coming from the monitor disappeared. "Jesus," she said. "Couldn't you see we're losing power? I mean, it's like, *gray* in here. Power losses can really fuck up a computer. I can't believe you left it on."

Suzanne looked around. The office was very dim—a twilight kind of gray. "Is that why I couldn't see to read? What's happening?"

Ronelle leaned back in her chair and stared at Suzanne. "It's the ice. Lines are down all over the place, I guess. The university has its own generating system, but it's only for emergency power. So it's like a major brown-out. They even let class out early, so they could cut the lights in all the classrooms. Where have you been? Everyone's yelling all over the halls."

Suzanne sat back down in her chair, pushing Sam and his harem of slim blondes out of her head. Charles, too. She rubbed her eyes. "I've been reading. I didn't notice."

"Jeez. Some powers of concentration. It's totally zooey, all over campus—kids running wild in the dorms, people trying to break into the computer labs and steal shit, while the alarms are out. People storming the kitchens and eating all the food." Her face lit up. "Hey, that might work—the computer labs, I mean. I could really use…."

"No. No, you're not even going to try. Charles has enough to worry about." She noticed Ronelle's puzzled expression. "Charles Clark, the university police guy. This must be his worst nightmare. You will not take advantage of this. You're not a common looter, are you?"

Ronelle sighed. "Hell, yes, if I can get away with it. But I won't, since you say so and you're the boss. And what's with the 'Charles'? Are you getting friendly with the fuzz, Ms. Brown?" She raised her eyebrows.

Suzanne slid down farther in the chair. "I thought I was. But not anymore. And I don't want to talk about it."

Ronelle stood up, stamping her feet. "Fine, be like that. But we can at least go out and play, right? I mean, you gotta see it out there. It's amazing. Come on. Put on your snuggies and come out and play with me. Come on. I'm the new kid on the block and I have no one to play with." She widened her eyes, batting her eyelashes. "Please? Pretty please?"

Suzanne had to laugh. "Christ—now you look like Bambi. I never could resist big-eyed critters. All right. We'll go out for a little bit, just until the lights come back and I can read again."

18

Bundled in many layers of assorted odd garments, Suzanne and Ronelle stepped outside the office door. They almost tripped over a young woman who was sitting on the floor outside their door. She was scribbling on a post-it note. She jumped up when she saw them. Suzanne felt her eyes grow big—this was one of the most gorgeous women she had ever seen. And oddly familiar although she was sure they'd never met. The girl was as tall as herself, but willowy and small-boned. Almost wispy, with long golden-red hair curling over her burgundy sweater. Her eyes were dark blue and her skin was perfect—peachy, glowing. Young.

The girl smiled, a small shy smile. "Oh," she said. "Sorry. I was about to leave you a note."

Suzanne felt her heart start to pound and her voice came out much louder and rougher than she'd intended. "What the hell kind of note?"

Ronelle shuffled her feet, staring at the girl and Suzanne, alternately.

The girl's face flushed and she took a step back. "I just wanted to talk to you. I just thought—well, here." She held out the little note, stuck to her index finger. Her hand trembled. Her voice was husky and she sounded near tears. "I just thought, well. You'll see." Using a perfectly shaped, pearl-tinted fingernail, she quickly peeled the note from her own finger and put it on Suzanne's gloved hand. Then she turned and walked quickly down the corridor, heading for the elevator.

Suzanne looked at the little yellow note stuck to her glove. There was just some writing, no nasty pictures, no obvious threats. Just someone asking for an appointment to see her, with a phone number. Just a normal student note. She shook her head, took the note, folded it, and put it in the pocket of her skirt.

Ronelle was still looking at her funny.

"What?" she said. "Come on, I thought you wanted to go out and play. Let's go."

"You were a tad snarky with that poor girl, boss. What's that about?"

Suzanne started walking. "I'm a little nervy, I guess. I thought it was—never mind. Let's go play."

Ronelle didn't move. "Nervy? Huh. I'd say, like, paranoid to the max. There's something you ain't telling, boss." She tilted her head, looking more like a terrier than ever. "I mean, how can I help you when you won't confide? I mean, am I your faithful assistant or what?"

Suzanne had to laugh. "Okay, Dr. Watson. I'll tell you. But let's get outside. This building is giving me the creeps." She realized that she'd been hearing the wheezing of the elevator as it slid downward and that it did indeed give her the creeps.

"Okey-doke." Ronelle bounced beside her down the stairs. "And you know, that girl was a little nervy, too. She looked really scared. And you know what, she looked sort of like you! I couldn't think, at first, why she looked familiar, but that's it. She looked like you, boss— only, like, twenty years younger and all."

Suzanne's boots hit each stair with a thump. That was it. The girl looked a little like her, only twenty years younger and at least forty pounds thinner. And a hundred percent more perfect. Great.

The sight of the world outside the building stopped all Suzanne's thoughts. Ronelle was right. It *was* utterly amazing out here. A world transformed. A world of blue moonlight on silver ice. A crystalline world, where every surface was smooth and glittery, charged with a kind of inner electricity, sparking cold shivers of light into the night air. Suzanne leaned on Ronelle's shoulder as they slid along the walkways. Everywhere, there were clutches of laughing people. Every face, too, was transformed; every face was tinted blue. Pale blue ovals for the white kids, deep midnight ovals for the black kids, and every shade in between. When anyone smiled or laughed, their teeth shone, suddenly sharp in the intense darkness of their lips. The students had brought out radios, CD players, all kinds of ways to make music. Most of the music was the pounding stuff the kids always listened to, but somewhere, someone had gotten creative, and bits and snatches of the Moonlight Sonata came through.

Lots of kids had gathered in the center of the campus, in the pool around the fountain. The shallow pool had been emptied for winter, but now it had filled with rain, then frozen into a single sheet of ice. The students were dancing there, many of them nearly naked, their limbs glimmering in the cold light. They held cans of beer aloft, sending silvery streams into open mouths. Their laughter was high-pitched, full of excitement. Couples wound together, so entwined that you couldn't tell where one body ended, the other began. Couldn't distinguish male from female, flesh from flesh. The dancing bodies looked like single beings, haloed in blue light. Strangers, maybe, until this night. People whose bodies came together in just this magical lunacy, this special dispensation from the gods. Carnival. All rules suspended. All bets off. Suzanne watched them, envious.

"Oh, man, this is unbelievable," Ronelle said. "It's a whole new world." She walked steadily, surefooted on the ice. "Oh, man, we've got to get to one of the big lawns, so we can skate."

Suzanne held her arm tighter. "I don't want to skate, Ronelle. I just want to look." She tilted her head back. "God, who knew there was a full moon up there? I mean, before, under all the rain clouds. It's so weird—like it came out of nowhere."

"Yeah. Like someone called it up. Ordered it to appear. Artemis, you know? Like the ice and the moon are in cahoots, huh?" Ronelle tugged at Suzanne's arm, leading her off the concrete walkways, away from the revelry of the students, toward the empty parking lots and the distant athletic fields.

Suzanne let the shudder run up her back. Artemis, Diana. Sam, called by the moon. Loony tune, moony, moonsick, moonstruck. Oh, Sam. Her lovely—and now, it seemed, faithless—Sam. Whom she hadn't, after all, known very well. About whom, it seemed, she had been deluded. Molly was right. She didn't pay enough attention. She leapt before she looked. She made mistakes. She looked up again, at the white globe of light in the sky. "It's scary," she said.

Ronelle laughed. "No, it's not. It's way cool. Like a country night. I hate the way the sky is always orange in the city, at night, all that fake light. That sucks. But this is real, natural, you know? With all the electric lights out. This is like being in the fields, out in the pasture, you know? Just you and the moon. And a few thousand frozen cow pies."

"How nice. See, you are a country girl, at heart."

"Yep. I miss the smell of cow shit, really. Come on, let's get way out, okay? Really out there."

Their walk across the baseball fields nearly retraced the footsteps Suzanne had taken in the afternoon, splashing angrily through the softened snow and earth. But this was a different place, one so taken by ice and moon that there were no familiar signposts or markers. As if, between afternoon and night, she'd moved to another planet. The snow was still there, but now it was crusted over with a sharp layer of ice. The wind came across the fields with great force, lifting, pulling, screeching. The music from the fountain was quickly snatched away, gone. The walking was hard, at least for Suzanne. Very hard. Her boots broke the surface ice with each step, crackling and jarring. Broken shards of ice scraped the sides of her boots with razor edges. She had to snatch each foot out of the sharp hole it had created, rupturing even more ice and feeling it slice against her boots. Imagining how easily it would lacerate bare skin. She was panting, sweating under her jacket. This was work, terribly hard work, getting tougher with each step.

But Ronelle slid easily along on the surface. Light and graceful. Her feet never broke through the ice. She simply sailed across, giggling, her arms held out like angels' wings.

Suzanne stopped walking, halfway across the field. She had a stitch in her side and bent over her ribs, gasping. "I quit," she said. She looked up. Ronelle was spinning in circles, far away. She tried to shout but her voice was weak and sucked away by the force of the wind. So she whispered, more to herself than to Ronelle, "Stop. I'm too heavy to stay on top. This is as far as I go." Then she just stood still. Ronelle moved even farther across the open field, becoming just a dark shape in the brilliant blue light. Suzanne sighed and stood straighter, watching as the shadow that was Ronelle danced away.

Well, okay. Here was a dilemma. Suzanne was exhausted, her hands stiff with cold. And she was sweating under her heavy coat and dizzied by the wind in her ears. There was nowhere to sit and nowhere to go. She'd just have to stay here, trusting that Ronelle would come back, once her moonlust was satisfied and she, too, grew tired. Suzanne turned in place and looked back at the campus buildings. Her breath, white clouds of it, lifted in front of her eyes and she gasped.

The campus was a magical sight. The four tall buildings, one at each corner of the campus, rose like blue-white spikes into the sky. There were no lights in the windows, no soft amber glows to soften the picture. This was a black and white snapshot, utterly clear and stark. She stared, her eyes dazzled. It was like looking at an X-ray film, she thought. Like seeing, for the first time, the actual skeleton of the campus. Bare building bones, thrust up against the night. Wind tearing at every corner, filling every atom of air with its cry. She'd never thought the campus was beautiful before. She'd just seen it as stark and uncomfortable, not built to human scale or suited to human comforts. She'd read about its famous architect, its daring design. But she'd only wished for softer benches, some color other than white. But here it was, beautiful. Maybe this was its trick, its secret—that it really wasn't built to human scale, but something grander. And that it wasn't at its best in sunlight. Maybe it needed darkness and distance. She settled her arms around her chest and leaned back against the wind and stared some more.

The thing that swept down from the sky came silently, or maybe its scream was covered by the wind. And it came from behind, without any warning at all. Just a sudden, brilliant flash of white wings—huge wings, whirring. It passed just above Suzanne's head, claws dangling. She screamed and fell to her knees, arms wrapping her head. She stayed there, crouched, cowering. When a weight fell on her shoulder, grasping, she only curled up tighter. The primitive, useless fetal curl—protecting her soft, vulnerable belly from the tooth and claw of the enemy. She whimpered.

Warm breath touched her ear. "Hey, boss, did you see it? Oh, man, you did, didn't you? Did it scare you?" Ronelle's hand shook her shoulder. "It was just an owl, Suzanne. A big ole owl, out hunting. It was so cool."

Suzanne unwrapped her arms from her face. She took a deep breath, long and slow, trying to will her heart to stop colliding with her ribs. "That thing was an owl?"

Ronelle was bouncing on her feet. "Yeah. I mean, I think so. I only saw it for a second. But no other birds fly at night, especially in winter. So, yeah, it had to be an owl."

Suzanne sat up. "No it wasn't. Owl, shit. It was a ghost, Ronelle. It was a fucking wendigo. That's what it was." She put both hands on the ice and pushed herself until she was standing. "It was pure evil. I smelled it."

"Yeah?" Ronelle tilted her head. "Huh. What does evil smell like?"

"Like rotten meat. It had old flesh on its claws. I swear." Suzanne looked down into Ronelle's face. Her eyes were just deep holes in the blue of her skin. Her lips were black. "I want to go back to the office. Right now." She turned and began walking toward campus, stamping each foot hard to shatter the icy crust.

Ronelle slid and danced along beside her, humming happily to herself.

When they reached the edge of the field, Ronelle stopped and looked back. "Hey, look!" she said. "Look at this—it's, like, some mystery thing! Like in a book, at the end, when the detective explains it all to his dumb sidekick. The whole solution, right here. Look!"

Suzanne sighed and turned back. "What? I see a field full of holes, that's all. My footprints look like big black holes. So what?"

"So what?! Think, boss. This is so cool—look. Two people walked out there, two people walked back. But what do you see? Come on, think."

Suzanne thought. "I see one set of footprints. Okay. I see that." .

"Yeah, yeah. Now, suppose, just suppose, that you'd killed me out there, okay?" She looked up at Suzanne, grinning, her teeth lit like Christmas lights.

"I can certainly imagine that. Okay, so what?"

"Look! Let's say I was lying dead in the middle of the field, in a puddle of blood. Yeah, like, a whole spreading lake of blood, all black in the moonlight. Like, with my throat slashed, okay?"

"Uh huh. Can you speed this up? I'm beyond cold here."

"Okay, so I'm dead and you walk back to campus alone and then you go and take off your bloody clothes and bury them in some dumpster, say, then you just go home and go to sleep, because the buses have started running again. And the next day, the cops get called and they come out and, voila! They've got a classic mystery thing going—only one set of footprints going out and a dead body. So, it's gotta be suicide, right?"

Suzanne looked back at the field. "No it isn't. You didn't cut your own throat, clearly. And there's a whole set of footprints coming back, too. They'd just think that I carried you out there and killed you and came back. No mystery."

"No, no. You're clever, Suzanne. You want this to *look* like suicide, okay? So, let's see." Ronelle tilted her head and thought. "Okay, I've got it. This is what you do. You cut my wrists, not my throat. Like I would do, myself. You drop the knife—no, a razor!—next to my bleeding body and you stomp back, very carefully, in your own footprints. And, then, let's say, the weather changes again and it gets kind of

warm and then the ice crust melts a bit and the footprints get all sort
of squishy and shapeless and—well, voila, again. Perfect suicide, only
it's really murder."

Suzanne jammed her hands into her pockets, looking at the field
and listening to the wind. "Okay. I can see this story emerging. But
you forgot some details. I mean, I'd be *really* clever, right? So I'd also
stick a piece of paper in your pocket, something you wrote, something that would look like a suicide note." She looked down into
Ronelle's blue face. "Did you ever write anything so depressing that it
sounds like you want to slice your own wrists?"

"Who hasn't? I mean—I can't think of anything, but, yeah, I must
have."

Suzanne closed her eyes for a minute. "Any poems? Anything like
that?"

"I don't do that shit. But there must be something you could use.
I really want you to get away with this, boss. So think of something."

Suzanne didn't even have to think. It was right there, in front of
her closed eyelids. A piece of paper that said THIS IS ALL
BULLSHIT!! She opened her eyes. "That thing you wrote on your
'Pointed Firs' response. That bullshit thing. Think that would work?"

Ronelle nodded. "Might. Not perfect, but it might. Or, hey, how
about this?" She started to giggle. "Listen—I was composing the perfect rejection letter. You know? Like you told me, for the magazine.
And it was hard to come up with the right words, so I started to get
silly and I wrote a real over-the-top one. Something like—*Oh, I am so
so sorry. I really am. I can't tell you how sorry I am. It's just not fair; it's rotten;
it's utter shittiness. And I really am sorry to have to reject your fine work.* Okay,
so you delete the last phrase and there you go. Typed on my computer, saved on my personal disk—it's perfect. See? Man, anyone can
get away with murder, if they're smart."

Suzanne nodded. "Maybe. Maybe, on a night like this, someone
could." She looked at the campus buildings, closer now, but just as
bony. "God, maybe someone really could." And maybe someone had.

So, for the rest of the way back, as they walked arm-in-arm, Suzanne told Ronelle everything: the horrible anonymous notes and phone calls, the night with Charles, the days and nights with Sam and his own strange sad history. The new bits, too—Sam's other Muse, this little Stella person. The angry Ajax. The melancholy Morris. She told Ronelle everything, except for the things she could not speak, could never speak—her true LaFleshe past, those terrible paint-stained days when her body had grown grotesque and had fed an artist's strange lust. And, that, surely, was not relevant anyway. Ronelle's face grew more and more still, as she listened with all her might.

At the doorway of Humanities, Ronelle stamped her feet, starting to grin. "Oh, man," she said. "A real mystery. Like, as in sleuth-city." She took Suzanne's arm in both hands. "Okay. By tomorrow, I'll have a list of suspects all typed up. Okay? And we'll start investigating. We'll work it out. We're two smart chicks, boss." Her eyes glowed with excitement. "And we'll get Molly to help. Shit, that old witch has, like, superpowers! Oh man—what a crime-busting team."

Suzanne sighed. She looked once more at the students, some, the hardiest—or the most drunk—still reveling in their icy moondancing. Then she looked once more up at the brilliant sky. She felt again the rush of white wings and she smelled evil, just like Molly had said. And Sam, she thought. She imagined that Sam smelled it too, in the air that rushed past him on the way to the stone floor in Humanities. It isn't a game, is it? It's a serious thing, being dead. Sam knew that. But maybe not Ronelle; Ronelle was still very young. She'd take it as a game. But it was not.

Suzanne tried to fall asleep in the big teal chair. She threw the red towel she'd brought for Ronelle over the window, to block out the weird blue light. She wrapped herself in her coat and put her feet up on the radiator. She willed herself to keep her eyes closed and to breathe regularly, in and out, gently, as if she was perfectly relaxed and comfortable. But she couldn't close her ears to the sounds of the revelry in the grad assistants' office; the music and shouting slipped in under the office door. She'd made Ronelle go to Leon's slumber party. She'd gone reluctantly at first, then returned with a glassful of vodka and a big grin, saying, "It's a great party, boss. Leon sent me to talk you into coming. Come on."

"No, thanks. You run along and play with the other children. I'm old and grumpy and I need my sleep."

Ronelle had shrugged. "Okay, then. See you later."

And, left alone, at least Suzanne was certain of getting the big chair. But it wasn't all that comfortable, as a bed. She was too big to curl up in its arms, like Ronelle did. And she was worried about her dogs and about Molly. She'd decided it was too late to call and check on them; she didn't want to wake Molly up. So she just worried. Finally, when it was apparent that she could not trick her consciousness into fading away, she sat up and opened her eyes. The office was filled with smoky blue light. She sighed. If the power came back on, she could at least work. She could turn on a light or start the computer, or something. She stood up, stretching. Maybe Rachel would take pity and cancel the dissertation meeting in the morning—anyone would, under the circumstances. She sighed again. Anyone except Rachel, who believed that work went on, no matter what. If they'd been under nuclear attack, Rachel would expect everyone to carry their laptops into the shelters. If the polar ice cap melted and the tidal waves were heading for their shores, Rachel would expect Suzanne to lash her books and notes to the life preserver and to write as she floated.

For awhile, Suzanne paced, walking back and forth in the tiny bit of floor space the office offered. Her back hurt. Her knees hurt. She wondered what Charles Clark was doing and felt guilty that she was whining about her own discomforts, when he was fending off all the forces of mayhem and chaos that 10,000 students could unleash in the dark. She paced some more, thinking of all the wendigo spirits, loose in the night, held aloft by the wind. In search of flesh, to warm their icy hearts. She stopped pacing. This was just stupid. She'd turn herself into a raving loony-tune if she stayed here thinking about that shit all night. Okay, then. It was a simple problem: she needed sleep.

Ergo, she needed a bed. A chair just wouldn't cut it. But, a couch. A couch would work. Okay. There were at least five couches in the newly furnished faculty lounge, right? (If Ronelle hadn't somehow shipped them off to her trailer-bound relatives by now.) Surely, one of those couches was free. So what if she wasn't faculty? This was a bona fide emergency and all of those fine class distinctions that the University held dear must have been swept away by the ice. This wasn't, after all, the Titanic.

Suzanne grabbed her coat and her backpack and slipped out into the hallway. The only light came from little emergency bulbs, placed along the floor, like the track lights running along the aisles of airplanes, the ones that were supposed to guide you out of the smoke-filled cabin, after disaster struck. Those lights that only reminded you of what could happen, calling up every scene of every plane crash on every news show you'd ever watched. These were just about as reassuring. Still, she could at least to see to walk. The music and laughter from the grad assistants' office came winding around the corner, cheerful but distant. She walked quickly down the hall. When she reached the center well, she could see much better, as moonlight poured down from the skylight. And that wasn't very reassuring, either, was it? She ducked away from the well, hurrying to the door of the lounge.

Once inside, she had to stand still to let her eyes readjust to the darkness. Someone had pulled the drapes and the only light came from the red "EXIT" sign over the door. There was at least one other person in here, though. She could hear breathing. She stood very quietly, staring into the red-tinted air until she could see, a little. There were couches lined up against the walls of the room and three of them seemed to have bodies on them, lumpy long bodies wrapped in garments, breathing. Okay, so some of the faculty were here, like her, seeking quiet and sleep. Okay. She could see one couch, on her left, that was empty. Hers. She tiptoed toward it, skirting the chairs and tables in her path, trying not to bump too loudly into anything. She couldn't help making some noise, though, and when her backpack knocked over a lamp, the body on the nearest couch said, "Jesus fucking

Christ," then rolled over and pulled its wrappings over its head. A male voice.

"Sorry," she whispered. She slid her butt onto her couch as silently as she could. She placed her backpack on the floor beside her, propped a cushion under her neck, and put her coat over her legs. She sighed, closing her eyes. It felt incredibly good just to lie down. This would be okay. She even felt comforted, somehow, by knowing that she wasn't alone in this room, that other people, however anonymous, were sharing her sleep. She began to relax, at last.

She didn't think she was asleep, not deeply enough to dream, anyway. She could feel that she was floating just under the surface of sleep, somehow both aware of where she was and not, simultaneously. So when the white wings of the owl brushed her face, her first thought was, "Who the hell opened the window and let that thing in here?" She smelled the foul meat in its grip and turned her face away. She saw Molly, then, Molly at a great distance, a kind of Molly, but much younger, much darker, as if enfolded in mist. This Molly swelled, suddenly, and wings grew from her shoulder blades and she lifted into the air. Molly's head tilted back and her voice rose in a high, hideous screech and she flew across a bulbous orange moon, laughing a cartoon witch's laugh: Hee hee hee.

Suzanne sat up. She shook her head and the vision cleared. But in its place was a pale face, inches from her own, staring into her eyes. She gasped, loud.

The body on the nearby couch said, clearly: "Shut up. Will you please shut the fuck up?"

And the face in front of her grew hands, and put one over her mouth. "Shhh, love, it's just me."

She tasted bourbon on the hand and recognized Morris' voice. She drew her head away.

Morris leaned forward, until his lips touched her ear. His whisper was so low that it was almost soundless. It was more sensation than sound, just a warm breath of air against her skin. "There are no more couches, Suzanne. May I share yours? Take pity on a poor shipwrecked

Crusoe, won't you? It's right up your alley, a man foundering about in a storm."

She shook her head. "No."

The body on the other couch rose up, like Jacob Marley in his shroud, and said, "If you people do not shut up, I will kill you. I will strangle you with my bare hands."

Suzanne looked past Morris's shoulder at the apparition on the couch. It was a tiny, white-haired man, shaking his fist in the air.

"Sorry, Dr. Littleton," Morris said. "So very sorry. We won't say another word, I promise. Go back to sleep." He lowered his voice, speaking again into Suzanne's ear. "It's old Little-dick, the ancient classicist. He really might strangle someone. Rumor has it that he once smacked the beanie right off the head of some unfortunate fraternity pledge boy. Back in aught-five or something. Really, love, there's no help for it. We'll have to share." He rose from his knees and slid onto the couch, wrapping his arms around Suzanne. She pressed her spine against the back of the couch, making room. He settled against her, his chin resting gently on her head.

She tried to raise her mouth away from his chest. "All right," she whispered. "But I'm trying to sleep here, seriously sleep. If you so much as move a muscle, I will kill you."

"Shhh," he said. "I'm not going to move. I'm going to sleep. I'm exhausted. Hush, now, love. Just relax and go to sleep. It's all right. It's just your Uncle Morris, here to hold you. Everything is all right."

Oddly enough, Suzanne did begin to relax. There were other people here, after all. It was an emergency situation, odd but tolerable. She shifted her hips, just slightly, trying to find a comfortable position. Morris's penis grew against her belly. She tried to pull back, but his arms tightened.

"Oh, come on," he breathed. "That's not a muscle and I have no control over it. Give a guy a break."

She couldn't help it—she giggled. Morris nodded, then his arms loosened and his breathing slowed. She felt herself begin to slide down into sleep, Morris's soft breaths ruffling her hair.

When she woke, blinded by the sudden fluorescence of the overhead lights, she was facing the back of the couch. Morris was curled behind her, his penis nestled snugly against her ass, her breasts cupped in his hands. She tried to sit up. All around her, she could hear that faculty wraiths were rising from their couches, muttering, coughing, cursing. A voice spoke from the doorway of the lounge: "Power's back on, folks. Buses are running. You can go home now."

Suzanne fought her way out from under Morris's arm. She sat up, pushing her hair from her eyes.

Charles stood in the doorway, looking at her. "Morning, Ms. Brown," he said. "Sleep well?" Then he closed the door gently behind him.

Part IV: *A Sober Cannibal*

Better sleep with a sober cannibal than a drunken Christian.

Herman Melville, *Moby Dick*

19

On the night of the ice, Diana did something a little bit odd. Not crazy, certainly not that. Just odd.

The idea took hold of her when she looked out her bedroom window. She'd been going through Sam's papers. Then the lights had flickered, once, twice, then out. She'd stood still, waiting to see what would happen next. What had happened had been lovely—cool blue light flowed into the room. She'd moved toward the ice-slicked window and the memory had come: once, Sam had made her watch a porn film with him. He'd said they were funny; she'd get a kick out of it. Well, of course, she hadn't. It was not one bit funny, just stupid and disgusting, people grunting like fat pigs.

But one thing from that film had stayed in her head, apparently. Because when she looked out the window, she remembered the thing the people in the film called the "Ice Cube Lick." It was when a woman held an ice cube in her mouth and sucked on a man's penis. Or, when a man held an ice cube in his mouth, and licked a woman's cunt. Either. Both. The film led you to believe that the Ice Cube Lick was quite a kick, that the cold against the warmth made the whole thing just incredibly stimulating. Sam had laughed at it, saying he didn't know many people who had the oral dexterity to keep the cube in place while licking.

True. But, still. On the night of the ice, it didn't depend on anyone else, did it?

So, somehow, on the night of the ice, Diana found herself drawn outdoors. She found herself, actually, out on her back balcony. She found herself naked, shivering at first, but then, oddly, warm.

She lay on her back and opened her legs. The ice collected on her skin, a lovely sheen. The ice ran across her naked, open tulip—frost on a spring flower. The ice slid inside her.

Diana raised her hips to the ice, holding her body like a cup. And she overflowed. She flowed into the night and the night flowed into her until she could not hold it all. Against the backs of her closed eyelids, she saw a shape—dark, winged—bending over her. She smiled at the face within the shadow. She knew him at once, had known him forever. Her lover—her true lover—here at last. She held out her arms and drew him in. Her body clenched around him, the cold inside her a magnificent solid core on which she spun.

When she was done, when she could not come any more or any harder, she folded her hands on her ice-slick chest and lay very still. Her lover lifted into the air, away. She watched him go, then closed her eyes again. Gradually, the ice sealed her eyes. It built a casing around her body. A perfect glass coffin. It was better than being dead, this shiny tomb. Really.

20

Seven a.m. on a bright, sunny, bitterly cold Saturday. Suzanne sat at her desk, groggy-brained and sorrowful, unspoken explanations to Charles jogging through her brain: I didn't want to sleep with Morris; I didn't mean to sleep with Morris; I didn't enjoy sleeping with Morris; and, come on, I only *slept*, as in *sleeping*, not *screwing*, with Morris. And it was an emergency, right? And why the hell should she think she had to explain anything to Charles Clark, any way? Okay, so maybe she was explaining to herself and who the hell cared? She had work to do. She had to focus. She looked around, shaking her head.

So this is what it's like to live in the office, she thought, sinking lower into her chair. Your eyes are full of grit, your throat is dry, your tongue is mossy, you haven't had a shower, your clothes are wrinkled, you think you probably smell bad—and you do. Your coffee is instant; your bread is untoasted, limp, damp, unbuttered. There are no dogs. No kitty. No Plum, Apple or Pear. There is no kitchen. No Molly.

She sat up and reached for the phone. It was too early to call—a night lover, Molly didn't exactly greet the dawn with joy—but she was going to anyway. The phone rang for a long time before she heard Molly's voice, scratchy and cranky: "What?"

"Mol, how are you? How are the animals? Are you all okay?" Suzanne stared into her coffee cup; slimy little lumps of Cremora were congealing on its surface. She pushed it away.

Molly sighed. Long and windy. A kind of whine in there.

Suzanne had never, ever heard Molly whine. "Come on," she said. "Are you guys all right? Should I come home? Talk to me, old lady."

Molly grunted. "Useless old lady. That's all. Weak-willed, soggy-spined, useless old crone."

"What? What's wrong?" Suzanne's throat got drier. Molly never complained, either.

"Well." Molly seemed to be shuffling something around now, making rustling noises. "Shut up, beasts!" she yelled. "Food is on its way. Well, I thought I had her, you know? I thought, just by sitting in my warm house and thinking, making mental spells, you know, I could do it. I must be getting lazy, thinking it could get done that way. I just didn't want to go out into that ice. Didn't want to break a hip." She snorted. "Ha. Here's today's headline: *Feeble Old Scaredy Cat Witch Stays Home; Evil Escapes.* Shut up, shut up. Here it comes." There was a loud thunk, as a metal bowl hit the floor. "There, you ungrateful wretches. You're sharing one bowl, like it or not. Well, look at this; Pear won't eat. He won't stick his noble nose into the same trough as Munchie and Apple. He's turned his back on the lot of us." She laughed and her voice settled into a steadier note. "Okay, old dog. You and I will eat later. By ourselves, like the civilized beasts we are. You're right. We don't mix our fine snouts in with their pointy little rat-faces, do we? No, we do not. Suzanne, are you still there? I think Pear is worried about you. Every time I say your name, his ears go up. Suzanne. Suzanne. See? Just like that."

"Stop teasing him, Molly." Relief began to break up the chill in Suzanne's veins. If Molly was laughing, she was all right. "What were you trying to do, anyway? At home, sending out spells, I mean?"

"Oh, it doesn't matter. It was just an experiment. It had to do with coldness and drawing like to like and things you don't understand. Pulling the winter woman into her own element and letting it freeze even her icy heart. Stopping that heart with the very stuff it's made of. Wind, water. Terrible cold." Molly's voice got cranky again, going higher. "You can't understand it. Don't bother. I wish—well, I wish that handsome Charles Clark's grandma was around. She'd know. Her

Indian name was Summer Hawk, did you know that? She had the strength of hot days in her blood, lots of good strong warmth, heat, fire. Well, who cares, anyway? It didn't work. When are you coming home? I'm sick of these miserable creatures and I want to take a nap."

Suzanne tapped a pencil lightly on the desk. She began to scribble on one of Ronelle's papers. What was Molly going on about? What kind of silly witch nonsense was she playing at now? "How do you know it didn't work, whatever it was? I mean, how can you tell?"

"Ha. The air still stinks. That's how. You been out? Use your senses, woman. Lift up your own damn snout and sniff! You've got to learn to notice, Suzanne. I keep telling you. I won't be here forever. So when are you coming home?"

Suzanne looked at the little drawing her pencil was making. There were wings there—big spreading wings. And claws full of flesh. "Did your whatever it was—spell—have anything to do with a white owl? A really big one? With stinky feet?"

There was a long sigh on the line. "No. That wasn't me." Molly's voice was soft and suddenly strong again. "That was the other side, getting away. Did it hurt you, Suzanne? Did it touch you? It didn't touch you, did it?"

Suzanne dropped the pencil. "No. I don't think so. It just brushed by. I mean, I didn't even know it was an owl. I thought it was the wendigo." She tried to laugh. "Ronelle said it was an owl."

"That Ron girl was with you? All right, then. It didn't find you alone. Thanks be. It probably did you some harm, but not too bad. She's got some gifts, that Ron girl."

"Gifts? Ronelle? I'm not sure. I mean, I like her. But I'm not sure I trust her, completely. She steals things," Suzanne said. "She lies."

"Of course she does. She's poor." Molly sighed again. "So of course she does. She should. But she was with you and so you're all right."

"I'm fine. Nothing hurt me." Suzanne pushed the paper away, hiding the feathery wings and scaly feet of the thing she'd drawn. She pictured Charles' face in the doorway, looking at Morris's hands on her breasts. She shook her head, clearing tears from her eyes. "I'm just tired. There wasn't anywhere good to sleep last night."

"Huh. There wasn't anyplace good at all last night, girl. The world was full of not-good, believe me. Come on home, Suzanne. I'll make some strong tea and we'll get better together. Pear wants to put his head on your leg. He's wasting away here."

"I can't, Mol. I've got a fucking dissertation meeting here this morning. I haven't written anything. I haven't read enough. I've got to do some work. Can you hold out until this afternoon? I'm so sorry. I'll make us supper, I swear. Waffles and bacon. Okay?"

"Huh. Okay. As long as it's real maple syrup. Six strips of bacon each and one for each dog and two for the cat, because she's been a whole less trouble than these damn dogs. I'm learning to appreciate cats, at my age. And sausage. All right?"

"Right."

"Okay then. I'll hold the fort. We're all going to nap anyway. Do your work, Suzanne. We'll be fine."

"Thanks, Molly. I owe you."

"You most certainly do. Listen, girl. Take care. It's still out there. All of it."

After doing what she could to wash up in the ladies room, borrowing the cherry red towel and brushing her teeth with her fingers and Ronelle's toothpaste, she gathered her books, heading for the library. She wondered, for a minute, where Ronelle was. Why wasn't Ms. Up-with-the-Chickens Farm Girl back at the office yet? Partied hard with the other grad students, she supposed, and slept in. But slept in where? With whom?

But she didn't have time to worry about it. She had only two hours to read, before the meeting. Outside, the air was so cold that it made her face hurt. She stopped short in the doorway of Humanities. The campus walkways were solid ice, gleaming in the sunshine. So bright she could barely see. Light leapt everywhere, flashing off benches, jumping from the concrete overhangs. Blinding icy light. She lifted her head and sniffed the air, feeling like a fool. Nothing. Molly was nuts with her evil smells and evil spells. Just plain nuts. She pulled her scarf tight around her face and took baby steps, shuffling her feet, all the way to the library.

Maybe, she thought, as she settled into her carrel, maybe no one would show up for this stupid meeting. No sane faculty would come in on an icy Saturday just for this. She sighed. There was no such thing as a sane faculty member, at least in the English department. Probably not in any English department, anywhere. And besides, Rachel would show. No doubt about that.

As she burrowed in her pockets for a pen, she felt the little yellow sticky note that the girl who could be her gorgeous younger/thinner self had given her last night, outside her office door. She unglued it from itself and read it: "Can I talk to you, Professor Brown? I was a good friend—really really good—of Dr. Tindell's and I need someone to talk to. I'm very stressed. I'll come by your office again. Thank you." It was signed "Tiffany Adams." The "I" in Tiffany was dotted with a smiley face. Dear goddess in the heavens. Another one of Sam's good friends. Another of his really, really good friends. This one a mere child named Tiffany. How many were there? She leaned her head back and looked at the ceiling. How many of *us* were there, Dr. Tindell? How many deluded, simple hearts did you need to worship you, just because your perfect Diana didn't? How fucking many? She crushed the little note in her hand and tossed it on the floor. She flicked the tears from her cheeks, bent her head over her books, and began to read as fast and furiously as she could.

Rachel did show up, of course. Rachel believed in work. It was her spiritual center, her goddess, her nirvana, her shrink. Rachel sat at her desk, hands folded on the pile of papers on her lap. She nodded to Suzanne, hovering in the doorway of her office.

"Of course we're still meeting, Suzanne," she said. "Come in. Sit down." She waved a hand toward the chair she'd clearly designated as

Suzanne's. "I have something to tell you."

Suzanne came in, plopping her backpack on the floor. She sat in the little folding chair Rachel had put in the corner of the office. There were two other little chairs, too, besides Rachel's desk chair, all arranged in a kind of semi-circle facing Suzanne's place in the corner. Set up for the inquisition. The panel of experts grilling the witness. The whey-faced senators interrogating Anita Hill. The good men of Salem leaning over Tituba. Suzanne shifted carefully on the tiny seat. This chair was definitely not made to LaFleshe specs. She was afraid it would collapse, crushed under her weight. She could feel it wanting to give in—metal stress, hairline fractures opening under her ass. She felt giddy, giggly. Sleep-deprived and silly. Just great. A fine way to impress her committee.

"Suzanne, before the others arrive, I just want to tell you that Dr. Rosensweig has taken a leave this semester. So she won't be able to sit on the committee." Rachel leaned forward, smiling, her hair like an aura around her face. "She's pregnant—twins, it turns out. And she has very high blood pressure. She has to lie on her left side or something, for three full months. So, of course, she sends her regrets. She also said that her delicate stomach couldn't take any more cannibalism. She hopes you'll understand."

Suzanne tightened the muscles of her ass, trying to sit perfectly still. "I do. I understand. I get nauseated myself, sometimes, reading this stuff." She tried to smile. "But who will replace her? I mean, I have to have three, right?"

Rachel nodded. "Yes. University regulations. So I called for a volunteer at our last departmental meeting and we were most fortunate to have someone agree to join us. It is unusual, having someone from the writing faculty sit on a literature committee. But these are unusual circumstances and we're most anxious not to hold up your progress. So we decided that…ah, well, here he is, now." She stood up and went to the doorway. "So kind of you to join the committee, Morris," she said. "Come in. I was just telling Suzanne how good of you it was, to take on this extra responsibility. Suzanne, do you know Morris

Russell? Our resident poet? Morris, Suzanne Brown."

Suzanne felt the prickle of annoyed sweat in her armpits before he was even into the room. She looked up from her corner seat.

He filled the doorway, all arms and legs. He ducked into the room, smiling like the most affable of uncles. He looked perfectly rested, perfectly groomed. "Good morning, Ms. Brown," he said. "I hope you slept well and are ready for our little confab here this morning. I am so looking forward to hearing about your fascinating work. Flesh-eaters, isn't it? Literary anthropophagy, yes? Yummy." He settled into his folding chair, his long legs inching across the floor until the toe of his rubber boot found its way to the leg of her chair and wedged itself there.

Suzanne pulled her feet under the chair, aware of her grubby boots, her stretched out tights. She looked at the floor, at the pattern of red lines in the gray rug. She'd seen the rug dozens of times, could even remember when Rachel had bought it for the office. Never before, though, had she noticed how ugly it was, how much the pattern ran on and on in front of your eyes, like blood and brains spreading out on a stone floor. She didn't look up again until the third committee member, white-haired, sweet-faced, sharp-tongued Dr. Angela Dillard had arrived. Then she raised her eyes and faced her inquisitors.

Rachel began. "Here," she said. She hefted the huge pile of paper on her lap and shifted it to Suzanne's. "I've gathered a few articles I thought you should read. There are more and more coming out every day, exciting new post-colonial inquiries into your topic. The British Empire as cannibalizing nation and so on. Fascinating stuff. You've really got to work to keep up."

Dr. Dillard shook her head. "I don't think post-colonial is quite the way to go, Rachel. It's been done. I think that what Suzanne needs is to break some really new ground here—create a kind of anthropo-logical/cultural poetics of the British novel. Cross-disciplinary work is so important these days." She dug into her bag and brought out a thick sheaf of paper. "I've made a quick list here of some things you must read, Suzanne." She put on her glasses and read from the top sheet: "*The Anthropology of Cannibalism* by Bergin and Garvey, fairly recent, 1999." She smiled happily. "And perhaps you could sit in on an anthropology course? Or two? You know, just to get your hand in."

Rachel tapped her fingers together. "Well, cross-disciplinary is just dandy, Angela. But she can't ignore the current work in literary theory, either. She has to read…."

Dr. Dillard's white curls shook vehemently. "There's no such thing as pure *literary* theory anymore, Rachel. Good grief. How outdated. She has to look into…."

Suzanne looked out the window, as Rachel and Dr. Dillard argued and then agreed to disagree, as long as both got to add more names to the list of Suzanne's must-reads. She shifted her knees slightly. Her thighs were getting numb from the weight of articles above and the sharp edge of the metal chair below. She saw, again, her tombstone, with its granite epitaph: *All But Dissertation. ABD. ABD, forever and ever and ever. Amen.* She felt dizzy and sleepy. She felt like closing her eyes and taking a nap. Curled up with the dogs and Plum, all together in a square of winter sunshine on her bed. Her eyelids grew heavy.

A sudden movement startled her. It was Morris, reaching out and catching a flurry of paper, just as the stack on her lap toppled. "Here, Ms. Brown," he said, "let me help you with that." His fingers brushed her leg and he smiled. "Let me take some of that weight for you."

Back in her office, Suzanne inhaled the last four packages of Ronelle's peanut butter crackers, letting the salt revive her. She threw the whole heap of articles and papers onto the desk top and just sat there, wolfing cracker after cracker, cursing. Fuckers. Motherfucking petty tyrants. Pettifogging, professorial power-hogs. Tormenting graduate students was the only fun they had, the only way to get revenge for their own torment at the hands of their professors. No better than the dumbest of dumb frat boys—hazing the plebes, torturing the pledges. God. Why didn't they just make her wear a beanie and march across campus with her clothes on inside out? Why not make her swallow live toads and whole liters of cheap whiskey? Stick "kick-me" signs on her back? Wallop her with sticks? That would hurt less than this—this endless endless piling on of ever more work. This Sisyphus crap. This utter absolute bullshit.

She licked the crumbs from the cellophane packets and let tears roll down her cheeks. Bastards. All of them. And Morris!! What an unspeakably wormy way to make sure she couldn't just ignore him. God.

The crackers were a dry lump in her esophagus. She stood up. And where was Ronelle, anyway? The hell with all of them. She was going home to her dogs. To her bathtub. To her own bed. She wrapped her scarf around her face and pushed her arms into the sleeves of her coat.

She had made it to the door when the phone rang. She looked at it, then trudged back and snatched up the receiver. "What?" she said.

"Ms. Brown? Charles Clark." His voice was neutral, professional. "I thought you ought to know. Mrs. Tindell is in the hospital, Albany Med. You remember, your friend Sam's wife. Diana. Suicide attempt, we think."

Suzanne's knees gave out and the crackers rose higher in her chest. She sat down, leaning in to the desk. "Suicide?"

"Maybe. She's not talking yet, so we're not sure."

"How? I mean, what did she do?"

"Exposure. Went out naked into the ice storm and laid down to die. Something like that. Like I said, she's not talking and the doctors said to leave her alone for awhile while she sleeps off the stuff they gave her. The doc from the ER called me, said she'd asked for me when they first brought her in but he just now got around to calling me. There were a lot of accidents last night. A bad night, he said, in the ER. Anyway, the most interesting patient of the night, this Diana Tindell, said that she needed to talk to the nice man who told her about Sam, that nice University cop. She said someone wanted her to die, someone was after her. And she probably would have died, except for a neighbor who decided to take a leak from his upstairs porch in the middle of the night and saw something lying on the balcony across the alley. Saw something all shiny in the moonlight. He said he thought at first it was a white blanket, or a snow drift. But then it moved, kind of moaned. Freaked him out—a snow drifted that cried. He called 911."

Suzanne sat still, the phone against her ear. Ice to ice, she thought. Like to like. Oh, god, what had Molly been doing, sending spells into the night?

"You there, Ms. Brown? You okay?"

She cleared her throat and swallowed hard, tasting bile and peanut butter. "Yes. I'm all right. Will she be?"

"Yeah. The docs said she has a bit of frostbite, nothing serious. Funny, they said. Her heart was barely beating and she was cold as stone. But it didn't seem to hurt her. Like she'd just turned into some kind of ice maiden, you know? The guy I talked to, the ER doc, he sounded like he was in love with her. Kept talking about how beautiful she was when they first saw her, all sort of blue-white, like marble. Like a statue. Perfect face. Silvery hair. But really thin, he said. Starved, maybe. Probably anorexic. Strange, hardly real. Kind of magical. The guy sounded, I don't know, kind of stunned by her. Knocked out."

Suzanne nodded. "Yes," she said. "Stunned. That's how Sam used to sound, too. Utterly stunned. Crazy about her. Couldn't get over her. How beautiful she was. Is."

There was a little cough, then Charles said, "More fool him, Suzanne. More fool him, to love an ice maiden, instead of warm flesh and blood. That woman sounds like pure wendigo to me, psychologically speaking. But I'm just a simple cop, not a shrink. You sure you're okay?"

She nodded again, unable to speak. Sam had, apparently, loved lots of warm flesh and blood. Or at least liked it. Enjoyed it. Fucked it. But he loved, she was starting to really understand, he really loved only Diana. And she, in her own strange way, must have loved him back. Enough to be in such despair after his death. And then, to be tormented by whatever the hell Molly did. Poor thing—poor icy thing.

"Suzanne? You want me to come over there?"

God, yes, she thought. But no. No. "No. I'm fine, Mr. Clark. I'm going home. Molly's alone with the dogs and I've got to get back."

"Uh huh. Well, I stopped by your place earlier, just to check, and I took the dogs out for a walk, so they're fine. But old Ms. Highsmith, she's looking pretty shaky. You're right, you better get on home. Need a lift?"

Suzanne stood up. "No. The bus is fine. But, thank you. For doing the dogs. And all."

"Right. For doing the dogs. You take care out there. It's still slippery as hell. And colder than Miss Molly's tit. You take care."

21

On the university bus home, Suzanne was packed in with a whole
sorority, apparently. A whole great gaggle of shiny-haired girls on their
way downtown to the bars, already. She looked at her watch. It was
just after noon, but these girls were clearly heading out for their week-
end bout of binge. They clustered three to a seat, laughing and whispering. Suzanne sat alone in her seat—well, she took up the entire
seat and no one wanted to try to squeeze in with her, obviously—and
looked at the girls. Pretty girls, most of them, in the ways that young
women are always pretty—smooth skin, glossy hair. And thin bodies,
most of them. She looked more closely.

Most of these girls weren't even wearing coats, much less boots.
They were already dressed for their evening out—tight shiny hip-
huggers in that new material that clung to flesh like black Saran Wrap,
tight little white sweaters that stopped above the navel. Slide shoes,
with high heels. She looked around, craning her neck to take in the
girls behind her. Yes. They were all dressed almost exactly alike. They
had the same kind of make-up, the same hairstyles. They were all
thin—thinner even than sorority girls had been in her day, and that
was thin enough. But these girls were almost skeletal, at least in the
arms. Bony little chests showed through the V-necks of the sweaters.
Bony little rib-cages poked out under the sweaters. Sharp hipbones
pressed against the pants. Bare ankles, blue and raw with cold, jutted
above the slippery little shoes. They all, it occurred to her, looked like
orphans in Victorian novels. Starved, chilled, always hungry, always

afraid, always angry and deprived. All dressed alike, like Jane Eyre's schoolmates. Huddled together against the world. She leaned across the aisle and nudged the girl closest to her seat.

The girl turned a pretty face toward her and raised an eyebrow. "Huh?" Her eyes were rimmed in black and she had glittery make-up on her cheeks. Her hair fell in perfect sharp points around her face, pin straight and precision cut.

Suzanne smiled. She ran a hand through her own messy, tangled hair. "Hi. I'm Suzanne. Suzanne LaFleshe." She waited for the girl to get it, to smile back.

The girl didn't. "Yeah?" she said.

Suzanne kept smiling. "I was just wondering where you girls are off to, all dressed alike and all. I mean, are you a chorus or something?"

The girl looked down at her black pants. "What? A chorus? Jesus, no. Do we look like a fucking chorus?" She turned to her seatmate and screeched. "This lady thinks we're a goddamn chorus, Amy! I told you to wear your other sweater. The pink one. Jesus. A fucking chorus." She leaned her head back against the seat and closed her eyes. Then she turned back to Suzanne, her dark red lips pulled into a kind of sneer. "Listen, Dr. Whoever-you-are, Professor Whatever, we're just going out, okay? I mean, it's a Saturday, right? We don't have to answer your questions today, all right?"

The lips were lined in purple, Suzanne noticed, and already the girl had bitten off most of the red in the center. Already she looked clownlike and sad. And her night had not yet begun.

"I'm not a professor. I'm not doctor anybody," Suzanne said. But the girl had already turned away, leaning into her seatmates and hunching her shoulders. Her shoulder blades stuck out, little white wings growing beneath her sweater.

Suzanne shuddered and looked out the window. Thin girls. Starving girls, out for a night of fun. How many of them would come back sick, too drunk to stand? How many would vomit up everything they'd put in their mouths all night? How many would come back heartbroken? Which one would be raped? Which one abandoned in the cold back alley outside some crummy college bar, left to freeze, unless her sorority sisters remembered to go back to look for her, to find her and wrap her in their bony little arms and carry her back to the dorm? She closed her eyes and saw Diana. Almost dead. Almost frozen to death.

What, what had gone on last night, in that awful moonlit cold? What drew a woman—a beautiful, beautiful woman like Diana—out into the bitter night, naked? A woman that Sam had loved. Truly, truly loved, no matter what.

And what, what had Molly been up to? Sending some kind of evil spells out into that same bitter night? She clenched her eyes tighter and Diana's perfect face rose there, a lovely crescent moon. What was wrong with Molly? She was old, she was getting battier and battier, as if she had delusions of some sort of witchy grandeur, a huge finale to her life in the craft. But it was worse than silly. It was harmful and stupid and just plain wrong. Molly hadn't mentioned Diana by name, but Suzanne knew, just knew that whatever terrible mischief Molly had got up to in the night, it involved Diana. Poor starved girl, husband dead, now tormented by some sort of psychic Molly madness. Suzanne sunk further into her seat. That poor girl. Her husband dead. Her unfaithful husband. She leaned her head against the bus window. Her own fault, too. Sam. The icy glass stung her cheek. But she, Suzanne La Fleshe, she at least hadn't meant any harm. But Molly? Molly had something to answer for. That poor, poor girl, out in that blue light, alone and freezing. *Moon dancer—fly me to the moon. And over you go.* Jesus H. Christ.

She let the front door slam behind her and ignored Pear's anxious eyes. She pulled off her boots and went straight to the little pantry door and shoved her way through. She pounded into Molly's side of the house and found her, asleep in the rocker, her white head buried in her black wool afghan. She stopped, looking at the small shape in the big chair. But she wouldn't let pity for an old woman quell her anger, not now. "Molly," she said. "Wake up."

"What?" The blind eye came out of the afghan first, like some mole from underground. "What the hell?" A wiry hand shot from behind the blanket and grasped Suzanne's wrist.

The hand was far stronger than she would have guessed and it hurt. Good—this was no feeble old lady but a willful, crazy old bat. "What did you think you were doing, Molly? You almost killed that girl. Do you know that?" She shook her arm, hard, and Molly's fingers fell away. She leaned over, clutching the arms of the chair, trapping Molly inside. "She almost froze to death. Do you hear me? You almost killed her, with your stupid spells. Are you crazy? She hasn't hurt anyone. She was Sam's wife. She's grieving, obviously. She's vulnerable. She told the doctors someone was trying to kill her. God, Molly, what were you thinking?"

Molly's good eye stared up into Suzanne's face. Her voice was very quiet. "You stupid, stupid girl. Get away from me. Let me up."

Suzanne leaned closer, putting her face right into Molly's. "What were you *thinking*?" she said. "How could you be so cruel?"

Molly's eye closed. She opened her mouth and spoke, very softly. "Munchie," she said.

Suzanne felt the teeth in her ankle, but she didn't believe it. Munchie—a white poodle no bigger than a good-sized squirrel, a curly-furred angel-tempered doggie—Munchie had his lips pulled back into a snarl and his teeth firmly clamped into her flesh. It started to hurt. "Jesus," she yelled. "Get off me, you stupid thing." She shook her leg and swatted with her hands. "Get off!" Blood was starting to ooze into her tights, but Munchie held on. His eyes were closed and he looked utterly peaceful, as if in prayer, but his teeth did not budge. Suzanne grabbed his head and pulled. It only hurt more. "Shit. Call him off, Molly. Make him stop."

Molly sat up, pulling the afghan from her head. She folded her hands in her lap. "You come into my house. You wake me up. You yell. You say stupid things. To me. To me. Ha." She stood up. "You're so smart. You know so much. You call him off. I'm going up to pee." She turned her back and marched out of the room.

Suzanne felt tears coming to her eyes. She sat down, hard, on the floor. She patted Munchie's head and whispered. "Come on, Munch. It's me. Let go." His eyes stayed closed, his little jaw locked. There was blood in the white fur of his chin. Suzanne sat back. She opened her mouth and yelled. "Pear. Come. Please."

In a minute, Molly's living room was aswarm with beasts. Apple was quivering and yipping in the corner; Plum was curled on the radiator, yellow eyes alight with interest; and Pear was standing over Munchie, drooling down onto his back, a deep low growl spilling from his throat. He opened his great jaws and put them over Munchie's neck, gently. He looked into Suzanne's face, a question in his eyes. Suzanne was crying. "Go on, Pear," she whispered. "Do it."

"If he does, if he hurts my dog, he will die a horrible death." Molly was back, standing over Suzanne. "And it will be your fault."

Suzanne's leg was burning. Sweat was pouring down her ribs. "It hurts, Molly," she said.

"Of course it does. But not that much. That dog's teeth are not very big. Sharp, though." Molly held out one hand and tapped Pear's head. "Let go, sweetie," she said. "You, too, Munch."

In one simple movement, both dogs' jaws opened. Both tails started to wag. Munchie crawled into Suzanne's lap, whining, and Pear put his head against her arm. Apple ran in circles, around and around them. Plum closed her eyes.

Suzanne pushed the dogs away and sat up, looking at her ankle. There were four neat holes in her tights, each one circled with blood. She could feel more blood, trickling toward her ankle. "God, Molly," she said. "It looks like vampire bites. Look."

Molly nodded. "It does, a little. Or snake bite. Doubled. Munch does have good sharp teeth, doesn't he? All that bone meal. Plenty of calcium. But, really, it's just a couple of small holes. Get up. I'll get some salve."

Leg up on one of Molly's kitchen chairs, stripped of tights, Suzanne sipped the bitter tea Molly had made and grimaced as Molly smeared some kind of greasy black stuff onto the holes in her flesh. It stank and it stung and she yelped.

"Oh, shut up." Molly rubbed her fingers into her cheeks, leaving streaks of black goo on her skin. "Good for wrinkles, too," she said, grinning.

Suzanne shook her head. "I can't believe you sicced that dog on me. I can't believe it." She looked at Munchie, sleeping peacefully on his rug. His chin was still stained with her blood, a rusty dark red. Pear was lying next to him, his feet jerking in one of his running dreams.

Molly sat down and picked up her mug. "Ha. I can't believe you thought I wouldn't. Haven't you learned anything? There really is an awful lot you don't understand, my girl. A terrible lot."

"God. He's tasted blood, now. He's tasted human flesh. He'll go wild. Turn vicious. Become a menace to the neighborhood."

"Oh, sure. The world is just terrified of were-poodles, isn't it? Don't worry. It's not his first taste of blood. He'll survive."

Suzanne tried one more sip of the thick tea and gave up. "Molly. I shouldn't have yelled. But you did something really wrong, really evil. You sent that poor girl over the edge. She almost died."

Molly looked into her tea, stirring the white flecks around with one finger. "So you believe in spells? You think I could just sit here in my house, an old lady alone, and make some poor innocent girl go out naked onto her balcony and lie in the ice? Come on, Suzanne. You know that's silly. Utter nonsense." She looked up, black lines on her face, eyes twinkling.

Suzanne shook her head. "I know. But I *don't* know, either. You know?"

"Ha. Wonderfully articulate, you are, for all your education." Molly leaned forward. "Listen, child. Nothing can *make* anyone do anything. Nothing I do or say in my little cave can make anyone go out into the night and do something silly. Nothing. All I do is this: I call like to like. I put thoughts into the air. If that woman finds herself drawn to ice, if it calls to her, well, that's that. Like to like. Listen. It's her familiar, ice. It's what she's made of. That's all." She sighed. "Yes, I'd be happy if she'd died out there, her cunt full of ice. It would make things easier, better. But it wouldn't be my fault. And she didn't die, did she? It didn't even hurt her. See? There's your evidence. Like to like. Familiars."

"Cunt full of ice?" Suzanne's own womb hurt, just thinking about it. "God. How do you know? What are you saying?"

Molly stood up. "I know what I know. And what Charles Clark told me. What the doctors told him. She'd filled right up with ice, like she'd mated with old man winter himself. And it hadn't melted. Not one drop."

"Oh, stop. You're making it up. Charles said nothing like that to me."

Molly put her mug in the sink, her back to Suzanne. "He wouldn't, would he? He wanted to see what you already knew. Like I told him— that's not much. You don't know much, although I'm trying to teach you. Just a little. Just what you'll need to survive, Suzanne. Just that."

Suzanne stood up. Her leg ached. "Fine. Speaking of survival, has that dog had his shots?"

Molly turned around, wiping her hands on a towel. The streaks on her face caught the fluorescence from the overhead light. "What shots?" she said, grinning. "If I were you, I'd get myself to the hospital, pronto."

It was what she'd been planning to do anyway, go to the hospital. Not, of course, planning to have holes in her ankle bandaged and a tetanus shot stuck in her arm, but the hospital all the same. She'd been planning to go see Diana Tindell. She'd hurt that poor beautiful girl, in more ways than one. She owed her a visit, at least. At least.

And she certainly hadn't planned on taking Molly along, but when the cab had arrived at the front door, there Molly was, face scrubbed, all wrapped in her ratty winter coat, holding her purse like any other harmless old lady. She put her arm through Suzanne's and smiled sweetly. "I can't let you go alone, you poor thing. Injured as you are."

In the cab, Molly chatted with the driver, telling him all about how her little poodle, Munchkin, had mistaken Suzanne for a burglar and how very sorry she was about it. Suzanne sat back and closed her eyes.

In the ER, after Molly showed them Munchie's rabies certificate, which she'd brought in her purse, they poured antibiotics into the tooth holes and stuck the tetanus needle into her arm. The nurse remarked that the holes were already closing, that she must have remarkable healing powers. Molly wandered from cubicle to cubicle, sticking her head inside the drawn curtains and offering advice to the patients and doctors and nurses. Just a harmless old woman, dithering.

Finally, as Suzanne was pulling on her boots and getting ready to go, Molly grabbed the arm of one particular doctor, a young man with sandy brown hair and tired eyes. She smiled at him. "My neighbor was brought in last night, doctor," she said. "Poor girl, out of her mind with grief for her husband. Tried to end it all. Diana, Diana Tindell. Do you recall her at all?"

The young doctor looked down at the tiny ancient woman on his arm. "Yes. I remember Diana."

Suzanne looked at his face and saw it—the same stunned worship she'd seen on Sam's face when he said that name. The doctor's face had softened, the lines of weariness around his eyes lightening. She stepped up to him. "Molly. Don't bother the man. We'll find Diana's room on our own."

The doctor looked up at Suzanne. He shook his head. "She's checked out. I just heard from the floor nurse. When she woke up and saw the IV in her arm, she freaked. She pulled out the line and checked herself out. That's what they said." Suddenly, his face brightened. "But you ladies know her, right? You can find out if she's okay. I'm kind of worried."

Molly smiled. "Oh, yes, we know her. We'll give her your regards."

On the floor, Suzanne spoke to the head nurse, a thin bearded man, while Molly cruised the floor, staring into all the rooms in turn. She wanted information from this man, so she turned on all her LaFleshe charm. Hell, if Molly could play the part of a sweet old lady, she could do her LaFleshe thing, surely. She smiled at him, leaning close. He had nice brown eyes and a web of gray hairs in his beard. She leaned closer. He looked at her breasts and smiled back. "Sorry," he said. "Mrs. Tindell didn't like us, apparently."

Suzanne shook her head. "Why not? I mean, you look like you'd take good care of a girl."

The nurse laughed. "Yeah, well, not that one. She said we'd been running pure sugar into her veins, without her permission. She said it was rape, having that thing in her flesh, filling her with sugar, with fluid. She was, I'd say, a bit upset. She pulled the line out herself." He shrugged. "Sometimes, you can't win."

Suzanne touched his shoulder and felt the tight muscles running up to his neck. "You saved her life."

He nodded. "Maybe. But she didn't seem real grateful." He leaned his head toward Suzanne's hand. "You've got a nice touch. Warm, gentle. Ever do any nursing?"

She laughed. "Not formally." She looked into his eyes—nice. She'd remember him.

Molly appeared at her elbow. "Come on, my dear. I've got pies in the oven."

Suzanne looked down. "You've got what?"

Molly pulled at her arm. "Oh, come on. Take your hands off that man and get me home."

The nurse laughed again. "You better get your grandma home, Ms. Brown. Thanks for stopping by. Listen—here's my card. Let me know if you see Diana. I would like to know that she's all right. She seems to have some problems with food, if you know what I mean. With nutrition. She needs some serious help, I'd say."

"Exactly," said Molly. "So let's get those pies to her, all right?" She pulled Suzanne away and down the hall. "Listen," she hissed, as soon as they were away from the nurses' station, "I found her room. You've got to see this." She trotted down the hall and then turned into one of the double rooms.

The bed near the door was occupied by a sleeping woman, with sheets and blankets pulled to her chin, but the bed near the window was empty. Next to it was an IV pole, a limp bag still hanging from it. The clear tubing snaked down across the rumpled sheets and the butterfly needle, with pieces of gauze and tape still attached, lay on the pillow. Across the bed ran a little sprinkle of blood drops and the needle itself was dark with dried blood. "See?" Molly pointed. "She pulled that right out and made herself bleed. A real lunatic, your sweet Diana." Molly bent over, slipping the pillow case off the pillow. She scrunched it into a tiny ball and slid it into the sleeve of her sweater. She grinned. "I can use this. A souvenir. A hair of the dog that bites, so to speak."

Suzanne looked at the empty bed. "How do you even know this is where she was?"

"Look around. Sniff. Feel. Notice, for once. What do you feel?"

"I don't know. I don't feel anything, Molly. You're nuts."

The woman in the bed by the door moaned, then spoke up. "Please. Will you ask the nurse for more blankets? It's so cold in here. I just can't get warm. Please."

Molly looked at Suzanne and winked. "Bingo," she said.

22

Diana lay on the floor in her kitchen. She had tried the bed, but it was too soft, too stiflingly warm. Her belly ached with emptiness but she could not eat. That was obvious. They had poured sugar into her veins—hundreds and hundreds of calories. Pure sugar. She pressed her spine against the cool linoleum.

She'd pulled the shades shut against the bright sun and the kitchen was dim. She closed her eyes. It would be hard, getting over the horror she'd suffered when she'd woken in that room and seen the needle in her arm. She was still shuddering, inside. And it had been a mistake, letting the ice call her, letting go, out there in the night. Letting them get their hands on her.

It was another worry. There might be inquiries. Social workers. Hospitals. Doctors. Psychiatrists. No. She shouldn't have let that happen. She'd been there before and she would not go back. She had been there. Before Sam, before anyone, when she was just a girl. Innocent, too simple to fight them. Oh, yes, she'd been there.

She turned on her side. She nestled her shoulder and hip against the cool floor. She bent her arm and looked at the small puncture hole they'd made in her flesh, just inside the elbow. A hole, just where the skin was so soft and vulnerable. Bastards.

She drew her arm closer to her face. She put out her tongue and touched it to the wound. There was still a touch of blood there. Salty. The perfect taste of her own sweet blood. She sucked, gently at first. Then, as the tiny hole broke open and bled anew, harder.

23

This was a dreadful Sight to me, especially when going down to the Shore, I could see the marks of Horror, which the dismal Work they had been about had left behind it, viz. The Blood, the Bones and part of the Flesh of Humane Bodies, eaten and devour'd by those Wretches, with Merriment and Sport.

Swell. Merriment and Sport. Suzanne leaned back in her desk chair at home, crunching Pringles and sipping milk. She stared at the page in her rumpled, dog-eared copy of *Robinson Crusoe*. Merriment and Sport. Maybe that was it. The whole key that would make the dissertation happen, fall together, coalesce, gel. It had been there all along, right in Crusoe, right where she'd forgotten to look, so busily pursuing other sources, hoping for help from the so-called experts. But here it was. Crusoe himself was hollering in her ear. Right here. She scrolled back to her magical title page. She could feel excitement building in her chest as the title she'd made up years ago flashed onto her screen: CRUSOE'S CHILDREN: EMBODYING CANNIBAL AND CARNIVAL IN FOUR TWENTIETH CENTURY NOVELS.

Her heart lightened. It was all there, all the connections she needed, all the little pieces that she could weave into a masterful analysis, a brilliant bit of scholarly sleight-of-hand. She grinned. Screw their postcolonial theory. Screw anthropology classes. She'd had it right in front of her, all along. CARNIVAL: revelry, mischance, mask, disguise, freedom from restraint, freedom from the real, from the rules. Orgiastic celebration. CANNIBAL: revelry, mischance (for the *eaten*, certainly), merriment and sport (for the *eaters*, indeed). Freedom from the restraint, et cetera et cetera. Orgiastic celebration. It was all about celebrating life, in its weird little way. Taking life, cooking it up and taking it in. For ceremonial purposes, sometimes. For religious, sometimes. Sometimes, for slaking simple hunger. But more often, for celebration, thanksgiving, acknowledgement. A party.

She laughed and bit into another Pringle. It was *fun*, her topic. She'd meant it to be. It had to be. Fun. She remembered when she came upon the idea, how perfect it had seemed. Because it was all about what she herself was about: flesh. But then she kept forgetting about having fun, kept letting the professors and the critics get in the way. Hell, she was just writing about flesh, after all. There was nothing here she couldn't do, if she was tough enough to do it her own way. She let her eye spin down the screen. When she came to her name, she grinned and deleted that boring "Brown." In its place, she typed "LaFleshe." By Suzanne LaFleshe. So there. And they could put that on the diploma, too—the one that would say Doctor of Philosophy. Whoopee. Probably, she was just barmy from lack of sleep, dog bite, Molly's insanity, pity for Diana, all of that. But, for the moment, she felt happy.

Her eye fell one line farther: In memory of Sam Tindell, PhD. Right. She closed her eyes. No matter what—no matter what, she and Sam had had something. Some kind of carnival of flesh. And he'd been alive. And now he wasn't. Shit, Sam, she whispered. I can do this. I won't let the bastards have their way. I won't let winter suck our marrow away. I will not allow them to freeze our bones. I'll stick with our warm-blooded, warm-hearted Fridays, our good-fellow cannibals, our flesh-loving friends. Our tropical, steamy topos. Heat. Celebration. That day in July. Heat-soaked, sweaty, steaming sex. Sam. Celebration.

She closed the title page file and opened a new one. She typed the beginning of a whole new introductory chapter. She called it *Merriment and Sport*. It would be all about fun. She thought for a minute about Crusoe's horror, his cringing before the bloody bones left behind after the cannibals' feast. Then she shook her head. Screw Crusoe.

She was taking Friday's side, all the way. She'd dip her fingers in the blood and paint crescents on her cheeks. She'd write in red ink.

She worked for a steady two hours before she looked up again. She was getting it, she thought. She was getting at the heart of the bloody thesis. She stretched. The red Pringles cylinder was empty, although she didn't remember eating them all. The window of her study was growing dark. It was past four p.m. The bright day was becoming a brilliant, brittle, bitterly cold night. She stood up and looked out into the back yard, where everything lay perfectly still, frozen in place. She shook her stiff shoulders. The sky was clear, that brilliant kind of lapis blue that preceded a clear winter night. Soon, she thought, the moon would rise. She looked at her computer screen, thinking "merriment and sport." But remembering, suddenly, the kind of cannibals who weren't fun. She remembered reading about wendigos. Hearts of ice, a filthy odor, snowshoeing their way across the subarctic barrens, luring people from their warm hearths and stealing their bodies. And then their souls.

Shit. She closed her file and snapped off the computer. She couldn't let that into her head. That was not relevant to her thesis. That was off-focus. Verboten. Unnecessary. She stared at the blank black screen. Really, it wasn't relevant, that's all. It was all North American stuff. Native American stuff. It did not matter to her British novels. It was altogether unnecessary for her to think about. Her cannibals were all warm-weather guys (and girls), all of them. England, she thought, didn't *have* wendigos. She was right to ignore them. Unless, unless— unless you considered subarctic Canada a part of England. Colonial. Post-colonial. Shit. She pushed her feet into her fuzzy moccasins and stamped out the room.

The dogs were sound asleep, Apple in her chair, Pear stretched on his bed. They opened their eyes and stood up, stretching and yawning, when they saw her. Then they went and stood in front of their food bowls, tails wagging hopefully. She filled the bowls. "Just eat and out, guys. No walk," she said. "It's too cold. You'll have to settle for the back yard." She opened the back door and they went, reluctantly, into the frozen dark.

She walked to the pantry door and slipped through to Molly's side. "Hey, Molly," she called. "You hungry?"

Munchie sidled up to her feet and lay flat, his white head pressed to the floor.

She looked down at him. He cowered, whining. "Oh, cut it out, you stupid thing," she said. "I don't blame you. You can't help what she makes you do. You're just a tool of Satan, you were-poodle you." She bent and patted his head. He sprang to his feet and started to lick her fingers, quivering.

Molly's voice came from the living room. "Watch your mouth, girl. Don't call Satan into my house. He thinks he's the boss of witches, poor deluded devil. Thinks he gets to control all the little women who worship him. Ha. Ha, ha, ha, I say. Like the Pope controls nuns. Ha. And, yes, I'm hungry. What are you making?"

Suzanne scratched Munchie's neck. "Meat loaf, I think. Garlic mashed potatoes. Corn. I decided against waffles. We need serious comfort food, don't you think?"

"I do. Make enough for meat loaf sandwiches, for lunch tomorrow. Make a big one, okay?"

"Okay. Dinner at six." She freed her fingers from Munchie's fur and stood up.

"Um, Suzanne. How's your ankle?" Molly's voice sounded ever so slightly penitent.

Suzanne looked down at the square of gauze taped to her leg, surprised. It didn't hurt at all. "Fine, I think. I forgot all about it. It must be fine."

"Well, of course it is. I told you that dog had tiny teeth. Mere pin pricks, that's all he gave you. Now go cook. And a warm dessert would be nice, too."

She had her hands deep in the mixture of eggs, bread crumbs, onion, garlic, spices, and ground meat when the phone rang. She picked up the receiver with a paper towel and tucked it into her shoulder. She put her hands back into the bowl, squelching the stuff around. "Yes?"

"Boss, it's Ronelle. I think I've done a bad thing. I didn't mean to, either. I mean, I do lots of bad things that I want to do, you know? But I didn't mean this one and so I'm kind of pissed about it. I hate to sin by mistake, you know? Why didn't you tell me Leon was married? I mean, Jesus, that's the job of the introducer, isn't it? To say, 'Ronelle, this is Leon. Leon's married. He'll try to fuck you anyway and he is cute, even though he's short, but remember, Ronelle, he is married.' I mean, it was your job to say that, wasn't it?"

Suzanne stopped squelching and leaned on the wall. "You slept with Leon? Jesus. Why?"

Ronelle's voice went higher. "Because I was drunk and stoned and we started fooling around and because you didn't say not to or anything. I don't know *why*. *Why* doesn't matter. I just did. And it was fun, you know? He's really cute. And smart. He knows a lot about Puritans and shit."

"Puritans. Perfect. Ha. Ha, ha, ha, I say." She realized she was quoting Molly and shook her head. "He's been trying to get me to sleep with him for years, Ronelle. He comes on to everybody. He's a legend in the department. I can't believe you fell for it."

"He has? Oh, crap. I really am the new girl in town, huh? What a jerk. But you should have warned me, really."

"What about that 'you're not my mother' thing you gave me the first day I met you? What about that?" Suzanne scrubbed the goo from her fingers with the paper towel.

"Well, you're not. Hey, was Leon trying to fuck my mother, too?" Ronelle started to giggle. "Maybe the next kid in the trailer should be named 'Leonette.'"

Suzanne laughed. "You're giddy, girl. You need a hot meal. Meatloaf at six. Me, Molly and the beasts. Be here." She hung up before Ronelle could answer.

While she was laying the strips of bacon over the shaped meatloaf, she thought about Leon and Ronelle. Skinny little Ronelle. Well, well. He didn't much care about flesh, then, did he? Or about friendship. Or about not taking advantage of the new kid in the program. Just wanted to hop on anyone's bones. Anyone's but his wife's, apparently. The skunk. He deserved never to finish his dissertation, to live in ABD limbo all of his days on earth. Praise be to an afflicting God.

But by the time the pan was in the oven, she'd realized that, by those standards, she too would never finish, merriment and sport notwithstanding. That if adultery counted as a sin to the dissertation gods, she too was doomed. She hung her head and started peeling potatoes.

By the time Ronelle rang the doorbell, sending a cascade of barking dog into the front hallway, the potatoes were boiling, the meat loaf was starting to smell good and the gingerbread batter was under construction. Suzanne yelled from the kitchen. "Come in."

There was a flurry of louder barking and rattling on the door. Then a long peal of the doorbell and a faint voice. "It's locked."

"Shit." Suzanne put down the jar of molasses and went to the door. Apple was making great leaps into the air, pounding against the heavy oak door on each descent. Pear was howling. "Shut up. Stop. Shut *up*!" She threw the bolt, turned the lock and swung the door open. "Jeez. Double locked—Molly must have done that when I was upstairs. She really is getting nervous."

Ronelle slipped into the hall. The dogs went into their "you're-a-stranger-but-she-let-you-in-so-we-love-you-anyway" mode—Pear leaning his whole great weight into her hip, Apple jumping and peeing in ecstasy, sending little droplets across the hardwood. Ronelle stood still, huddled in one of Suzanne's huge sweaters. Then she said, "Control your dogs, boss."

Suzanne shrugged. "I can't. They always do this. I'm sorry."

"Huh. They do, do they?" Ronelle leaned over and put her forehead against Pear's. "Go away," she said, quietly. She pushed against his head with her own. He backed up and walked away, tail down. Then she grabbed Apple by the scruff of spotted fur at the back of her neck. She didn't say a word to the yelping, peeing dog—she just tossed her like a rag doll, all the way down the hall. Apple screeched once and headed for the kitchen. Ronelle grinned at Suzanne. "Down on the farm, we know how to deal with dogs. Dogs are not pets; they're slaves. I can't believe you let them be so obnoxious."

Suzanne looked at Pear. He didn't seem offended or upset. He was curled up against one wall, licking his feet. Then he sighed and closed his eyes.

Ronelle slipped out of the sweater. Underneath she had another sweater, belted like a dress, and under that, it looked like, yet another. She pulled a knitted cap off her head and her hair sprang out in frizzy tufts. She looked all puffy and wooly—a kind of sheep-girl. "See? Once dogs understand the ranking system, they relax. Hey, nice house." She walked into the bare living room, looking up at the high, carved ceiling. "Wow." She turned in a circle in the center of the wooden floor. She swept one arm out into the empty space. "Cool way of having no furniture, too. Like you don't even care."

"I don't. I live in the kitchen and the study anyway. Come on in." She led Ronelle down the long hall, through the equally empty dining room and into the kitchen.

"Oh man. It smells great in here." Ronelle slipped into a kitchen chair, curling her legs under her. Her boots crashed to the floor under the chair and she wiggled her toes inside her socks. "It's cold enough to stop lower limb circulation out there, I'll tell you. I think I might have frostbite."

Suzanne thought of Diana and nodded. "Could happen." She handed Ronelle a knife, a cutting board and a clove of garlic. "Here, chop. Mince it really fine, for the potatoes."

Ronelle looked at the garlic for a minute, then picked up the knife. When she pressed the knife blade into the clove, it slipped away, shooting across the floor. In one second, Apple had pounced and swallowed it whole. "Oops. Bad doggy breath, coming up. Sorry—it was a slippery little devil. Can I try again? I'm not much good at this."

Suzanne stared at her. "You don't know how to chop garlic?"

"Hey. The trailer kitchen is as big as a bread box and Mom never let me in it. Anyway, we don't do garlic—that's for spics, according to Ron. And greasy guineas. We do plain meat. Plain potatoes. No fruit. No veg. Nothin' fancy. Ron always says, 'Don't try to sneak no strange shit onto my plate. I like to know what I'm eating.' Chef Boyardee is a little too exotic for Ron. Here, give me another try."

Suzanne handed over another clove and turned her back. "I can't bear to watch," she said. She measured molasses into a cup and added it, with hot water, to the flour and spices in the bowl. She stirred the batter, smoothing away the lumps. It smelled wonderful—cinnamon and cloves and ginger and molasses. She listened to Ronelle curse and fret, amid wild chopping noises, while she put the batter in the pan and slipped it into the oven. The meatloaf, brown and fragrant, with the bacon crisped on its top, was ready to come out and she put it on the warming shelf above the stove.

"There." Ronelle sounded triumphant. "That sucker is minced, but good. Looky here, boss." She stood up and handed the cutting board to Suzanne. The garlic was minced, indeed. It also had quite a few speckles of blood mixed in, here and there. Ronelle grinned. "Knife kept slipping."

Suzanne sighed. "I'll rinse it."

Ronelle was licking her fingers. "Uum." She sat back down in the chair and tucked her feet under her again. "Okay. Now talk to me about Leon, okay? Tell me I'm an utter ass and make me feel better. I know I'm an utter ass and it will be good for me to moan and weep about it. Come on, boss, let me have it."

Molly answered from the pantry, her voice coming before her face into the steamy kitchen. "Who's Leon?" She stopped in the middle of the kitchen, Munchie at her heels. "Smells lovely in here. Warm, too." She sat down at the table. "Hello, Ronelle. What have you been up to?" She winked her blind eye, grinning.

Ronelle sank into her chair. "Forget it. I don't want to talk about it now, with all these witnesses. But, hey. Look at what I did here." She pulled a typed list out of her pocket. "I've made a list of suspects."

Suzanne was mashing potatoes, feeling the steam curl her hair into tangles. "What? When did you do that?"

"Well, you know how it's sometimes hard to sleep after you've had sex with a new guy? I had some time on my hands." She looked up. Molly nodded. "Absolutely—new guy, no sleep. So what's this about suspects? What have you girls been up to, while I was working my ass off all alone in the night?"

Suzanne kept mashing, harder, more vigorously.

Ronelle sat up straight. "Sleuthing," she whispered dramatically "We think…." She glanced at Suzanne. "Well, I think that Suzanne's friend Sam didn't do himself in. There's some evidence that he was, in fact, happy and cheerful, full of life plans. Ergo, we've got a murder." Molly folded her hands on the table. "Huh. Maybe. I don't know. Go ahead."

"So, I made a little list, from what Suzanne told me last night. Here it is: I call it People Who Wanted Sam Tindell Dead."

"Catchy. Just read it, girl." Molly was drumming one bent finger on the table top. "I'm hungry and haven't got all night for nonsense. Read."

"Okey doke. Suspect Number One: Suzanne." She grinned. "Not really, but that's what the cops might think, if they find out Diana was pregnant."

"Ha!" Molly slammed a hand on the table. "That woman is not pregnant. I would never call ice to a pregnant woman, never. I'd know. You're crazy."

"Fine. I'm just thinking here. And I don't know what ice you're talking about. Okay, okay. Don't freak. Okay. Number Two: Ajax Swenson, crazed poetry geek out for an A." She looked up. "You don't know him."

Molly nodded. "Uh huh— but I know the type. Go on."

"Number Three: Girls Sam fucked. Silly enough to fall in love,

crazy enough to kill when he rejected them. Unknown quantity."
Suzanne bent her head lower over the potatoes.

"Huh. Go on."

"Number Four—and this is my pick." Ronelle gave a little pause
for effect.

"Oh, can it," Molly said. "I know your pick. It's mine too. Diana."
She shivered. "There is something seriously bad about that woman. I
can barely stand to have her pillowcase in my house. It makes me
sick."

"What pillowcase? What are you talking about?"

"I'll tell you later. Just finish your silly list, girl."

"Well, yeah, Diana was my choice." Ronelle put the paper down
on the table. "But I put one more, just for fun. Number Five: Anyone
Suzanne was fucking, who might be jealous of Sam." She raised her
voice. "Unknown quantity. Right, boss?"

Suzanne turned to look at her. "Yes. Unknown numbers of men.
Lines of them. Right, Mol? Lines and lines, up the front walk, around
the corner. Every damn night." She slammed the pot of potatoes
onto the counter. "This is almost ready. You guys want to make stupid
lists or eat? Listen, you two, this isn't some stupid mystery novel. It's
real life and I'm cooking here. You want to eat or not?"

"Eat. We want to eat. But, Suzanne, you'll need another plate,"
Molly said.

Suzanne turned to look at her. "No, we've got three out."

Molly looked tired, frail. But her eyes were bright. "Four. We'll
need four. I asked that nice Charles Clark to join us for supper."

"Oh no. You didn't." Suzanne ran her fingers into her hair, looking down at her sweatsuit and ratty moccasins. "Shit." She put some
heated milk into the potatoes and kept mashing. She added a big chunk
of butter, some dill, pepper. She tipped the garlic in, as well. "Molly,
you had no right. I don't want to see...."

The doorbell rang and all three dogs began a scrabbling dash down
the hall. Ronelle stood up and bellowed, "Stop. Right there." And
they did, slinking back to their places, tails and ears low. "I'll get it,"

she said, and trotted out of the kitchen.

Suzanne bit her lip. "I can't believe you invited him without telling me. What the hell is your problem?"

"I do not have a problem. This is my house, right? And I told you to make a big meat loaf, didn't I? And a nice dessert? Well, then. You were warned. And you've made a fine meal. He'll appreciate it, a single man like himself."

Charles had brought a good merlot and he poured it into everyone's glasses, avoiding Suzanne's eye as she put the dinner on the table and sat down. He smiled then, and tapped her leg under the table. "It looks great," he said. "Pure home." He dipped a spoon into the potatoes and dropped a great dollop onto his plate. "Man, these smell good. All garlicky and hot. And, look, you even put paprika in, like my grandma always did. What a treat." He passed the bowl to Molly.

Suzanne sat still. She had not put paprika in. She also had not remembered to wash Ronelle's blood from the minced garlic. She dropped her eyes. When the bowl of potatoes got to her, she took a nice big helping. Merriment, she thought, and sport.

24

By the time she'd heaped the whipped cream onto the warm ginger-bread, Suzanne was almost relaxed. She'd had enough meatloaf and corn and mashed potatoes to lull her nerves. Everyone else seemed totally relaxed, jovial, best-of-friends. Molly had been mostly quiet, but Ronelle and Charles laughed and chatted, all through dinner, instant buddies. Now Ronelle was quizzing him about the ethics and legal ramifications of date rape on the University campus.

"So, like, if a girl is stoned out of her mind and she, absolutely by mistake, happens to fall into bed with some guy she just met, is that a crime?" She tucked a fuzzy braid behind an ear and licked whipped cream from her fork.

Charles hunched over his coffee cup. He'd taken some of the cream from his gingerbread and he stirred it into the coffee. "Well, maybe. But she's already in trouble, because she had whatever she got stoned on on campus, right? Illegal stuff, we'll presume. So she's not going to complain to us about this little inadvertent sex thing. Nope. She's going to shut up and hope like hell she remembered to take her birth control pill. And in a week or so, she's going to go to the clinic and get a blood test for HIV. She's going to cry to her roommates and she's going to curse her fate, but she ain't coming to me." He sipped his coffee.

Ronelle's white face grew even paler, her freckles standing out like bruises. "Uh huh. But it's not, like, her fault, legally, is it? And what if he gave her the weed, this creepy guy, in the first place? And she's not morally at fault, say, if the guy turns out to already have a steady girlfriend? Or a wife?" She lowered her fork onto her plate.

Molly started to chuckle. "And what if his name is Leon? Does that help? Ethically, I mean."

Suzanne kicked Molly's foot. "Shush," she said.

Charles's eyes lifted to Ronelle's face. "I don't know about the ethical, moral stuff," he said. "But, hypothetically, no, it's not really this girl's fault. She's the victim, legally. But she's also the one with the herpes, the HIV, the chlamydia, the crabs—whatever he carries around in his crotch, this wonderful guy. And maybe she's the one with the baby or the abortion, too. Hypothetically, of course."

Ronelle sank into her chair. "Jesus." Tears came into her eyes.

Suzanne stood up, pushing her chair back. She started gathering plates. "Oh, come on. Don't dramatize. Hypothetically, the guy probably had the sense to wear a condom. And, he probably doesn't have a thing wrong with him, other than basic horniness. If he's got a dorky name like Leon and he's really, really short and he's married, for Christ sake, he doesn't get a lot on the side, that's for sure. He's safe as houses." She nudged Ronelle's shoulder. "I cooked. You do dishes. I presume you know how."

Ronelle stood up, a little less pale. "I suppose I can figure it out. In the trailer, we use paper plates."

Charles stood up. "I have the feeling we're not all having the same conversation here. But I know how to do dishes, too—in the long house, we use real plates. Hand over that sponge, Ronelle. I'll wash. You dry." He looked over his shoulder at Suzanne. "You look after Ms. Highsmith. She looks done in."

Suzanne looked at Molly. She was trying to stand up and push her chair away, but even that seemed difficult for her. She had both hands on the table and she was swaying. "Okay. Come on, Mol. Let's go to your living room, where there are real chairs." She took Molly's elbow and steadied her. "Let's go put our feet up and let the youngsters clean up, okay?"

Molly looked up at Suzanne's face. "Don't you patronize me, my girl."

Suzanne rolled her eyes. "Fine. Just get your ass into your own side of the house then, you old wart. Come on." She tugged on Molly's arm.

When she'd gotten Molly through the pantry door and into her own kitchen, Munchie worrying at her feet all the way, Suzanne stopped. Molly was leaning her whole weight against her. It wasn't much weight, since Molly was small, but it was enough to alarm Suzanne. Molly didn't usually lean. She tightened her arm around Molly's shoulders. "You want to sit in your rocker, Mol?"

Molly sighed. "No. I want to go to bed. I've been sitting up too many nights. I've been trying too hard. Maybe even looking in the wrong direction, fighting the wrong force. I don't know. Even that child Ronelle has ideas I didn't think of." She reached up a hand and rubbed her eyes. "I'm not what I used to be. I wish, now, I'd taken an apprentice, some hearty young witch to teach. But, hell, I thought I'd last forever, you know. But I'm getting tired." She shook off Suzanne's arm. "Not so tired that I need to be tucked into my bed like a child. I'll go up on my own, thank you."

Suzanne watched as Molly, Munchie at her heels, walked slowly across the kitchen. At the dining room doorway, Molly turned and spoke. "You all can sit in my living room, if you want to. I'd like that Charles Clark to stay around tonight, Suzanne. All night, if he will. And that mixed-up, skinny Ronelle—she should not go back and sleep in that office, in that nasty empty building tonight. She can take my couch." Molly straightened her shoulders. "Listen to the wind, Suzanne. It's picking up. Sniff the air. There's still a lot of stink to it." She lifted her head, listened and nodded. "Stay in. Stay warm. Lock the doors. Don't answer the knock, okay?"

"What knock?" Suzanne felt an icicle slip down her back.

"Ha. Any knock. Any one at all."

But in the few minutes she'd been gone, Ronelle had already an-

swered the front doorbell. Pear, seeing Ronelle heading down the hallway, hadn't even dared to bark. Apple had stayed in her chair, nose
tucked firmly under her tail. So it had been a quiet entry when Morris
came into the house, a burst of freezing air at his back, a bouquet of
red roses in his hand.

Suzanne stopped short in her kitchen. Charles was standing at the
sink, soapsuds dripping from his hands. Ronelle, towel over her shoulder, had ushered Morris into the kitchen and now stood, looking at
Charles, who was looking at Morris with distinct displeasure.

Ronelle turned to Suzanne. "Um, boss? You got a visitor."

Morris smiled broadly and held out the flowers. "Ah, Ms. Brown. I
had a thought about your dissertation. I just had to tell you my idea.
And I know how much you like roses, in winter, especially in your
bath." He turned to Charles. "You've hired a domestic? How nice."

Charles shook the suds from his hands and stood up. "Professor.
Charles Clark, Chief of University Police." He took the towel from
Ronelle's shoulder and dried his hands, slowly and thoroughly, every
finger separately. "I think we've met. You were very drunk. You were
bothering Ms. Brown. Maybe you still are." He handed the towel back
to Ronelle and turned to Suzanne. "This man bothering you, Suzanne?
Or did you invite him to your house?"

"Oh come now." Morris put the roses on the table. He was still
smiling. "I don't need an invitation, Mr. Clark. Suzanne and I are old
friends. I've had free entry here for a long, long time. We are great
friends, aren't we, my dear?"

Suzanne stood very still. "We used to be, Morris."

"See? I think Suzanne wants you to leave." Charles moved to the
table and picked up the roses. "And you can take these with you. Flowers out of season stink of fakeness, I always think. They're just not
real."

Morris looked over Charles's shoulder, at Suzanne. "Real enough
last time, weren't they, when you were so lusciously naked in your
bath? Petals like little red tongues against your skin. You appreciated
my winter roses then, didn't you?"

"Fuck that, Professor. Leave her alone, okay?" Charles moved very close to Morris. His shoulders were tensed. "She doesn't want your lousy roses. Do you, Suzanne?"

Everyone in the room stared at Suzanne, waiting for her answer. Then Ronelle chirped out, "Oh, my. Look at the time. I gotta run. I got work to do. Come on, boss. Walk me to the door?"

Suzanne shook her head. "Ronelle, you're not going anywhere. Molly wants you to stay. Morris, please go. Things are very confusing right now. Charles, you go too." She raised her chin and looked into Charles's dark eyes. "I mean it. Please."

Morris stepped forward. His face was blank, impossible to read. "I really did have a thought, Suzanne, about your work. I honestly did think I could help you out. I'm sorry if I intruded. I see that you are determined to go it alone and I've always respected that. And you. Please remember that." He leaned over and picked up the roses. "Mr. Clark. Clearly these ladies wish to be alone. Shall we go?"

Charles didn't answer. He was already heading for the door.

Ronelle collapsed into a kitchen chair. "Showdown at the OK Corral!" she said. "Two guys fighting over you! How cool was that?"

Suzanne lowered herself carefully into another chair. Her legs were shaking. "Not cool at all. It was stupid. Men are the stupidest things in the world. All of them."

"Yeah, well. That's true. But still." Ronelle twisted a braid around a finger. "Um. You been with both those guys? As in, been with? I mean, they both seemed to think they had some kind of claim, you know? Like they'd pissed on the same tree, marked their spots."

"No one has a *claim*, Ronelle. No one has pissed on this tree. And, even if they have, it washes off. Always remember that—it washes off." She stood up again. "Come on. I meant what I said. Molly says it's too cold for you to go out again. She wants you to sleep on her couch. I'll take you over."

"Way cool." Ronelle stood up. She reached a hand out and touched

Suzanne's arm. "Hey. What about that Sam guy? The dead guy? The poet. He have a claim?"

Suzanne felt her eyes fill up. "No. He had no right to a claim. He was married, remember?"

"Oh yeah. I remember. That spooky blond wife. Jesus. Why can't these married dudes save it for the home front? Why bother us? What's their problem?"

"I don't know. I don't care. I'm going to bed. Come on. Your couch awaits."

But, of course, when she got into bed, Plum curled up in the curve of her back, a purring pillow of warmth, Suzanne couldn't sleep. She closed her eyes and relaxed her muscles, one by one, but her brain churned. What a day. So unlike Crusoe on his island, alone with the wind and the sand and the goats. And one lousy umbrella. Her day was loaded with other characters. She started ticking them off on her fingers, going chronologically since dawn: Charles. Morris. Rachel, Angela, Morris (again). Charles, on the phone, telling her about Diana. Some child named Tiffany (by note). Molly. Munchie, possessed by a demon. The ER. That cute nurse. Ronelle. (Leon, in spirit.) Molly (again). Charles (again). Morris (again). She rolled onto her back, up-setting Plum, who stalked to the end of the bed and jumped down. The thing was, she realized, that she didn't trust any of them. Not really. Well, Molly—but even Molly was admitting that she was fallible and that was a scary thing. She sat up, plumping the pillow behind her. What a pathetic state of affairs: she had all these people buzzing around her and she was leery of most of them. Downright scared of some. She thought: Morris had been a friend for two years. They'd had sex without strings, affection without love, companionship without commitment. But, now, he seemed to want more. He didn't seem so undemanding. But that was probably her own fault—he was probably just a bit miffed about Charles. Charles. She felt a softness in her thighs, just whispering his name. She was afraid she could really fall for Charles.

He'd been lovely in bed. But she couldn't trust him either. He was a cop; he looked at her, sometimes, as if she was nothing more than a suspect. And he'd seen that drawing, that fat, greedy, toothed-cunt drawing and he'd known it was her. Automatically. Recognized her. She clenched her hands. Charles was a cop. She would not forget that again. Leon. Another long-term friend, turned skunk. Rachel et al, dissertation committee. Too horrible to contemplate. The cute nurse—someone to hold in reserve, for when she was ready to let her LaFleshe side loose again. Ajax and his poor Jennifer. Diana. She shuddered, pulling the blankets to her chin. Totally spooky—Ronelle was right. Well, then, Ronelle. A thief, liar, wild child. Winning, smart, needy, but, essentially, unknown. Molly. She closed her eyes. Molly. She tried to get comfort from Molly; she wanted to think of Molly as wise-woman, helper, mentor. Grandmother. Guide. But Molly was slippery, evasive. Called herself a witch, seemed to know things—but who knew what. And Molly had made her dog go nuts. She had let that little poodle turn vicious and she'd made him actually *bite*. What could you think about that?

She pulled her knees up and ran her hand down to the gauze on her ankle. True, it didn't even hurt. True, the holes were almost closed, as if Molly's black goo really did have some sort of healing magic. Still. Still. What kind of grandmother turned her dog on you?

And Sam. Sam was gone. He'd checked out, early. On purpose, maybe. And he hadn't, it seemed, exactly been the fine soul she'd thought. And now he was gone.

And someone hated her enough to draw those pictures, to drop off those notes. Someone who knew where to find her and how to hurt her.

That was it, wasn't it? That was enough, surely. Lots of people to distrust. But someone to trust, completely? Someone who was totally and absolutely on her side, come hell and high water? There was no one—no one like that. She turned back onto her side. "Come on, Plum," she called. "I won't move again." But even the cat had abandoned her, curled up now on the radiator, tail swinging.

The wind came up suddenly. Fiercely. All at once, it seemed, things began crashing around outside. Suzanne woke up afraid, with strange noises in her ear. Plum was on the window sill, back arched, fur bristling. Suzanne got up and went to the window. Tree limbs were waving wildly against the sky, backlit by the moon. Scraps of cloud rushed across the moon's face, solid one minute, torn apart the next. Objects—pieces of paper, plastic bags, garbage can tops—were running ahead of the wind, sailing across the icy ground.

Plum's eyes were disks of yellow. She was making a noise Suzanne had never heard, a kind of low growling in her throat. "Come on, kitty," she said. "It's just the wind." She reached out and touched the spiky fur on the cat's back. Plum looked at her and hissed. Suzanne backed up. She switched on her bedside lamp and looked at the clock. Three forty-eight. She was searching for her moccasins when the light went out. The little green numbers on the clock, too. She sat down on the floor. Fine. Great. Just like every bad movie ever made. She heard Pear start to whine, outside the bedroom door. And Apple's nervous toenails, clicking up and down the hall. All right, she thought. There are candles in the kitchen. This is not supernatural; this is a winter wind storm. In Albany. In January. This happens, all the time. Naturally. This is not the wendigo, come to call. She stood up, barefoot. The room wasn't totally dark, after all. There was enough moonlight to see. She could certainly find her way to the kitchen. The minute the bedroom door opened, Apple launched into the room, quivering and leaping. Suzanne ignored her, found Pear's solid head under her hand and let him lead her down the dark staircase. The noise of the wind was all around her as she followed Pear through the dining room and into the kitchen. She looked out the windows into the back yard. It was full of movement and whirl. Snow blowing, trees bending, broken branches skittering along the ground. A kind of constant screeching howl.

She fumbled inside the junk drawer next to the sink until her fingers found matches and some candle stumps. She lit one and set it into a saucer. She shoved the others into her pocket. "Come on, dogs," she said. "We better check on Molly."

In a line, Suzanne, then Pear, then Apple headed into the pantry. Plum slipped in behind them, her back still arched, her tail a thick broom of bristles.

Molly's living room couch was empty. Suzanne called, trying to whisper and yell at the same time. "Ronelle? Where are you?" No one could hear her over the wind, she realized and she headed for the stairs.

When she got to Molly's bedroom, the door was open. She felt odd, going in. She'd never been in Molly's room before. She stopped in the doorway. "Ronelle?" she whispered. "Are you in here?"

Molly's voice was sharp above the wind. "Oh, yes. She's here. This child was made a bit uneasy by the wind. I let her climb in with me."

Suzanne held the candle higher and went into the room. Molly's bed was an old four-poster, covered in quilts and blankets. Up against the pillows, Molly sat, propped against the headboard.

Ronelle sat beside Molly, leaning against her shoulder. Her eyes were wide. "Hi, boss," she said. "I freaked. Trailers blow over in storms. I got scared."

Suzanne shook her head. "This house is a hundred years old. It won't blow over."

The words weren't out of her mouth before sounds of crashing came from above their heads. Both dogs slid under the bed. Ronelle slipped down into blankets and put her hands over her head.

Molly started to laugh. "Yep. Hundred year old slate roof. Some of those suckers always come loose in this sort of wind. Fly all over the place." A huge gust of wind shook the window. Suzanne could see dark squares flying past the glass. Molly sighed. "See? They'll be all over the yard, tomorrow morning. Once," she added, poking Ronelle's shoulder, "once, a slate came right through the dining room window. Shattered the glass and stuck into the hardwood floor. Like a thrown knife, embedded in that wood like it was jello. Quite a thing." Ronelle groaned.

Molly sighed. "Come here, Suzanne. You might as well get into bed, too. We're better off together, night like this. Those dogs have the right idea—Munchie's been under the bed for an hour, even before it got bad. Munch knows trouble when he hears it."

Suzanne slipped out of her bathrobe and put the candle on the bed table. Awkwardly, she got into Molly's bed. It was very high—an old-fashioned bedstead. The mattress was hard as a rock. Her bare feet were icy and she rubbed them together. The wind continued to hurtle slates past the window. She could hear them crashing to the ground. "Jeez, Mol," she said. "Does this happen often? I mean, won't it cost a fortune to repair the roof?"

Molly laughed. "Not often. This is rare. This is just a bit special, I think, this kind of winter wind. Happens more often in summer, in big old thunderstorms. Anyway, I won't have to the pay to fix the roof, not this time."

"Why not?"

Molly shifted against the pillows. "You'll see." She poked Ronelle's shoulder again. "You're surrounded by woman-flesh, my girl. You're safe."

Ronelle sat up. She squiggled her skinny shoulders up against the headboard, nestling between Suzanne and Molly. "All right," she said. "Cool. Now, why doesn't someone tell me a story? I need a night-night story. Come on, aunties, tell little Ronnie a fairy tale."

Suzanne groaned. But Molly nodded. "Fine. Let me tell you the one about the girl who leaves the path in the forest. The girl who meets the wolf. The girl who opens the door to Bluebeard's secret room. The girl whose stepmother demands her bloody heart on a silver tray. The girl who pricks her finger, bleeds and falls asleep. The girl who's always losing her first-born, her first love, her stupid little heart…."

"Stop. Okay, stop. I get it." Ronelle sank back under the covers.

"They're all horrible, aren't they? All the stories?"

"Of course they are," Molly said. "They're warnings, about real life. They are absolutely real. Pay attention. Keep safe." She rested her head against the pillows and sighed. "Now go to sleep, all of you. I'm tired."

Suzanne felt herself growing warm and sleepy, despite the howling, screaming wind. She felt as if Molly really were taking care of her, letting her sleep, making her safe. She blew out the candle and curled up, moving Ronelle's sharp elbow from her side, and slept.

In Suzanne's dream, the owl landed on the bed post. She knew it by its stench and she pulled her feet away. Molly and Ronelle were sound asleep and so only she saw the owl. It was holding something in its talons, something feathery, limp and dead. A bird of some kind, small. The dead bird was still warm, blood still dripping from its torn throat, its black eyes open and empty. The owl dropped the dead bird on the quilt and began to tear into it with its sharp beak. It gouged pieces of guts and flesh and feather out of its soft belly and swallowed them. Its round yellow eyes glowed and its beak shone in the moonlight, wet with blood. Its own feathers were sleek and healthy; they glistened. The owl ate, greedily and steadily. When there was nothing left of the little bird, not a beak or a bone, the owl unfurled its great wings and beat them, hard. Soft little bits of down floated up, tiny bits of feather. The wings made a noise like the wind and the owl opened its throat and screeched. It lifted off the bed in a great rush of feather and stinking claws. It disappeared, out the open window, into the frozen night.

In her dream, Suzanne understood perfectly. She knew what it meant, the owl, the wind, the bloody cannibal meal. Like to like. It was profound and simple and satisfying, this knowledge the owl had brought. But when she woke up, she'd forgotten what it meant and she could not get it back.

25

The wind had stopped. The sky was now gray with clouds and it had grown quiet. Suzanne opened her eyes into soft dawn light and tried to remember where she was. Ronelle, curled up against her side, reminded her. She sat up, slowly and quietly, looking at the faces of the women in bed with her: Ronelle looked about ten years old, her face smooth, her breathing deep and steady. But Molly looked about a hundred. She was still propped against the headboard. Her mouth was open and her breathing was rapid, shallow. Her eyelids twitched and her fingers scrabbled at the edge of the covers. Her forehead was coated with a wash of sweat. She kept muttering and jerking; she sounded angry, as if she was fighting someone in her sleep. Suzanne watched her, for a minute, wondering. Who was it that attacked Molly in her sleep? Who dared?

She felt a wet nose in her side and turned to see Pear standing beside her. He'd just come out from under the bed and he looked worried. He pushed his nose into her ribs and whined. He wanted, she could tell, to be back on his own side of the house. He wanted things to be normal. She nodded at him and touched one soft ear. She slid her feet from under the covers and stood up. Apple's pointy little snout emerged from under the bed. Suzanne reached down and scooped her up, before she could start bouncing and wake everyone up. "Shhh," she said, clutching the wriggling dog to her chest.

She bent down and tried to see Munchie below the bed, too. She couldn't. If he was there, he was too far under to worry about. She held Apple tight and let Pear go ahead, down Molly's stairs and into her living room. Plum was curled into Molly's black wool afghan and she didn't look like she was ready to get up. "Fine," Suzanne said. "Sleep in. I'll make breakfast for everybody."

The trip around the block with the dogs was interesting, to say the least. The neighborhood was strewn with junk. Branches lay cracked across the sidewalks. Slates from everybody's roofs were stuck in the snow like black arrowheads, sharp and deadly. Pear picked his way delicately, looking up at Suzanne with every step. His tail hung low and heavy. "I know, I know," she told him. "It's a mess. But you didn't make it. It's okay." As they walked, light snow began to fall.

She was glad to get back to the warmth of her kitchen. The power had come back on and the furnace was working. The lights and the stove, too. She opened her fridge and got out eggs and buttermilk. She went to the pantry and got the flour and maple syrup. She hadn't made Molly's waffles last night, after all. But she could have pancakes this morning. She'd surprise her—bring her breakfast in bed. Both of them—Ronelle and Molly. She felt bad that she'd doubted them, last night. They were her friends. Of course they were. They'd kept each other safe in the wild windy night. Of course they were safe, she thought. Safe as houses. She started to hum, pouring flour into the mixing bowl.

When the phone shrilled, she grabbed it on the first ring. "What?" she said. Jesus, it was early on a Sunday morning. Who would have the gall? "What?" she repeated into the silence.

A voice grated in her ear. "I'm sorry to call you at home, Ms. Brown. It's Ajax Swenson."

She groaned and picked up a measuring cup. "What do you want?"

"I just wanted to assure you that things are going well with the tribute to Dr. Tindell, the student magazine. The outpouring of material has been gratifying. Not all of it is good, of course. I've had to make choices. And I wondered if I might ask you—is it, do you think, appropriate to print pieces from people who—ummm—seemed to have an unusually close relationship to Sam? As in physical relationship. We've gotten some poems that, well, are a bit explicit."

The smarminess of his voice nearly oozed through the phone line. Suzanne closed her eyes. "No, it is not appropriate," she said through gritted teeth. "Dr. Tindell has—had—a wife, Ajax. Think about her."

There was a long pause. Then he said, "That smacks of censorship, don't you think? As editor, I have to uphold my belief in free speech. I have to…."

Suzanne heard the snarl in her own voice as her eyes snapped open and she slammed a metal spoon down. "Listen, you little prick," she said. "Dr. Tindell's wife has enough grief. And you might think a bit. You say that Dr. Tindell changed your grade, the night he died. You say that you saw him, that you went to his office. And I don't believe you, not for a minute. I was in the building that night—and I never saw you. I think, Mr. Swenson, that you are a lying little prick. That you filled in that change-of-grade form yourself and signed Sam's name. You're taking advantage of his death." She caught her breath and waited. She hadn't thought of any of this before. It just came out, now. But now she was certain. The slimeball kid had fudged that form to get his beloved A. Or, even worse, he had been there that night. He'd fought with Sam and…. She felt dizzy.

The voice was smooth and undisturbed. "You're mistaken, Ms. Brown," he said. "I saw Sam; he gave me the form. I left the building, apparently, before you arrived."

She leaned against the wall. "Have you told this to the University police, Ajax?" she asked.

"Of course I have. I spoke to Mr. Clark personally. Perhaps he just hasn't shared all his information with you, Ms. Brown. Thank you for your advice on the magazine. I will take it into consideration." He hung up before she had a chance to slam the phone in his ear.

Ronelle surprised her, slipping into the kitchen before even the first batch of pancakes was done. She was yawning, pulling her sweaters on over her head. She stopped and sniffed. "Oh, man. You're cooking again? That smells so good."

Suzanne, waiting for the little holes to appear in the tops of the pancakes, looked up from the griddle for only a minute. "You're up early," she said.

"With the chickens, I told you." Ronelle yawned again. "I got to get some work done, boss. I mean, I have these classes, you know? I got to get back to the office, to my files." She sat down at the table. "Is there coffee yet?"

Suzanne nodded. She flipped the three pancakes over. "In the pot. I was going to give you breakfast in bed, but since you're up, you can eat here. Is Molly awake?"

Ronelle was pouring coffee into a mug. "Nope. She was perfectly quiet when I got out of bed. Sound asleep."

"Okay, then. You eat, then I'll bring her some." She slid the pancakes onto a plate and handed it to Ronelle. She took the pan of maple syrup, gently heating on the stove and put it on the table. "And, while you eat, I'll tell you what an utter ass you are, okay?" She thought of telling Ronelle about Ajax's call, to let her know that her little list of suspects might be on target, but she thought that perhaps it was best to focus on Ronelle's personal transgressions, keep her humble a bit longer.

"Great." Ronelle grinned. "As long as you keep feeding me like this, you can tell me anything you want."

Suzanne stood by the stove and poured more batter onto the griddle. Then she turned to watch Ronelle eat. It still did something to her, to her heart, to watch that skinny girl fill herself up with good food. It touched something she hadn't known was in her. Something, God forbid, motherly. So she folded her arms over her chest and started: "First of all, you should have *asked* if Leon was married. Asked me or asked him. I'd have told you. He'd have lied, but you'd have been able to tell. Second, you shouldn't have been screwing around anyway, with someone you'd known like, what, five minutes? Third…wait a minute. I have to think of a third." She turned back to check the pancakes.

"Yessir, boss," Ronelle said. "You're right. You're absolutely right. Just keep cooking, okay?"

So, Ronelle wasn't humble; in the night, she'd somehow recovered her cockiness and confidence. Well, good food would do that to a girl, wouldn't it? Suzanne smiled at her and poured more batter onto the griddle.

After she'd seen Ronelle out the door, she fixed a tray for Molly. It was fun, making it up. A nice hot mug of coffee, a steaming stack of buttered, syruped pancakes. A glass of orange juice. A pretty napkin, silverware. Fixing something nice for someone else could keep her worries at bay. She wished she had some flowers, to put in a little bud vase. She should have kept at least one of Morris's red roses.

Still, the tray looked lovely. She carried it through the pantry door carefully, barring the dogs from coming with her. Then even more carefully up the stairs to Molly's bedroom. When she got to the bedroom door, she spoke. "Surprise, Mol. I've got your breakfast. Are you awake?" There was no response, so she went in. She set the tray on the dresser and turned toward the bed. "Smell that? Your pancakes, madam, special delivery."

Molly sat propped against her pillows, her head back, her mouth open. Curled on her chest, teeth bared, was Munchie. A low growl came from his throat.

Suzanne stood very still. She could feel a spot of ice begin in her chest. It expanded. It was heavy and it was stopping her heart.

"Molly?" she whispered. She took two steps toward the bed.

Munchie stood up. He was shaking. His sharp feet were digging into Molly's chest but she did not move. He growled again.

Suzanne stood still. The ice in her chest spread to her belly. Then to her legs, creeping down, filling her whole body. "Oh, God," she said. She took two more steps. She held out one hand, leaning toward the trembling little poodle. "Hush. It's just me." The dog's tail gave one small wag and the growling stopped. He started to whine. He walked down Molly's body, inching toward Suzanne.

When he reached her, he pushed his curly little head into her hand. When she came around the side of the bed and took Molly into her arms, he leaned against her, every muscle in his body quivering.

She held Molly's head against her breasts. She rocked. She rocked and rocked, crooning a little song she didn't know she knew. She rocked, stroking the old white head. She ran her hands across Molly's face, closing the open eyes. She rocked.

Far away, on the other side of the house, Pear started to howl. Apple's voice joined his. Long and wild, the oldest song in the world. Keening. Beside her, Munchie put up his tiny jaw and added his voice. In the middle of the dogs' grief, Suzanne rocked and sang.

She saw Plum jump to the top of the dresser and begin to lick the butter from the pancakes as they grew cold. She saw the clouds outside the window thicken and the snow falling, fast and hard.

She rocked.

Part V: *Conspirator with Starvation*

Windigo is a conspirator with starvation.

Howard Norman, *Where the Chill Came From*

26

Terrible dreams filled Diana's head, the night of the wind. In the dreams, she was being fed. Tubes forced down her throat, horrible foods sent down the tubes and into her belly. She couldn't see the stuff they were shoving into her, but she could smell it. It was vile—creamy, fatty, thick, sweet. Chokingly sweet. Honeyed, sugared, milky stuff. She fought. Of course she did. Her limbs were strapped down but her mouth was free. She spat and bit; once, at least, she felt her teeth meet in the flesh of someone's arm. But they were stronger and there were more of them. Doctors in green masks. Nurses in stained white. They chattered among themselves, laughing as they fed her. They spoke her name: "Diana," they said, "Diana, be still. Relax. We are trying to help you."

Her belly grew so full that it ached. It blew up into a round ball of pain. It pushed down into her groin and up into her chest. It filled every space in her body. It bent her rib bones out and pressed against her heart. She could not breathe. She could not move. And still the happy doctors and nurses pumped in the food.

She awoke in the black, howling night wind with such a weight on her chest that she could not sit up. She lay pinned to the hard bare mattress. Her chest was pressed down, aching. Her belly was a ball of fire. She set her teeth and thought: Perhaps it is just a dream. Just that thing that Sam called the Night Mare, the horse who sits on your chest in the night, crushing. It will go away by morning.

But she did not believe in Sam's silly stories. She did not believe that it was just a dream. She knew it for what it was: someone who hated her; someone who wanted her dead. Someone whose great weight, lifted by the winds, came flying through the night and landed here, on her heart. Someone fat and heavy and crushing.

Oh yes. Diana knew what she knew and she gritted her teeth. Diana was strong. Diana was a match for this. She tightened every muscle in her body and she lay rigid under the great weight, under the fire. She endured.

When the wind died and the gray dawn lightened the sky, the weight lifted. Not like a dream ending but like the end of a war, the cessation of a long siege. The enemy's unwilling surrender. She heard the groan, felt the wrenching away as the crushing force rolled like a huge stone from her body. She watched it go—a jagged, solid thing that rolled across the floor, getting smaller and smaller as it went. In the end, a pebble. Nothing. She sat up. She took in air. She smiled. She almost laughed; she had won.

She stood. Her legs were weak but they did not shake. She would not let them shake. She had work to do. She sipped water and ate nothing. It did not matter—she'd had victory for breakfast, hadn't she?

Diana headed into the gray morning. She slipped outdoors and stretched her arms. She was invisible. A mere sliver of morning moon, hidden by clouds. Still there, still pulling against the sea. Still the center of powerful gravity. Still the mistress of tide and time. But unseen. Walking quickly in the dawn light, Diana disappeared.

27

Suzanne did not know what time it was or how long she'd been sitting with Molly's body in her arms. But when the phone rang, she felt as if it had pulled her back from a very long way away. She laid Molly's head on the pillow and stood up. She pulled the blankets up and tucked them carefully around Molly's shoulders. She nodded to Munchie, who jumped onto the bed and curled into a tight ball against Molly's side. Then she left the room, picking up the breakfast tray on her way. She closed the door behind her.

By the time she stood in her own kitchen the phone had stopped ringing. She thought. She would have to call someone. She would have to do things, now. She sat down at the table and put her head in her hands. Pear, whining, laid his head on her knee. She grabbed a chunk of his fur, wrapping it in her fingers. Molly had no children, she knew that. No family at all, that she knew of. There must be someone, though. Surely Molly had someone. But she didn't really know. No one much had come to see Molly, not that she had paid much attention to whomever knocked on Molly's door. Occasionally, she'd spotted some oddly dressed women she'd assumed were witchy types. Women dressed in capes, wrapped in dark colors. Earth worshipers, pagans, wiccans, something. But no one normal. No one you could call and say, "Please take care of this. This death." Make it go away, clean up the mess. Take my dear dead friend out of my house. Please. She leaned over and put her head into the thick black scruff of Pear's neck. Please, someone.

The phone rang again and she stood up and answered. "Yes?" She could hear that her voice was thin and shaky, a mere thread of sound. She cleared her throat and tried again. "Hello?"

"Is that you, Suzanne? You sound like you're on Mars." Ronelle's voice was unnaturally high and it, too, was shaky. "Listen. Someone trashed the office. I mean, like trashed. Stuff thrown all over."

Suzanne leaned on the wall. "What?"

"Like trashed. As in broke in and made a fucking mess. And, um, left a message on the walls and all kinds of other shit." Ronelle sounded like she was chewing on her fingers. "You better come on down. I've already called Charles. He's on his way."

Charles. Thank God. "Listen, Ronelle," she said. "Tell Charles to call me, the second he gets there. At home. Right away. It's urgent. Okay?"

"What? Are you listening? This is serious. Aren't you coming? It's your office, Suzanne. Your magazine. I'm just the hired help. I can't deal with this alone."

Suzanne closed her eyes. "Call Rachel. Her number's in the desk drawer. She'll come over."

Ronelle's voice rose into a wail. "But I want *you*, boss. This is some nasty shit and I want *you*."

"I can't come. I cannot leave the house. Tell Charles to call me. Please." She hung up on Ronelle's next wail and sat down to wait for the next ring of the phone.

Charles came. Then the ambulance came, two men with a stretcher. Suzanne stayed on her own side of the house, in her own kitchen, while they took Molly away. Charles brought her Munchie to hold in her arms, howling and shivering, while the men lifted and wrapped Molly and took her away. When the ambulance pulled away into the softly swirling snowfall, Munchie leapt from her lap and walked stiffly to the back door. She let him out and he stood for a very long time in the snow, his head lifted, sniffing the air. Then he bent his white muzzle and started to eat snow, gobbling it like meat, like he'd been starved. She watched him. What was he doing, the foolish little dog?

"Freezing his pain."

She jumped at Charles' voice, close beside her.

He put a hand on her shoulder. "Inducing numbness. My grandmother said that when her daughter—my mother—died, she ate ice for weeks. Nothing else. Cracking it in her teeth. It hurt, she said, all the way up her cheekbones and into her skull. It hurt like hell. She couldn't get enough of it, that pain. It took her mind off the other pain, she said. A little." He leaned against her. He was warm and solid and she leaned back. "You okay, Suzanne?"

"I don't know." She watched the white dog in the white snow, gorging himself with cold. She rested against Charles. "I feel like someone's ripped my heart from my chest, you know? Like there's a big hole in there. It doesn't really hurt yet, but it feels really odd. A big empty spot, right here." She put a hand between her breasts. She could almost feel it through her clothes, the empty spot that was getting ready to throb. She clutched her bathrobe. God, she'd never even gotten dressed. She pulled away from Charles's warmth and opened the back door. "Get in here, Munch," she yelled. "Stop that. Get in here."

The dog's ears dropped and he drew his muzzle from the snow. "Now."

He walked slowly back toward the house and came in, his head hanging. His little white snout was coated with icy rime.

She shut the door behind him and watched as he walked into the pantry, standing by the door to his side of the house. "Oh, God." She bent to pick him up, bringing him back into her kitchen and slamming the pantry door. "Stay on this side," she said. "Stay with us." She put him down on the floor. He wouldn't move. He just stood there, shivering. "Jesus. He's pitiful. What will I do with him?" She looked at Charles.

"Well, hell, I don't think there's a thing we can do." Charles stepped to the kitchen door and yelled. "Pear. Apple. Get in here and help your fellow canine. Now."

And they did. Pear nudged Munchie with his nose and Apple licked his cold fur. Together, they moved him into the corner, by the radiator. There, they all slumped down into a doggy heap, with Munchie on the bottom, warmed by their bodies. They all closed their eyes, and went to sleep.

Suzanne looked at Charles. "Miracle worker," she said.

He smiled. "Wish it were so simple, for us. I'd like nothing better than to take a nap. All wrapped up with my fellow human." He touched her cheek. "And you look like you haven't slept in a week."

She shook her head. "I slept last night. I slept right next to her, Charles, and I never noticed she was dying. My God." She closed her eyes, seeing Molly propped on the pillows, her brow wet with sweat. "I didn't *see*. I looked right at her, this morning, and I didn't *see*. If I wasn't so blind, so stupid, I'd have seen that she was in distress. I'd have called someone. But I'm so blind, so fucking blind. Why didn't I see?"

"Sit down, Suzanne." Charles led her to the table and into a chair. He sat down across from her and took her hands in his. "Listen to me. Molly Highsmith was well over ninety years old. She had a shaky heart—had it for years, knew all about it, chose to do nothing. Hear me? She *chose* to do nothing. She died in her sleep. It was an easy death. No one pounded on her chest, snapping her ribs. No one shoved tubes down her throat. No electric shocks, none of that. There was no hospital, no nursing home. Exactly as she wanted it. Peaceful, simple. Quick."

Suzanne pulled her hands from under his and looked into his eyes. "No it wasn't. Not peaceful, anyway. She was fighting, fighting like hell in her sleep. I saw that. She was doing battle."

He looked away. "Maybe. But still, wouldn't she want to go out fighting? Come on, Suzanne. She would. She did. Now, I'd like some of her tea if you'd care to brew up a pot. I'll call her lawyer; her affairs are all arranged. She told me that. There won't be a lot for you to do.

She'd taken care of all of it, I understand."

She grabbed his hand. "Wait. How do you know? How do you know all this?"

He leaned forward. "I told you. I've known Molly Highsmith a long time. She and my grandmother were good friends. So she called on me, once in a while, for legal advice and whatnot. She told me things—not a lot, but what she thought I should know."

She felt the empty spot in her chest begin to fill up with something thick and warm. Anger, building. "What kinds of things? She never told me. Never told me she had a 'shaky' heart or who her lawyer is. Never confided in me. Why the hell would she talk to you? Why didn't she tell me?"

He shook his head. "You ever ask, Ms. Brown? You ever volunteer to help, should she want it? Or were you too busy? Spending days with your cannibals and nights with your many friends?" His eyes grew narrow. "She was ninety years old, for God's sake. How many times did she walk your dogs for you, out in the cold? How many nights did she sit here, all alone, fighting whatever fight she felt needed fighting?"

Suzanne stood up. Her chest felt tight and hot. She could feel sweat run between her breasts. "I was her friend. I was. I cooked for her. All the time. I was her friend."

He stood, too. His voice softened. "I know you were, Suzanne. She told me you were. She said she was working on you. She loved you, I think. She said you'd brought warmth back into this old house, just when she most needed it, in her waning. She told me she was teaching you to see—trying to, any way. She thought you were teachable and, for her, that was something."

She sat back down, hard. Tears began to run down her cheeks. "But I didn't see. Just like Sam. I did not see. Didn't see that he was miserable. Didn't see that he was fucking his students. Just plain did not see. Worse. I *would* not see."

"Yeah, well. Maybe now you will." He leaned over and placed a kiss on her hair. "Go on. Go up and lie down for awhile. And then

you'd better call Ronelle. She's scared to death and she needs you. I've
got to go back on campus for awhile, but I'll come back later. You get
some rest."

Suzanne did go up to her room. She shut her door, for quiet, but she
knew she could not rest. Would not be able to sleep. So she picked up
the phone and called her office number. It rang all six times before
the machine picked up and Ronelle's official recorded phone voice
said: "You've got the Editorial Office, Fat Mag. Leave us a message.
Or not." Suzanne sighed and talked to the machine: "It's me, Ronelle.
Call me at home."

She sat back against her pillows and looked out the window. Snow
was falling harder now. God, she thought, will this winter ever end?
She closed her eyes. And how could they bury Molly, in frozen-solid
ground? Jesus. Would Molly's poor old bones have to sit around in
some—what? Crypt? Vault? Refrigerator?—all winter, waiting for the
spring thaw? There must be some system, here in the northeast, for
winter storage of bodies. Some kind of giant refrigerator/freezer
things. For human meat. That's all we are, really. Meat that spoils fast
if you don't chill it thoroughly. She felt tears building in her head but
they would not fall. They just sat, just behind her eyes, burning. The
phone shrilled and she jumped to pick it up. "Yes?"

There was loud snuffling, then Ronelle's voice. "Oh man. I am so
bummed. I can't believe I slept next to a dead woman. I can't believe
it."

Suzanne sat up, thumping her feet onto the floor. "This is not
about you. Get over that shit, Ronelle. You're lucky to have even known
her." She ran a hand through her hair and felt that it was sticking up
into greasy spikes. "And if you're sitting right there, why didn't you
answer the phone?"

"I was scared to. I was afraid the psycho who trashed the place
would call. And Charles said not to, anyway. He said to let anyone
who called talk to the tape. Then maybe we'd have some record, if the

nut bag did call. I'm just obeying orders here, Suzanne, and you don't have to get snotty with me."

Suzanne sat back. "All right. All right. I want you to tell me what happened."

"Hold on." Ronelle's voice got muffled, then came back. "Okay."

"Is someone else there? Who were you talking to?"

"Um. Just Leon. He came to help pick up the mess. I mean, he came over with some coffee and donuts and when he saw the mess, he offered to help."

Suzanne put both legs up on the bed and crossed her ankles. She noticed that the gauze square was gone from her ankle and she bent her knee, staring at the four tiny pin prick holes in the skin. No red-ness, no swelling. Molly had been right; that bite was nothing. "Leon?" she said, trying to sound entirely neutral.

"Uh huh. Now, do you want to hear what happened or not? I mean, maybe it's just too much, with Molly and all. Maybe I should wait?"

She rubbed her ankle. It didn't hurt, not at all. Why had she made such a fuss about it, anyway? "No. Tell me. Things can't get much worse, so what the hell."

"Okay then. Here goes. I got here nice and early, even though the bus had to go around all the tree branches in the street. Anyway, I came up on the elevator and as soon as I got into our hall, I knew something was wrong." Ronelle's voice was warming up. She was making a story out of it, already, an adventure.

"Uh huh. How did you know that?"

"Oh, man, the hall was freezing cold. And there was this funny breeze, like. And it smelled weird."

"Uh huh. Like what? I mean, what kind of smell?"

"Like silage! See, I know that smell—a kind of rotten-sweet fermenty smell. So anyway, I go to the office and I stop, right in front of the door. Because it's open a crack and that cold air is coming from our office! Right around the door—cold air. So, I get freaked, and I stand there for a minute, but then I just say "Shit" and I open the door. And there it is—the world's biggest mess. And the window is broken and…."

Suzanne sat up. "The window? That, like, triple-paned industrial-strength university window was broken?"

Ronelle's excitement was audible. "Yeah, yeah. Like a rock went through it, you know. A big, jagged hole through both panes of glass. So papers were, like, blown around and the computer was tipped on its side and all my food and clothes and stuff were dumped on the floor and, like, trampled and smashed and the shampoo poured out and…." Ronelle's voice paused "And then, I see the worst thing." Longer pause.

"Stop the drama, Ronelle. Jesus. Just tell me."

"The worst thing, boss, is that someone wrote on the walls. Like with black markers." Her voice lowered into a whisper. "Like I put on the chair, but now no one will blame me—they think the nut bag did that, too. Anyway, there were nasty words, in big black letters. And disgusting drawings. Charles said he'd send someone over to paint the walls, after the university police took a whole bunch of pictures of the writing. They were here all morning, doing that. They put plastic over the window. And I called Rachel and she came by, too, and took notes about it, to tell the other faculty what happened. There's going to be some kind of emergency warning to everyone in the building, you know? To keep their doors locked and stuff."

Suzanne closed her eyes. "What kinds of pictures?"

"Sick, nasty stuff, boss. Big, well, cunts, I guess. That's what the words say, too—"Fat, greedy cunt"—stuff like that. But the pictures are really ugly. They're like—what did you call them, Leon?"

Suzanne heard Leon's voice say clearly: "Vagina dentata. Like the Indians used to tell stories about. Vagina dentata."

Ronelle's voice cut back in. "Yeah, yeah. 'Vagina dentata.' As in 'toothed cunt.' Pretty vicious. Leon's been explaining, like from his Puritan research, some Indian tribes had stories about these, like, hungry cunt creatures, and…."

Suzanne's hand clenched on her ankle. "I know the stories, Ronelle.

I don't want to hear about it." She could feel the tears, pressing harder behind her eyes now. "And I don't want to see it. I won't come back in until they're painted over. I can't deal with this now, Ronelle. I'm sorry, but it's up to you."

"Yeah, well. I guess I can deal with it, now that Leon's here. I just didn't want to be alone here, you know. I was freaked at first. But I'm okay now. Except… about being here at night, you know? I kind of don't want to sleep here anymore. Leon says he can lend me some money to rent a motel room, though."

"No. No. You can't take Leon's money—he is *married*, remember? God, do you want to be his little kept floozy, the little piece on the side, in some sleazy motel room? Think about it."

There was a little silence. "I don't have a lot of better offers going on here, boss."

"Of course you do. Do you think I want to be alone in *this* house right now? You'll stay here. Tell Leon to stuff his motel room, the slimy bastard. He's just taking advantage of circumstances. Tell him to fuck off."

"Yeah, all right. I will. Later, you know—when the office is picked up and the donuts are gone. But, Suzanne, there's one thing I didn't tell you. The worst thing, I think."

"What? Let's have it."

"The picture. The vagina dentata thing—it's got a label."

Suzanne nodded. She'd known it would. "Let me guess. It says 'LaFleshe,' right?"

"Um, yeah. But a little worse—it says '*Suzanne* LaFleshe.' Right across the, um, lips, you know? And there's a huge breast, with this little guy sort of sucking…."

"I know. Don't tell me any more. I'm going now." She put down the phone. So, Charles had seen it again, that drawing. Huge, now. A wall mural, larger than life.

And Ronelle had seen it. And Leon. Rachel. Who knows how many university police. Who knows how many painters. And the word would get out—the ever-efficient university rumor-mill would grind until every graduate student and every professor would know, would laugh behind their sympathetic eyes. Morris. Dr. Littleton. Angela. Everyone.

The tears finally came, hot. Everyone had seen. Everyone knew. She was the fat, greedy cunt, the man-killing cunt. The great gaping vagina, always hungry. It was her and everyone had seen it. Her enemy was strong—and daring. And there was no Molly to help her. She pushed her face into her pillow and cried, ugly choking sobs, so hard that they hurt her ribs, tore her throat. But she could not stop, could not control herself. She stuffed the edge of the pillow into her mouth, but it didn't help. She heard the dogs whining outside her door; she heard them begin to howl in sympathy and distress. But she could not stop—nothing could make her stop.

She'd been asleep, finally, when the phone rang again. Her hand shot out and grabbed it, before she was fully awake. "What?" she said.

"Hey, listen, Ms. Brown. Okay, I admit it, I changed my poetry grade myself. I just faked Sam's signature on the form—piece of cake. Okay? But Sam would have signed it, you know, if he'd been still here. He said he would. So I don't think I should be punished, just because some teacher makes a mistake and then goes and fucking dies. I don't think that's exactly fair. Everyone knows I deserved that A—everyone. And…."

Suzanne heard her voice crack, its pitch was so unnaturally high. "Ajax, shut up. Just shut the fuck up. No one cares. No one cares about your goddamn grade. No one." She slammed the phone down and sat up, shaking.

She stood up, dizzy with anger and fear and sorrow. The closed door of her room moved slightly and she watched as an orange paw crept under the door, feeling for her, patting the floorboards. She heard soft, questioning mews and sniffs. The paw became a whole leg, stretched to its full length under the door. She sighed. The dogs had sent Plum to scout her out. The animals needed her.

28

The short day had fallen quickly into darkness. Snow was still falling and Suzanne did not bother to walk the dogs after she fed them. Munchie wouldn't eat out of the bowl she gave him and she couldn't make herself go into Molly's side of the house to get his own. "Sorry," she said, looking down at his curly head. "I just can't. Eat, or not. I can't." He sighed and walked back to the radiator and curled up against it. Apple moved quickly from her bowl to his and began to wolf his food down. Pear looked at Apple, seeming to consider whether he too should share in the bounty, but then he just walked away. Suzanne nodded at him. "You are a noble and dignified beast," she said. "You have true class and will not stoop to stealing the food of those in mourning."

She thought about making herself something to eat. It occurred to her that she hadn't eaten all day, not one bite. She opened the refrigerator and looked at the remains of the meatloaf, neatly wrapped in plastic wrap. She felt bile rise into her throat and slammed the refrigerator door. She wasn't hungry. She stopped to think about that. It was a strange sensation, not wanting to eat. She didn't even want to finish the gingerbread, snug in Tupperware on the counter. She didn't even want to dip a spoon into the bowl of leftover whipped cream. Nothing tempted her. Maybe this was what other people felt like when they said, "No, thanks, I'm not hungry." She, Suzanne Brown/LaFleshe, was *always* hungry, always had been hungry, and so she'd always assumed that other people were lying when they said that. But maybe not. Maybe that was something else she'd been wrong about. She put a hand against her belly—it felt already full. It was not demanding; it was quiet. It really did not want to be fed. She leaned against the counter and decided that tea would be enough. Simple uncomplicated Lipton, made with a good old American tea bag— none of Molly's strange stuff. She turned the flame on under the tea kettle. When the tea was ready, she found she didn't even want sugar in it. Nor honey. She squeezed a wedge of lemon into the cup. She wanted tart on her tongue, not sweet.

The doorbell rang and she hurried down the hall, hoping for Charles. Even Ronelle. The house was way too empty, now that darkness had fallen. Solitude was not what she needed. The dogs, as if permanently trained by Ronelle, did not stir from the kitchen. They lifted their heads at the sound of the bell, then buried their noses back into their tails and ignored it. It was strange, opening the door without a tumult of dog around her feet. Better, but kind of lonely. She swung the door open.

It was not Charles. Not Ronelle. No—her front porch was full of women wrapped in shawls, women holding baskets and bags. Their heads were covered by scarves and their shoulders were coated with snowflakes. There must have been a dozen of them, counting the ones who stood below the porch, ankle-deep in new snow. They stood quietly, but around them there was a kind of hum, some kind of energy. She stepped back into the hallway, wishing that Pear were right here, barking his big-dog bark. "Yes?" She heard the fright in her own voice.

The woman closest to the door stepped forward and pushed the wrapping away from her head. She was tall—taller even than Suzanne. Not many women were; it was an odd sensation to have to tilt her head up to meet the woman's gaze. Suzanne looked up into a square face, with high flat cheekbones and pale eyes. The woman's hair was dark, streaked with white bands.

"We are sorry to trouble you," the woman said. Her voice was low, gentle. But she did not smile. She spoke solemnly, formally. "We did not want you to be frightened when you heard us in Mother Highsmith's house, that is all. We wanted to let you know we were here. We will be here all night. There will be chanting, some banging. We do not want you to be frightened. It is as it should be. Your house will be free by morning."

Suzanne stepped back again. "Who are you?"

The woman bowed her head and gestured behind her. "We are a coven. We have come to honor our Mother, who has left us. We have rituals to perform. We clean the house of any evil it still holds; we open the windows to let the good air in. We make sure her spirit is free to fly out into the night, unhindered. We tell the other spirits she is on her way, so she will be welcomed. It is really very simple. And it is necessary. You will be glad we have come. By morning, you will have nothing to fear, in your house at least."

Suzanne swallowed. Her chest hurt and she clasped her robe against her breasts. "I am afraid." She heard the strange formality in her own words, the stilted diction that mimicked that of the woman. What, she thought, suddenly wanting to giggle, aren't witches allowed to use contractions? She tried again. "Actually, I'm scared shitless."

A tiny smile broke the solemnity of the woman's face and she nodded. "You should be, Suzanne. You have every right to be."

A tremor slid down Suzanne's spine. "You know my name?"

"Oh, yes. We certainly do." There was a stirring among the other women, a hint of subdued laughter. One of those on the lawn stamped her feet, shaking snow from her boots. The woman in the doorway leaned forward. "We will go in through Mother Highsmith's front door. We have a key." She turned to leave, pulling her wrap back over her hair.

"Wait." Suzanne leaned forward. "Could I come? I mean, could I watch your ritual?"

The woman turned back and her face was no longer pleasant. It was hooded under the scarf and very still. "No. We have decided that you may stay on your side of the house—and even that is unusual, a concession to our Mother's affection for you. But you will not watch and you should not listen. You are unable to understand and it will only confuse you. And," she leaned forward, "you, yourself, are a cause of some of the disturbance in this house. You have brought something in." She sighed. "We do not think that you meant to and Mother Highsmith was quite certain that you did not. But still, there is something strong working its way toward you, full of hate. We will do our best; that is all we can do." She tapped a finger against the doorframe. "Please send the dog over. The silly little Munchkin. He is needed."

Suzanne leaned her back against the door after she'd closed it. She heard Molly's front door open and she walked back to her own kitchen, shaky-kneed. Her Lipton was still steaming on the table. The whole encounter hadn't taken a minute but it had sucked all the strength from her legs. She dropped into a chair, then noticed Munchie whining at the pantry door. She stood up and let him into the pantry. She slipped the connecting door open and he dashed through, a little white arrow, heading home. She couldn't hear or see anything from Molly's side of the house but she felt cold air rushing through the door. Apparently the windows were open already.

She sat back down. Neither Pear nor Apple had moved. They lay quiet, curled up, asleep. She shook her head. Some guardians they'd turned out to be. A whole coven of crazy women had invaded their house and the dogs didn't seem to give a hoot.

The phone woke her from the stupor she'd fallen into, sitting upright in the kitchen chair, the tea cold in the cup in front of her. It hadn't been a nap exactly—surely she wasn't becoming someone who fell asleep in hard kitchen chairs—just a kind of tired, half-dream state. She'd been watching the steam from the tea, and she'd been looking for Molly in it. That was something her grandmother had taught her, that the spirits of those you had loved and lost could sometimes be spotted in the little twists of steam that rose from cups of tea, just a hint of a smile, a beloved face. "Only those who were at home in your kitchen, lovey. Only those who loved you so hard that they cannot quite leave." Suzanne hadn't remembered that, not for a long, long time and she'd almost forgotten that her grandmother called her "lovey," embarrassing her with the endearment all through her teenaged years. She'd tried to forget how desperately she'd looked for the images of her parents in every cup of tea she'd seen, for many years after their death. They'd never taken form there, never appeared to her and she'd thought, for some of those years, that that meant that they really hadn't loved her enough.

She hadn't seen Molly in the steam either but she had felt that Molly was there in the half-dream, just out of sight. A kind of presence, just beyond the edges of her vision. In the center of sight was the owl, huge eyed and still. It did not fly or move. It simply fixed her with its stare. Its beak was hooked and sharp, its talons dark with blood.

The shrilling of the phone was a relief, as it chased the owl off, flapping out the window into the black sky. She jumped up and grabbed the receiver. "Yes?"

"Hey, boss. Just me. I wanted to tell you that I'm not coming over to sleep at your house tonight." There was a rustle, as if papers were being shuffled. "Okay?"

Suzanne sat back down on the chair. "Ronelle, I don't want to be alone here." She thought about the women in the other side of the house—she was hardly alone. But still. Was the idea that the witches were here supposed to comfort her? She thought not. "And where are you going to go?"

A longer silence and more rustling. "I'm, um, going to Leon's place."

"Uh huh. And will Leon's wife be serving dinner for the three of you?"

"Look. It's none of your business, okay? But she's out of town."

"How nice." She made her words as dry as she could. "How very nice."

Ronelle's voice got louder. "Cut it out. You can't exactly claim the moral high road here, Suzanne. And he's been really good. He's been here all day, cleaning up and helping me deal. So just get off my case, okay?"

Suzanne slid down in her chair and took a sip of tea. It was bitter and cold. Horrible. "Fine. It's your life."

"Yep. It sure as hell is. And, oh, you won't be alone tonight, anyway. Charles told me to tell you that he'll be there, just as soon as he's done work. Around eight. And, Suzanne, he painted the walls of the office. All by himself—took him most of the afternoon, but that shit is gone. Well, not gone, I guess. But it's covered over. Not visible. As good as gone. And he replaced the windowpane, too. So be nice to him, okay? I think he really likes you. *Really* likes you." The phone clicked as Ronelle hung up.

Suzanne looked at the clock. Seven-thirty. She had sat in her stupor a long time. She got up, headed for the bathtub. Definitely time to wash this day from her skin.

Charles was there by 7:45. He stood outside the bathroom door and said, "Hey, Ms. Brown. The dogs didn't even come to the door and you'd left it unlocked. Are you nuts?"

Suzanne sat up in the hot water. She thought about inviting him in, but she remembered Morris, the last man she'd let in to share her bath. The last man she'd allowed to comfort her in the aftermath of sudden death. The last man who'd shown her that her body—her greedy, greedy body—did not respect grief, even her own. Her hungry body that responded, no matter how sorrowful her soul felt. She would not repeat that little mistake. She began scrubbing her arms, hard. "I'm fine. There are a dozen witches only a few feet away. No one in their right mind would come into this house tonight." She raised her legs and scrubbed them, too. "I'll be out in a minute. There's food in fridge. Help yourself."

"Thirteen," he said.

"What?" She began to pour shampoo onto her head.

"Thirteen witches. I think. I'd bet that's the whole coven, over there."

She used her fingers, hard, massaging her tired head. "Great. Whatever." She paused. "Aren't you even the tiniest bit concerned? I mean, aren't you worried about whatever shit they're doing over there? It's probably not even legal."

"Not my worry. I prefer not to mess with those people. My grandma was on good terms with witches, all her life. Not Indian-type witches, you understand. They're always evil. But the white women—pagan-type witches. Whole different thing. Anyway, they were the only white people she could stand. Except for my grandpa, apparently. And him only for the couple of nights it took to create my mother. It's wise, you know, to keep on the good side of the witches. So far, they don't seem to dislike you. If they did, you'd know it by now. So, you got leftover meatloaf in that fridge?"

The water from the handheld spray hose was running into her ears. She shook it out. "How would I know, if they disliked me?"

There was a snort, a kind of barking laugh. "Oh, you'd know. And gingerbread?"

"Yes. Everything. Go down there and have whatever you want."

"You don't want me to stay up here? Dry your back or anything?"

The water swirled down her shoulders and breasts, warm. She did. She did want his hands on her back. And on her front. She wanted him to wrap her in the biggest towel she owned. She wanted him to dry every inch of her skin, everywhere, slowly and carefully. She clenched her teeth. "No. I want you to go downstairs and eat. I am not in the mood for anything else, believe me." She waited, hoping that he wouldn't believe her. She certainly didn't believe herself.

"Right. I'll make you a sandwich." His footsteps moved away from the door and down the stairs.

She sighed. She stood up in the tub, looking down at her body. Her skin was pink and smelled sweet from the bath. Her breasts were heavy on her chest, the nipples prickly with desire. Little rills of water ran down her belly into the red-gold curls of her crotch. What a waste.

What a silly, weak, empty virtue abstinence was. How little comfort it
was, to be sensible. She closed her eyes, thinking of calling him back,
of opening her arms and her legs and letting him in. She tilted her
head back and pictured it, the pleasure of letting him fill her with
warmth and strength. But, suddenly, the picture was invaded by black
lines. On her closed eyelids, spidery lines crept and grew fat, weaving
themselves into a shape. The drawing—the monstrous woman with
the fierce cunt, drawn in thick black lines. He seen it; she'd seen it.
Neither of them would be able to forget it. She opened her eyes and
grabbed a towel. She rubbed herself so roughly that it hurt, until every inch of her body was dry. Then she dressed in a heavy wool turtleneck and stiff jeans. Nothing silken and nothing soft.

He'd made two sandwiches, piled high with meatloaf, cheese, onion,
lettuce, and tomato. He'd also made fresh coffee and the kitchen
smelled like home. She sat down at the table and watched him bite
into his sandwich. "Heavenly," he said. "Heaven is a cold meatloaf
sandwich."

She picked up her sandwich and took a bite. It felt like sand in her
mouth and she could barely swallow. She put the sandwich back on
the plate and sipped her coffee. She tilted her head toward Molly's
half of the house. She couldn't hear anything. "What do you think
they're doing over there, really? Do you have any idea what this ritual
entails?" She watched his face as he chewed. He really was handsome,
in a hawklike sort of way, his straight white hair, cut short and bristly,
a sharp contrast to the dark skin. His eyes were a deep brown, flecked
with green lights. She wanted to reach out and lay a hand on his cheek,
feel the muscles in his jaw. She folded her hands tightly in her lap.

He swallowed. "I don't know. I was taught to keep my nose out of
spirit-business. I was told to mind my beeswax and look the other
way. Better not to know. Good advice." He took another bite of his
sandwich.

She nodded. "Yeah, but it's happening in my own house. And they said it has something to do with me. Something about evil following me home. Nonsense, I'm sure. But still."

He reached across the table and tapped her plate. "Eat, Suzanne."

She picked up her sandwich. Her throat closed. She put it back down. "I can't. I'm not hungry."

"Uh huh. When did you last eat anything?" He was leaning across the table, his eyes intent.

She thought. "Last night, I guess. With you and Ronelle. And Molly." She felt her eyes filling up. "I just haven't been hungry, since then."

"Drink some coffee, at least. I put whipped cream into it." He pushed her cup towards her.

The coffee smelled wonderful, but when it touched her lips, it tasted like gall. She swallowed a tiny bit, for show, and wrapped her hands around the cup for warmth. She heard a noise coming from the back yard, a kind of high wail. She stood and went to the window. Snow was falling, straight and soft, big fluffy flakes. She listened. The wail came again, longer, full of wavering trills. She shivered. Apple and Pear were sitting up, their ears pricked, their noses twitching.

"Chanting." Charles had come to stand beside her. "They've got the windows open and they're chanting. That's all."

She stood beside him, their arms just touching. "See? You do know."

He shrugged and put an arm over her shoulders. "I've heard it before, that's all." He leaned over and put his head against hers. "It's all right, Suzanne."

She turned toward him, raising her face. She leaned against him. "Charles, I…."

The thud against the window came suddenly. She spun to see a flurry of white feathers and wings and a cruel hooked beak. Orange eyes, round and open, staring into her own. Claws spread for a second against the glass, then gone. She heard herself shriek. A stupid, girlish, terrified shriek that she could not pull back into her throat. It kept coming, a horror movie scream that she couldn't control. She put her hands over her eyes, as spinning darkness filled them. Her ears were thick with the pounding of her blood and she felt her knees give.

She was back in her chair and Charles was kneeling in front of her, his hands on her shoulders. He was speaking. At first it was just a jumble of syllables, but gradually, the words began to make sense. "Are you okay? What happened?"

She felt a warm wet nose against her elbow and looked down into Pear's eyes. He was whining and shaking, his whole black body trembling. She put a hand on his head. "Good dog," she said. "It's all right."

Charles shook her shoulders. "Jeez. You scared the shit out of me. What were you screaming about?"

She looked into his face. It was pale across the cheekbones. She shook her head. "You saw it. The owl that hit the window."

He leaned back, dropping his hands from her shoulders and laying them on her knees. "I saw a bunch of snow blow against the glass, Suzanne. What owl?"

She stared at him. "The owl. It hit the window with a big thud. You could see every damn feather. That was not snow."

He stood up quickly and turned his back. He went to the window. His shoulders were hunched under his corduroy shirt and he held his elbows in his hands. "You been seeing a lot of owls, Ms. Brown?" He spoke toward the window and his breath misted the pane.

She stroked Pear's wide head and she let Apple jump into her lap. Both dogs were still trembling. "I guess so. I've been dreaming about an owl."

"Yeah? Since when?" The circle of mist widened.

"Since the night of the ice storm, I guess. I saw it for real then. Ronelle did, too. And now I can't get it out of my head." She wrapped one of Pear's silky ears around her fingers. "But it's real, Charles. I'm not, like, imagining it. Ronelle saw it; she told me it was an owl."

He took a palm and wiped the windowpane before turning back toward her. "I know it's real, Suzanne. It's real as hell." He came back to her chair, laying a warm hand on her still-damp hair. "Listen. I have a story to tell you. I want to sit up tonight, stay awake, while those ladies are busy next door. I kind of want to keep watch. And I'll stay awake better if I talk. So let's sit down somewhere and I'll tell you one of my grandma's stories."

Suzanne didn't look at him. "There's nowhere to sit except my bed."

He laughed. "That's fine with me." He reached for her hand. "But, listen, pal. We don't make love until the ladies have done their thing. It's better not to mix death chanting and sex. In fact, it's kind of a rule—for lots of folks, actually. You know—a time to embrace and a time to refrain from embracing. So tonight I'm refraining. Don't even try to tempt me."

Suzanne was under the covers; Charles was on top of the covers on the far side of her bed, sitting up. He held Plum in his lap, flicking his fingers against her pointy ears. The cat purred, obviously in some kind of feline ecstasy. Both dogs, strictly against household rules, were curled at the foot of the bed. Charles had invited them up, saying "It's an unusual night. The dogs need their pack." Charles had also instructed Suzanne to wear her warmest, least sexy nightgown. So she was neck high in flannel, curled up against her pillow.

Charles leaned his head back against the headboard and began to speak. "This is how I heard it told. There is remembered, from a long time ago, a winter of great difficulty." His voice sounded different, soft and slow, rhythmic. Deeper.

Suzanne touched his arm. "What's with the voice?"

He shrugged. "Give me a break. I haven't got much practice at this. And this is how you tell it. That's all."

"Tell what?"

He sighed. "You are one ignorant white woman. Stories. My grandmother's stories. You sit quietly by the fire—or in bed, if that's all you've got—and you repeat the tales you've heard a million times before. Cree stories. From way up north. That's where she came from, my grandmother, way up there in Canada before she moved down south to New Hampshire. Only my grandmother would call New Hampshire 'south,' I know. But she grew up way way up there. Land of the northern lights. Lakes and trees and snow and animals and not much else. But lots of stories."

Suzanne sat up a little, leaning on an elbow. "I'd like to hear about her. My grandparents were from Maine and I thought that was pretty far north—and pretty damn cold."

"Ha. You don't know cold, girl. And I'll tell you about my grandmother some other time. Tonight, you get to hear this story. So lie down and listen." He put a hand on her head. "Lay your head down and stay quiet."

She snuggled back down under the covers. "Okay. Tell."

He nodded. "This is how I heard it. The winter was terrible and there was little food. Wapukasew lived near Black Ice Marsh and sometimes, when he was checking his traps and his nets, he slept on an island in the middle of that swamp. It was a bad place, always foggy, always dark. You know what that is—a place of twilight, all day. A place of steaming, misty light. They never fished in that marsh. One day, Wapukasew saw a heron walk into that marsh. It walked in on two good legs but when it touched that marsh water, its legs disappeared. The heron had to rise and fly. When it did, it had no legs hanging behind it. That heron's legs were gone. It had to fly forever because it could not stand. Wapukasew saw this. You can see why he did not fish there.

But I will tell you that Wapukasew did sleep out there on the island, alone, one winter night. It was a bad winter, a terrible cold, hungry winter and the people were starving. Wapukasew was looking for animals for meat and he thought he could find some, if he stayed out there all night, where no one else dared to hunt. Even though others had told him that a Wendigo lived in that marsh. They told him to keep the fire going strong all night if he went out there."

Suzanne tapped his arm. "Wait, wait. Tell me exactly what that is, a wendigo. I read a little but I can't quite picture it."

Charles's voice came back to normal. He shifted, pulling on Plum's ear. She squeaked and he let go. "Lucky for you. If you could picture one, I mean really see it in your head, you could become one. Even if you dreamed about one, it could happen. So don't try."

She nodded. "All right. But you've got to explain a little."

"Yeah, a little. Okay. A wendigo, at least in my grandmother's version, is a skinny bony thing, all covered with ice. It's a winter creature, living in the coldest, darkest time of year. Its skin is sort of transparent, bluish. Its hair is like icicles, all long and stringy and pale and drippy. It's always starving, so it eats people. But even after a hearty meal of human flesh, it's still starving. Its belly is always empty, always hungry for the taste of human meat. It can never rest from killing and eating. And it moves fast. It travels on the cold winds and nothing much can stop it."

"Huh. I read it was a giant monstery thing, walking across the woods on snowshoes made of the tops of pine trees. Like, huge."

He sighed. "Will you shut up? I'm telling you what my grandmother told me, not what some white anthropologist doink put in a book. Now shut up, okay?"

She smiled to herself: white anthropologist doinks were worthless. That's what she'd tell her committee, next time they brought up that crap. "Okay."

"So. My grandmother's wendigos were dried-up, skinny, starved, mean-spirited people who started to look at their own families funny—started to look at their own daughters and sons and mothers and husbands like they were meat. If the wendigo spirit steals into someone's heart, the heart turns to ice and the teeth sharpen and the belly screams for human meat. Wendigos walk the woods, yeah, but they also walk the village. That's the worst kind. So there are two kinds—the wild woodsy kind and the right-in-your-own-backyard kind. Got it? This story is about the wild kind."

Suzanne scrunched her pillow under her neck, settling in to listen. "Got it. Go on."

"All right." The storytelling voice came back. "This is how I heard it. Wapukasew did not come home. Several days passed and still

Wapukasew was not seen. The people in the village believed that the Wendigo had surely killed and eaten him. They knew then that they had to kill the Wendigo before it grew so bold that it left the marsh and flew to the village, on the ice winds. Five of the bravest men were chosen to kill the Wendigo. They didn't want to go, but they did. Out they went to the frozen marsh. They found Wapukasew's camp, but he was not there. Also, there were two heron feet stuck on the ice—no bird, just feet. Then they found blood splatters in the snow, all leading to a big black iron pot. In the pot were bones and bits of leather from Wapukasew's pants.

It was very dark, very cold. They sat very close to the fire. One of the men volunteered to keep watch while the other men slept. But then a loud screaming woke them up. 'What was that?' one of the men whispered, his voice shaking.

'It was a big old white owl,' said the one who had stayed awake. 'I saw it. It reached for your hearts, but it missed.'

They went back to sleep. The screaming came again. One of the sleeping men sat up quickly. 'It is back to get our livers and our lights,' he whispered.

The man who stayed awake said, 'Huh, owls can take all of you. Either stay awake or stuff your ears with deer hide. Sleep like you are deaf.' The men pushed pieces of their sleeves into their ears and went back to sleep, hearing nothing.

In the morning, the man who stayed awake was missing. The others found big red spots where he had been sitting. They set out to look for him. They found his bones, stuck into the black ice of the marsh like little white sticks.

'Huh," one man said. 'That was no owl. It was a Wendigo. We stayed safe because we slept and did not hear it call to us Not hearing the Wendigo's voice saved us.'.

The others agreed. They left the marsh and they did not return until summer, when the hot sun should have melted the Wendigo's heart of ice and the marsh had swallowed the dead men's blood and bones. They did not fish and they did not hunt. All the meat from that place was poison and they did not go there again. That is how I heard it." Charles's storytelling voice stopped. He scritched Plum's neck. She stretched under his hand, yawning, her pink tongue and sharp teeth visible.

Suzanne spoke into her pillow. "Wow. But what am I supposed to learn from that? I know there's a lesson here. Right? So just tell me."

He folded his arms behind his head and leaned back. "If I knew, I would. These stories don't come out and preach anything directly. Or even indirectly. They're not parables; they're just stories. You just listen." He leaned over, his warm breath ruffling her hair. "It's just the owl thing—it struck me, your seeing the owl in your dreams. It's not a good sign. Dreaming about owls is never a good sign, in any of the stories. It portends death. And owls and wendigos tend to hang out in the same stories, you know? Night creatures and so on. I don't like the owl dreams, Suzanne."

She shivered. "Well, neither do I. So, I should be deaf? Blind? I shouldn't try to see? But Molly told me I had to learn to see, better." She tried to laugh, poking his thigh through the covers. "I'm getting mixed messages here, oh wise shaman. And I don't believe any of it, anyway. Wendigo, shmendigo."

He laughed, his lips against her hair. "Yeah, well. I don't actually believe it either. But, hell, a little deliberate deafness can't hurt. Especially tonight. And, just sitting here, I'm getting a little tempted." He stood up, dumping Plum unceremoniously to the floor. "So you go to sleep, Ms. Brown, and dream that you're deaf. All right?"

She tipped her head and looked up at him. "What are you going to do?"

"Me? Drink coffee, eat gingerbread and read magazines. Down in the kitchen."

"Uh huh. Then you're the one the wendigo will come for, right?"

"Right. That's the plan. You sleep, me fight monsters. Deal?" He whistled and two dog heads lifted from the bed, yawning. "Come on, beasties. You're coming with me." The dogs stretched and all three animals jumped down from the bed, following him to the bedroom door.

Suzanne could feel sleep building behind her eyes, already. She felt perfectly warm, perfectly safe. "Deal," she whispered.

Suzanne slept the sleep of a child—dreamless, warm, deep. And, apparently, deaf. She heard none of the witchcraft on the other side of the wall. There were no wings, no screeches to invade her sleep. What finally woke her, near dawn, was a clutch of iciness against her legs. She woke in panic, all her muscles frozen. There was a shivering, bony, cold thing in her bed, touching her. She would have screamed, if she could have. She lay perfectly still, clenched in horror. She could feel the skeleton of the thing and it was made of ice. She took a deep breath, preparing to leap from the bed.

A tiny voice from beside her said, "Sorry, boss. I didn't mean to wake you up. Charles said I could sneak in with you. There's no other bed."

The fear flew from her limbs and hot indignation surged in. She sat up, reaching for the lamp switch. Its flood of light showed the tangled hair and pale face of the bony cold thing in her bed. "Jesus fucking Christ, Ronelle," she said. "You scared the shit out of me." She started to sweat and shake. She swung her legs out of the bed and stood up. Her long flannel nightgown was rucked up around her hips and sticking to her damp chest.

Ronelle looked up from the pillow. "You look like an avenging angel. Your hair is like a halo, I swear."

Suzanne ran her hands through her hair. It was sticking straight up, like some cartoon version of sudden fright. She must look like a bad joke. She pulled her nightgown down and took a deep breath. "What are you doing here?"

The pale face crumbled. "Oh, God. She came home, Suzanne. Leon's wife came home. She walked into her own house in the middle of the night and slipped into her own bed, with her own husband. And found me. Oh, God. It was awful." Ronelle's thin fingers clutched the covers to her chest. "I mean, the woman was right there, two inches from my sorry naked self, screaming in my face. It was the worst. The absolute worst. I ran out and I walked and walked, in the snow. I didn't know where I was, at first, until I found Western Avenue. And then I walked, like, three miles, uphill, until I got here. I'm so fucking cold." Ronelle opened her mouth and started to wail.

There wasn't much choice. Suzanne sat back down on the bed and took Ronelle into her arms. She held the weeping child against her breasts, rocking and saying, "It's all right. Shhhh." The bedroom door opened and Charles's face appeared.

"Christ," he said. "What was that horrible yell?"

Suzanne looked up at him, patting Ronelle's heaving back. "Nothing. Girl stuff. We're all right." He shook his head and closed the door. Suzanne reached around Ronelle and flipped the lamp off. She settled back into bed, watching the winter dawn lighten the sky. The snow had stopped and the sky was clearing. Ronelle slept, her head on Suzanne's shoulder. When the sun broke over the treetops, Suzanne heard Molly's front door open and close. The witches, she thought, were done with their work and her house was free from evil.

29

Suzanne walked quietly down the stairs. The house was utterly quiet. There was bright light coming through the windows, the sunshine brilliant against the new snow. She stopped in the hallway, looking into her empty living room. She raised her head and sniffed the air. It smelled clean; it smelled as if the witches had done good work. She went looking for Charles.

He was asleep in the wicker rocking chair, Apple curled on his lap, Plum nestled on his shoulder, Pear at his feet. Only Pear bothered to look up at Suzanne as she stood in the kitchen doorway. His tail thumped gently on the floor. She put her finger to her lips. "Shush," she whispered.

She sat down at the table and looked at the man who was sleeping under the furry blanket of her animals. His face was relaxed in sleep, his fingers curled loosely on Apple's spotted back. His feet, in thick socks, were crossed at the ankles. He looked perfectly at home, perfectly part of the household. He didn't look like a cop, someone who carried a gun. She thought about that. This man, who told stories and made coffee and who had had a good strong grandmother, also carried a gun. Presumably, he'd used it. Never, ever in her life had she thought that she'd love a man who might, at any time, have to shoot someone. Or—her heart thumped at the idea—be shot by someone. The university wasn't exactly a raging war zone, but there were the inevitable crazies, the kids who brought guns to classrooms, knives to frat parties, pipe bombs to the cafeteria. Even to the library, holy of holy places, weapons were carried. She remembered one incident from her own time there, a few years ago. There had been a father whose daughter had gotten drunk, gotten pregnant, a father whose daughter had had an abortion and who had been dumb enough to tell her parents all about it, weeping, repentant, begging forgiveness. She'd told her father all about it, her fanatic fundamentalist, enraged father. The father brought a shotgun to the health center and aimed it at the receptionist, ranting about murder, murder, his grandchild, murder, his grandson, his flesh and blood, murderers, murderers. He hadn't killed anyone, in the end, because a university cop had grabbed the gun out of his hands. Was that Charles, that cop who had talked gently and quietly to that ranting man, who had agreed and sympathized and chatted with that man—yeah, it was a shame, what these kids got up to; it was a shame that our taxes went to supporting schools where girls were lured into sin—lulling the frantic man into a sense of security, then snatched the gun from his hands and cuffed him, facedown on the floor? She didn't know. She hadn't known him then. She'd only read about it, in the papers. She looked at him sleeping in her kitchen. It could have been him, it sounded like him, something he would do. She shifted in her chair. He could, she supposed, say anything to anyone, in pursuit of justice. Someone who hadn't told him the truth, hadn't told him half of what she knew. He could get, one had to presume, pretty ticked off about someone like that. She stared at his face. Couldn't he?

Pear stood up, slow and stiff, and walked to her chair. He put his heavy head into her lap. She rubbed his ears. Suddenly, his head lifted and he put his nose into the air. He sniffed, then started to whine. He walked to the pantry door and pushed his nose against the crack below the closed door. He breathed in great gulping sniffs, whining louder. He turned to look at Suzanne; he raised a paw and placed it gently on the door.

"What?" She stood up and opened the door, flicking on the pantry light. Pear walked into the pantry, straight to a red box on the floor, right in front of the connecting door to Molly's kitchen. He put his nose on the top of the box and sniffed again. His tail went down, his ears back. He turned, brushing past Suzanne's legs, his whole body low to the floor and slunk out of the pantry, whining.

She looked at the box. It said "Nine West" on the top, in dark blue letters. It was just an old shoebox—no, bigger. A boot box. She remembered bringing home her high-heeled boots in it and taking them into Molly's side of the house, to show her, happy with her purchase. Molly had kept the box, saying it was a useful size and had all that nice tissue paper in it, hardly even rumpled. She felt her chest tighten. She thought about waking Charles and making him open it. She shook her head: wimp. Wuss. She stepped forward and lifted the box from the floor. It was heavier than when it had held boots, definitely. She swung it to her chest and carried it back into the kitchen. She put it on the table. She looked for Pear, but he wasn't in the room. Apple's eyes were open, but she stayed curled on Charles's lap. Plum, too, was gone.

She lifted the top of the box. Pink tissue paper was wrapped carefully over the little body but it couldn't quite contain the bits of white poodle fur that curled around its edges. She felt a scream, like the owl-scream, building in her throat but she held it down. She stifled it, sending it down into her chest, stuffing it away in her pained chest. She put a hand out and lifted the edge of the pink paper.

Munchie looked peaceful, as if he'd just settled down for a nap in the box. His fur was unnaturally clean—soft and springy. Newly bathed. Carefully brushed. He smelled sweet, like fresh summer air, like a garden. White sage and lavender. Rue and hyssop. His collar was gone, replaced by a soft necklace of braided ribbons, all colors, gaily intertwined: yellow, blue, pink, green, purple.

Suzanne bent her head over the box. Tears were running down her face and she swatted them away with an angry hand. She started to shake. She turned toward the rocking chair and yelled. "Fucking witches. How could they? How dare they? Bitches. Did you know they'd do this? Did you?"

Charles woke up completely, no grogginess, no slowness. He stood up, knocking Apple to the floor, and looked into the box. "Shit." He ran a hand over his hair.

She grabbed his arm. "Did you? Did you know and not tell me? Did you let this happen?" She shook his arm, hard. "You bastard. You know about this witch stuff. You knew, didn't you?" She could feel blood thumping in her ears, boiling with anger.

He put a hand on her shoulder. "Hey. Cut it out." He sighed. "No, I did not know."

She looked into his face and saw something, some kind of shutter inside his eyes, a shutter that snapped closed. Right then, she saw it: his eyes turned into cop eyes, secretive, untelling. "You liar." She shook off his hand and stepped back from the table. "You knew. You let this happen. Jesus, Charles. A tiny little dog."

He lowered his eyes. "All right. I suspected. Munchie was her familiar, right? Isn't that what she believed? That he carried part of her spirit? So yeah, I did sort of wonder."

Suzanne felt herself sway, her legs weak. She stepped back, nearly tripping over Apple, who was crouched at her feet, making high-pitched growling sounds. She looked again at the box—a freshly bathed, beribboned animal. A sacrifice. She thought she would throw up.

"Sit down, Suzanne. I'll make you some tea." He turned toward the stove, reaching for the tea kettle.

She swallowed. Her belly was knotted into a fist. "Get out. Get out of my house."

He stood still. "Listen. I'm sorry. But they do what they do for a reason. Molly knew. She knew exactly what would happen to Munchie, when she died. She didn't try to stop it, either. It must have been, I don't know, necessary, somehow."

She clenched her jaw, trying not to cry. If she cried, she'd weaken. If she cried, he'd comfort her. With his guilty hands. She felt the muscles of her jaw strain. "Get out," she whispered.

He nodded. "Okay." He reached for the box.

Her hand shot out, clutching the edge of the box. "Don't touch him. I'll bury him. Don't you touch him."

But the ground was frozen under at least a foot of new snow and old ice. Burial would not prove easy. Suzanne stood staring into the back yard. She'd need help. She stomped upstairs to get Ronelle.

She'd woken Ronelle by shaking her hard. Ronelle was oddly unperturbed by the sight of Munchie's cold little corpse. She'd run her hands through her tangled hair, then set them on her hips, looking into the box on the kitchen table. "Well, jeez," she'd said. "He sure looks clean."

Suzanne stared at her. "Clean?"

"Well, yeah. You know? All fluffy and nice."

"Ronelle, the dog is dead. They killed him. I can't believe you think he looks nice."

Ronelle yawned. "He does look nice. Smells great, too. And, look, he's all decorated and all. They did really neat work here." She ran a finger along the braid of ribbons. Then she turned and looked at Suzanne. "Hey, you look really upset. It's just a dog, boss. You know? It's a *dog*."

Suzanne closed her eyes for a minute. "I know he's a dog. I just want to bury him, okay? You have to help me."

Ronelle looked toward the window. "You can't bury nothing in January, boss." She bent her head, thinking. "I guess we'll have to burn him." She smiled, looking incredibly cheery. "Yeah, we'll have a funeral pyre. That'll be cool." She reached for the box and took it into her arms. "But first, breakfast." She turned, the box held against her chest, and walked out of the kitchen. "Come here, animals," she called.

"Where are you taking him? What the hell are you doing?" Suzanne followed her out into the living room.

Ronelle bent and put the box on the floor, right in the center of the room. She looked up. "The other animals have to see him, smell him," she said. "They have to know he's dead, or they'll wait around for him to come back." She stood up. "Watch."

Pear moved on stiff legs, his fur bristling up in black tufts. Apple crawled on her belly. Plum stayed on the radiator, her eyes following every move. When Pear got to the box, he put his nose inside the box, reaching right into the nest of paper. He snorted, stepped back, and sneezed. Apple ran round and round the box, yapping.

"Shut up, you." Ronelle kicked the racing dog. "Okay, everybody cool with this?" Both dogs wagged their tails and sat down. "Good. We'll burn him later." She bent down again and picked up the box. "Got the lid?" She turned to Suzanne.

"It's still in the pantry, I think."

"Okay." Ronelle carried the box back into the kitchen, got the lid and put it on. Then she opened the back door and set the box into the fresh snow on the back steps. "There." She came in, blowing on her hands. "Man. It is brutal out there. A fire will feel great." She stomped her feet. "You making breakfast? I'm starved."

Suzanne looked into Ronelle's face. "You can eat?"

"Eat? Of course, I can. I'm starved. If you're going to cook, I'll get dressed." She shivered. "I'm still chilled, from last night. Wait'll I tell you. That was the worst horror show you have ever, ever seen." She shook her head. "Oatmeal? You got real oatmeal anywhere? Brown sugar?" Seeing Suzanne nod, she smiled. "Cool. I'll be down in few."

Irish, steel-cut oats, boiled in half 'n half, with brown sugar, cinnamon, nutmeg, raisins and a pinch of salt, then baked in the oven for thirty minutes—the oatmeal of the gods. Making it kept Suzanne's hands busy. Her brain, she tried to keep blank. But it wouldn't stay that way. It kept seeing Munchie, innocent and happy, surrounded by witches. She wondered what they'd actually done to him. He'd looked perfect, no wounds. Just dead. She shuddered.

Ronelle came back into the kitchen, her hair slightly neatened, her body wrapped in a whole array of sweaters. "Oh, man," she said. "Smells great."

Suzanne heaped oatmeal into a bowl for Ronelle. She half-filled a bowl for herself. Ronelle set a glob of butter into the center of her oatmeal, then poured cream over the whole bowlful. "This is great," she said, holding her first spoonful in her mouth.

The first bite that Suzanne put into her mouth sat on her tongue like cement. She put down her spoon. "Okay," she said. "Tell me the horror story. I mean, what could possibly be worse than getting up to find dead bodies, two days in a row. Actually, three, counting Sam. Three in a week, if we're really counting."

Ronelle rolled her eyes, her cheeks full of oatmeal. When she'd swallowed, she said, "Today it was just a *dog*. You got to keep a sense of proportion here. Really. Let me finish, then I'll tell." She bent over her bowl, shoveling in the cereal.

Suzanne sat back, playing with her spoon.

When Ronelle's bowl was empty, she gestured at Suzanne's. "You eating that?"

"No. Take it." She pushed the bowl to Ronelle's side of the table.

"Cool." When at last she'd had all she could hold, Ronelle leaned back, pushing both bowls to one side. "Oh, man. I am so stuffed. Okay, now here it is, in all its awfulness. Ready?"

"Ready as I'll ever be. Don't dramatize, Ronelle. Just tell me what happened."

"Okay. You remember that Leon came to the office, right? Okay, so he sees the mess and he helps me all day, a perfect angel. He doesn't bug me, he just cleans and helps and is nice as pie, you know? Then, he hears me call you and knows I can come back here and all, but he comes over and he says that his wife—first time he's mentioned her, of course, and only after some other guy blurted it out the other morning, so he knows I know—is out of town and he'd really really like it if I came to stay with him. I, of course, give him hell about even having a wife and not telling me *last* night, but he says that they aren't compatible at all and that…"

"Ha."

"What? Don't interrupt. I know—it's lame—but, I don't know, he seemed to mean it. He looked all sad and said they hadn't even slept together in a long time and...."

"Ha."

"Yeah, well. So, anyway, I go with him. He drives this piece of shit car, but it gets us there, some little street way downtown. And up we go, like ten flights of stairs, and he shows me around the apartment, which is just two crappy little rooms and a kitchen. Smaller than a trailer, I swear." She stopped for a minute, twirling a bowl on the table, then looked directly at Suzanne. "And, yeah, there's only one bedroom and only one bed, so I kind of think that Leon does sleep with his wife—only maybe they just sleep, not fuck—but by then it doesn't matter." She looked back down at the table. "He's being really sweet, you know? And we go into the bedroom and have a lot of fun. The bedroom has a brick wall right next to the bed—great toeholds. Anyway, then we fall asleep."

"Uh huh." Suzanne taps her spoon on Ronelle's wrist. "Go on."

"Well, all of sudden there's this whirlwind in the room, somebody yelling and hitting and punching and screaming." Ronelle's eyes are wide. "Like a maniac. Like Bertha just broke into Jane Eyre's room, you know? A raving madwoman, all hair and flaming eyes, flinging stuff around and screeching."

"Well, Bertha thought Jane was after *her* husband, too. And she was."

"Yeah, I know. Anyway. I hear Leon saying stupid things like 'Wait, Lee Anne, don't hurt her,' and I just shoot out of there like a greased piglet. I mean, I book. I grab my clothes and I'm gone." She shook her head. "Down those stairs like I have wings. Then, I'm outside, it's snowing, it's absolutely freezing and I have no fucking idea where I am. So I just head uphill, figuring that I'll hit a street I know sooner or later. And I do. And I get here, and I knock and Charles lets me in. He laughs his ass off and sends me up to sleep with you." Ronelle sat up, pushing her hair out of her face. "Why he's not in *your* bed, I can't figure. But hell, I'm not asking. Anyway, you know the rest."

Suzanne looked at Ronelle's pale, thin face. She shook her head, sighing. "What a scene."

"Yeah. I felt really bad, once I had a chance to think about it. I mean, what a nasty shock, for that woman. She did go crazy, but who wouldn't. I mean." She stood up, pushing her chair back and picking up the bowls. "That's it, for me. I will never, ever make that mistake again. Trust me, boss. I am a sadder but wiser person, really." She walked to the sink and turned on the faucet. "Really."

"Uh huh. Me, too."

Ronelle turned, her hands in the steaming sink. "You? What did you have to learn?"

Suzanne shrugged. "Same thing. Not to trust any guy to tell you the truth, ever. Any guy. Any time. Any where." She dropped her spoon into the sink. "I'm getting dressed. We've got a dog to cremate."

The stone bench in the center of Molly's frozen herb bed was the site of Munchie's pyre. The garden was a winter wonderland—every shrub veiled and rounded in its new coat of snow. Every tree branch hung with garlands of white. Like a wedding chapel Suzanne thought, looking around. Everything white and pure and decorated with ruffles. Only cold. Unbelievably cold.

Ronelle found all sorts of twigs and fallen branches and she bunched old newspapers into a wad, then placed sticks around them in a rough triangle. She placed the red box on top, balancing it carefully. She stepped back from the bench, blowing on her hands again. She looked at Suzanne who was standing in the snow a few feet away, Pear leaning against her thigh. Apple was jouncing about, up and down the yard, nearly buried in snow. "You want to say something, boss?" she said. Her breath rose in a thick white puff.

Suzanne's lips were frozen, clinging to her teeth. The hairs in her nose were frozen and her sinuses ached with cold. She shook her head. "No. Just do it."

Ronelle nodded and struck a match. She cupped the match in her hand and touched it to all four corners of the box. At each, a little flicker of flame began to climb, bright orange against the red. When she was satisfied that the flames had caught, she stepped back, stamping her feet. "Burn, baby, burn," she said.

The flames grew quickly, rising straight up into the cold air. They licked around the box, sizzling at the edges of the writing on the lid. But only for a moment—then the whole thing became a rush of heat and fire. For one terrible second, Suzanne saw the box dissolve and its tissue paper ignite in a flash of blue. Then she saw the fur on Munchie's body start to scorch. Then he, too, was just a flare, reaching for the sky.

The air filled with the smell of roasting meat and Suzanne closed her eyes. Cannibals, she knew, often began with dogs, before progressing to meals of human meat. Merriment. And sport. Her throat ached.

When the flames were gone, leaving only a greasy black circle on the bench, Ronelle said, "Okay, then. I'm getting my ass back inside. Come on, boss."

But Suzanne stood for another minute, breathing the last scent of the pyre. Then she whispered, "And heaven swallowed the smoke."

"What?" Ronelle's face was nearly blue with cold. "What did you say?"

Suzanne stamped her feet. "Nothing. *Beowulf.* Poetry, that's all. Nothing." She reached for Pear's head. "Come on. It's freezing out here."

30

Diana no longer needed sleep. Food, she'd given up days ago. She needed nothing at all. She was finally free of her body. She was pure spirit. She could rise into the cold air like vapor. She could lift like smoke.

Oh, she still had legs. And feet. Muscle and bone. Blood and flesh. But they did her bidding now. She was not a slave to them. Her belly was closed. Her breasts flat. Her Tulip clean and quiet. Purged. Tight. Shriven. Like the knights of old, she'd been purified before the battle.

Diana had only one thing left to do and it was getting easier. Now that she could move through the world without making a sound, without leaving shadow or footprint behind, she could go anywhere, anytime. She could follow LaFleshe, she could point the finger of righteousness at that body made of filth. Diana's arm would rise like a glinting sword and glisten with the blood of truth. Everyone would see the fat whore for what she was, at last. Everyone would know.

Diana, goddess of the moon, would shed her light on earth, silver and clear, and everyone would see. The night of revelation was at hand.

31

Tuesday, January 28, was a new day. Suzanne sat in her office at the University and decided that that's how she'd think about it. The office smelled of fresh paint. The walls were a clean, empty ivory. Whatever had been scrawled there was completely covered, gone. The worst was over. She would do what she'd always done—count up her losses and move on. So, the losses: Sam was dead. Molly was dead. Munchie was dead. (Okay, okay, just a dog. But still.) Morris had turned a bit strange. Leon was a shit. Charles was untrustworthy, an accomplice in dog-murder, and a cop. Her dissertation was a heap of crap. *Largesse* had gotten absolutely nowhere. Well, maybe not. Maybe *Largesse* was actually coming along okay.

Ronelle had been working, at least. And she'd been productive. There were neat little folders of manuscripts rescued from the mess the intruder had made. There were neatly printed out letters for both acceptance and rejection. Two, actually, for rejection, one—pink—encouraging ("We would like to see more of your work"), one—yellow—discouraging but not downright cruel ("We are sorry that your work does not meet our present needs"). There was a sense of efficiency, of businesslike calm, especially since Ronelle had removed all of her personal belongings—the ones that hadn't gotten destroyed by the intruder—yesterday afternoon, packing everything up and bringing it back to Suzanne's house. Ronelle had moved into Molly's side, saying she was sure the witches had taken care of any ghostly stuff and that she'd be fine. Besides, she said, Molly's side had furniture.

Suzanne stared out the window at the white campus. She would have to remember that it wasn't Molly's house anymore. It was, in fact, Suzanne's house. She'd have to start to thinking of it as her own. Because, early this morning, Molly's lawyer had called with the news that she, Suzanne Brown, aka Suzanne LaFleshe, was Molly's only heir. Molly had left her the house, the one thing she'd owned. Suzanne had listened to the man on the phone, her head swimming. "Me?" she had asked, over and over. "Me?"

"Yes," he'd said. "There's no question at all. Ms. Highsmith made a will a few months ago. She was very clear and very coherent."

Suzanne had cleared her throat. "Who was it going to, the house, before that?"

"I have no idea. This was, as I understand it, Ms. Highsmith's first and only will." He'd laughed, a short lawyerly laugh. "She said that she'd always planned on being immortal, but had changed her mind."

Suzanne's eyes had filled. "I wish she hadn't. I wish she'd stayed."

The lawyer had coughed. "Of course. Well. She also left instructions that there were to be no services, of any kind. Nothing. Absolutely nothing. She left her body to Albany Medical College, for the students to, uh, study anatomy."

"For the medical students? You mean, to dissect? To cut up?" Suzanne's stomach had lurched. She could picture Molly's body on a stainless steel table, surrounded by medical students, Molly's blind eye watching as the scalpel made its first cut.

"Well, yes. Essentially. She said that she'd made old bones, that she had all her teeth and all her marbles and that they might learn something from that. Again, she was very clear in her instructions. In any case, there will be probate, but essentially, the house is yours, Ms. Brown. It is entirely paid for. You will, of course, be responsible for taxes."

"Of course," she'd said. "Of course." She'd hung up the phone, blinded by tears. What was the name for what Molly was now? What was that horrible word? *Cadaver.* That was it. That was the word.

The campus was bustling, students rushing along the cleared paths. An ordinary Tuesday at what was still, despite the dramatic events in her life during the past ten days, the start of an ordinary semester. Kids were everywhere, laughing and talking, their breath puffing out in air that was still bitterly cold and clear. Suzanne watched for a while. She tried to clear her head. She was a homeowner. She was an editor. She had a dissertation to write. She was done with men. She had work to do. She would get a grip.

She turned from the window and checked the door. The security people had installed a new lock on the door, a working lock, and she made sure the door was firmly shut. Out in the corridor, people were still whispering, still giving her sidelong, sideways, sidling glances. They were still talking, she was certain: *That's the one, the fat cunt. That's the one.* She leaned against the door. Fine. She'd stay inside her office; she'd do her work; she'd ignore them. She had work to do.

She sat down at the desk and picked up the phone, pushing the little red button that said, "Message waiting." She closed her eyes when she heard Morris's voice: *Suzanne. I'm sorry. We've gone astray somehow. No, I have gone astray. I would like to apologize. I would like to begin anew. Please call me.* She just hadn't the energy; she pushed "erase." The next voice was Charles: *Ms. Brown, keep the office door locked when you're here. Security will be checking your corridor regularly. We tried to lift fingerprints from your walls and from that drawing we received but there are none. The person doing them is smart enough to wear gloves, apparently. Remember, you have someone seriously upset with you, Ms. Brown. Think about it. Who might want to hurt you? Think hard. And be careful. Call me if you have any problems.* She pushed "erase." The next message was brisk and businesslike, Rachel: *The Largesse office has been restored to normal, Suzanne. I'm sorry for any inconvenience. And I'm sorry that you've suffered another loss. Ronelle mentioned the death of your landlady. Keep working on your dissertation. It's the best therapy.* She pushed "erase." The last message was Charles again: *Suzanne, I'm really sorry about the damn dog, okay? I should have told you to keep him with you. But I didn't want those women messing with you. They were going to take him, one way or another. But maybe I should have tried. But…shit, I'm sorry.* She nodded, and pushed "save."

Suzanne worked for a whole day. It was much easier to get things done, now that she didn't need to eat. She wasn't distracted by her stomach; she didn't even notice when lunchtime came and went or when tea time came and went. She ate a couple of pretzels, drank a lot of tea, and kept on working. There were books to read, references to check, notes to make—cannibals, cannibals everywhere. But sterile, book-dwelling cannibals, incapable of harm. Her cohorts, her always-helpful Fridays. She worked, calm and disciplined and alone.

The winter dusk came quickly and the sky outside the office window turned a deep turquoise. She stood and stretched. The wind was coming up again; she dreaded stepping out into the icy night to walk to the bus stop. She could stay awhile, keep working. Ronelle had promised to take care of the dogs. She was getting tired, and thinking about putting in another hour or so of work when the envelope slid quietly under the door. She stared. It was a plain white envelope. She bent and picked it up. She put it on the desk, her hands shaking. Another? Another horrible little missive from her enemy? Another note from yet another one of Sam's sad conquests?

It took a minute for her to realize that the person who'd put it under her door might still be there, standing in the hallway. She opened the door. There was a rush of cold air, but nothing else. The elevator was vibrating; she could hear its hum from down the hall. She stepped out and walked toward it. The elevator doors were closed. She looked up at the deep blue skylight and down the deep well. Some students were chattering on the floor below and they craned their necks up as she bent over the rail. She could feel the pressure of her weight on the railing and she held on with both hands. She called down. "Did you guys see anyone get off the elevator?" The students shook their heads. "Nope," one said. "No one." She nodded and turned away.

The envelope was still on her desk and she wondered if she should pick it up with gloves, bag it or something. Preserve the evidence. She didn't touch it. She flicked on the overhead light, the glaring fluorescent thing that she hated. She looked at the walls—clean, fresh, ivory paint. But she thought, suddenly, that in this light she could see black marker lines under that surface. The marker, she thought, must be bleeding through. She could see, just barely, the scrawled words, the awful images. They were still there and they were coming through. They would always be there, even if no one could see them. She looked at the envelope on the desk. She shouldn't touch it, should she?

Then she shook her head. She was going nuts. She picked up the envelope and tore it open. Inside there was a sheet of paper, neatly typed. It was addressed to her.

```
Dear Suzanne Brown:
I'm hoping that you will be willing to help me. I have
been terribly distraught, facing life without my hus-
band, Sam Tindell. I have been despairing. But today an
idea came to me and I believe it is a good idea. A
wonderful idea, really.
As you probably know, Sam left behind a large number of
poems. I would like to try to find a publisher for his
work, as a final tribute to his memory. I know that Sam
valued your expertise and advice about his work. Per-
haps you would agree to work with me on putting to-
gether a presentable package of his poetry for poten-
tial publishers?
I am not knowledgeable about literary matters. You
are. I would be honored if you would agree to serve as
editor for Sam's work. It would, I believe, be a way of
healing, for both of us.
You may reach me at the following number: 454-5207.
Perhaps we could meet on campus this week, if that is
convenient. Thank you for taking the time to consider
this project.
```
Sincerely, Diana Tindell

The signature was tiny, neat, slanting toward the left. Suzanne sat down, holding the letter in her lap. Dear God. Something positive and real she could do for Sam. Something she could do to make up for hurting this woman, his wife. The woman who was, after all, Sam's beloved Diana, no matter how strange she seemed. Dear God. She read the note again. Diana certainly seemed perfectly sane. With a perfectly rational idea: get Sam's work published. So simple and right.

Without taking a minute to think that the woman couldn't possibly be home yet if she'd just dropped off the letter, she dialed the number. She got the machine—and the voice on it was Sam's. Her knees went watery at the sound: *Hey. The Tindells aren't home. So leave us a message, okay?* She lowered the phone and hung up. She put her hands over her head, cupping her ears as if she could somehow hold on to the sound of his voice. How could she have forgotten it, Sam's voice?

She sat still. The message made it so clear. Diana and Sam really and truly were married; they had shared a house, a name, a phone. A whole world in that simple phrase, said so naturally: *The Tindells.* Plural: two. A couple. *Us. Home.* She hadn't thought about all that, last summer or last fall, when she'd been enjoying Sam in her home, in her bed, in her life. She'd been playing and she'd played by the rules, as she'd understood them—the unwritten rules for the other woman. She'd never once called him at home, never risked getting Diana on the phone. So she'd never heard that message, with all its cozy coupleness. She'd put all that aside, ignored it, his life with his wife, even when it screamed up from every poem—*Diana, Diana, Diana.* She dropped her hands into her lap, ashamed.

She held her head down, pulling her scarf around her face, as she walked toward the University bus stop in the cold wind. It was dark already, but the campus was well-lit. Orange-tinted lights everywhere, along with the little blue emergency lights that marked places to call Security, directly. There were students everywhere, bustling, laughing, yelling to one another. Full of energy, full of youth. She sighed. She was watching her feet on the snowy cobblestones that led to the bus stop when she collided with a solid form. She gasped and looked up. Morris. His head covered in a wool cap, his feet in his ridiculous rubber boots.

He grasped her arm. "Suzanne. I've been waiting for you. No. Please don't back away. I'd like to talk. I need to apologize."

She sighed, her breath whitening in the air. "Morris, you don't have to apologize. I'm not mad. I'm just tired. I want to go home." She looked up into his face. His cheeks were drawn in, his lips blue with cold. "Good grief. How long have you been out here, waiting for me? And how did you know I was even here?" She shook her arm from his hand. "Are you stalking me or something?"

He smiled. "Well. Perhaps. I saw the light in your office. I saw you moving around in there. I knew you'd come down eventually, to go home for supper. I just, well, hung about. Waiting. Not stalking."

The bus was pulling into the circle, slowing for the stop. She stamped her feet. "Look. I'm going home, okay? I've had a rough week. Please—let me be, okay?" The wind was icy on her face.

He walked with her to the stop. Groups of chattering students were climbing the steps to the bus. Suzanne placed herself in the line waiting to board. He put a hand on her shoulder. "Let me just say this one thing, Suzanne. I have been acting like a fool. I didn't know. I didn't realize how much I cared about you. I know I haven't shown it in the best ways. But do forgive me, Suzanne. I cannot bear to see you hurt. Or angry at me. Please. I really cannot bear it." His voice was rising and the little clutch of girls behind them in line began to giggle.

Suzanne shook her head, embarrassed for him. "It's all right, Morris. Don't worry about it." She put one foot onto the bus step, then turned to look back at him. "Just promise you'll approve my dissertation, okay?" She smiled at him.

He smiled back, a sudden glowing grin. "Of course. Of course I will, my dear. Whenever it's done, it's got my approval. Automatically, no questions asked. *Voila*—PhD."

Suzanne stepped into the overheated bus, steamy with the exhalations of young bodies. One of the girls behind her touched her back. She turned.

"Is that, like, legal?" the girl asked. "I mean, can you get a professor to do that, just by, you know, asking? Just because he likes you?" The girl tipped her head to the side, her glossy dark hair sliding over one thin shoulder.

Suzanne nodded solemnly. "Yep. Just by asking. Just because he likes you. A lot."

"Cool," the girl said.

Ronelle had made supper. Sort of. She'd cooked a whole pound of bacon and set it to drain on paper towels. She had beaten up a dozen eggs in a bowl and was waiting to cook them when Suzanne came in. Suzanne stopped in the kitchen doorway. The dogs were sleeping peacefully and Plum was perched on a radiator. The kitchen was warm and smelled like bacon. Ronelle, standing near the stove, began pouring eggs into the frying pan. "Wow. What a cozy little domestic scene," Suzanne said. "Someone cooking supper for *me*. Wow."

Ronelle nodded, pouring the eggs into the skillet. "Yeah, well. I thought you'd be starving. I haven't seen you eat much over the past few days." She lifted a piece of bacon from the paper towels and held it out. "Here, have an appetizer."

The bacon was good, warm and crispy. But it kind of stuck in the throat. Suzanne swallowed hard. She shook her head. "I don't know what's wrong with me. I can't eat right. I think I've lost my lifelong hearty appetite. Food isn't going down right."

Scraping cooked egg to the side of the pan, Ronelle shrugged. "It's the stress, boss. You're all tightened up. You need to relax. Have some wine." She pointed to the bottle on the table.

It was a nice red. "Where did this come from? You didn't buy this, did you?" Suzanne looked at the label and the price. "Surely not."

"Hey. Now that I'm not homeless, maybe I can afford some of the finer things in life. Today, wine that goes with bacon and eggs. Tomorrow, wine that goes with peanut butter. Eventually, wine that goes with Kraft Macaroni and Cheese. Sit. The eggs are ready." Ronelle piled about eight strips of bacon on each of their plates and scooped heaps of egg beside the bacon. She set down the plates and sat down. "Supper of the gods. Yum."

Suzanne slid into her place and lifted her fork. "Come on. Where'd the wine come from?" She took a bite of egg—it felt thick and heavy on her tongue, but she swallowed it. She took a few more bites, forcing each one down.

Ronelle was shoveling egg into her mouth at a stupendous rate, alternating with bites of bacon. She waved her fork. "Oh, it was a peace offering from Leon. He left it on the doorstep, with a pathetic note." She kept eating.

"Oh my God, Ronelle. You shouldn't have accepted it. What about your vow? What about his wife?"

Ronelle's fuzzy head barely lifted from her plate. "Wine's wine, boss. I don't have to like him to drink his wine, do I?" She looked up. "You going to eat that?"

Suzanne looked down at her nearly full plate. "I've had enough." She pushed the plate to the other side of the table.

When they were done eating, Suzanne volunteered to do the dishes. Ronelle smiled. "Thanks, boss. I'm going to my side of the house— geez, I like to say that—and do some work. You know Molly actually has a desk and chairs and reading lamps and rugs. It's really, like, civilized over there. A great place to study. Oh, and I left some reading materials by your bed, too. I've been writing an article for the mag." She tilted her head, looking like a cocker spaniel. "That's okay, right? I mean, can assistant editors contribute stuff?"

Suzanne poured bacon fat into a can and thought about that. "I don't see why not. But I don't see how you'll have the time, either. What are you writing about?"

"It's a kind of list thing. You know—Good Fat Books vs. Bad Fat

Books. Like those 'What's In, What's Out' articles you see in stupid magazines. It's a kind of take-off of that kind of thing. But it's serious, too, you know? Showing our readers that they might decide to read certain things because of how they portray fat women. I decided that it wouldn't even matter if the authors were men or women. What matters is how they show fat women—good or bad. And I'm skipping all the earth goddess crap. I can't stand that stuff. I thought we'd do just fiction, for the first issue. A kind of Oprah thing—you'd think, given her weight issues, she'd have already thought of this. But she hasn't. So we could be the first, you know?"

The water was running into the sink and Suzanne added detergent. "Uh huh. Like the Catholic church used to do? Recommend only uplifting Pope-approved books and blacklist others? Seems a bit extreme. But it might be interesting. Sort of like giving books the *Good Housekeeping* seal of approval." She swished her hands into the water. "But are you finding many *Largesse*-approved books? I mean, are there that many actually out there that we could recommend?"

"Yeah, I think so. Well, not many. Not enough. But a start. Like I said, I put the lists—with sample passages noted—by your bed."

Suzanne looked into Ronelle's eager eyes. "Really, where do you get the energy and time to do all this, kiddo?"

Ronelle smiled. "Clean living and a solid upbringing, boss."

"Ha. And you're really okay on Molly's side? I mean, you're not scared or freaked by anything over there?" She realized, suddenly, that she hadn't told Ronelle that the house was hers. She wanted, she thought, to keep that to herself for awhile, think about it.

"Nah. I get nothing but good vibes. That old witch liked me, I can tell. She still does, I think. And, hell, like I said, it's got furniture. And, if you need anything, I'll be right there." Ronelle turned toward the pantry, then stopped. "Okay? You just yell and I'll be right here."

Suzanne looked at her. Her pale eyes were half-closed, but watching. "Why would I have to yell, Ronelle?"

The eyes opened wide, completely innocent and without guile. "Can't imagine, boss. But that nice Charles Clark, he mentioned that I might want to keep my eyes open. And my ears, too." She cocked her head. "And, you know, I've been thinking that maybe I could trail that creepy Diana. You know, stake out her place, see what she's up to? I mean, no one knows what she's up to, really. And she's obviously crazy as a loon."

Suzanne felt her empty stomach lurch. "You leave that woman alone, Ronelle. Molly did enough harm. Diana's perfectly sane; she's just hurt, that's all."

Ronelle tipped her head to the side. "Huh. You sound pretty certain. You been talking to people behind my back, boss? I mean, Molly thought...."

"Molly was wrong. She was very old and she was wrong, that's all. Molly made a mistake. Now you leave Diana alone. Do your work, Ronelle. Just do your own fucking work, okay?"

Suzanne didn't even have to look at the number Diana had given her; it was burned into her brain. The Tindells' number: 454-5207. She sat on the edge of her bed and dialed it.

The voice that answered was soft and high-pitched. "Hello?"

Suzanne cleared her throat. "Diana? This is Suzanne Brown." Her heart was pounding and she didn't know why, exactly. Embarrassment, maybe. Shame. Knowing that this woman knew what she'd done with Sam. Knowing that this woman was Sam's wife. Still, Diana had asked for her help—surely she held no grudges. She waited through a long moment of silence. "You left me a note? About Sam's poetry?"

"Oh, yes. Suzanne. How good of you to call. I've been so looking forward to talking to you. To meeting with you." The voice was breathy, childlike. Gentle.

Suzanne felt as if a balm of forgiveness was coming through the wires. Her eyes filled with grateful tears. "I'd be honored, Diana, to help in attempting to get Sam's work published. He was a fine poet."

"Yes, he was. Well, so everyone said. I can't really judge. And, of course, I can't be impartial, can I? So many of the poems are about me."

Yes, Suzanne thought, they are. Diana, goddess of the moon, the only woman Sam had loved. She cleared her throat again. "Yes. Sam wrote about you in nearly every poem."

The childlike voice sounded surprised, delighted. "You saw that? You knew, even when he hid it under all that moon symbolism? Still, you knew?"

"I did. I knew that."

"Lovely. I'm so pleased. Well, when shall we meet? Soon, I hope. I'm so anxious to begin. I've been, well, ill. But I'm much better now and I'm ready to begin."

"Of course. Well, then, how about tomorrow? At my office? I'm flexible, so name your time."

There was another longish silence, then Diana's voice. "I'm flexible, too. I am not working at the moment. Bereavement leave, they call it." She sighed. "Yes, I am bereaved. I'm a widow. Imagine, at my age, a widow. It's very odd. Well. How about three tomorrow afternoon?"

"Yes. Fine. Three. I'll see you there—you know where my office is?"

"Indeed I do, Suzanne. I certainly do." The child's voice gave a little giggle and then it was gone.

Suzanne held the receiver in her hands. Bereft, she thought. That's the right word: it isn't "bereaved"; it's "bereft." Diana didn't know that and she did. That was important, a little thing like that. Words mattered to Sam.

Blankets pulled to her chin, she picked up Ronelle's neatly typed list of Good vs. Bad books, judged on a scale of fat-approval. She skimmed down the bad. Oh, she knew them. She didn't need to even read the list to know them; they were part of her. She'd absorbed every one of those characters, somewhere along the way. All those hideous, greedy, devouring fat women. Fat, filthy cunts. She knew them all already.

She flipped to the good. The list was alphabetical by author, with title, publisher, date, and a brief passage from each book, highlighting a fat woman. Each entry was also followed by an annotation, by Ronelle herself. That girl was indeed a wonder. Ronelle would no doubt finish *her* dissertation in six months, after passing *her* doctoral exams "with distinction." She sighed, settling into her pillows. A few good fat women passages were exactly what she needed. She jumped down the list to the B's—a book called *Water Music* by T. Coraghessan Boyle—her eye caught by the words "erotic charms." About a fat woman! Yes, this certainly was what she needed.

Fatima's erotic charms are predicated entirely on a single feature: her bulk. In a bone-thin society, what more appropriate ideal of human perfection? Fatima weighs three hundred and eighty-two pounds.... Ali comes in off the desert, blood and sand in his eyes, and plunges into the moist fecundity of her flesh. She is a spring, a well, an oasis. She is milk overspilling the bowl, a moveable feast, green pasture and a side of beef. She is gold. She is rain. (24)

Suzanne closed her eyes and smiled. Yes, this is what she needed. She opened her eyes again to read Ronelle's note: *Well, other than that "side of beef" remark, this is pretty cool, huh? Although the way in which Fatima was forced to become fat (26) is pretty awful. Still....*

Damn. Fatima was forced to become fat? Suzanne was glad that she didn't have the book at hand, couldn't check page 26. She just wanted to loll in the words before her. Milk overspilling the bowl. Someone named Ali lustily plunging into abundant flesh. Moist fecundity. Rain. Green pasture. Spring, she thought. Someday it would be spring and this long, long winter would be over and honest rain and verdant green would return to the earth and she would be able to work in her—yes, *her*—garden, in *her* backyard. She could feel sleep pulling at her.

The phone shrilled beside her. She groaned but picked it up. "Yes?"

"Ah. Answered on the first ring. I surmise that you are in your bed, Suzanne. As I'd hoped. As you should be."

She groaned again. "Morris, what do you want?"

"Just to reiterate my apology, my dear. I am fretting, not really sure you'd truly forgiven me. I wanted to hear your voice."

"Well, here it is. I've forgiven you. I said I had and I have. Really, I have. Now let me go to sleep." She was about to plop the phone receiver into its cradle when he spoke again.

"I can just see you there, Suzanne. Sitting up, leaning against your pillows, your breasts swelling out above the sheets. Great mounds of sweet-smelling, sweet-tasting flesh. My God, how I'd like to be there with you, right this minute, tasting every inch."

Suzanne felt a slight loosening in her thighs and thought that perhaps she really had forgiven Morris. He hadn't, after all, done anything so very terrible. He'd gotten drunk; he'd been a bit persistent; he'd obviously been jealous of Charles; he'd wangled his way onto her committee. Still. Weren't those all signs of affection? An enduring, perhaps stronger than she'd suspected, affection? And was that so bad? Morris, at least, was neither married nor a cop. He had never, as far as she knew, collaborated in the death of a small dog. "Uh huh," she said.

"Oh yes. I would like to be just at the start, just opening your thighs, taking that first deep plunge. I would like, my love, to be just beginning to lose myself in you."

She shook her head. All this plunging, just when she'd been thinking about it herself. Her crotch felt warm and tingly. "Go on."

He laughed. A deep, throaty laugh. "Oh, yes. I will go on. I would like to have my tongue on one of your nipples. Have I ever mentioned, my dear, how very lovely they are? Each as round and pink and smooth as an old-fashioned rose. Yes, I would like to take that nipple into my mouth—very, very slowly, just drawing it in, drinking, you know, its sweetness. I'd like to feel it get hard in my mouth—all tight and yearning, ripe as a raspberry. I'd like to hear that sound you make—you know the one—when you put your head back and gasp, in surprise almost, at the feeling. I'd like to hold that nipple in my teeth, quite gently, of course, sucking and sucking. Perhaps not so very gently. I know exactly what your cunt does then, Suzanne, while I suck. It begins to move; it begins to suck, too, moving to my rhythm. It begins to tighten and loosen. Tighten and loosen. Around my prick. I can feel it now. It has muscles. It has great strength. It is like a lovely, hungry mouth, pulling and pulling. Wanting, wanting. It is a prodigious, wondrous thing, your cunt. Magnificent."

Suzanne took her hand away from her crotch, where it had gone, all by itself. She opened her eyes: she saw the drawings. The thick black lines. The little man attached to the great breast. The huge toothed vagina swallowing him up.

Every inch of her body went cold. It could not be. Could it? Morris, drawing those obscene pictures?

Her voice was cool and steady when she spoke. "I'm tired, Morris. I'm not in the mood. I'll see you later." This time, hanging up was easy.

Of course, that was absurd. Suzanne was tossing in her bed, thinking. Morris would never do such a thing. She'd known Morris for a long time—longer than any of them, really. Morris had been her first friend in Albany. Her first lover. Before Sam, before anyone. Morris could not wish to hurt her. But who would? Who, who would? She heard Molly's voice, every time she fell toward sleep: *Who is your enemy?* It woke her—she didn't know who. When she did fall asleep, she saw the owl at the edge of every dream, its white wings outspread, its talons hanging near her face.

When the phone rang again, it broke into a dream of watching a little white dog being buried in ice, the owl swooping overhead, its claws coming closer and closer to the dog's eyes. In the dream, she couldn't move, couldn't even look away from those sharpened claws. Her ears screamed with the terrified cries of the trapped dog. When she realized the phone was ringing, she was sure she'd hear the voice of the wendigo and that there was nothing she could do to stop it. She picked up the phone and did not speak, waiting for the voice to come across the wires, excoriating, pitiless, wailing of its endless hunger, its need for living flesh.

"Suzanne, are you there?"

It was Charles. She sat up, relief rushing through her as the ice of her dream melted away at the sound of his voice. "I was asleep. Is something wrong?"

"No. I just wanted to check on you. You okay?"

She began to wake up fully. "I was *asleep*, Charles. I'm fine." She sat up and shook her hair out of her eyes. She looked at the clock; it was after midnight.

"Uh huh. Listen, I want to ask you something."

"It's late, Charles. Is it important?"

"Might be. Um, is there anyone there with you?" His voice sounded strained.

"Oh for God's sake. Is that why you're calling? To check on my sex life?" She flung her feet out from under the covers and onto the floor.

"No, that is not why I'm calling." He coughed. "I'm just worried. I don't think you should trust anyone right now and so I wouldn't recommend taking anyone home with you."

"Taking anyone home! As in, going to bars and picking up perfect strangers and coming home and fucking them blue? God, is that what you think I do?"

His voice rose. "Listen, Ms. Brown. About 10 minutes ago, some guy was seen entering your house. Carrying a bunch of boxes. Okay, he was going into Molly's side, but still. I am checking, that's all. This isn't personal. It's my job."

Suzanne stood up, looking out the window. Some guy? She saw nothing but a quiet, snowbanked street. On the other side was a line of parked cars—all dark. "How do you know this? You must have what—a stakeout? A stakeout! In front of my house? That's absurd. It's crazy." She leaned over, trying to see if any of the cars was occupied. It was impossible to tell.

"Listen to me. It's not crazy. Someone wishes you harm. I'm keeping an eye out. It would help if you'd talk to me, Suzanne. Has anyone said or done anything odd? Anyone approached you in some new or different way? Anything weird happened?"

She sat back down on the bed. She thought of Diana's call. Stupid annoying Ajax's call. Morris's call. None of which she wanted to talk to Charles about. Sam's poetry was none of his business; Ajax's damn grade obsession was too petty to even think about and none of his business; her own reaction to Morris was definitely none of his business. "No. Everything has been perfectly normal. Oh, except for some witches. Except when people killed an innocent little dog in my house. And that you know about."

"Jesus Christ," he said. She heard some object crash in the background, as if he'd thrown something. "I said I was sorry." He took a deep breath. "This is serious, Suzanne. You could be in real danger. Those drawings were pretty vicious. I don't want you meeting up with the person whose mind they came from, especially when you don't even know who it is."

The drawings. She could not escape from the drawings, their black lines like scars on her skin. She couldn't bear to think that Charles had ever seen them, never mind that he was apparently obsessing over them. "I can take care of myself, Charles."

"Fine. So who's over on Molly's side of the house?"

She thought about that. "I don't know. Ronelle is staying over there. She may have—um, a guest."

"She's what? I told her to stay with you. Damn it. I'm coming over there."

"No you're not. Ronelle is a practical farm girl, so she's staying where there's furniture. A bed of her own. And you had no right to make her my keeper, anyway. She's just a kid."

He snorted. "Smartest kid I ever met. That girl was born old and sneaky. All right. You go over there—no, call over there on the phone. See what's up. Then call me back. I'm in the office. If you don't call in 10 minutes, my guy will come in and check. Do not argue. Do it." He hung up.

Feeling like a fool, Suzanne dialed Molly's number. No one had told the phone company that Molly was dead. So it rang. And Ronelle's voice, sounding perfectly awake and cheery, answered. "Hallo. Whassup?"

"Ronelle, it's me, Suzanne. I got a phone call from Charles. He says some guy came to your side of the house and he's making me check to see who it is. I think I can guess—Leon? Right?" She tapped her fingers on her knee, waiting through the silence.

Then Leon's voice came onto the phone, talking a mile a minute. "Hey, Suzanne. Yeah, it's me. My wife tossed my ass out. Ronnie took me in. Do you really mind? If you do, I'll hike out into the cold, cold night and you'll never see me again. I'll just keep walking until my feet freeze and bleed. I'll walk until I drop. Someday, they'll find my mummified corpse in a frozen bog and I'll be the anthropological wonder of the 23nd century. Praise be to an afflicting God."

Suzanne sighed. "Shut up, Leon. Put Ronelle on."

"Yeah?" Ronelle sounded a bit defiant.

"*Ronnie? Ronnie?* Sounds like a certain senile former president. Okay, listen. It's your life to fuck up. I just don't want to see him, okay? He is not to step on my side of this house. Ever. Got it?"

"Well, yeah. I think it's a little harsh but…."

"Got it?" Suzanne was yelling. "This is *my* house now. I do not want some wise-ass, philandering, annoying, extremely short man bothering me. Do you understand? We will discuss your rent later. But I do not want to see that man's face."

"Yass'um, boss. I got it." There was a moment of sulky silence, then Ronelle's cheery voice returned. "Hey, is it really your house now?"

"Yes, it is."

"Cool. Night, boss."

Suzanne called Charles back. He answered on the first ring. "It's no one you need to worry about," she said. "It's Ronelle's, well, boyfriend

I suppose. You've seen him around—Leon, another English grad student."

"Uh huh. Leon who? What's his last name?"

"Jesus Christ! His name is Leon Jacob Dingleheimer Schmitt, for all I know. You're the one with all the spy resources at your command, you find out. And leave me alone. Call off your fucking goons." She slammed down the phone and stomped to the window. None of the cars across the street pulled away. She thought, for a minute, of doing something she's always wanted to do but never found the right occasion. She thought of mooning the officer who sat in one of those cars. She thought of putting her big white buttocks right against the glass, huge crescents of flesh. She thought how good it would feel. And how grotesque it would look. She thought about how many of Charles's men had already seen images of her ass and decided against it.

She pulled down the shade and turned on the light, sliding back into bed. Since she couldn't sleep, she might as well read. She picked up Ronelle's good-book list and skimmed down to the E's. Penelope Evans' book, Freezing: *Big Angie...A woman, larger than anyone I have ever seen, making a perfectly normal doorway look small. Despite her size, she was dressed in a towel so tiny that conscience made you look away, only to look again, despite yourself. The impression was not so much of flesh as scenery. There was so much of her she seemed to be flowing above and below the towel like an uninterrupted landscape rolling before your eyes (68).* Below that Ronelle's note: *Okay, great character, Big Angie. She's kind, smart, etc. But, of course, the guy falls for a skinny girl instead and BA meets a nasty end.*

Shit. The guy falls for a skinny girl and lovely Big Angie meets a bad end. Couldn't she have just predicted that? Sam loved Diana, after all. This reading was not helping. She tossed Ronelle's list on the floor.

Still, there was always something else to read, some new bit of literary cannibal research. She sighed and picked up the heaviest book on her night stand and opened it, balancing its spine on her belly.

Part VI: *Queen of the Cannibal Islands*

O's Song

Doobee doobee dubio
Doowop welladay
Hugga bugga yumma yum
How do you like your buggers done
Boiled in bug juice, boiled in rum
Says the Queen of the Cannibal Islands
Love love
Love will get us out of here.

Jaimy Gordon, *Bogeywoman*

32

On the night before she would meet the enemy face to face, Diana ate. She hadn't taken solid food in days; she'd known that once she'd started, she would not be able to stop. But now it didn't matter. She was so strong that nothing, now, could hurt her. She giggled as she set out her offerings. She hoped that the filthy fat beast, her now-dear friend Suzanne, was eating too. Weren't the condemned always allowed a last meal? A great feast? A final feeding of the flesh, before the spirit struggled free of its carrion body?

She'd chosen carefully, even though she'd been dizzied in the market—the great huge palace of food on Central Avenue. The MegaMart, temple of excess. She'd almost turned away, almost vomited at the sight of heaps of melons, greasy slabs of meat, fish piled into cold pyramids. But she had steadied herself and chosen well.

She had put out the antique plates Sam had bought her, when they were first married. Cobalt blue edges rimmed in gold, flowered centers. Only seven plates, an odd number. Sam had found them at a yard sale. Three were cracked. Two chipped. All faded. She'd hated them from the moment he'd carried them into her house, grinning with pleasure at his find. Every time she'd looked at them, she couldn't help but see all the food they'd held, all the years they'd been used, all the mouths hanging above them, dripping with saliva and gluttony. She'd rarely used them, told Sam they were too lovely for everyday use.

But here they were, all seven of Sam's precious plates, each with its separate offering—all the foods she had found most tempting and troubling, all her life. They were arranged in a circle on her table: Smuckers butterscotch ice-cream topping; Oreos; McDonald's french fries; bacon, limp and undercooked; Cheezits; Cracker Jack; ground beef, raw. Diana looked at them, nodding. She'd chosen well.

She circled the table five times, humming to herself. She walked very slowly, very smoothly, keeping in control. She was naked, her body freshly bathed and shaved. She reached one finger out, oh-so-slowly, and scooped a glob of butterscotch onto its tip. She shuddered at the feeling of its sugary grip on her skin, its slide under her fingernail. But she was brave. Oh, she'd always been so brave. They had no idea, any of them, how brave she'd been. She raised the finger to her lips and licked. As the sugar glazed her tongue, she let herself go: she fell upon the food like a wild thing, sucking, licking, biting, slurping, guzzling, swallowing, swallowing, swallowing, swallowing.

In the end, Diana sat on her kitchen floor, all seven plates smashed around her. Their breakings—each sent crashing to the floor when it was empty—had left cuts along her ankles and calves and feet. Her hands were coated with muck, her chin smeared with juices. She smiled.

33

The morning of Wednesday, January 29 was warm and cloudy. Warm for Albany in January, at least. As Suzanne made her early-morning trek around the block with the dogs, she could smell moisture in the air, a kind of loosening of winter's iron grip. The surface of the snow was softening. The dogs kept their noses high, snuffing at the possibility of warmer, happier days.

As she started off, Suzanne woke the sleeping University cop in the car across from her house. In the daylight, it was easy to spot—a plain dark car with a man in uniform resting his head on the back of his seat. She knocked on the car window and the poor man jumped. She smiled. When he rolled the window down, she tapped him on the shoulder gently. "Morning. I'm safe and sound. Go get coffee. Go home."

The man shook his head. His blond hair was sticking straight up in the back—a real case of sleep-head. He yawned. "Morning, Ms. Brown. Nice dogs." He patted Apple, who was bouncing up and down outside his window. "Hey, don't tell Mr. Clark I nodded off okay? He's a real bear about that kind of thing."

She nodded. "I won't be telling Mr. Clark anything. Don't worry. Have a nice day."

After the walk, she ate one piece of dry toast and drank half a cup of coffee. This loss of appetite, she decided, was making her life a whole lot easier. No cooking, no dishes to wash. She noticed, when she got dressed, that her good wool skirt was loose in the waist. Her long sweater hung a bit on her hips. She was dressing carefully for her appointment with Diana and she looked, well, fine. She smiled at herself in the mirror. What the hell, maybe by spring, she could buy some new clothes—bright, lightweight summer clothes, in normal sizes. Maybe starvation was the way to go, after all.

Diana smiled at herself in the mirror. Her hair, newly washed, fell like a cloak of light down her back. She dressed carefully, although, really, it didn't matter. Still. She chose a soft gray blouse, silk, and a long black skirt. Her silver watch. She slid her legs into fine gray hose, pointing her toes and arching her strong calves. She slipped into slim black boots.

She spun before the mirror, a girl off to a party. She nodded to her reflection.

She made her one phone call, her voice sweet and thick as honey. Then she sat down to wait. The morning would be quiet. The afternoon, what she had of it here, in peace, before she had to leave for her appointment, would be quiet, too. She would sit, here in her clean and silent house, and make herself still. She had spent all night cleaning, purging. Her body and her house. It was all done—every surface scrubbed and clean. The house, her self. Clean and ready.

It was interesting, she thought, as she folded her hands in her lap and settled herself into stillness. It was interesting, just to sit here and contemplate the fruition of her plans. Today she would meet both her enemy and her closest friend, together. Her enemy would be vanquished and her friend, her best of all friends, her winged lover who wore a black cloak and kept his face hooded, her friend would meet her at last, would finally deem her worthy, and sweep her up into his strong arms. He would, she was certain, uncloak his face at the very last and allow her to gaze into his shining eyes.

Suzanne paused before she left the house. Ronelle's side was quiet. Well, Ronnie and Leon's side, she supposed. They'd probably been up late, having happy wife-free sex on Molly's bed. She made a face. Still, between the two of them, maybe they could afford to pay a real rent. She'd have to think about that. She was a landlady now, a homeowner. And she'd need help with the taxes. Repairs. Whatever. She shook her head: the damn dissertation would have to get finished, now. A job would have to be found. No more screwing around.

She left a note on the kitchen table: R., *I'll be working in the office. Do not come in—I don't want to be disturbed. Don't let Leon into my side. Let beasts out periodically. Eat whatever you want. S. P.S. I like the list.* Largesse Seal of Approval *will reassure fat chicks all over the globe, sort of. But aren't there any fat female characters who actually get the guy, live happily after, etc.? Oh, well, we can dream. See you tonight. P.P. S. Don't bother to make supper for me—I'm not hungry.*

The office was quiet and empty. No notes, no intruders, no scrawls of hatred on the wall. Suzanne sat down at her desk, cannibal books and articles piled around her. She turned on the office computer, slipped in the disk labeled "Dissertation," and began to work. She worked well, worked hard. She ignored the phone; she didn't respond to the little flashing light that said "Message waiting." Whoever it was could wait. She was working. She didn't look up from the screen until well into the afternoon

When it was time, Diana wrapped herself in a fine black shawl and left the house. It wasn't far. Sam had found them an apartment near the University, so he could walk to classes. She kept her head down as she passed along the sidewalks. She was quite sure that she was invisible, now, so thin and dark and shadowy she'd become. Still. She kept her head down until she reached the long quiet sweep of snow that led to the pond. She looked across its shining face and stepped out, gently, one black-booted foot just testing the surface.

She smiled. She'd been right. She was, easily, so easily, light enough to skim across the top of the snow. She could glide like an angel right across the surface and leave no trail. She was, at last, mere air. Ether.

When Suzanne did check her watch, she was startled to see the time: nearly three. She felt her chest tighten. Almost time for Diana. She stood up and stretched her stiff back. She would make a pot of tea, she thought. She wanted something to serve Diana. She wanted to be a civilized, kind woman—a woman with a responsible job, a respectable woman. She did not want to be Suzanne LaFleshe, woman of appetites. LaFleshe, fat filthy cunt. Woman who slept with other women's husbands.

She smoothed her skirt with her hands. She could fit two fingers inside the waistband of the skirt. And she hadn't thought of food all day. Maybe she really was losing her appetites, all of her fleshly desires. Maybe, she thought, she was becoming respectable, after all. Maybe, she would drop the "LaFleshe." There was nothing wrong with "Brown," really. Dull. But respectable.

She carried the tea kettle to the bathroom and filled it. She washed the mugs. She came back to the office and turned off the computer and then sat still, hands folded in her lap, waiting for Diana to come, bearing Sam's poetry in her slim young hands. She put her head back and closed her eyes. Behind her eyelids, she remembered Sam. Not as she'd last seen him, a bloody mess on the stone floor, but as she'd seen him when they were talking about his poetry: Sam, excited and worried, running his hands through his hair, saying, "What do you think, Suzanne? Is it okay? Is it any good? Is it absolute shit?" And remembering herself, intoxicated by the physical nearness of Sam, the smell of his skin, the touch of his elbow, praising, soothing, smiling. Seducing, she realized, all the while she was acting as his literary advisor. Because she'd always known, really, that there is no better way to seduce a poet than by praising his poems. Poets feel those strokes of praise for their words like other men feel a soft palm sliding down the belly. Poets respond like other men do to the slide of a tongue across a thigh. Poets' needs are simple: a line admired, a word appreciated, neat meter applauded. After that, the rest was easy. Yes, she'd taken advantage. She'd drawn Sam into her bed, into her body by first—first—drawing him into her web of poetic affirmation.

She felt tears on her face. But Sam was a good poet. She hadn't lied, hadn't led him down some garden path. Sam was beautiful, yes. She'd hungered for Sam's body, yes. But that didn't mean his poems weren't good. They were. And she would help Diana show that to the world.

When the clock said three-thirty, she suddenly thought of the messages and sat up. Diana's voice was on the first message, light and clear: *Suzanne? Diana Tindell. Sam's wife. It's such a lovely day. Let's meet outdoors, shall we? I'll be waiting for you at the University pond.* There was a pause, then: *It seems odd, I know. But it was one of Sam's favorite places. Once, we made love at the very edge of the water, hidden by the reeds. It was early fall, the start of the semester. People walked right by but we were very quiet and no one saw us. Sam said, that day, that he was the luckiest man on this earth, to be married to a woman so small, so hushed that she could be hidden by a single reed.* Another pause, then: *Always the poet, yes? Well. See you at three, then? On the stone bench by the pond.*

Suzanne played the message twice, before she hit "erase." A woman small and hushed. That's who made Sam happy. That kind of woman. She shook her head and hurried into her coat and boots. She was late and Diana was waiting.

It was, of course, to be expected that the careless LaFleshe would be late. Diana looked at her silver watch. It didn't matter, really. No matter when she arrived, the outcome would be the same. Diana would be there, floating free, and LaFleshe would be there, weighted by all that she was: heavy, bloated, sinful. And LaFleshe would know herself for what she was. LaFleshe would suffer.

Diana smiled into the air and began, slowly and carefully, to remove her clothes, the last things that held her to the ground. First, the boots, unzipped down her calves, a shiver of cold as she stepped out of them and onto the hardpacked snow. The shawl, fine lace, brought from Spain, long long ago, by her father, who had loved her so very, very much. The fine silk shirt, shimmering with its own light. The skirt. Last, the hose, gossamer. Nothing at all. She bent, feeling the cold air slide across her body like a caress, and folded the clothes. She created neat, perfect edges. She left the clothes at the edge of the pond, hidden in the reeds where, she'd told LaFleshe, she and Sam had once made love. She tilted her head, trying to recall. Was that true?

It was funny, she thought. She put one foot forward and felt the thrill of the ice on her sole, shooting up her whole body, raising her nipples into tight points of desire. It was funny that she really couldn't remember, now, anything about Sam at all. As if he hadn't really mattered at all. As if he had never touched her. As, indeed, he had not. Diana put both feet onto the ice and danced to the center of the pond, her hair spinning around her like moonbeams.

The inner campus was full of noisy students but the wild area near the pond was empty and quiet. Suzanne trudged through squashy snow, her feet soaked and heavy, trying to hurry, sweating in her heavy coat. She wasn't doing well, in the respectable, responsible line, was she? A woman who couldn't even answer her phone; wouldn't even listen to messages, until it was too late. A woman who kept another woman waiting, while she sat remembering the touch of her husband's hands. She stomped harder, trying almost to run. Breathless, flustered, her legs tiring, snow caking on her boots.

The wind was picking up, clouds scuttling across a clearing, deep blue sky. The early winter dusk was already falling and the warmish air was changing back to cold. She kept her head down, stamping along the rough path that circled the pond, the dark woods to her right. The bare tree branches tossed and crackled in the wind, lifting their black arms to the sky.

When she reached the stone bench, it was empty. She held her hand above her eyes, looking into the woods. "Diana?" she called. There was no response. Then she looked toward the edge of the pond, still solid with ice. It was ringed with frozen reeds, singing in the wind, a high wailing sound that ran up her back like a cold hand. She stepped to the edge of the pond and looked toward its center.

The body in the ice was very hard to see. It was so small that it barely disturbed the surface. It was simply a mound of pewter-gray in the darkening silver of the ice. But it was a body. It was human—she could see that. She could feel that, right to the center of her bones. She leaned forward, trying to focus in the failing light. Yes. It was a body. The body of a slight, frail, naked woman, splayed across the ice, right in the center of the pond. The woman's shining hair was spread in a circle around her head, catching the last of the daylight, a halo of silver. "Oh God," she whispered. "Diana."

She put a foot onto the ice and stepped forward. The ice cracked, then splintered. Her foot splashed through, hitting the cold water below with a shock. She pulled it out, looked frantically toward the still body in the center of the pond. She realized what Diana had done. Diana— tiny, almost weightless—Diana had walked on the ice to the middle of the pond. And there, she had lain down to die.

And Suzanne, Suzanne LaFleshe, could not follow, could not take that same simple path across the ice. She was much too heavy. She could not save Diana. The ice would not bear her weight. She stood at the edge of the pond, her fists clenched. "Help her," she screamed. "Someone, please. Help her." But the wind took her words and tossed them away.

The body in the ice seemed to stir at the sound of her voice. The hair lifted and the pale blue face turned toward Suzanne. "Oh my God," she said. She put a foot, again, onto the ice. It broke through, again. But she realized that the pond was not very deep; the foot only fell a few inches in the icy water before it hit bottom, a mushy, mucky bottom. She stood still for a moment, clenching her jaw, then she stripped off her coat and walked forward.

Each step meant breaking through a sharp crust of ice. And each was a torture of cold. But Diana's eyes were open. They were looking into the sky and they were watching. They were waiting for her. The water reached her knees and her skirt pulled down, its fabric heavy and soaked, clinging to her legs, slowing and tangling her progress. She stood still, unbuttoned the skirt with shaking hands and let it fall from her legs. She stepped out of it and it sank, sodden and muddy. She went on, step by icy step. Her flesh went numb, everywhere below the waist.

Diana kept her eyes wide open. She heard the crashing footsteps of LaFleshe. But, really, she didn't care, any more, about that. And that was her great joy. Her final gift. She'd gone beyond the flesh, at long long last. She could feel every pore in her body open up, every cell of her body lifting up to meet the wind. The ice below her was like a bed of cloud—comforting and clean. She smiled up into the sky. It was happening, just as she'd willed it. Just as she'd planned. She was here, dissolving, giving up her body to the air. Lifting like steam from a cup. Weightless. Nothing. At last. And her friend, her only friend, her true lover, was coming. He was here. She could smell his breath in the air. He bent over her, whispering her name: Diana. His hood was flung back and she could look, at last, into his face, into the ice-gray eyes encircled in pure, shining bone. He was beautiful. She arched toward him. And he took her, fast into his grasp, and carried her away. Over the ice they sped, together. High, fast, flying. Lifting into the wind. Together. Away.

By the time she could reach out an arm and touch Diana, the water was a tight band of terrible cold around her chest. It had soaked her sweater and penetrated to the skin below. Her breasts were floating in its icy grip. She took one more step and grasped Diana's shoulder with a gibbering, terrified hand. It was like grabbing a statue, the flesh was so solid, so hard and ungiving.

She tried to shake the shoulder, looking into the staring eyes. "Diana, get up. Get up."

The shining eyes were empty. There was no movement, no breath. She looked at the chest. It did not lift, did not fall. There was no sign of breath. The body was completely naked, completely smooth. The breasts were mere swells, the nipples blue. The bones of the hips were sharp; each rib was distinct under the merest curtain of flesh. The genitals were hairless, smooth and pale as ivory. This, she realized, was the body of a starved child. The face was beautiful, its cheekbones sharp and pure. The hair was frozen into its icy halo. She reached out and pulled the body into her arms. It didn't come easily. Some of its flesh stayed with the ice, frozen there, clinging in little blue crystals. She had to pull the hair away from the ice, strand by strand. But when she finally set it free and lifted it, the body weighed nothing.

The trip back to the shore of the pond was much easier. Perhaps she'd simply grown used to the cold; perhaps she was too numb to feel it. But it was easy. Suzanne was strong; she could carry this tiny body forever, if she had to. Diana's head rested easily against Suzanne's chest. Her bare feet dangled, brushing the surface of the ice. She was very very light. Nothing, really, but air.

When she reached the shore, Suzanne stepped out and carried Diana to the stone bench and set her down, as gently as she could. She arranged her, lying on her back, arms folded over her pathetic ribs. Diana's wet hair fell to the ground like a rope of eels. Suzanne stood above her, shivering violently in the cold wind. She knelt by the bench, looking into Diana's eyes. "I'm sorry," she whispered. "I am so very sorry." Then she stood, fetched her coat from the ground, and covered the body.

Finally, she began the long cold walk to the security building, to find someone. She knew how she'd look, bursting through their doorway, bare-legged, shaking, crazy with cold. Still, it had to be done. She would have to tell someone. As she walked, stumbling on her frozen feet, she felt ice forming on her wet flesh, felt her skin grow brittle and hard.

Five steps from the warmth of the building, she heard the owl calling to her. She looked up. There it was, huge and white, its wings spread against the rising moon, the moon that was just a slim copper crescent hanging in a dark, dark sky. The owl swooped down, silent, and fastened its talons in her hair.

34

Suzanne awoke in her own bed, curled on her side, covered with blankets and quilts. Pear was sleeping against her ribs. Apple was curled against her thighs and Plum was lying right across her ankles. She felt warm and happy, for a minute. Then she remembered. She tried to sit up.

Ronelle's hand was on her head, gentle but strong. "Stay there, Suzanne," she said. "The animals are warming you up. Jeez, you scared the shit out of us. You were, like, blue from head to toe."

Suzanne closed her eyes. Ronelle's hand gently stroked her hair. "Who brought me home?"

"You don't remember? You were talking and all, almost like normal. You were very polite and calm. You said, 'Thank you for your help.' You said you didn't need to go to the hospital, that all you needed was a cup of Molly's tea and your own bed. You really don't remember?"

"No. I do not. Who brought me?"

Ronelle's fingers kept stroking. "Charles's guys. Two of them. They kind of led you in the door, all wrapped in a blanket, your teeth chattering, your face like, slate blue, I swear. You looked like something from *The Night of the Living Dead*, swear to God. I like to died. Pear went nuts. He growled and snapped at them and I couldn't make him stop. He didn't shut up until we got you into bed and then he climbed in with you, right under the covers. Dogs aren't dumb, you know. He knew you needed body heat."

Suzanne reached down and scratched Pear's head. He sighed, moaning slightly in his sleep. She opened her eyes. "So. You heard about Diana?"

"We heard something about some dead chick. I didn't have time to listen. I was pouring tea and bourbon down your throat and getting your wet clothes off." Ronelle stopped rubbing and sat back in her chair. "I was scared, boss. I really was. And do you know that you don't even have a fucking heating pad in this house? Or a hair dryer? I mean, what's a person supposed to use, to heat someone up? Christ, even the trailer had a heating pad."

Suzanne turned over so that she could see Ronelle's face. The dogs readjusted; Plum slid out from under the covers and went to sit on the windowsill. The air in the room was stifling, dry and hot. "My God, did you turn the heat up to 90 or something?" She looked at Ronelle, who was pale and sweaty, dressed only in a tiny tank top and underpants.

"Shit, yes. You don't seem to get it. You were, like, totally frozen. I mean, your skin was all weird, kind of splotchy and gray. You had icicles hanging from your hair. You really don't remember, do you?"

"I remember Diana's body and the owl and walking into the door of the security building, blubbering like a giant baby. That's about all." She pushed her head against the pillow. She wished that she could have forgotten all of it—every single moment from the time she'd listened to Diana's voice on the machine, talking about making love to Sam by the pond. The last time Diana spoke, probably, ever. "Listen," she said. "It was my fault. I didn't pick up my messages. I was late. I couldn't walk on the ice." Her voice began to crack, grow thin and wobbly. She put her hands over her face. "Ronelle, I couldn't get to her fast enough. She was still alive and I couldn't get there fast enough. You could have. Remember the night of the ice storm, the footprints? You could have run across that ice just like she did, fast, and reached her. I couldn't. I broke through, Ronelle. I was just too fucking heavy."

Ronelle's hand fell on her shoulder. "It's not your fault, Suzanne."

A laugh, a horrible kind of bubbly laugh, broke from Suzanne's throat. "No? Diana *and* Sam? Both dead. Molly. Munchie. Jesus, Ronelle. Who's the windigo now? Who's got the heart of ice, who preys on the ones she loves? The owl, Ronelle, I saw the owl."

Ronelle stood up. "You're babbling. None of this shit is your fault. You just know some crazy people, that's all. But you look better— sort of pink and normal. I better turn the heat down before the whole house combusts. Go back to sleep, boss."

To her own surprise, Suzanne did fall asleep again, the dogs sighing against her warming skin. When she woke again, the room was still hot but less Saharan. The light was off, but someone was sitting in the chair beside her bed, a dark quiet bulk limned in faint moonlight. She sat up.

"Hey, there," Charles said. He reached out and put a hand on her arm. "You okay?"

"I don't know." She pushed the covers away from her chest. Her naked breasts tumbled out. She pulled the covers back up to her neck and shook off his hand.

Charles laughed. "Don't do that, Ms. Brown. Not for my benefit."

"How come I'm not wearing clothes, if everyone was so anxious to warm me up?"

"Best thing to do. Your little Ronnie's a smart cookie. If you've got to warm someone fast, go skin to skin. And skin to fur, in this case. But she got into bed first, even before the dogs, she said. She stripped to her skinny little bare-naked hide and held you in her arms till you stopped shaking, she said. She's a practical girl. Knows almost as much as the animals, by pure instinct."

She kept the covers high, but sat up all the way, leaning back against the headboard. She couldn't see Charles' face clearly in the faint light, just the gleam of his eyes. She was glad. She cleared her throat. "Tell me what happened," she said. "Everything you know, all right?"

Charles shifted in the chair. "It's not pleasant. You might want to wait until morning."

"No. I want to hear it now, in the dark. Really." She folded her hands on top of the covers, tight. "Please."

Charles gave a grunt, then a sigh. "Okay. Don't interrupt. I only want to say this once."

"Okay."

"All right. Here's what we know, so far. We went to her apartment. It's a little place, almost bare of furniture. It looked stripped, like she'd gotten rid of things. I don't know. It was all just kind of empty, like no one ever really lived there. But the kitchen was a mess—broken plates all over the floor, globs of food. Vomit. A whole lot of vomit, splashed on the floor, on the walls even. Vomit streaked with blood."

Suzanne shuddered. "Why?" she whispered.

He shrugged. "You're interrupting, Ms. Brown. Looked like she'd had some kind of big meal, then thrown it all up, half her stomach coming with it. Some kind of ritual thing, we guess, since this was clearly not a woman who ate a lot. The medical examiner—I spoke to him about an hour ago—he said she was incredibly malnourished. Just a walking skeleton, really. If she hadn't died of exposure out on the ice, she'd have dropped from starvation anyway. Internal bleeding. Either way, very soon."

"I carried her, Charles. She was light as a child." She gripped her hands tighter. She remembered the feeling of Diana's head against her breast. Like a child.

"She was no child, Suzanne. She was a grown woman and crazy as a loon. And, well, sick. Molly would say evil. My grandma would say evil. I don't know. But I know I got chills down my spine when I walked into that kitchen. And my balls just seized up."

"But…."

He raised a hand and held it out. "No. Just listen, okay? This part is hard to say. In the kitchen sink, there was a whole heap of ashes. Like lots and lots of pages had been burned, all black and greasy. And—well, shat on. There was a pile of bloody feces, right in the center of the ashes." He stopped, then cleared his throat. "And there was a note, right in the middle of the kitchen table. And a picture."

She felt a thread of iciness spin itself around her chest, just as if she'd never warmed up.

Charles's voice was low. "The note read, as follows: *The poems are gone. Sam is gone. I am gone. Blame Suzanne Brown. The fat bitch killed us all.*"

The ice crept into her throat and lungs. She whispered around it. "And the picture?"

"You've seen them before. This one was only a little different—it had both a man and a woman attached to the huge woman's breasts. And a man and a woman being swallowed by her.... Well, you've seen them. I don't have to say it."

"Cunt," Suzanne said. "You know the word, Charles." Her teeth began to chatter, as the ice filled her. "The fat, devouring cunt. Mine."

Charles stood up. His voice was thick. "She was a crazy woman. Listen to me. She was purely evil. Wendigo, if I ever saw one. She killed herself—and not just today. She'd been hurting herself over a long long time, way before she ever met you. Her arms, legs, they were a welter of scars, old and new. You had nothing to do with it. You're not at fault."

Trembling, Suzanne felt the fat on her belly wobble and shake. She felt her heavy breasts jiggle. She threw off the covers and stood up, naked in the moonlight. "Look at me, Charles," she yelled. "I am a fat, filthy cunt. I did kill them both. I did."

He reached out and took her shoulders in his hands, roughly. He shook her. "Stop it. She was crazy. She was a starved, vicious, crazy bitch. She did it, not you."

The bed erupted with barks and growls. Pear's great black head emerged, his teeth bared, his fur bristling.

Charles stopped shaking her. He drew her into his arms. He put his mouth against her ear. "Listen to me, Suzanne. Please, just listen. She was possessed. She killed *herself*. She may even have killed him. Who knows? It seems real probable, though."

Suzanne stood stiff in his arms, shivering.

"Even if she didn't push him over that rail, she killed him. No man could live with that stick of ice and bone. No one." His arms tightened. "Jesus, Suzanne, a man needs warmth, flesh. She was barely even human. She was the monster. Not you. You're a beautiful woman."

She felt the warmth of his body, smelled his skin. She felt, against her naked belly, the stirring of his penis and her own automatic, helpless response, the softening and weakening of her flesh. She pulled out of his grip. "No, Charles. She was right. Somehow, she is right. I don't understand it. Even Molly didn't understand it. But somehow, it's me. It is me the owl comes to, every night. Me."

She sat down on the edge of the bed, pulling the sheet to her shoulders. She touched Pear's tense neck. "It's all right," she said to the dog. "I'm all right." She felt his fur go down, heard the thick thump of his tail, wagging under the covers. She lifted her head and spoke quietly. "Please go now, Charles. Please. I need to be alone."

Charles shook his head. "All right. But you call me. You hear? I think it's all over, really I do. I think the world is free of that stink Molly kept talking about. But you need rest. You're not thinking straight. So you call me in the morning. All right?"

"Yes. In the morning. I will." She tried to smile at him. "And thank you, Charles. For seeing this through, you know?"

35

In Victorian novels, women who are having a particularly tough time often take to their beds. It's a time-honored and effective therapy, always assuming that there is someone in the house to fetch and carry, bring food, take away empty trays, answer every ring of the bell. A good stretch of bed rest requires devoted servants.

Ronelle was, apparently, sick of playing her part. By Saturday afternoon, she was standing by the side of Suzanne's bed, her hands on her hips, her hair frizzing out in an angry circle around her head. "Get the fuck up," she said.

Suzanne looked at her. "I can't," she said. "Every time I even stand up to go the bathroom, I get all dizzy."

Ronelle rolled her eyes. "That's because you *only* get up to go to the bathroom. You walk a grand total of, like, twelve steps a day. Your muscles are all mushy and weak. And you haven't eaten shit, for three days. You're wasting away; your hair is all greasy and stuck to your head and, well, you don't smell so hot. It's time to get up. You've been lying here for three days. It's time for the goddamn resurrection." She reached over and flipped the covers away from Suzanne's legs. "Now. I'll start the bath water."

Suzanne groaned, feeling the chill of the air on her legs. She knew she should get up. She knew she was being a terrible baby, weak and spineless. But she just couldn't. She's grown used to lying here now, the dogs by her side, Ronelle taking care of all the things she couldn't face. Ronelle feeding and walking the dogs; Ronelle answering the kitchen phone—she'd unplugged the one in her bedroom—and the doorbell, telling people to go away. Ronelle carrying up trays of food—strange food, yes, cooked by Ronelle, but food still—that Suzanne barely picked at. Ronelle yelling at Leon downstairs. (Yes, Leon was on Suzanne's side of the house sometimes, but she didn't have the energy to care.) It was simple, it was what she needed. Rest. It wasn't that much to ask, really. Just rest. She sat up. "Ronelle, I'm really tired. Really really tired."

"Yeah, well so am I. Up." Ronelle whipped the covers all the way off the bed, exposing sheets coated with dog hair. "Yuck," she said. "Look at this. You might as well be sleeping in the barn. This stinks."

Suzanne was cold, exposed. She could see that her sheets were disgusting but she couldn't care. That was the thing: she just could not care. "All right," she said. "I'll get up and take a bath. You can change the sheets while I'm in there. But then I'm coming back to bed. I am very tired."

Ronelle's voice was a low hiss. "I can change the sheets? I can?" She bent over the bed, staring into Suzanne's face. Her pale eyes were bulging and her freckles stood out like gravel in her skin. "I can run the magazine; I can feed the dogs; I can take my classes; I can write my papers; I can deal with Leon's wife and her lawyers; I can talk to Charles, who calls daily; I can talk to Rachel, who also calls daily; I can talk to that slimy kid Ajax; I can talk to some little airhead named Tiffany that I've never even met; I can talk to your friend Morris who calls, like, hourly. I can cook, I can clean, I can do the laundry, I can do every fucking thing on the whole fucking planet? I don't think so." She leaned very close. "I do not fucking think so. I quit." She turned on her heel and left the room.

Suzanne heard her footsteps go down the stairs and out the front door.

Sitting in the tub, Suzanne started to think. She hadn't been able to, for three days. She had only been able to grieve. She wasn't even sure what for. It was all mixed up in her head. For Molly, surely. For Munchie, even. For Sam, of course. And for his wife, maybe. Maybe there was enough room to feel sorrow for Diana. Yes, it was Diana who had been sending those horrible notes, horrible pictures. Diana had hated her; under her honeyed, child's voice there was a forked tongue and venom. And maybe Diana had even been a murderer. Maybe, like Charles said, she'd killed Sam. But, still, she—Suzanne LaFleshe—she'd been the catalyst. She'd worked on that sick girl's mind like acid, eating away at whatever sanity remained.

She ran water over her head, down her neck, thinking. So maybe she was really grieving for her alter self, her largesse. For Suzanne LaFleshe, who was also dead, she thought, drowned in the waters of that pond. Replaced by Suzanne Brown. Dull, without hunger, sad—but safe. Suzanne Brown would not get in trouble, would not hunger after other women's men, would not devour. Would not want. Suzanne LaFleshe was all desire, endless hunger. It was better she was gone. What a lot of trouble she'd been.

She rubbed the bar of soap over her chest. She was definitely thinner—her breasts looked like deflated balloons, lying flat against her ribs. Her thighs—she lifted them one at time and stared—were flabby, loose. But much slimmer. When she stood up, the water sluicing down her body, she felt lighter, smaller. Things were changing. She might, she thought, actually become normal. She began to dry herself, feeling unfamiliar bone under the flesh.

There was a tentative knock on the bathroom door and Leon's voice. "Hey, Suzanne. Do you know where Ronnie went?"

She stood, one foot on the toilet, drying her leg. She felt a little dizzy. "Ronelle got a little upset. She went out."

There was a sigh. "Yeah, she's been a bit testy. Can I talk to you?"

"No. I want to be left alone, Leon. And you're not even supposed to be on my side of the house, remember?" She reached for the talcum powder—Summer Hill. The scent of roses. She thought of summer. Would it come, ever? Would she be stuck in this endless, haunted winter forever? She sighed and sprinkled powder into her palm.

There was a sound like a long slide, then a plop. Leon had obviously just sat himself down, leaning against her bathroom door. He groaned. "Listen, Suzanne," he said. "I'm really sorry that this all happened. And all at once—a whole bunch of strange shit to come crashing down at one swell foop, as my father used to say. But, hey, Ronnie and I are going to give it a go. We're really going to try. To be a couple. I—I think I might really love her, Suzanne. Really."

She pulled her bathrobe around her shoulders. Her head was spinning and the steamy air was making her feel just a little sick. She sat down on the toilet and put her head into her summer-scented hands. "Jesus Christ. What about your wife, Leon?"

"Ha." His head banged against the door. "She's nuts. She's got a whole pack of lawyer-wolves, already. They're, like, slavering at the door. She hates my guts. She is after my hide, really. She wants my head, stuffed and hanging on the wall. All glassy-eyed. She'd eat my liver if she could, fried with bacon and onions. It's scary."

Suzanne nodded into her hands. Her head was clearing. "Do you blame her?"

"Yes. Yes, I do." He turned and put his mouth against the keyhole. "Listen, Suzanne. Ronnie told me how you think you're to blame for Sam, for his wife. How you think it stinks that Ronnie and I are together, since I'm married. Like it's Ronnie's fault or something. But you are wrong."

She lifted her head. "Give me a break. I don't want your input, Leon. You lied, you cheated, you're a prick."

His voice came through the door like a rocket. "Fine. It's all me and my slutty girlfriend, right? We're the sinners here. But how about her, the little wife at home? How come she gets to be the saint? Oh, yeah, she supported my useless ass while I was trying—trying—to finish my piddly little degree. She did that and she always reminded me that she was doing it, every single day. Hourly. Minute by minute updates on how useless and ungrateful I am. And maybe I am, ungrateful. But maybe that's because there ain't a whole lot to be grateful for. Did you ever think that maybe I haven't had a smile or even a goddamn pat on the head for, Christ, years and years and years? Not a kind word, not a soft gesture, not a kiss? Do you know what's it like to live with a stone, Suzanne? Jesus Christ. Okay, so I'm the sinner here. Fine. But don't you think there are other kinds of sins? Her kind? Sins of omission. No joy. No laughter. No sex. No warmth. Not one stitch of generosity? Jesus." His fist hit the door and he stood up. "Ronnie is the only joy I've known, for years and years. At least our sins are sins of commission. At least we are fucking alive. We are alive and fucking. I'm not giving that up."

The quiet in the bathroom was almost startling, after Leon had stomped down the stairs. Suzanne realized that her head was perfectly fine. She wasn't even a bit lightheaded anymore. The heat of Leon's words had cleared the air and her mind, like a good solid smack on the cheek. She opened the bathroom door and walked into her bedroom. She didn't even feel like going back to bed anymore. She gathered up the dirty sheets and shoved them into the laundry basket. She shook out a clean set and began to make up her bed.

By the time Ronelle came back, Suzanne had cooked dinner. There wasn't much in the house but there was olive oil, butter, garlic, and pasta. That was all, really, anyone needed to make a meal. Leon had walked the dogs and taken the laundry to the laundromat on the corner. He'd washed and dried and folded every last thing. He'd picked up a loaf of Italian bread at the bakery next door and a bottle of cheap chianti to go with it.

When Ronelle walked into the fragrant kitchen and saw Suzanne up and dressed and standing at the stove, dropping handfuls of linguine into a pot of boiling water and Leon putting three plates on the table, she started to cry, tears streaming down her spotty, pale cheeks. "Oh, man," she said. "A fucking family. Look at us. We're a goddamn family."

Suzanne smiled. "Yep. Sit down. I owe you a meal."

Suzanne still couldn't eat much, just a few bites really, but she enjoyed watching Ronelle and Leon slurping up their pasta, laughing and talking. She didn't have much to say, either, but she enjoyed listening to them. Ronelle was telling Leon exactly how to finish his dissertation—she seemed to have read a whole lot of Puritan literature in the past few days—and he was nodding, agreeing, his eyes lit up with energy and hope. It was, Suzanne thought, as if they were both her children. Wayward, imperfect, but hers.

When the phone rang, Ronelle stood up, but Suzanne waved her away. "I think I can take my own phone calls, now." She picked up the receiver and said hello.

"Thank God. It's you, in person, Suzanne. I've been nearly frantic."

"Yes, it's me, Morris. I'm sorry to have worried you. I've been—resting." She leaned against the wall. Ronelle and Leon were both watching her. "Wait a minute. I'll go to the other phone."

In her room, she sat down on her neatly made bed and plugged in her phone. She lifted the receiver. "You can hang up down there," she yelled and she heard the click of the kitchen phone. "I'm back, Morris. As I said, I've been resting."

"As you should, my poor dear. Are you well now?"

"I think I am. I feel all right." She thought about that. She did seem to feel all right. "Kind of limp. Deflated. Sad. But all right."

Morris make a kind of tsking sound. "I don't like the sound of that 'deflated.' Your best quality has always been your inflation, Suzanne. Your fullness and buoyancy. Your ebullience. I hope that returns."

She laughed. "Actually, I'm hoping to become a whole lot less full. But, thank you." She felt, suddenly, enormously grateful to Morris. He'd been her friend before anyone, before she'd gotten so messed up with Sam. And he'd stuck. He'd never left her. "Really, thank you, Morris. You've been a real friend."

There was a long moment of silence. "Have I, Suzanne? I didn't think you felt that way, anymore."

She was ashamed. "I've been a bit confused. I think I'm coming out of it."

"Then, I have a suggestion. Perhaps you could join me for a drink? At my apartment? I have a lovely bottle of wine or two, lying about the place."

She heard the strain in his voice. She had never been to his apartment, not ever. No one she knew had. She didn't even know the address, come to think of it. He was, as he'd always told her, a bit of a hermit. A kind of new-age Crusoe. A man who lived alone, who wrote alone, who did not share space easily. She hadn't cared; she'd understood. Her house had always been fine, for their brief and infrequent encounters. "Your place? Are you sure?"

He laughed, a little ruefully. "A kind of new start, perhaps? A new phase in our friendship? Here, on the first day of a new month. Our February 1st transformation. Hell, why not? Yes, I'm sure. 653 State Street, on the park. The number 10 bus comes right along the street, my dear. I'll be waiting."

She dressed carefully, conservatively. She was not, not, going out as Suzanne LaFleshe, but as Suzanne Brown. Her clothes were all loose, anyway. She found, at the back of her closet, an old dress, dark red velvet, high in the neck, long in the skirt. She put it on and looked at herself in the mirror. The dress hung gently over her. She was very pale, with dark circles beneath her eyes. But her hair was clean and curling and the dark dress set it off. She looked like a tired child, dressed up for a party. She stopped only for a minute to call through the pantry door to Ronelle and Leon, who had gone back to their own side of the house, leaving the kitchen neat and clean.

"Hey, you guys. I'm going out. Back in an hour or so."

She stepped out into the cold night, wrapping her scarf around her face. She hadn't been outdoors in three days. The walk was slick with ice. She'd almost forgotten how cold it could feel, the winter night. She pulled her coat tighter around her chest. God, she'd become so sensitive to cold. She was shivering already. She'd just reached the sidewalk, when her front door was flung open. She turned to see Ronelle framed against the light, Pear at her side.

"Hey. Where are you going?"

"I'm going out. I told you." She stood on the sidewalk, stamping her feet. "Close the door. You're letting all the heat out."

Ronelle put her hands on her hips. "Out where? Charles said I shouldn't let you go out alone. He called off the guys watching the house, but said I might want to keep an eye on you, anyway. He thinks you're still—well, a bit emotionally fragile, he said."

"Oh, did he? Well, tell Massa Charles that I went to see an old friend, all right? Tell him that the bogeyman—bogey woman—is dead and that I'll be fine. Ding dong, the witch is dead." She began to walk away. Pear, suddenly, bolted from the doorway and ran to Suzanne's side, whining. He dug his head into her thigh. She grabbed his collar and shook it. "Get back in there, you bad dog. Go." Pear didn't budge. He pushed his nose harder into her leg. "Go. You're a bad dog. Bad dog. Now go back." He looked up at her with huge sad eyes, then turned away and walked, very slowly, back into the house, head and tail hanging.

Ronelle ruffled his ears. "Listen, boss. You're still a little weak. Be careful, okay? Don't, like, fall down or anything."

Suzanne waved and walked away. Halfway down the block she heard, out of nowhere, Molly's voice, as clear as day: *It's easy to fall down when you're already hurt.* She shook her head. Really, Mol, she thought, you can give it up now. I'm okay. The bogey woman, the one you tried to warn me about, the one you fought, she's dead. It turns out that you were right, all along. You smart-ass witch you. And it's all right now. You won, Molly. You did.

She put her head down and headed to the corner, to the bus stop. As she stood there waiting for the downtown bus, she looked up at the sky. The moon was just a tiny shaving and there were stars. Even above the orange city lights, there were stars.

36

The bus was full of chattering, laughing students, heading down to the bars on Lark Street. Suzanne got out two blocks above Lark. She walked down State, looking into the lit windows of the beautiful old buildings that lined the left side of the street. It was one of the loveliest streets in the city, with it row of three-storey brownstones and brick buildings, each with a historic marker near its door. 1815, 1822, 1798, 1848. Old houses, houses that seen much life and many deaths. Many of the windows were stained glass—twining flowers and seashells, lit from within. Many had wrought iron window grates and boxes, too. The boxes were piled with winter greenery; some still glittered with tiny white Christmas lights. She stopped in front of 653 and looked up. It was a solid, strong brownstone. Like all of the houses, it faced Washington Park—now a huge lawn of white snow, with the bare branches of hundreds of trees swinging in the night air. In spring, she knew, many of the trees would bloom, along with the thousands of tulips, lilacs, and roses that made the park so beautiful. In spring, she thought, Morris must wake up to bird calls and sweet scents. Perhaps he walked in the park, early, before anyone else, when the grass was still wet with dew and old cobbled streets were still. She smiled. Perhaps, this coming spring, she would wake here with him some day, in this gracious home. She climbed the steps and rang Morris's bell.

He opened the door himself. He looked awkward, formal. He even gave a funny little bow. "Welcome, Suzanne. Oh, you are so welcome." He took her into the hall and helped her off with her coat, running a hand over her back. The hall was elegant, with a high carved ceiling and oak-railed stairs leading to the upper floor. "What a lovely dress," he said. "So soft and warm. Come in." He opened a set of French doors and led her into a living room of simple luxury.

She looked around: high ceilings, dark green flocked wallpaper, comfortable furniture. Hardwood floor, an oriental rug in soft, faded greens and blues. "Oh, Morris," she said. "This is beautiful. I had no idea."

He smiled. "Well, I have tried. I've been a professor a long time, you know. They pay me well and I have no one to spend it on." He laughed. "Very well, actually. When I came in, eons and eons ago, as a Yale Younger Poet, I was considered quite a star, for the department. Well, in latter years, with my star shining very much less brightly, they may have regretted where my salary started, since it had to keep going up, proportionate to where it began. I do love our professors' union." He put a hand at the small of her back. "Listen to me, nattering on. I believe I'm nervous. I so rarely entertain. Do sit down."

Suzanne sat in a cozy armchair in front of a cheerful fire, burning in the living room grate. The mantelpiece was made of green marble, swirled through with black and white lines. Above it was a painting, a medieval-looking madonna and child, the child suckling at his mother's breast, quite beautiful. She looked around the room and relaxed.

Morris handed her a glass of a very nice wine, in a very nice glass that she held in both hands. The color of the wine matched her dress— a pleasing little coincidence. Morris sat across from her in a blue velvet rocker. Its arms were carved into the shapes of swan's heads, beaks bent and settled into the feathers at their necks. "It was my mother's, this chair," he said. His long fingers gripped the swan on his left, stroking. "I've always been fond of it." He raised his glass, tilting it toward her. "*Salud*, my dear. *A votre sante*. Down the hatch. All of that. Welcome to my home."

She tipped her glass in his direction. "*L'chaim*. Bottoms up. All of that." She sipped the wine; it was slightly warm, wonderful. "Ummm," she said. "Lovely."

He nodded. "Thank you." He sipped. "Well, it may be a bit too warm. I kept it near the fire, all the while I was getting up my nerve to invite you over. It is, perhaps, overly heated."

"It's perfect. I seem to like things warm these days."

"Understandable." He leaned back in his chair, his long legs flung out before him. He looked into the fire. "I must apologize, again, Suzanne. I was very much out of line on the phone a few days back— I had been drinking. I do that, way too much, I now realize. A function of loneliness, I think, of living alone for so very long, with just my thoughts, my work, for company. And my work, of late, has been a bit dark. Disturbing. Still, I mustn't turn to the bottle for comfort, must I? I've vowed to be more careful." He took a sip of wine and laughed. "Notice how very slowly I'm imbibing."

She smiled. "Yes."

He sat back up, glass on one knee, and leaned toward her. "And I have a bit of a confession."

Her relaxation fled. She held up a hand. "I don't want to hear it, Morris. I've been pretty much of an ass myself. I've been wrong about almost everyone I know. And wrong about myself. I've been an utter ass. I don't need apologies and I sure as hell don't need confessions. You haven't done anything wrong."

"Oh, but I have. I've been selfish, self-absorbed, unwilling to share my work—or my life—with you. I haven't allowed you to see how much you mean to me, Suzanne. I've hidden my feelings."

Suzanne looked at his face, lit by the fire. It was tense, full of concentration. The fingers around his glass wine were tapping, jumpy. Oh my God, she thought. He's going to say something I don't want to hear. This is some sort of declaration. She leaned forward and put a hand on his knee. "Morris, don't," she said. "I really can't deal with anything intense tonight. I just want to sit here and be warm and drink wine. That's all I can handle, all right?"

His lips tightened. "But it is time. It really is. More than time. I've been through a lot, the past few weeks. I've been—distraught. Disturbed. Ever since the beginning of the semester, I've been, well, shaken. Since last semester, really. Last summer, even. I've been—ill. I really would like to settle things, between us." He laid a hand over hers; the fingers were cold and she jumped. His fingers tightened.

"Where to begin? Well, with Sam, I suppose." He nodded, his eyes on his wine glass. He swirled the wine in the glass, gently. "Your friend Sam. I was very angry at your friend Sam, Suzanne. I had been, all during the fall, but somehow, over the Christmas break, when I was entirely alone, it became, well, difficult. Quite terrible, really." He looked into her face. "Quite terrible, my state of mind. I don't think you quite realized how much it hurt me, last summer, when you began— well, seeing—Sam. Perhaps you didn't mean to, but you quite dropped me. Do you recall? I believe I only saw you once or twice, during the whole fall semester. Do you recall, Suzanne?"

Suzanne felt her mouth go dry. She thought back, to days of fall-ing leaves and blue skies. To Sam in her bed, in her back yard, rolling in leaves, laughing. Their Thanksgiving feast, in her kitchen. Yes, she recalled. She had dropped Morris. Had not called, had barely remem-bered to say hello, when she ran into him on campus. When, before Sam, they had been friends and lovers. Occasional lovers, casual lov-ers. She'd thought they were only very casual lovers. She looked into Morris's face and saw the pain there. Oh God, could there be anyone in her life she hadn't hurt, hadn't wounded? She leaned forward, closer. "Yes. Oh Morris, I certainly didn't mean to hurt you. I thought—well, I thought that you and I were, casual. You always seemed not to care, not really. I didn't know that…."

He laughed, a short bitter laugh. "You didn't know that I would sell my immortal soul for you?"

She sat back, her lips trembling. She took a sip of her wine, trying to think of what she could possibly say. "No, of course I didn't think anything like that. That's silly. That's just an exaggeration. You never once indicated that…"

"That what? That I would have followed you to hell and back? That I have, in fact, followed you to hell and back? Across the Styx, forgetting everything? That I have given up everything, just to keep you? To fuck you?" His voice rose and she tried to pull her hand away. He held it, his fingers like bands. "That my whole life, all my days and all my nights are full of wanting to fuck you? To sink into your flesh? To bury myself inside that incredible cunt? To lick your juices from my fingers?"

His spit wet her face and she cringed. "To fuck you, Suzanne, to fuck you until you screamed my name—my name, not some pissant graduate student. Me. I want to fuck you, day and night. I see it in my dreams, Suzanne—your cunt. I taste it. I cannot, cannot live without it."

The glass fell from her hand and she watched as the wine stained the rug—a spreading circle of warm red on the cool green, cool blue. He set his glass down carefully beside it. His voice fell, became soft, gentle. He licked the spittle from his lips. "Oh, my dear, I'm sorry. I've frightened you. I become, sometimes, too vehement. Too plainspoken." He shook his head. "Perhaps I should just show you my little secret."

She stood up, his hand still gripping hers. "No. I'm going home." She shook her arm. "Let me go, Morris. You're frightening me."

"Yes. Yes, I am. I apologize." He made a wry face, but his grip didn't loosen. "Come, my dear. I want you to see my study." He stood up. He kept her hand enclosed in his and wrapped one long arm around her shoulder, placing the other hand on her breast. He pulled her hip against his and spoke into her ear. "This way, Suzanne. You'll understand, I think, once you see my study."

She tried to pull away, but he was very strong and his fingers dug into the soft flesh of her breast with every step. He walked her to a door at the end of the living room, the door to what must have once been a family dining room. He opened the dark oak door. "My study, Suzanne. My lair. Where I work and dream and long."

She stepped inside, and suddenly, he gave one hard shove on her back and then let her go. She stumbled forward and found herself standing in the center of a dark room, as he slipped back into the hall and slammed the door behind him. She heard a key turn in the lock.

His voice, through the heavy door, was gentle. "The light switch is just to your right, my dear. Turn it on. You'll see."

She stayed still, waiting for her eyes to adjust but the room was very dark. She leaned toward the door. "I don't want to see, Morris. I want to go home. Please just let me go home, all right?"

"Of course I will, Suzanne. But I'd like you to look around first. Perhaps what you see will convince you that I am—well, sincere, to say the least. Switch on the light, love."

There seemed to be no choice. She felt about with her right hand until she found the switch. She flipped it on and held a hand over her eyes in the flood of brightness that blasted into the room. There were white spotlights, everywhere, casting unrelenting beams at the walls.

"Ah. There you are, then. You see? Aren't you lovely?" His voice whispered through the door.

She lowered her hand and the walls of the room sprang to life. Painting after painting. She read the labels: *Suzanne LaFleshe 23. Suzanne LaFleshe 118. Suzanne LaFleshe 39. Suzanne LaFleshe. Suzanne LaFleshe. Suzanne LaFleshe.* She turned slowly, in a circle. She was everywhere. The room swelled with fleshtones, with pinks and mauves and amber. She filled every inch of the walls—flesh, rolls and rolls of it. Thighs, breasts, buttocks, belly, shoulder, calf. Hair, hands, eyes, neck. Feet. Acres and acres of flesh. She remembered posing for some of them. She remembered how her husband had lavished the paintings with light, how his brushes had limned every surface of her body with warm pink light. She remembered how he'd asked her to lean this way, that, to sit here, there, to open herself to the light, to him. She could remember it all. The days she'd learned, she remembered, to hate herself.

But here. So many of them, here. They cost a great deal of money, she knew that. So many of them. A terrible excess of flesh. The room was hot; it smelled like oil paint. It was making her ill.

"Do you see, Suzanne? I've purchased every one I could find. I've taken trips to the City—to all sorts of galleries. I've plumbed the internet auction sites. There are ways to find them, still, the paintings of you. So you see, I live with you, all the time. I write with you. I watch you. I—well, I confess—I masturbate to your image. I do homage. I fall to my knees, prick in hand, and I worship. Do you see? How lovely you are, in my eyes? Do you see, now?"

She closed her eyes, her head swimming. She heard Molly's voice, a mere thread of sound in her ear: *You must learn to notice, Suzanne. You must learn to see.* And then a question, the one she'd never learned to answer correctly: *Who is your enemy?* Dear God. She'd never answered it correctly, the crucial question. Never.

She walked to the door. "I do see, Morris. I do. Now, please, let me come out."

There was silence on his side of the door. Then a long, long sigh. "I think you do not understand, Suzanne. Even though it is right there, before you. All my adoration, laid at your feet."

She put a hand on the door. "No, I understand, Morris. I do. But it's—it's a bit much, to take in. I need to go home, to think about it." She heard the tremor in her own voice, the patent fear. She tried to sound normal. "I'll call you tomorrow and we'll talk about it. But I need to come out. I'm hot. I'm feeling sick. I'm still weak. I haven't been eating. I'm faint, Morris. Please."

He groaned. "I am not a fool, Suzanne. I recognize lies."

She leaned against the wood. "Please, Morris. Let me go."

The key turned. The door shook with the violence of his kick. And then he was in the room, holding her arm, his fingers bruising the flesh. "No. You have to know the rest. You, perhaps, will understand then. But it will be too late." She cringed, looking away from his face. It was suffused with blood, dark, sweating.

He put a hand against her throat. "It will be too late." He smiled. "Well. Still. Knowledge for its own sake, then? Never to be scorned. Not among academics, my dear. And poets. So. Top drawer of the desk. A manuscript. Completed, just today. You may remember, I told you about it, some time back? In the bar? You seemed—how shall I say?—somewhat less than impressed. Well, that is understandable. What I described was a very crude version. Now it is refined, polished. Perhaps now you will see its genius. Perhaps. Read it, Suzanne.

I will wait here. I will be right here, on the other side of the door, awaiting your astute critical response." He pushed her again and slid out the door.

There was nothing else to do. She was, after all, a reader. She could do this. And maybe, while she did, she could think of some way to make him see reason, to let her go free into the cold night.

But after she'd read the pile of pages, she really did understand. He was right—it was work of genius. An epic poem, beautifully crafted. It was a narrative of lust and vengeance and jealousy and great struggle—as all the epics are. Spun out in perfect iambic pentameter. Heroic verse. The plot was classic, the characters vivid and simple. The story as old as humankind—the old, wise, true lover vs. the young, handsome, foolish lover. A clash of warriors—the upstart with his shining shield and the true knight, the knight with dented, hard-used armor. The knight with truth in his heart. The knight with guile and ultimate courage. The wily knight, the old knight.

And the woman? Oh she was beautiful—large, a bounteous woman. The descriptions of her would make Ronelle's good list in a moment. Her body, with every inch limned in glorious words, her generous body—she was the object of the old knight's quest. Of course, she was not really human, not fully a person. She was simply flesh. She was all body. And it was her flesh that was the prize over which the two men battled, each in his own way.

There was jousting—wars of words. Challenges. Boasting. And treachery: the old knight slipped a note to the young knight's wife, telling how the young knight worshipped another woman. The young knight's wife grew to hate him, grew cold, added layers to her heart of ice. Oh, yes, there were tricks, feints. And then the invitation to do battle. The young knight invited to the old knight's lair. The foolish, simple young knight, accepting in good faith, the invitation. The young knight, unschooled in treachery, came alone.

And there was the final battle—a cold cold night in January, under the light of the moon. There was a well—a deep stone well, its floor gleaming white in the silvery light from above. In the end, it was all very simple, just as the old knight had planned. The weapon? None, really. Nothing that could be traced, nothing to raise suspicion. Just a railing, and far below, a floor of stone. A cry. Wind with weight. A terrible leaden thud. Blood. Brains. Victory.

She wiped tears from her face and stood up. Her horror was like a fierce hand inside her chest, squeezing. She saw, branded on her eyelids, Sam's shattered body, the outflung hand with its curling blond hairs. She felt, burned into her skin, Diana's child-body in her arms. She stood up and walked to the door, surrounded by accusing mirrors. *Suzanne LaFleshe. Suzanne LaFleshe.* But she thought before she spoke, carefully.

"All right, Morris," she said. "I understand. You are a wonderful poet. It's an astonishing work. It will make you famous. It is simply stunning." She listened. Maybe, maybe it would work. The old trick. The old seduction. The way to a poet's heart. He would want to hear more, want to hear it forever, and he would let her out, to whisper her praises in his ear.

There was a soft exhalation. "Is it, Suzanne? Is it good work?" The key turned.

She closed her eyes. "Yes. It is. It is fine, fine work."

Morris laughed, sounding like a boy. The door swung open. "Yes, I know that it is." He put both hands on her shoulders, smiling down into her face. "And perhaps now you'll understand why I did what I did. Not only was that man, your precious Sam, a fool, he was a bad poet. A silly, spoiled brat—not a real poet at all." He laughed again, a soft ironic chuckle. "Well, then, I suppose I won't need this knife then, the one I'd been keeping in my pocket." He pulled it out—a sharp kitchen knife, shining in the brilliant light.

He held it up, close to her eyes. "Come, Suzanne, tell me. Do I need this?"

She took a deep, shaking breath. Her eyes could not leave the silver blade of the knife. She swallowed. "Please, Morris. You don't want to hurt me."

He looked startled and then he chuckled. "No. Of course I don't. You are being silly, my dear. That's not like you. You are usually far more astute. Well, of course, you're upset. But it's quite clear. See? I've even drawn dotted lines, right along my wrists. I thought perhaps you wouldn't come this evening. I thought I might need them." He lifted the edges of his white shirt sleeves and he had, really had, drawn long broken lines, lines that traveled up his arms, in blue ink. The lines crossed the flesh like rivers on a map.

He looked at her, his head tilted slightly, the knife held close to her throat. "You see? But you have come and you do see. You must forgive me, for loving you. That's all it is, Suzanne. Love."

She nodded, her blood pounding in her ears. "I do, Morris. I do forgive you. Please, put the knife down."

He lowered the knife. He pressed it, lightly, against his exposed wrist. "Well, then, I won't need this. But I did wonder, what it would feel like." He pressed the blade into his skin, gently but firmly. A thin line of blood appeared and he smiled. He lifted the wrist to his mouth and licked the line of blood. "There, that wasn't so bad. It's very sharp. One can hardly feel it cut." He held the wrist to Suzanne's lips. "Take a taste, my dear." She tried to turn her face away but he pressed the knife against her throat again.

"Oh come, my dear." He pressed the wrist against her lips and she tasted salt and copper. She licked her lips and swallowed. "Ah, there! You've done it. Now there is a blood pact. Something strong between us. For you must promise never to tell. You must agree that it isn't for anyone else's ears, this story. That poem—it is just for you. I will never be able to publish it, of course. And that's a shame, because it is so fine. It really is fine. But, then, I wrote it for you, really. Just for you." The knife scraped her neck. The blood from his wrist was warm on her lips. She swallowed again.

"I wrote it so that we'd share that secret, the wonders of that night, you and I. I need you to see it, Suzanne. How lovely it was, in all that blue moonlight. The simplicity. It wasn't really planned, but it was so easy. It was so easy that it had to be fated. It happened like a lovely dream, with no effort at all, really. One little tap, that's all. To send that silly boy on his last long journey. And then, a moment later, standing over his body, like a dream again, but a strong, sexy dream. I stood there, my penis hard as a sword. Oh, it was amusing, my dear. He tried to speak, through the bloody hole that was his mouth. He tried to say something that sounded like 'Diana.' That was his very last word. Silly little prick, loving to the end, his lovely cold Diana. Oh, I wish you'd been there. How you would have laughed. You'd have understood."

He took his wrist from her mouth but not the knife from her throat. He bent, awkwardly, and kissed her bloody lips. His tongue forced her teeth open. Her jaw clenched itself against him.

He pulled back, just a little. "Oh come, Suzanne. Surely you see the beauty of it. The irony. Because, as it happens, you were there, the whole time, in your office. I knew that you were there. I'd watched you enter. It was the knowledge of your presence that gave me the strength. And, do you know what else, my dear? Oh, this is too precious! He was still alive when you left. Oh, yes, still whispering into that cold floor, still moaning. Still calling for Diana. So silly of him." He shook his head. "Well, then. Surely you don't want to continue this little drama. You don't want to have me bleeding at your feet. Surely not. Ah, you don't answer. Shall I, then? Shall I use my silly little dotted lines?"

She felt her anger rise like a serpent. She spat—his blood, her saliva—aiming for his eyes. Her voice, when it came, was not her own. It was a voice of ice, of venom and cold hate. The voice slid from her throat like oil, coiling into the air. "Do it, Morris. Do it. Cut your wrists wide open. Wide, wide open. I want to see you die."

37

She could, of course, have fled. She could have called for help, she could have walked out and taken the bus back home. She could have phoned for an ambulance, could have screamed. She could at least have turned out the lights so that she didn't have to see so clearly the blood pooling around him and the light leave his eyes. She could have done any number of rational things.

But what she did was not rational. It was primal, it was primitive. She had tasted his blood. She had entered the realm of the cannibal, where the enemy must not only be defeated but consumed. To the victor go the spoils. If someone had handed her his liver, she would have devoured it. She would have.

She crouched, not three feet from his head and watched him die. He died slowly, shaking with cold, crying with thirst. His last words, though, were gentle—*Suzanne, my dear, Suzanne, my love, please*. She listened with a heart of ice. She watched the last rise of his chest with joy. She sat, surrounded by images of her own living flesh, and watched the life leak out of his. To the victor go the spoils.

When it was done, she stood up, smoothing the hem of her red velvet dress. She remembered that the wendigo could only truly be destroyed by fire, that only flame could melt its icy heart and return it to human form. Only fire could give the monster back its humanity. She thought about that, that she could give him that. A log from the fireplace, a simple burning coal tipped out onto the rug. She could give him that.

But she didn't. She left his last poem on his desk—his confession, his suicide note. She went into the living room and picked up her wine glass from the rug. His glass, she tipped over, knocking it down with her boot, adding its contents to the stain from her own. She carried her glass into the kitchen and washed it. She held it with a towel and put it back into his neat cupboard. Then she picked up her coat and simply left his house. The air outside was sharp and clean. She walked into the park across the street. She stepped into the deep, untrodden snow, white and clear under the stars. She bent and took a handful of snow and rubbed it across her face. Over and over, she scooped the snow and scrubbed her face, until surely his blood was gone. Erased. When she looked back, there was only one set of foot-steps leading into the snow and one coming back out. The perfect crime.

She took the bus home. She picked up the phone and she called Charles's office.

She told the officer who answered her story—how she'd just gone to Morris's house and how she'd found him there, dead. She told them to send someone over to 653 State Street. The door, she said, was open.

Ronelle asked, only once: "But you left so much earlier than you said. Where were you, all that time?"

She looked into Ronelle's pale eyes and said, "Where do you think?"

Ronelle looked back. "I think it doesn't matter. I think you did whatever you had to do, boss. Fuck 'em if they can't take a joke."

Apple bounced, sniffing at the hem of her dark red dress. Plum looked out from orange, glistening eyes.

When Charles came, he folded her into his arms and whispered into her hair. "It's all right, sweetheart," he said. "I'm so sorry. But it really is all over now. It's all right."

And Pear forgave her for calling him a bad dog. In the light of dawn, he curled beside her in her bed, sighing with satisfaction. All he'd ever wanted, his whole long life, was for her to come home safely. And now she had.

38

The May wind ruffled Suzanne's hair. She was sitting in a folding chair on the dock that stuck out into the lake. Apple was snuffling on the rocks that ringed the shore, waves lapping gently against their granite feet. Pear was lying on the soft gray wood of the dock, hanging his head and front paws over the side, watching for fish. His reflection wavered and glistened in the clear amber water. When a fish came by, his ears perked and he drooled.

Suzanne lifted her sunglasses and looked across the water from her island in the center of the lake, her small mound of land that rose from the water. On the mainland, trees were green with new leaves— soft, fuzzy chartreuse green, young and fresh. She sighed with pleasure, folding her hands on her belly and sipping from her ice cream soda. Vanilla ice cream, cream soda. Thick and white. Sweet, rich. Food of the gods. Her appetite was coming back, full force. Everything tasted good again. She stretched her legs and looked down over the sun-warmed field of her flesh. She was getting herself back, pound by precious pound. She smiled.

The air was sharp with the smell of wood smoke, coming from the cottage behind her. She looked up, watching a curl of smoke drift across the sky. Soon, she thought, she wouldn't need to light the stove, even at night. February and March and even April had been tough. She'd had to struggle to keep the cottage above freezing. But she'd remembered old skills—how her grandfather had stoked and babied the old iron stove in his print shop in Maine. The stove in this cottage—Charles's grandmother's cottage in New Hampshire—wasn't much different. She'd remembered that she had a knack for keeping a fire alive.

She looked down at the letter in her hand. It was from Ronelle:

Hey, boss-Things are cool here. The house is fine. Leon fixed the loose shingles on the roof. Plum is exactly the same as ever. She doesn't seem to miss you at all - cat's a cat a cat. All the legal papers on the house are ready for you to sign - Molly's lawyer says to tell you he's sending them up. You'll be an official homeowner. Maybe then you'll let me pay you some rent, okay? What else? Oh, yeah - Leon's legal papers came through, too. He's almost divorced. Maybe we'll make an honest woman of me - but maybe not. Can't decide if I want to. Please advise.

And the mag is coming along - I think we'll have an issue in the fall, no shit. And I'm getting A's in my classes (did you ever doubt?) and the semester has only two weeks left - whooppee! Oh, and Rachel called - said to tell you that your committee - minus one member, ha ha - has granted you an extension on the diss. Due date is now in December. That's a long time away. You'll get it done by then, easy. How's it coming, by the way? Pat those stupid dog noses for me - would you believe I actually miss those beasts? Love, El. (I'm dropping the Ron, I think.)

She sighed. December. It was a very long way away. But still—there it was. The laptop was in the cottage. The cottage floor was covered in books. The shelves were adrift in paper, sheets and sheets of paper, typed, scribbled over, crumbled. It was in there, a skull on the shelf, still. But, first, before the dissertation, before she even thought about returning to her cannibals, there was the pile of Sam's poetry, waiting to be retyped, to be sorted, arranged. Diana had burned his copies, had crushed his disks, smashed his computer, even. But Diana had forgotten one thing: Suzanne had copies. Sam had always given her copies, at least of the ones he'd written for Diana. If there really were others, others written for other girls, they didn't matter. These were Sam's heart. She could almost feel them beating in her hand. Sam's poor wounded heart. They were Sam's legacy. And they were her work to do, to find a publisher for *Moon Dancer: An Elegy*. If she did it well, Sam would live on. Wouldn't he?

She shook her head and watched clouds pass through the scrim of pine needles above her head. She breathed deep and thought about supper: she'd gotten out the grill, for the first cookout of the season. She'd bought steaks and they were already marinating. She'd scrubbed potatoes to bake in the coals; she'd found a batch of lovely new fiddle-head ferns, curled like babies, right in the woods behind the cottage. She'd baked a rhubarb pie and whipped cream to put on it. She'd bought wine and beer and made a pitcher of lemonade. She nodded. It would be a good supper, a lovely LaFleshe meal. When Charles got here, after the long car ride from Albany, he'd at least get fed well. More than that, she couldn't promise. But she might take him for a ride in his own canoe, out under the soft spring stars. She'd been practicing and was now a good paddler, strong and well-balanced. He deserved that. He'd waited; he'd left her alone for three months. Back then, when her terror and sorrow had taken over and she'd thought she would lose her mind, he'd given her the key to the cottage, no strings, no questions.

When she'd arrived in early February, the lake was still solid with ice. An old local man had carried her across the ice in his snowmobile, the dogs trotting along behind. Before he'd roared away, leaving her alone at the cottage, he'd turned to her. "Don't you go walking out on this ice, young lady," he'd said. "Just cause those dogs did it. Ice is tricky.

You never know about it. This old lake's full of currents. Don't you trust her. Ice is tricky stuff." Suzanne had nodded and waved. Oh, she knew that: icy is tricky stuff.

All winter, men had skimmed across the ice on noisy snowmobiles. They had cut holes in its surface and drawn up fish from its waters. At night, the holes closed back over, the ice forming a new skin. When the men came back and opened up the holes, steam rose into the air from the waters below.

During the cold months, she'd stayed inside, close to the stove, watching the men through closed windows, wrapped in the warmth of the cottage. The old man came back weekly, bringing groceries and dog food. She's stayed inside, alone on her island. She was never bored. Only very, very tired. The cottage was full of Charles's grandmother's things. Tins of strange teas. Bits of leaves and bark. Figures in clay and in cloth. Masks. Turtle shells. Rocks and stones. Pine cones. Hand-stitched quilts. Shining pieces of amber, with insects frozen inside. Animal skulls. Bones. Acorns. Fossils. Dried wasps' nests. Mussel shells, shiny black, opalescent, piled in mounds. As the days warmed, she'd ventured out more and more, walking the snowy woods, rejoicing when spring turned the paths muddy and soft. The nights, always, were very still and very lonely. She had to wake up and stoke the stove, at least once every night, and when she did, she often couldn't get back to sleep. So she thought too much. She got scared. Things came back to her, haunted her. She feared the owl, although she never saw one, never even heard its cry. Still, at night she walked the cottage floors, touching the grandmother's things like charms, like totems to keep herself safe and sane. They reminded her of Molly.

The sun on the dock was very bright, almost hot. She closed her eyes and red circles spun on her eyelids. Some days, everything reminded her of Molly. Molly had been wrong—she'd fought the wrong battle, against the wrong foe. She'd feared the ice of Diana, not the heat of Morris. She'd made a mistake. She'd gotten old, as she said, confused. She'd been wrong.

Ha, someone said.

The wind tugged at her hair and her eyes sprang open. She heard it again: Ha.

She looked up into the branches of the pine above her head. There was a blue jay there, looking down, its head tilted. She shaded her eyes, trying to see the blue bird against the blue sky. It shook its wings and looked down at her, closing one eye in a jaunty wink. She stood up. Pear raised his head, his lips dripping with happy drool, his tail waving like a flag.

Her eyes followed the bird as it lifted from the tree and crossed the sky. Blue against blue. Like to like.

She nodded. She started up the path to the cottage, looking forward to good food. And to Charles. Still, every time she left the dock, she looked for a footprint in the sand of the little beach—the telltale print, bare sole, wide toes. So far, she'd never seen one. So far, there were no intruders on her island, no Friday to break her peace. No wendigo. No cannibals. Except, of course, for herself. And that, she understood. She got it now—blood lust. Victory. The fallen enemy at your feet and the desire to consume him in your heart. She was learning to live with the terrible truth of cannibal knowledge. She thought it would make for a better dissertation, this hard-won knowledge. She started up the path, smiling. Merriment. And sport.

Ronelle's List of Books Receiving
the *Largesse Seal of Approval*

Atwood, Margaret. *The Edible Woman*.

Boyle, T. Coraghessan. *Water Music*.

Dawson, Carol. *Body of Knowledge*.

Evans, Penelope. *Freezing*.

Jarrell, Donna and Ira Sukrungruang, eds. *What Are You Looking At? The First Fat Fiction Anthology*.

Koppelman, Susan, ed. *The Strange History of Suzanne LaFleshe and Other Stories of Women and Fatness*.

Newman, Leslea, ed. *Eating Our Hearts Out*.

Powell, Leslie, ed. *Food and Other Enemies: Stories of Consuming Desire*.

Seamon, Hollis. *Body Work*.

Spark, Muriel. *A Far Cry from Kensington*.

Partial Bibliography of Suzanne's Research Sources on Literary Cannibalism and Wendigo Legends

Atwood, Margaret. "Cannibal Lecture." *Saturday Night*. November 1995. 81-90.

Colombo, John R., ed. *Windigo: An Anthology of Fact and Fantastic Fiction*. Saskatoon, Saskatchewan: Western Producer Prairie Books, 1982.

Crain, Caleb. "Lovers of Human Flesh: Homosexuality and Cannibalism in Melville's Novels." *American Literature*. 66:1. March 1994. 25-53.

Davies, Nigel. *Human Sacrifice in History and Today*. NY: William Morrow, 1981.

Doody, Margaret. *The True Story of the Novel*. NJ: Rutgers U. Press, 1996.

Gill, Sam and Irene Sullivan. *Dictionary of Native American Mythology*. NY: Oxford U. Press, 1992.

Gliserman, Martin. "*Robinson Crusoe:* The Vicissitudes of Greed—Cannibalism and Capitalism." *American Imago*. 47. Fall/Winter 1990. 197-231.

Glover, Douglas. *The Life and Times of Captain N*. NY: Knopf, 1993.

Hilliard, Raymond. "*Clarissa* and Ritual Cannibalism." *PMLA* 105:5. October 1990. 1083-1097.

Howe, Winona. "Charles Dickens and the 'Last Resource': Arctic Cannibalism and *The Frozen Deep*." *Cahiers Victorians and Edwardians*. 44:6. 1996. 61-83.

Kilgour, Maggie. *From Communion to Cannibalism: An Anatomy of Metaphors of Incorporation*. Princeton: Princeton U. Press, 1990.

Lyons, Paul. "From Man-Eaters to Spam-Eaters: Literary Tourism and the Discourse of Cannibalism from Herman Melville to Paul Theroux." *Arizona Quarterly*. 5:2. Summer 1995. 33-62.

Norman, Howard. *Where the Chill Came From: Cree Windigo Tales and Journeys*. San Francisco: North Point Press, 1982.

Rigby, Nigel. "Sober Cannibals and Drunken Christians: Colonial Encounters of the Cannibal Kind." *Journal of Commonwealth Literature*. 27: 1. 1992. 171-182.

Tannahill, Ray. *Flesh and Blood: A History of the Cannibal Complex*. NY: Stein and Day, 1975.

Warner, Marina. "Cannibal Tales: The Hunger for Conquest." *Six Myths for Our Time*. NY: Vintage, 1994. 83-102.

Acknowledgments

Thanks to all who pointed me in the direction of fleshy women, wendigo, and/or cannibal sources: April Selley, Tobias Seamon, Brio Burgess, Gretchen Ingersoll, Joanne St. Hilaire, and Barbara Ungar. Many of those same people, and others, read early versions and/or parts of this novel and gave me reactions; to all of these I owe a great debt: Judith Fetterley, Tobias Seamon, Gretchen Ingersoll, Libby Dyksen, Melissa Lassor, Grace Rielly Tierney, and Doug Butler. I also want to thank those who have been fans of Suzanne LaFleshe, in all of her incarnations, for a long time, and who have supported me as a writer at every turn: Gene Mirabelli, Margaret Black, Susan Koppelman, Nalini Jones, Jacob Seamon, Thomas Seamon, Dan Dyksen, Susan Nelson, Sally Olmstead, Priscilla Branch, Stacey Mascia, Bill and Pamela Lowe, Maria de la Camara, Melanie Bowman, Deborah Zlotsky, and Doris Butler.

Extra thanks to Tobias Seamon for permission to use his poem, "The Aloe Symphony" and to April Selley, whose poem "For My Student Who Dreamed That I Was Trying to Kill Her" got me thinking about a particular place and means of death.

Note: Although the State University of New York at Albany is a real place, I have taken great liberties with its architecture, its law enforcement system and its people, including both faculty and students. In my own time there as a graduate student, I met only kind, intelligent, reasonable people—not a wendigo among them. And sincere apologies to my friends who are painters; none is anything like the painter in this novel. All characters and events in this book are entirely fictional.

Recommended
Memento Mori Mysteries

Luanne Fogarty mysteries by Glynn Marsh Alam
DIVE DEEP and DEADLY
DEEP WATER DEATH
COLD WATER CORPSE
BILGE WATER BONES

Viv Powers mysteries by Letha Albright
DAREDEVIL'S APPRENTICE
BAD-LUCK WOMAN

A Katlin LaMar mysteries by Sherri L. Board
ANGELS OF ANGUISH
BLIND BELIEF

Matty Madrid mysteries by P.J. Grady
MAXIMUM INSECURITY
DEADLY SIN

A Dr. Rebecca Temple mystery
by Sylvia Maultash Warsh
TO DIE IN SPRING

AN UNCERTAIN CURRENCY
Clyde Lynwood Sawyer, Jr.
Frances Witlin

THE COLOR OF EMPTINESS
a crime novel by Cynthia Webb